A LOVE DIVIDED

"I can wait no longer to kiss you," he said huskily, lowering his lips to hers.

Moaning with pleasure, her pulse racing, Zondra twined her arms around his neck and returned his kiss twofold.

Strange feelings swept through her. The aching, sensual throbbing was almost unbearable. A force within her made her lean her body into his. . . .

Suddenly afraid, and breathless, Zondra drew away. Breathing hard, she turned her back to him. "Please don't," she said, a sob catching in her throat.

"You do not want me to awaken more feelings inside you . . . a woman's feelings?" Lone Eagle asked.

"No, please don't," Zondra said, doubling her hands into tight fists at her sides, for everything she was saying now was a lie. Oh, Lord help her, she wanted to give her all to this man.

But she just couldn't allow herself to give in to her feelings. She was too afraid to be owned again. . . .

Lone Eagle

Cassie Edwards

A TOPAZ BOOK

TOPAZ
Published by the Penguin Group
Penguin Putnam Inc., 375 Hudson Street,
New York, New York 10014, U.S.A.
Penguin Books Ltd, 27 Wrights Lane,
London W8 5TZ, England
Penguin Books Australia Ltd, Ringwood,
Victoria, Australia
Penguin Books Canada Ltd, 10 Alcorn Avenue,
Toronto, Ontario, Canada M4V 3B2
Penguin Books (N.Z.) Ltd, 182–190 Wairau Road,
Auckland 10, New Zealand

Penguin Books Ltd, Registered Offices:
Harmondsworth, Middlesex, England

First published by Topaz, an imprint of Dutton NAL,
a member of Penguin Putnam Inc.

First Printing, December, 1998
10 9 8 7 6 5 4 3 2 1

 REGISTERED TRADEMARK—MARCA REGISTRADA

Printed in the United States of America

BOOKS ARE AVAILABLE AT QUANTITY DISCOUNTS WHEN USED TO PROMOTE
PRODUCTS OR SERVICES. FOR INFORMATION PLEASE WRITE TO PREMIUM
MARKETING DIVISION, PENGUIN PUTNAM INC., 375 HUDSON STREET, NEW
YORK, NEW YORK 10014.

I wish to dedicate *Lone Eagle* to the following fans, who have become very special to me—

Arlene Klimek
Linda Duca
Wanda Trager
Linda Paul
Jean Ann Dunn
Vivian Castrodale
Cindy Strothers
Alice Stickles

Love,
Cassie

THE PEOPLE

The days were long, the work was hard,
They lived off the land, they loved and
prospered.
Their Great Father above, their world that they
loved,
Their winds and their weather, nights dark, days
bright, were true.
The buffalo running in the sun, made their
world supreme,
Their knowledge, visions and dreams, made their
lives sublime.
Faith and hope were theirs for a while, then the
white man came,
And following came darkness and disaster.
Treaties were signed and treaties were broken.
Promises were made and all promises were
broken.
Now tell me, if you please, why all these things
happened?
Why did the white man's words prove false, and
why were The People forsaken?
Why all these things so cruel, when man's prom-
ise should hold truth?
Treaties should not be broken, these are the
words The People have spoken.

—MARIETTA L. GUNTER, Poet

Chapter One

Complete thy joy—
Let not my first wish fail!

                    —JOHN KEATS

The Yellowstone River Basin

The heat was oppressive. The sun was high and bright, beating down on Zondra Poole as she reluctantly wielded a hoe in the garden of her father's vast ranch. Sighing, she stopped and wiped the sweat from her brow with the back of her hand, taking a short break from her tedious labor.

She gazed around at those who were also working in the garden, lifting their hoes up and down as though they were mechanical dolls. The difference between Zondra and the other workers lay in the color of their skin, for while Zondra's was white, theirs was black.

This difference was easy to explain. Zondra's mother was black, her father, white. But the fact that Zondra's skin was white and her father owned this vast land made no difference in how she herself lived. Her mother had been born to slave parents and was still a slave, as was Zondra. Except for being the daughter of the rich landowner, Zondra was like the other slaves in every way.

Just as she had when she lived on her father's vast plantation back in Mississippi, Zondra lived in one of the small, hot, drab slave shacks at the far back of the ranch. She ate the same meals, which amounted to little more than beans most of the time. She wore the same lifeless cotton frocks that were always wrinkled from not being ironed, since an iron was a luxury only rich white people owned. The same could be said of fancy hairbrushes.

Seventeen, and so badly wanting to dress and look beautiful like her two white sisters, who lived in the huge pillared house with their two white brothers and mother, Zondra could not help but be bitter over how her father treated her so differently from his other children. The fact that he *was* her father was rarely discussed by anyone; certainly it was a forbidden topic among the slaves.

On the very rare occasions that Zondra's father gave her any attention at all, she would secretly meet with him far from the ranch and he would allow her to go horseback riding with him. She didn't own a horse, of course. Her father would choose one for her to ride from his huge herd. For the moment, while she rode alongside him, she *did* feel special, for she had never seen any of her sisters or brothers horseback riding with their father.

Zondra knew that her father had singled her out for this one special treat only because he felt some guilt over not having openly claimed her as his. And . . . because he still loved her mother with all his heart and would have divorced his wife, Sylvia, long ago and claimed Zondra's mother as his woman . . . had her skin not been black.

Her mother and father still shared *their* secret trysts. And Zondra knew where. Her father had built a pretty little cabin deep in the woods, far from his large mansion, where her mother could pretend, if only for a little while, that she was the queen of her castle. But Zondra's mother could only go there and enjoy the luxury of her "castle" when Zondra's father allowed it, and when he would be there, to meet her and make love with her.

So hot and thirsty, and wanting to get away from these thoughts that troubled her deep inside her soul, Zondra dropped her hoe. Without checking to see if her father's overseer was watching her, hardly caring, Zondra ran into the nearby forest.

Feeling momentarily free, Zondra wove her way through the thicket, where the lighter tones of the willows contrasted with the deeper hues of the hardwoods. Just as she'd done many times before, she sought the sweet peacefulness of a stream that wound lazily through the trees.

Finally reaching it, she fell breathlessly to her knees and splashed water on her face, then cupped the cool, refreshing liquid in her hands and gulped it greedily. She then leaned even closer to the water and hung her long raven-black tresses in it. The water soaking into her hair, reaching all the way to her scalp, felt deliciously wonderful.

When she heard the snapping of a twig behind her, she knew she was no longer alone and yanked her head quickly from the water. Tossing her hair back over her shoulders, the dripping tresses soaking the bosom of her dress, Zondra leaped to her feet.

Expecting to find the overseer there, come to scold her for having grown lax in her garden duties, Zondra made a quick, haughty turn, her chin lifted defiantly. She gasped with shock when she saw a Crow Indian warrior on a beautiful black mustang, slowly approaching her through the trees, his eyes intently on her.

As he continued moving toward her, Zondra stood her ground and stared at him. She was very aware of who he was; she had become infatuated with the Indian, admiring him from a distance while horseback riding with her father.

She had frequently accompanied her father to a bluff that overlooked the Crow village nestled in a heavily timbered bottom on the banks of a stream. Father and daughter were both curious about Indians, having arrived at the Yellowstone River Basin only a few months earlier from Mississippi. They had watched the Crow people as they moved among their skin lodges, involved in their daily activities.

She had become intrigued by one Indian in particular. Her father had pointed out Lone Eagle to her, telling her that he was the chief of this village of Indians. Her father had asked around about the Indians who lived in this area before settling here. He had been told that Lone Eagle was honored among his people. He was stoic, with the stealth of a mountain lion.

Zondra knew that Lone Eagle was a wizard at handling horses. He was also skillful at breeding horses, his herd often numbering a thousand. She had been in awe of the vast herd the first time she had seen it. The hills around his village swarmed with the animals. Zondra knew that horses were one of the Crow's most valued possessions, and the training of horses was considered a valued pastime.

What made Zondra feel comfortable and unafraid in Lone Eagle's presence today, as close as they were, their eyes locked, was the fact that thus far there were few recorded instances of hostilities between the Crow and non-Indians. Neither Lone Eagle nor any of his warriors had been any threat to her and the others who had come with her father from Mississippi to make their home in this giant, beautiful wilderness. Lone Eagle's clan was known for their love of peace.

Zondra was awed to think that a man as young as Lone Eagle could be a great and powerful chief. She was also smitten with his utter handsomeness! These past weeks, after having seen Lone Eagle more than once from the bluff, and to help while away her time working among the slaves, she had begun to fantasize about how it would be to come face-to-face with Lone Eagle, to actually know him, one-on-one.

Today . . . oh, today . . . was it truly happening? Could it be that he would soon be only inches away from her? He was close enough now for her to see his features.

She could hardly control her thunderous, racing heart, as she was finally able to see just how handsome he was. He wore fringed leggings, along with a fringed shirt and moccasins. A bow was slung over his left shoulder, an arrow quiver of otter skin, embroidered in quillwork, was positioned across his back.

His coal-black hair was so long she had seen it sweep the ground as he walked among his people. His jaw was lean and sharply angled. His deep-set brown eyes seemed to be looking clear into her soul, sending shivers of wonder throughout her. His hands—oh, how large they were, and how powerful they surely must be!

As Lone Eagle slowly approached Zondra on his steed, he stared at the woman, his pulse racing, for ever since he had seen her that first time riding a horse so skillfully across the land, and then during those times when he had silently observed her as she labored in the large garden, he had nursed a tormenting desire to see her up close.

Now that he was able to gaze upon her, he knew he would never forget her loveliness. Her skin was as white as clouds in a spring sky, yet her hair was as dark and long, as glossy black, as his own.

She was gracefully shaped, with a tall, supple body. Her eyes were large, brown, and shining, and had a flash of spirit in them. There was no fear in those eyes as she stood there awaiting him. He had never seen her drop her eyes submissively to anyone, as the others who worked with her in the large garden sometimes did.

Lone Eagle inched his horse even closer to her, then stopped. "White woman, it is good that you show no fear of this Crow Indian," he said in clear English. "I have come to you in friendship. My name is Lone Eagle. I am of the *Absaroga,* bird people, from which comes the name Crow. I am of the River Crow, while others of my own tribe are of the Mountain. I am of the Buffalo clan, who are friendly with White Eyes. And what is *your* name?"

"My name is Zondra," she said softly, his friendliness making her feel comfortable enough to talk with him. "It . . . it . . . is a pleasure to meet you, Lone Eagle."

So in awe of being this close to him, actually speaking with him, Zondra suddenly felt shy and at a loss for words. She was glad when *he* began talking again, his voice so deep and resonant, his tone so kind and gentle. If she'd been enamored of this handsome chief before, it was even more so now. Her knees were weak from her feelings for him!

"Your name is intriguing, as are you," Lone Eagle said. His dark eyes slowly swept over her. But seeing that he was making her uneasy, he looked directly into her eyes again. "I have been watching those of you who recently came and settled on this land," he said. "I am especially intrigued by the huge white house the tall white man I have seen riding horses with you lives in. This house, with its strange white columns, is as nothing I have ever seen before. It has many eyes that look down from high places."

Hearing him describe the windows as "eyes," the innocence of it, made Zondra totally relax with him. "The eyes are windows, and yes, it is a huge house, with two stories," she said, smiling. "The owner took great pains to bring special lumber for this house to the Yellowstone River Basin from his home in Mississippi. He is a man who is used to living elaborately."

She had purposely not referred to the "man of the house" as her father in the presence of the Indian chief. It was always hard to explain her association with her father; she was ashamed that a father would, for the most part, treat her as though she were anything *but* a daughter!

"How do you and your people feel about settlers coming to land that once belonged solely to your people?" Zondra dared to ask when he didn't respond to her explanation about her father's house.

"White woman, how would *you* feel if our roles were reversed?" Lone Eagle asked, his jaw tightening.

Zondra wished she could tell him that she wished their lives *were* reversed. Thus far his people had not been forced onto a reservation. They were still *free*. She was a slave, anything but free. But she saw that he didn't see her as a slave, perhaps unaware of such a word and its meaning, so she left the thought unsaid.

"I have not yet taken a wife," Lone Eagle said. "Have you taken a husband?"

Stunned that he would talk this openly with her, especially about something so personal, Zondra was momentarily speechless. She wasn't sure how to react to his question. Should she be honored to be questioned so intimately, or wary of his open boldness? All she was certain of was that she had many questions that she would like to ask about him and his people.

And, oh, how it would thrill her to be able to sit down with him and get to know him better. She even wished for more than that, yet knew it was foolish to allow herself to wander that far in her intrigue with this man. She belonged to her father.

"You do not respond to my question," Lone Eagle said, his eyes locked with hers again. "You are a wife, or you are not. Which is it?"

"No, I'm not married," Zondra blurted out.

Then, afraid of her deepening feelings for this warrior, and possibly his for her, and sure nothing could ever come of it, she spun around to leave, but stopped with a start when he asked her something else.

"Why does everyone who labors with you in your garden have black skin and yours is white?" Lone Eagle asked as she turned and faced him again. "And I have never seen black skin before. Do they paint their skin that color? If so, why do you not paint yours? Why are *you* different from the others?"

Zondra gave him a wavering stare, stunned by his innocence. Not wanting to talk about the color of her skin, and why it was white instead of black, she hurried away from him.

When she reached the garden and resumed her hoeing, she thought further about Lone Eagle's question, bitter over the true answer. She wasn't even free to claim her father's last name! How often had she lain awake at night, whispering her true last name to herself, since she was forbidden to say it aloud? From the moment she had realized she could not use her father's name, she had felt cheated. She couldn't help but aspire to it, even while knowing the futility of wishing so hard for the impossible.

The only time she felt she and her father had any kind of relationship was when they sneaked away together to go horseback riding. Only then was she allowed to feel how it might be if he truly claimed her as his daughter! But she knew this would never happen, just as she knew nothing could ever come of her having such delicious feelings for Lone Eagle. To him, surely *she* was forbidden fruit!

She turned and looked into the distance just in time to see Lone Eagle riding across a vast stretch of land that lay just beyond that which her father had laid claim to upon his arrival in the Yellowstone River Basin. A sensual shudder of ecstasy overwhelmed her as she saw how majestically tall he sat in his saddle and how beautiful his hair was, the long locks floating behind him in the wind.

Ah, such grace in motion, this man on his horse, his hair seemingly his wings, she marveled to herself. Her pulse racing, she swallowed hard and turned her eyes away.

Chapter Two

Thou has sought in starry eyes,
Beams that were never meant for thine.

—Percy Bysshe Shelley

His eyes narrowing angrily, Red Moon of the Wolf Clan of the Crow Indians stared at White Bead of Lone Eagle's Buffalo Clan. Her long black hair blowing in the breeze behind her, White Bead forced herself to stare back, continuing the standoff between herself and Red Moon, who sat dressed in his finest attire on his proud steed.

She found it hard to believe that he would dare come again into the village of his enemy clan and persist in asking for her hand in marriage when she had told him countless times before that, although she was highly proficient as a tanner and bead worker, and was of marrying age, her people came before marriage. She was the Buffalo Clan's prophet, a holy, virginal woman held in high regard by her people, who looked upon her as a special maiden.

White Bead could hear the silence all around her as her people stood outside their tepees, watching and waiting to see how she handled Red Moon this time. Knowing that she was the only reason Red Moon came to her village, and realizing he meant her people no harm, White Bead had told Lone Eagle's warriors to allow Red Moon to move freely about the village. He was only a threat to the Buffalo Clan of Crow if his warriors met Chief Lone Eagle's out on the open plain with drawn weapons.

But even those warring times were long past. Ever since Lone Eagle became chief of their village, he had striven to keep peace among all the neighboring tribes and Crow clans. A wise man for his years—he was only twenty-eight—Lone Eagle had looked into the future and concluded that all Indians must present a united front against the onslaught of whites in the community. He had watched how the white man had come into Indian territory, taking land, killing the game, and flooding the streams for his own selfish purposes.

White Bead understood the concerns of her cousin, Chief Lone Eagle, and she saw the need to keep herself available to him and their people should the time come when warring against the whites became inevitable.

Red Moon's heart beat like angry thunder inside his chest over White Bead's ongoing rejection. Here he was, a brave, noble man showing her the respect a man shows a woman he wants to marry. His frustration was great today, for this was the fourth time he had come to try and persuade the beautiful woman to be his wife.

He had told her how their marriage would bond the two enemy clans into a force strong enough to resist the influx of whites. He even knew without a doubt that deep inside her heart she loved him.

When Red Moon and White Bead were young and could look beyond the feud between their clans, they had met a few times, alone, and played among the wild creatures in the forest, laughing and enjoying being together as friends. This had stopped when Red Moon's father caught them one day and forbade them from ever seeing one another again.

Now Red Moon's father was dead, no longer there to forbid anything. Red Moon was a powerful chief who gave orders, not took them. He could give a woman much love, yet still White Bead ignored him, treating him as something less than dust that blows in strange circles on a hot summer day!

How could she reject him when she knew that she was wasting her life away as a spinster? How could she reject him when he knew she wanted him? It was in her eyes every time she looked at him! He wanted her more than anything else on earth. She was so beautiful she stole Red Moon's breath away. He had left his pride behind in order to come today into his enemy clan's village and once again speak of his feelings to White Bead.

"White Bead, did you not hear me tell you of the gifts I would offer your family and the rest of the tribe if you would agree to be my wife?" Red Moon asked warily. White Bead's sparkling dark eyes and her lifted chin still showed her stubbornness, proof that nothing he said today was going to change her mind.

"Red Moon?" White Bead finally breathed softly through her luscious lips.

Red Moon's heart skipped a beat, for White Bead's speaking to him with softness made him think that perhaps he had finally convinced her that marriage was best for her after all, better than being a virginal spinster. There were many in her village who were way less lovely and could better serve their people as their prophet, for they were the ones who would not have men all that eager to take them for wives.

Whereas, White Bead, oh, White Bead, in her loveliness, could have any man on the face of the earth
as her husband. Even white men would surely die to
have her in their beds!

"Yes, White Bead?" Red Moon said. He knew that
he had responded a little too anxiously, yet there was
no hiding the intensity of his love for her. He had
shown it too often to her people; he had already left
the village three times looking the fool over this
woman. He now had hope he would not be leaving for
a fourth time with his heart dashed as though against a
stone and his pride torn asunder.

The fringes on her buckskin sleeve fluttering as she
lifted her right hand, White Bead pointed to an evergreen bush that grew on one side of her tepee. "Red
Moon, do you see the leaves of that evergreen bush?"
she asked, watching his eyes move to the bush, regret-
ting what she was about to say, for she loved this man
with all of her heart and soul. Yet she must make him
understand that he should not come again for answers
she just couldn't give him!

"Yes, yes, I see," Red Moon said, then slowly slid his
eyes back to her, puzzled as to what the bush had to do
with the matter at hand. "Why do you point it out to
me when there are more important things to discuss?
Like horses, White Bead. I will bring your family many
horses if you will say today that you will be my wife."

"You have evergreen bushes in your village, do you
not, Red Moon?" White Bead said, her voice still soft,
her eyes still steady on Red Moon's, her heart breaking.

"Yes, there are many," Red Moon said, idly
scratching his brow. "Why do you ask, White Bead?
What is the importance of you knowing about bushes
in my village?"

"Because it is important, Red Moon, for you to

keep watch on them every day," White Bead said, forcing her voice to sound sullen and cold. "When the evergreen bushes turn yellow, come again, Red Moon, and ask me to marry you."

Instantly anger flashed in Red Moon's eyes. His jaw tightened. He now knew that White Bead had been toying with him. She had purposely humiliated him in the presence of her people, for he knew that the reference to the turning yellow of evergreens indicated to the Crow people the impossibility of something. She was telling him in this way that she would never marry him. Her decision was that final. That insulting!

Knowing this, Red Moon felt that he had no choice but to stand up for his honor by, in turn, humiliating White Bead. He knew now that he could never have her. She had just severed all ties by rejecting him so completely in the presence of others.

As he wheeled his horse around and rode off, White Bead stood quietly among her people, their eyes following his departure. He shouted at the young Indian woman over his shoulder. "Doll Woman!" he cried sneeringly, then said something that was a terrible insult to any Crow woman. "You do not know how to dance, nor will you ever be able to! Your testes are hanging down in the way!"

He ignored the gasps of horror behind him as he rode away from the village and headed his horse in a hard gallop toward his own.

He most certainly wasn't aware of how White Bead ran into her lodge and threw herself onto her pallet of furs, crying. But he knew that he felt an intense ache, an emptiness, for there was no satisfaction in his heart from what he had just said to White Bead. He even realized that he might expect retaliation of some sort from Chief Lone Eagle when he returned to his

village and was told of Red Moon's visit there today,
and how he had behaved toward Lone Eagle's people's prized prophet.

Downhearted over knowing that he would never
have White Bead as his wife, Red Moon did not even
care what Lone Eagle would do about the insult di-
rected at his village prophet today. It had to be said,
or Red Moon would lose more face than he already
had among the Buffalo Crow.

His head hanging low, sighing deeply, he rode onward, trying not to care . . . not to want . . . not
to desire.

Filled with the wonder of having finally been with
the white woman of his midnight dreams, Lone Eagle
rode tall and proud into his village, where his people's
conical tents were set up in no special order, and
where, instead of scalps dangling from the tips of their
scalp poles, pennantlike streamers of red cloth waved
in the wind.

It didn't even matter that Zondra had run from him
and returned to her gardening chores, for he knew
that it had not been out of fear or distaste for him
that she had done this. He had seen in her eyes the
tumultuous emotions she felt just being near him. He
knew by the way her eyes spoke to him that she was
as enamored of him as he was of her. In time they
would share the ultimate of emotions, of passion.

His intense joy soon faded into a brooding wonder
when he looked around his village and saw no smiles,
only a sullen quiet as his people nodded a silent greeting to their chief. Even the children were not playing.
They were sitting outside their lodges, their eyes filled
with a strange sort of sadness.

Fearing someone dear might have died, afraid to

know who, Lone Eagle rode on to his father's magnificent tall tepee with its paintings of buffalo on the outside skins. He dismounted, handed his reins to a young brave who held his hands out for them, then went on inside his father's lodge.

Relief flooded his senses when he discovered his father was all right, for Mad Buffalo was an aged warrior whose time to travel the road to the hereafter could come at any given time. A member of the honorary club called the Bull Buffalo Society, and one who, with the approval of the council, had given over the title of chief to his son of twenty-eight winters, Mad Buffalo sat today resting before his lodge fire, puffing on his long-stemmed pipe.

His sunken, aged eyes looked over at Lone Eagle as he came and sat beside him. Nodding a silent greeting, he reached over and rested a hand on his son's shoulder.

"Father, what causes such a quiet sadness in our village?" Lone Eagle asked, as his father eased his hand away and rested it on his lap. A red-striped blanket lay around his thin shoulders. "Father, what has happened in my absence to cause such feelings among our people?"

Mad Buffalo took his pipe from between his lips and rested it on a rock. "My son, it is feelings for White Bead that cause such sadness among our people," he said, sighing.

"Has something happened to our prophet?" Lone Eagle asked, a keen panic detectable in his voice.

"Humiliation," Mad Buffalo said, again sighing heavily.

"Humiliation?" Lone Eagle said, raising an eyebrow. Then his eyes flared angrily. "In my absence did Red Moon come again into our village with his

ridiculous proposal of marriage?" he asked. "Did he
humiliate our lovely White Bead again?"

"Yes, he came, and this time his humiliation was of
the worst kind," Mad Buffalo said thickly. "It was
worse than all other times he came to speak face-to-
face with White Bead, offering her horses and whatever else to get her to say she will marry him. When
she refused him again, his response to her was said
with much humiliating, disgusting disrespect."

"That *chien,* son of dogs, what . . . did . . . he say
to her?" Lone Eagle asked, his eyes gleaming even
more angrily as he envisioned his clan enemy, knowing
Red Moon was capable of anything, even hurting a
pure woman, one who was revered by all, a woman
who should never be treated with disrespect.

With a hollowness in his voice, with much sadness,
Mad Buffalo repeated what Red Moon had said to
White Bead, about her having testes.

An anger so deep, so piercing, more intense than
he had ever felt before for Red Moon, grabbed at
Lone Eagle's heart.

"My son, Red Moon came to our village knowing
that White Bead would not marry him," Mad Buffalo
said. "He purposely came with a mock proposal to
cause more dissension between his clan and ours."

"Then the Buffalo Crow must retaliate this time
against Red Moon, who continues, it seems, with the
feud between two clans that began long ago with his
father," Lone Eagle said tightly. "I alone will avenge
White Bead's shame. I will make Red Moon wish he
had never ridden that first time into our village as
though he were welcome, when in truth he is an object
of all of our people's disgust!"

"*Di-a,* do it, go ahead. Go to White Bead, my son,"

Mad Buffalo said, once again placing a hand on Lone Eagle's shoulder. "Help erase White Bead's sadness."

"*Ahh*, yes, I must go to her," Lone Eagle said, giving his father a long embrace. Then easing from his father's arms and gazing into the old man's eyes, he said, "Father, when I first came into the village and saw the forlorn looks on our people's faces, I thought something might have happened to you. For a moment my heart stopped!"

"As you see, this father of yours is still alive and kicking," Mad Buffalo said jokingly, his way of teasing his son when Lone Eagle showed too much concern over his health. He motioned with his hand toward the entrance flap. "Now go, Lone Eagle, where you are more needed. This old man is quite content sitting beside his lodge fire, smoking his pipe as he dreams of what was, and what could have been."

Lone Eagle placed a gentle hand on his father's copper, weather-lined face, then left the lodge and went to White Bead's tepee.

When he spoke her name outside her private lodge, a few footsteps away from her parents' lodge, she bade him enter. He went inside and became angry again at Red Moon when he saw White Bead's lovely face so tear-streaked.

He went and sat down beside her on her pallet of furs beside her lodge fire and took her in his arms and comforted her. "Cousin, at your age of twenty years you are so beautiful," he said softly. "This is why warriors dare come and speak so foolishly amid their enemy clan!"

He purposely didn't tell her that surely her humiliation was planned to purposely arouse the Buffalo Clan into wanting to war with the Wolf Clan.

"I am that beautiful?" White Bead said, leaning

away from him, searching his eyes. "You see me as this beautiful?"

"My sweet cousin, you are more beautiful than all of the stars in the heavens," Lone Eagle said, quickly reminded of another woman whom he saw as beautiful. Zondra. Oh, what a beautiful woman, with such a beautiful name! His heart ached to see her again already and he had just left her only a while ago!

"But do you know the disgusting thing Red Moon said to me?" White Bead said, visibly shuddering at the mere thought of the word "testes" being spoken in the same breath as her name.

"*Ahh*, yes, Father told me, and Red Moon will pay for openly insulting you in this way," Lone Eagle said with conviction.

As White Bead's eyes wavered, she lowered them so that Lone Eagle would not see them, or he might be able to see how she truly felt about Red Moon. Yes, she was angry and hurt over Red Moon humiliating her in such a disgusting way. But she understood why he'd done it! He had to save face over her having given him a final negative answer to his proposal of marriage and over the way she had done it.

Because she loved Red Moon, she wanted to beg Lone Eagle not to do anything to Red Moon, the chief of his clan of Crow. But she kept her silence, for she knew better than anyone else that such a love was impossible.

She had chosen the life of a prophet when she was twelve winters of age and a vision came to her, telling her to be this special religious person for her Buffalo Clan. She just couldn't admit to loving a man. Especially not Red Moon, who was of the enemy clan!

"I must go now, White Bead, and have council with my warriors," Lone Eagle said, framing her face, with its delicate features, between his powerful hands. "Will you be all right?"

"*Ahh*, yes, I am fine now that you have come to me, special cousin, and helped me in my time of sadness," she murmured. She flung herself into his arms. "Thank you, cousin. Thank you."

He held her for a moment, then eased her from his arms. "If you need me after my council, send for me," he said, rising to his feet.

"Yes, I will do that," White Bead said, slowly nodding. "Again, thank you. You are always there for me when I need you."

"As I always will be," Lone Eagle said, then turned and left.

Running her delicate fingers through her long tresses, drawing her hair back from her face as she stretched out on her pallet of furs beside the fire, White Bead tried to focus on the hurt inflicted on her by Red Moon, searching for a way to hate him.

Yet all she could think about was how it might feel to be held in his arms. She knew he hadn't truly meant what he said to her today when he taunted her with the nasty word "testes." Because she'd rejected him again, he was forced to say the worst thing that he could conjure up to inflict as bad a hurt on her as she had on him.

"You could never mean that," she whispered to herself. "I know your love for me is as deep . . . as . . . mine is . . . for you."

Tears streamed from her eyes. "But you will never, never know, Red Moon," she whispered. "Never . . . never . . ."

Chapter Three

The moon made thy lips pale, beloved—
The wind made thy bosom chill.

—PERCY BYSSHE SHELLEY

The moon's glow coming through the open window above Zondra's bed was the only light in the drab one-room cabin, but she could see well enough to place the last of her meager possessions in a travel bag that she had sewn from a flour gunnysack confiscated from her father's kitchen pantry.

Late this evening she had also stolen some food. She had made sure to take only as much as she could carry, and food that would not spoil too quickly. She wasn't sure how far she would have to go to find a way to establish a new life for herself.

She was going to make her escape from slavery tonight. She had thought often of doing this, especially after arriving in this new land and getting a taste of freedom, riding alongside her father on their secret outings.

All this afternoon she had made her plans of escape. When she had stolen the gunnysack from the pantry that day many weeks ago, she had known why she was taking it. That very evening, while her mother slept, Zondra had made the travel bag while sitting by

the window so the moon could give her the light by
which to sew. Since then it had been hidden beneath
her meager, thin mattress.

"Tonight, oh, tonight, can I truly be doing this?"
she whispered to herself, jumping with a start when
she heard something move behind her.

Cautiously she turned around to see what had made
the sound. Surely it was only her cat, Ralph. Zondra
had given her precious coal-black cat the name before
she realized the kitten her father had presented her
with was a female. Moments earlier she had checked
on Ralph, and she had found her asleep beside the
door, as though she were waiting, having somehow
sensed Zondra's plan of escape.

Earlier this evening, while Zondra's mother had
been taking a walk, Ralph had sat on Zondra's lap,
purring contentedly, as the girl made a carrying bag
out of another stolen gunnysack, so that when she left
she could carry her cat with her.

Her eyes peering through the darkness, Zondra saw
that Ralph hadn't made the noise she'd just heard.
The cat was still snoozing beside the door. What Zondra had heard was her mother tossing in her sleep on
her bed across the room from Zondra's.

When Zondra heard her mother saying something
in her sleep, she tiptoed over to her bed, bending to
her knees to listen. Her heart ached when she heard
her mother talking, as though someone were there in
the room with her. It was Zondra's father's name that
her mother was softly speaking in her sleep. She was
telling him that she loved him, that she wished to be
his wife, that she wanted to give Zondra the same
lovely things that her white sisters had.

Not wanting to hear any more, knowing that the
dream proved what her mother's thoughts were when

she was awake, Zondra went back to her own bed. It
hurt Zondra to realize that her mother was pining
away for a man who would never claim her as his
wife, never openly acknowledge her as his mistress. It
was obvious to Zondra that her father would always
guard well this secret affair with a woman whose skin
color did not match his own.

Never more certain than now that she must leave
this life of heartache and shame behind her, Zondra
prepared her escape into the night. She wasn't afraid
to leave on her own. Anything would be better than
this life she had been born into.

A slave.

A white slave!

She knew that back in Mississippi many men had
gawked at her as she had worked all her daytime
hours alongside the blacks. She would never forget
the smug looks on her father's friends' faces, knowing
they understood too well why she was there, laboring
with the blacks, even though she was white. They
knew that the man who had fathered her was also
her master.

Many plantation owners openly displayed to their
men friends the white children they'd sired with black
slaves, as though the child were something akin to
a trophy.

Zondra hated being a trophy. She hated being a
slave!

She despised her white brothers and sisters, who
lived like royalty in their large house, their rooms
filled with precious, valuable possessions.

She hated having to watch each and every movement she made now that she had matured into a
woman. She realized her father's ranch hands saw her
as fair game since her mama was black. And not only

did she have *them* to fear, there was also Guy, Zondra's half brother.

No, she had no choice but to leave and try to find a new life elsewhere. Settlers were moving into the Yellowstone River Basin every day. Perhaps she could just become one of them, with no past, but hopefully a future much better than what it would be should she stay at the ranch.

She paused for a moment and climbed onto her bed. She crawled to the window and stared at the two-storied, pillared, magnificent house as the moon's glow silhouetted it against the black sky.

She looked up at one window in particular on the second floor of the house. She knew by having seen him standing in the window many times, staring down at the slaves' quarters, that it was her father's bedroom.

Her thoughts drifted back to when her father, Harrison Lester, had left his vast plantation in Mississippi to escape with all his slaves when he had first heard whispers of a war that was going to break out among the slave states, resulting in the freeing of all slaves.

Her father, owning fifty slaves . . . men, women, and children . . . hadn't wanted to chance losing them. He had made a quick sale of his plantation to a neighbor who was going to stay and wait out the rumors of war, hoping they were just that—rumors. Then Zondra's father had brought his wealth, his white family, and his slaves to the Yellowstone River Basin.

Zondra's mother had shared a bed with the wealthy plantation owner from the moment she had been purchased at an open auction in Georgia many long years ago. And Zondra wasn't the only child born of her mother and her white father's forbidden union. There had been seven other children, boys *and* girls. Having been born with dark skin like their mother's, they had been sold to other plantation owners for huge sums of money as soon as they were old enough to work in the fields.

Zondra was the only one who had been allowed to stay, but even though her skin was as milky white as her father's, not only had she been denied her father's last name, she had also never been allowed inside her father's mansion to share the family riches with her four white brothers and sisters.

"I should be there with my own private bedroom, and when people speak my name, they should be calling me Zondra Lester, not Poole," she whispered bitterly to herself.

But she had known long ago that that would never happen. To her white brothers and sisters she was an outcast—that is, until recently, when Guy, her twenty-seven-year-old spoiled half brother, began finding ways to be alone with Zondra. A few days ago he had followed her into the forest, where she had gone to seek some solace from her tormented life, and had grabbed her and wrestled her to the ground.

She felt sick to her stomach even now as she remembered his big hands groping anxiously up under her skirt, his wet lips pressed hard against her mouth in a slobbering kiss. As she lay there, utterly helpless, the fight having drained from her, she had known that she must flee this life that had become unbearable.

She could never forget how her father had ridden up on his majestic white stallion that day just in time to save Zondra from being raped by her very own blood kin, for her half brother saw her as nothing more than a slave, someone to use as one saw fit to use.

She shivered now, remembering the snap of her fa-

ther's whip when it come down hard across Guy's bare
rump, and how Guy had shrieked and yelped with
pain as he rolled free of Zondra, then scampered
away, stumbling into his breeches.

So tall, so blue-eyed and handsome, her father had
hurriedly dismounted and held Zondra close to comfort her.

She had always felt torn about her father's af-
fections through the years; he was only there for her
if no one was around to witness him making a fuss
over an illegitimate child born of his union with a
slave.

"Oh, Mama," Zondra whispered, a sob lodging in
her throat. "Mama, I so wish it could be different."

"Child, what are you doing? Why is that bag on
your bed? Zondra?"

Her mother's voice brought Zondra quickly out of
her reverie. She turned with a start and found her
mother standing behind her, so beautiful and delicate
in her white cotton gown, a look of keen puzzlement
in her dark, velvet eyes.

She had not wanted to awaken her mother, knowing
that she would plead with her not to go. Zondra now
knew how wrong that would have been. It would have
been cruel for her mother to have awakened and
found her daughter gone.

Zondra realized that her sweet mother would have
conjured up all sorts of dreadful thoughts about where
Zondra might be. Her mother knew about Guy. She
had warned Zondra time and again that he might try
and find a way to avenge the beating his father had
given him over the incident with Zondra, for even
after having received such a beating he had surely not
understood why and blamed her.

"Zondra, child, answer me," Ada said softly. She

walked barefoot to the bed and touched the garment bag and gave Zondra another look. "Where did you get this? What's in it?"

"Oh, Mama, please try and understand," Zondra blurted out, tears filling her eyes. She crawled from the bed and stood beside her mother. "I have to go, Mama. If I stay, I will die slowly inside. I must leave while I have the spirit and courage to leave, or forever live in the shadow of slavery."

"Child, I ain't never heard you talk like this before," Ada said, lovingly running her long, slender fingers through Zondra's lustrously thick black hair. "But I can understand your feelings." Ada dropped her hands to her sides. "And, Lord help me," she murmured, "I approve. I even urge you to go. This ain't no life for someone like you. Away from slavery, you will look as normal as all other whites. You can mingle with them with your chin held high." A sob caught in her throat. "Daughter, away from this place of misery, you can make somethin' of yourself."

"You truly do understand," Zondra said, flinging herself into her mother's arms.

"Yes, I understand," Ada said, her arms trembling as she hugged her daughter to her. "But I'll worry. Oh, how I'll worry."

"Please don't," Zondra murmured, slipping from Ada's arms. She took her mother's hands and gently held them. "Mama, I can take care of myself. I'll find a white family who'll take me in for the time being. I'll work for my keep, but not in the capacity of a slave. I'll be paid for my services, Mama, like a normal person—I'll be *paid*."

"But what if you don't find someone who'll take you under their wing?" Ada asked, tears flooding her eyes. "What if you're all alone and someone evil finds you?"

"All I can tell you, Mama, is that I'll do my best," Zondra said, releasing her mother's hands. She grabbed up her bag and placed the long strap she had sewn onto it over her shoulder. "And, Mama, I promise that I'll somehow find a way to send for you. I'll find a way to free you, Mama."

Ada swallowed hard. "I couldn't leave your father," she said, wiping tears from her cheeks with the backs of her hands. "I live for those shared moments with him. He has my heart, Zondra. All of it. I wouldn't want to live without him."

"But, Mama, in his eyes you are still a slave," Zondra pleaded. "Don't you work the gardens alongside the other slaves? Don't you live in poverty?"

"Yes, for the most part I live the life of a slave; but, Zondra, those times alone with Harrison are my true world. He is a gentle, loving man. Don't you know that if it was possible, he'd have me with him in his home instead of that woman who has ice flowing through her veins?"

"Mama, you know it'll never happen," Zondra said, her voice breaking.

"But still, I live for those moments with your father," Ada persisted. "And I always shall, as you will one day when you meet the perfect man."

Zondra thought quickly of Lone Eagle. If she had her choice of men, he would be it. She wished that she could somehow find a way someday to be a part of his life.

But as it was for her mother, impossible to live with the man she adored, so it was for Zondra. Although she had been with Lone Eagle just that one brief time, it was obvious how he felt about her. He surely would never consider marrying her. They were worlds apart in their beliefs. And he was a powerful chief. Surely an Indian chief would never take a white woman into his life, especially to have her as his wife!

"Zondra, where has your mind taken you?" Ada asked, taking Zondra by the hand. "You suddenly seem so distant . . . so quiet."

"It's nothing," Zondra said, sighing. She took one long, last look at her mother, for she was afraid she might never see her again. Zondra had just been dreaming to believe they could be reunited eventually, for it was obvious now that her mother would never leave her lover.

Her mother gazed questioningly at the garment bag. "You didn't answer me before when I asked you where you got this bag," she said, recognizing that it had been made from gunnysacks. "What's in it? And now I see another bag on your bed. What is *it* for?"

"Mama, I stole two gunnysacks from Father's kitchen pantry. I made a travel bag for me from one, and another one for Ralph so that as I travel on horseback the cat's bag can hang from the pommel of the saddle, you know, like a sling," Zondra said softly. "And, Mama, tonight, after everyone was asleep in the big house, I stole some food from the pantry. Who knows how long I'll be traveling alone? Also, I've placed what clothes I own in the bag."

"You've been planning this escape for some time?"

"After Guy came close to raping me."

"If he had tried to rape a woman who wasn't a slave, he'd have been put behind bars," Ada said bitterly.

"Yes, it's an injustice I will never grow used to, Mama," Zondra said sullenly. "But by leaving I am

making sure Guy never gets the chance to even so
much as touch me again.''

"Zondra, I'll worry so about you," Ada said, another sob lodging in her throat. "Please be careful.
Don't take any chances.''

"God will be with me," Zondra said quietly.

She gave her mother a last, lingering hug, then
rushed to the door. She scooped Ralph up, and the
cat, awakened so suddenly, hissed at Zondra. Laughing softly, bubbling over with excitement, Zondra gave
Ralph a hug, then slipped her into the sling bag.

Zondra opened the door, flooding the room with
moonlight. She turned one last time toward her
mother. She blew her a kiss, then stepped outside into
the warm, fragrant night air.

She didn't look back as she ran across the yard
toward the stable. When she reached it, she rushed
inside, choosing the strongest, best, and fastest horse
to get her far from the ranch as quickly as possible.

"Speedie, you're going to be a part of my and
Ralph's adventure," Zondra whispered as she saddled
her father's favorite steed. She felt a deep attachment
to this powerful white stallion. Her father had sneaked
Zondra into the barn on the very night the horse was
born. He had even given her the honor of naming the
lovely foal. At first she had named the horse Beauty,
but as it matured into a steed powerful and fast, she
had, with her father's approval, renamed the horse
Speedie.

Zondra knew that her theft of her father's favorite
steed would enrage him, but she couldn't think of that
now. Hopefully by the time he missed Speedie, Zondra would be long gone. And she doubted her father
would ever find her. He was too new in these parts
to know the lay of the land well enough to be able to

track her. And the ranch hands that he had hired were drifters, themselves ignorant of the area.

She doubted that her father would go to Fort Bass, a post established on the Yellowstone River for trading with the Crow, to report her missing, for that would draw attention to himself. He had fled to these parts because he owned so many slaves. That was a fact he would want to keep from the authorities in case the government eventually chose to order all slaveholders to set free their slaves.

Riding off into the black of night, weaponless, totally alone for the first time in her life except for the company of her cat, Zondra couldn't help but be afraid. Surely she had just lost every chance of *ever* being able to claim her true last name.

Strangely, that no longer seemed all that important. Being free had become more of an aspiration than claiming a name that had for so long been denied her.

Won't he be surprised? Zondra thought, in her mind's eye envisioning the expression on her father's face when he discovers she's gone. Somehow she didn't see rage, but instead, concern and loss.

"You do love me, Papa," she whispered. "I *know* you love me!"

Chapter Four

For each ecstatic instant
We must an anguish pay
In keen and quivering ratio
To the ecstasy.

—EMILY DICKINSON

In Chief Lone Eagle's council house, a large tepee of fine buffalo hides, a fire was burning in the central fire pit. Lone Eagle's warriors were seated in a circle around the fire. Men of consequence, they were all stripped to their breechclouts.

Lone Eagle removed his clan's sacred pipe from its red cloth cover. Passed down through a long line of ancestors, it was flat-stemmed, of Dakota pattern. Tobacco was one of the three holiest objects of worship, hence all children wore a small necklace of it as an amulet.

Smoking was strictly ritualized. After lighting the tobacco in the bowl of the pipe, with a ceremonious sweep Lone Eagle handed it to the warrior who sat at his left side. No one ever took more than three puffs at their turn.

When the pipe had made a full circle around the council house, and had returned to Lone Eagle, everyone was quiet as he knocked its bowl clean of tobacco, then restored it to its red cloth cover and laid it on a stone before him.

This was the second important council in two days. But tonight all talk centered on one thing—how to avenge White Bead's shame.

"Chief Red Moon should not feel free to come into our village anytime he wishes and bring shame into the lives of any of our people, especially our women," Lone Eagle said angrily as his gaze swept slowly from man to man. "Especially not our prophet woman."

"*Ahh*, yes, that is so, my chief, but is it not White Bead herself who has said we should not stop Red Moon from entering our village?" Fox Crossing said as he gazed with intense, dark eyes at Lone Eagle.

"She has only done this because she has always hoped his people would one day meet with ours as one people instead of as enemy clans," Lone Eagle said flatly. "Because of Red Moon's behavior today, White Bead now sees how wrong she has been to think it is possible for our two peoples to come together as one, although it has been my own deepest wish that it could be that way also. But too much bad has happened between our two clans for us ever to be friends. For the most part this is the fault of Red Moon's chieftain father. Even though Red Moon is now chief, peace is still beyond reach. And Red Moon's actions are too often the mirroring of his father's."

"Then what do you suggest is the best way to avenge White Bead's shame, if not by going to war with the evil-mouthed Red Moon?" Two Chances asked, leaning over to place another log on the lodge fire. "Red Moon was foolish to come today on such a misguided mission and think he will not have to pay in some way for it."

"*Ahh*, yes, that is true. He will not get away with it," Lone Eagle said, running his fingers slowly through his sleek black hair, drawing it away from his sculpted face.

"Then how is it to be, Lone Eagle?" another warrior asked as he leaned closer to his chief. "Tell us how you wish to seek vengeance for our sweet White Bead."

"How is it to be done?" Lone Eagle asked, folding his arms over his bare, powerfully muscled chest. He smiled cunningly at his warriors. "Tell me, brothers, what is most cherished by all male Crow? Besides their horses and women, that is."

"Their hair," Two Chances said with a smile. "As do you, Lone Eagle, with your long and flowing hair that reaches the ground when you stand, so does Chief Red Moon take much pride in *his* hair."

"Yes, that is so," Lone Eagle said, laughing ruefully. "And it is his hair, and thus his pride, that will suffer as a consequence of what he did today to our most chaste woman."

"How?" Fox Crossing said, his eyes gleaming. "And *when*?"

"Soon," Lone Eagle replied, lifting the sacred calumet again, filling the bowl with tobacco.

Two Chances held a twig in the flames of the fire, then touched the lit end to Lone Eagle's tobacco, drawing it away again when the tobacco began to glow orange. Lone Eagle took a long drag from the pipe, removed the stem from between his lips, and let the smoke roll slowly from his mouth.

"Tell us, Lone Eagle," Two Chances said anxiously. "We are eager to know what you plan to do with Red Moon's hair . . . how much you plan to remove." He chuckled. "*I* would take much pride in taking his *scalp*."

"No scalps hang from scalp poles in our village now,

nor will they ever," Lone Eagle said, giving Two
Chances a scolding look. Then he smiled slowly. "No.
The portion of hair that I remove from Red Moon
will be left behind in his lodge for him to find and
grieve over, perhaps even cry over, since the loss will
be so great."

"So you plan to remove only one lock of his hair
rather than much of it?" Two Chances said, a keen
disappointment evident in his voice.

"One lock is adequate to teach Red Moon a lesson," Lone Eagle said, finding his mind drifting to
someone else's hair. The white woman's. Strange how
her long black locks looked so much like an Indian's.
Even her eyes were like those of an Indian.

Lone Eagle wondered if Zondra might be a breed.
He wished now that he had been bold enough to ask
her. In fact, he wished to know everything about her.

Since she had eluded his innocent questions today,
however, how could he ever expect her to respond to
something so seriously personal? No one admitted
easily to being a breed. The word "breed" was one
of shame to many people. Perhaps she had been afraid
he was getting close to asking her that, and that was
why she ran away from him today and returned to her
labors alongside the people with black skin.

The color of her skin compared to the skin of those
who worked with her still confused him. Hers was
pearl-white. Those she labored with had black skin.
The people who lived in the huge pillared house had
the same skin color as Zondra. The man he had seen
her riding horses with had white skin. Lone Eagle had
surmised they were father and daughter, yet . . .

"Lone Eagle, did you not hear what I said?" Two
Chances said, bringing Lone Eagle quickly from his
reverie.

Embarrassed, having never allowed his thoughts to stray beyond the council before, especially to a woman, Lone Eagle looked awkwardly around the circle of men and found all of their eyes on him.

"Your question was?" he said, now centering his attention solely on Two Chances.

"It is my deepest desire to ride with you to avenge White Bead's shame," Two Chances said. "She is not only your cousin, Lone Eagle, but also mine. I wish to have a part in the revenge."

"I understand, but I cannot allow it," Lone Eagle said, nodding a thank-you to several women who entered the lodge with large trays piled high with an assortment of food. He waited until they were gone before speaking his mind to Two Chances. "I plan to sneak into the Wolf Clan's village, cut an opening at the back of Red Moon's lodge with my knife, then enter and hurriedly cut Red Moon's hair," he said. "If more than one of us attempted this, it would double the risk of making noise that could get us caught."

"But you should not go alone and chance being caught," Two Chances argued. "You are our chief. You should not take that risk without someone being there to guard you. You are a valuable man. You are everything to our people."

"Was I not chosen to be chief after my father because of my courage and cunning ways?" Lone Eagle asked, looking slowly from man to man. He then gazed intently at Two Chances. "Cousin, do you question my ability to carry out the vengeance that we all seek?"

"If it seemed as though I was, then I apologize," Two Chances said, humbly lowering his eyes.

"Then it is settled," Lone Eagle said, leaning closer to the fire to knock the tobacco from the bowl of the sacred pipe into the ashes. He replaced the pipe in its wrappings.

"It is settled," Two Chances said, nodding.

"Then let us talk no more of it," Lone Eagle said, sliding one of the platters of food over to Two Chances. "Cousin, fill your stomach with food and let the pleasures of the food erase the worries about your chief from your mind."

Two Chances nodded and, with his fingers, plucked a piece of roasted venison from the plate.

"Now let us all eat and speak of more pleasurable things," Lone Eagle said, then took a bite of succulent wild turkey.

"Like women?" one of his other warriors said, chuckling.

"*Ahh,* yes, like women," Lone Eagle said, once again finding his thoughts drifting to the tall, willowy woman whose name was as intriguing as she was.

"Mine is heavy with child," Two Chances said, puffing his chest out with pride. "In two moons I will be holding a son in my arms. Then I will ask my wife for a daughter."

"When will you choose a woman and mate with her, Lone Eagle?" Fox Crossing asked. He bit into an apple and waited for the chief's answer.

"When?" Lone Eagle said, directing his gaze toward Fox Crossing. "When the woman sees me as the man she will proudly choose as her husband."

"*The woman?*" Fox Crossing asked, raising an eyebrow. "You say that in a way that makes me believe you have your eye on a particular woman, yet I have not seen you looking at anyone special when we are visited by other Crow clans, or when we visit them. Is there a particular, special woman, Lone Eagle? If so, please share her name with your brothers."

Lone Eagle suddenly felt trapped. He didn't want to reveal anything about the white woman to his men, especially not when he was unsure of whether there could ever be a possibility of them getting together as he wished them to be. His one encounter had proved way less than promising. But having been that close to her, having talked with her, he knew that he would not give up on her all that easily. Yes, they would meet eye-to-eye again. He would not let her get away from him another time without getting answers from her.

"No, no particular woman," Lone Eagle said, hating to lie, yet knowing he had no other choice but to. "You misinterpreted what I said, perhaps because you want too much for this chief to have a wife."

"It is time, do you not think, to think of not only a wife, but also children?" Two Chances dared to say.

"Are you saying your chief is not getting any younger?" Lone Eagle said, chuckling as he tried to lighten the mood around the lodge fire, and cleverly leading Two Chances away from prodding Lone Eagle about marriage and children. In time, yes, in time he would give them all an answer, but only after he had one himself!

"I did not mean to imply . . ." Two Chances began, then stopped and laughed softly, his eyes twinkling when he caught on to Lone Eagle's teasing.

"Let us speak of our horses!" Fox Crossing said, seeming to understand why Lone Eagle did not wish to speak of things that did not please him today.

"*Ahh,* yes, our horses," Two Chances said, a look of satisfaction entering his eyes at the mention of something so precious to him it made his heart soar. "Soon there will be many foals born into our herd. The mating of our most prized studs has been as I have never seen it before. Have you ever seen such huge—?"

A woman came into the lodge with more food, and Two Chances abruptly stopped what he was about to say, since he knew it would embarrass, even offend, any woman who heard that part of a horse's anatomy mentioned in her presence.

When she left, the men burst into howls of laughter, then continued their conversation about things only men talked about.

And when they were contentedly full of the delicious food, drowsy from it, and had talked enough about things that were forbidden around women, they left the council house and went their own ways.

The talk of horses mating, of studding, had stimulated Lone Eagle, as he knew it had the rest of the men in council. He expected that most of them would immediately take their wives to bed, whereas Lone Eagle's bed of blankets was empty.

Unable to get Zondra off his mind, he swung himself into his saddle and rode in a hard gallop away from his village. He rode until he reached the bluff where he had so often viewed the activities of Zondra from a distance.

He drew in his reins and stopped his horse, gazing downward. It was past the midnight hour, now, and all of the lanterns in the huge, pillared house had been extinguished. Nor was there any lamplight in the cabins at the far back of the white man's property, where Zondra slept.

Lone Eagle had watched Zondra go to one cabin in particular and knew that it must be where she lived. This had puzzled him then, as it did now. Why did she not live among the other white people in the larger house? Surely white daughters and white fa-

thers slept in the same house so that the daughters
would be under the protection of their fathers.

Zondra and the white landowner *must* be father and
daughter. While together, riding their horses, the
white man always looked at her as though he adored
her . . . the way fathers gaze at daughters. Lone Eagle
had seen it among the families of his village. Daughters were cherished by fathers!

He was more confused now than ever and he would
seek more answers from Zondra the next time he
chanced an encounter with her. And he would be with
her again, for he would not rest until he convinced
her to love him!

He wheeled his horse around and rode back toward
his village, the loneliness he felt tonight for a woman
surpassing any loneliness he had ever felt before. He
could hardly bear the thought of going to his blankets
alone again.

Yes, there *had* been women in his past to feed his
hungers. But now those women were not enough, not
when his heart and mind were filled with someone
else!

And even though her skin was white, and children
born of Lone Eagle's and Zondra's love would be clas-
sified as "breeds," he was sure that she was the only
woman he would ever desire.

"I will have her!" he shouted to the dark heavens,
his eyes widening when a huge star fell in a white
streak from the sky.

Surely that was an omen, he thought to himself.
Was it a good one? Or bad? Did it have to do with
Zondra, or something else?

Chapter Five

More inward than at night or morn,
"Sweet Mother, let me not here alone
Live forgotten and die forlorn."

—ALFRED, LORD TENNYSON

Tired and aching from the long ride and night chill, Zondra felt that she had gotten far enough away from her father's ranch so that it was safe for her to stop for the night. She rode onward for just a while longer, her eyes searching through the moon-splashed night for a safe haven.

She soon found herself riding in a deep valley surrounded on both sides by high walls of rock. When she spied a lone overhang that might give her more shelter from the dampness, she reined in Speedie beside it.

After unsaddling her horse and taking Ralph from the sling, she spread a blanket beneath a cottonwood tree and prepared to eat a quick snack before going to sleep. She chose a chicken leg for she knew that it was the most perishable of all that she had brought. She broke off a few small pieces of meat and laid them beneath Ralph's nose, laughing when her precious cat eagerly began to eat them.

"You're as hungry as me, aren't you, Ralph?" Zondra murmured, then dove into the chicken herself. She couldn't recall having ever been this hungry in her life. Earlier, back with her mama at their supper table, she had been too excited about her plans to eat much of the bean soup her mother had placed before her on their shabby dining table.

But now, with so much ahead of her that could be exciting—most of all, her freedom—Zondra's appetite had returned, twofold.

She gobbled down the last of the chicken, then took a bright red apple out of her bag and ate it leisurely as Ralph lay beside her, cleaning her paws with slow strokes of her tongue.

"Sweet cat, tonight is just the beginning of our fun," Zondra said, tossing the stripped apple core into the darkness. "But now I need my sleep." She swept Ralph up into her arms and hugged her. "Ready to snuggle, sweetie?"

Ralph's purrs were the cat's way of contentedly responding.

Zondra smoothed her hand over her cat's sleek black fur, then shivered as the night wind swept through the valley.

"We need a fire," she said, laying Ralph down beside her on the blanket. "But we don't dare build one. I still don't feel comfortable enough with the distance we've put between ourselves and Father to build a fire." She knew that a campfire could draw her father, outlaws, or hostile Indians to her.

She shook out another blanket and covered herself up to her chin, smiling when Ralph snuggled up next to her face. "We'll keep warm enough, won't we?" Zondra whispered.

As Zondra lay there, staring up at the sky as she drifted off to sleep, her heart skipped a beat when she caught a slight reflection of fire in the dark heavens.

She knew it was the Crow's fire. She had seen it before
and had questioned her father about it when they had
been horseback riding.

He had told her that the Crow keep an outdoor fire
burning through the night in an effort to keep wild
animals from straying too close to their lodges in their
village. Also, he said he thought it might be a comfort
to a people whose enemies could strike at any moment
during the night.

Who could be an enemy to Lone Eagle? she thought,
remembering his kindness . . . his gentleness.

As her eyelids grew heavier with sleep, she continued to watch the glow in the sky from the Crow's fire,
her thoughts lingering on Lone Eagle. She doubted if
she would ever see him again and regretted having
run off like a scared rabbit during their one chance
meeting.

But his questions! They had become too personal.
She hated having to tell her life's story to anyone . . .
how she happened to have white skin when she had
a black mother.

No, she just couldn't bear to explain it to Lone
Eagle. She could tell that he was born of pure-blood
parents. She doubted he would understand the circum-
stances of her parentage.

As her eyes closed, she pushed aside thoughts that
pained her and instead thought of how it might feel
to be held by Lone Eagle and to be kissed by him.

"Lone Eagle," she breathed softly, shivering with
ecstasy at how it sounded to speak his name aloud as
though he were there to hear her.

As a nearby stream murmured its song over rocks,
and her cat lay peacefully curled up beside her, Zondra drifted off to sleep.

The sudden hunting cry of a cougar, sounding like

a woman in agony, broke the silence of the night. Her mouth dry with fear, Zondra sat up, grabbed Ralph, and looked guardedly around.

She noticed that the moon was no longer visible, there to give her light by which to see. It was covered by dark clouds. When the cougar let out another piercing cry, Ralph leaped from Zondra's lap and scurried into the inky black of night.

Panic seizing her, so afraid that her cat might be killed by the larger animal, Zondra scrambled to her feet. She called for Ralph, but knew not to stray far from camp herself. If she got lost and couldn't find her way back to her horse, she was doomed. Tonight she might become the cougar's meal.

Losing all hope of finding Ralph, Zondra downheartedly returned to camp. She was torn about what to do. She felt that she should move onward, but if she did, Ralph would be lost to her forever.

No, she decided. She must stay the night. Perhaps at morning's light Ralph might find her way back. They could resume their journey and forget the trauma of their first night.

"Please let it be so," Zondra whispered as she positioned herself between the blankets again. Her cat's fur on the top blanket reminded her of Ralph's sweetness. Tears came to her eyes, for she was afraid, deep down inside herself, that her cat was gone forever.

"Damn the cougar," she muttered harshly.

Just as she said the word "cougar," the large cat let out another cry, this one closer than the last, which had to mean that the cat was closer to Zondra!

Her heart pounding with fear, Zondra was too afraid to stay there alone any longer.

Lone Eagle! She could go to his village and seek asylum there just until her father gave up looking for her, then move on. Maybe by then her courage would be stronger.

Perhaps she might even be able to secure some sort of weapon from Lone Eagle to take with her on the next leg of her journey. And maybe Ralph would show up at the Crow's village, looking for her.

"I'll do it," Zondra said, her jaw tightening with determination.

She knew exactly which lodge was Lone Eagle's. While watching his village with her father, she had seen Lone Eagle come and go from his tepee more than once. Except for one other large tepee, Lone Eagle's was larger than the others, which seemed right, since he was his people's chief.

Yes, that's what she would do. She would go to his lodge, and she would ask Lone Eagle to keep her presence a secret from her father should he come looking for her.

She knew the *true* danger of being with Lone Eagle was her feeling of attraction for him. Although she had fantasized about being with Lone Eagle, sometimes even imagining herself as his wife, and deep down inside truly wishing it could happen, she was afraid of having a man in her life. Even a man who made her melt at the mere thought of his name!

She had seen how men's minds worked, how devious and overbearing they could be. And possessive! She hated that her mother loved Zondra's father when, in truth, her mother should hate him for using her as though she were nothing more than an animal.

It would be hard for Zondra to trust any man, knowing what they were capable of. But still she was going to seek Lone Eagle's help. While in his presence, she would guard her feelings well. She most certainly wouldn't allow him to know how she felt about him, although he might already know. Surely he had seen it in her eyes. Surely he had heard it in her voice!

Afraid that the cougar might be slinking about somewhere even closer now, sniffing her scent and envisioning her as its next meal, Zondra hurriedly gathered her things together and soon had them positioned on Speedie.

Feeling very sad about Ralph, Zondra mounted the beautiful white stallion and rode off at a lope, her eyes constantly searching around her for her cat. The cat had been a part of her life for so long now. How she would miss her purring; how she would miss her soft fur as she brushed against Zondra's bare legs.

When she heard the cougar's cry again, and realized that it most certainly was closer than the last time she had heard it, Zondra knew that the important one to worry about now was herself. She must get to safety!

Oh, why hadn't she thought ahead to the dangers of cougars . . . of wolves . . . of all the many things that would enjoy feeding off not only her cat's tender flesh, but also her own? What else was out there that could threaten her on her journey? She now felt so naive, so vulnerable!

She dug her heels into the flanks of her horse and rode in a thunderous gallop through the darkness, her eyes never leaving the glow in the sky from the Crow's fire, using it as a beacon in the night to guide her to their village.

Before going on into Lone Eagle's camp, she rode to the bluff that overlooked it to see if everyone was asleep so that she might enter the village without alarming anyone. The only one she wished to awaken was Lone Eagle. She hoped when he found her standing in his lodge, he would welcome her.

She *had* fled that day when he had come to talk

with her. If that had humiliated him, how might he treat her now? Might he see her as an enemy and turn her away, to find her way through the darkness again to another safe haven while the cougar continued to be a threat to her?

Sitting in her saddle high on the bluff, Zondra gazed down at the village. The fire was flaming high into the sky, but there was no other activity. She didn't detect any sentries sitting guard on the outskirts of the village.

Her eyes were drawn by a movement in the dark shadows where the Crow's horses were corralled behind the lodges. Her heart skipped a beat when she realized a man had just ridden into the corral. He was dismounting.

As he busied himself removing his saddle, the clouds slipped away from the moon and Zondra had just enough light to see who the lone figure in the night was. She knew this man! How could she not recognize him by his long, flowing hair, his impressive height, his majestic way of walking as he left the horse and corral behind and entered the village?

Yes, it was Lone Eagle!

Her pulse racing, she watched him, expecting him to go to his lodge. Instead, he went to another.

She wondered why. Whose could it be? Jealousy sprang into her heart when she thought that he might have a woman waiting for him in the lodge. Perhaps that was where he kept his women for his nightly pleasure, using his other lodge for meeting with his men.

She waited and watched for him to leave the lodge, and when he didn't, she suddenly realized this was the opportunity she had been waiting for. With Lone Eagle someplace other than his lodge, it would make her entrance much easier. She could be there waiting for him in the dark. Or she could simply hide at the back of his lodge behind his belongings. That might be best. He would go to his bed and not even notice her until morning. That would give her the opportunity to get some sleep before he decided what to do with her the next morning.

Deep down, she hoped he wouldn't resent her being there, but would be willing to lend her a hand. One night and one day of lodging was all she would ask of him.

Her heart pounding, she began her slow descent on her father's horse down the side of the hill to enter an Indian village for the first time in her life.

Chapter Six

Within my reach!
I could have touched!
I might have chanced that way!
Soft sauntered through the village . . .

—EMILY DICKINSON

Breathless with a mixture of fear and excitement, Zondra unsaddled, then freed Speedie among the many other horses. He could blend in with the herd as though he were one of them so that he would not quickly be recognized as an intruder. It was best that he was there among the many other horses in case her father might happen along searching for Zondra. Zondra just hoped that her father wouldn't take the time to look down at the village and the horses from the bluff. From that vantage point he would surely make out his white stallion!

Her heart pounding, her throat dry, Zondra grabbed up her makeshift travel bag and ran quietly to the village, sneaking in behind the lodges, then hurrying around to enter Lone Eagle's, slipping, hopefully unseen, through the entranceway.

Never having been in a tepee before, she stopped long enough to familiarize herself with it. Smoke rose slowly upward, escaping through a smoke hole, from a fire that burned low in the center of the lodge. The fire was surrounded by comfortable-looking mats and blankets. Looking into the shadows, she saw buckskin parfleche bags, weapons, more blankets, and other things she could not make out in the dark.

She looked at the buffalo-hide walls of the lodge and saw beautiful paintings of animals, the buffalo most prominent of them all. She also saw what might be a calendar, on which were drawn objects that she also could not make out in the dark. To her left, she saw something standing just inside the door. She couldn't tell what it was. It was wrapped securely in skins.

Afraid she had taken too long looking around the interior of the tepee, and suddenly feeling a desperate need to hide, Zondra tucked her bag into the crook of her left arm and hurried to the back of the tepee, directly opposite the entranceway. Breathless, she fell to her knees behind a stack of blankets, then waited.

She became aware of the night noises. Everything was so much more clearly defined during this time of night, when, except for a few night creatures, everyone slept.

Somewhere close by, in the forest behind the lodge, an owl hooted, went silent for a moment, then hooted again. Farther away, in the winding stream, a loon's cry echoed across the water. Zondra could hear horses neighing softly in the corral.

Crickets sang to their mates in the grass. Frogs croaked. And a sound now all too familiar to her, a cougar's screech, came from afar.

That made Zondra's thoughts return to her precious cat. Where could Ralph have gone? Had the cougar found her? Was Ralph dead? Or was her precious cat out there, as frightened as Zondra had been, running frantically through the night, not knowing where?

Thoughts of Ralph and the cougar were quickly interrupted when Lone Eagle came into the lodge. His entrance was so abrupt, so sudden, that Zondra flinched with a start and knocked over the stack of blankets that she had been hiding behind.

Now on her knees, her eyes wide with dismay, she stared at Lone Eagle as he gaped openly at her, the fire's glow casting dancing shadows on her lovely face.

"You!" Lone Eagle said, quirking an eyebrow. "Zondra? Why are you here? How did you get here?"

For a moment Zondra was at a loss for words, for now that Lone Eagle was so close, his eyes locked with hers, she could hardly believe herself that she was there.

She wondered if he saw her presence there as the act of a desperate woman. Or might he believe it was for some other reason . . . that she had come to offer herself to him?

That thought made her rush to her feet to give him at least part of the true explanation. She didn't want to confess everything to him. She still did not want to have to explain to him how it was that her skin color differed so much from her mother's.

"I . . . I . . . had a need to leave my home," she stammered, her pulse racing.

"You were unhappy?"

"Yes, unhappy and . . . and . . . something more."

"What else?" Lone Eagle asked, taking a slow step toward her.

Zondra stiffened, for she just now thought of how vulnerable she was, all alone in this man's presence. If he wished to, he could overpower her and . . . take her for himself.

"What else?" she said, gulping hard as he took another step toward her. "It was the men who worked there," she said in a rush, noticing how that made

Lone Eagle hesitate, and how his eyes narrowed. "I felt threatened by them."

"Threatened in what way? Afraid they would take advantage of your lovely innocence?" Lone Eagle said, anger rushing through him at the thought of any man wrongly approaching this beautiful, sweet woman.

"Yes. To some men, women are objects to be used, not respected," Zondra said, in her mind's eye seeing her half brother Guy leering down at her as he held her to the ground, just before he tried to rape her.

"Why is it that your father did not make things right for you?" Lone Eagle said, again approaching her. He held his hand out toward her. "Your father should have given you a life free from fear. Why did he not do this? Does he not treasure you as the Crow treasure their daughters?"

That question caused a pain, deep and searing, to enter Zondra's heart. She went stone-quiet, for she just could not explain the relationship between her and her father. To do that would be to reveal too much that was uncomfortable for her to talk about. How could she tell Lone Eagle that the man who fathered her was also her slave master?

No. She could not belittle herself in the eyes of this wonderful man by allowing him to know that her father felt so little for her that he made her live the life of a slave. Lone Eagle would never understand.

The Indian chief didn't understand Zondra's sudden silence, but he didn't press her for answers. It was enough that she had come to him in her time of trouble.

"Are you hungry?" Lone Eagle asked.

Relieved that he wasn't going to try to get more

answers out of her, Zondra smiled at him. "No, thank you," she murmured. She felt her eyes burning with the need for sleep. "But . . . but I'm so very sleepy."

Finding this almost too good to be true, that Zondra was there, and that she was comfortable enough with him and trusted him enough to actually sleep in his lodge, Lone Eagle reached down and grabbed a blanket and held it out for her.

"This blanket is yours to use tonight," he said, glad when she took it. He nodded toward a pallet of furs on the right side of the lodge. "You can sleep there. I will sleep on the other side of the fire, away from you so that you will have your privacy."

Touched by his kindness and gentleness, Zondra gazed at him for a moment, then spoke. "Why are you doing this?" she murmured. "Why are you being so kind? So generous? I'm an intruder in the night. I came into your lodge without being invited."

Lone Eagle wanted to tell her how wrong she was—that, in truth, she was no stranger in his lodge, for she had been there with him many times before in his dreams, as well as in his daytime fantasies!

But until she felt more comfortable with him, so that she could open up and share her deepest thoughts, he felt it was best not to be as open with her, as well. It was enough that she was there, that she trusted him.

"Would you not be as kind, as generous to me, were I to come to your lodge unannounced, seeking shelter and escape from a life that was not good to me?" Lone Eagle asked softly, daring to reach out to place a gentle hand on her cheek.

To Zondra, his touch was heaven, momentarily stealing her breath away. She had to fight against revealing to him all she was feeling, now that she had

actually been touched not only by his hand, but by
the deep longing she saw in his eyes.

"Yes . . . I would do the same for you," Zondra
said, her voice a breathless whisper. "I would offer
you shelter. I would offer you food. I . . . would . . .
offer you . . . my bed."

Realizing what she had just said, that she would
offer him her bed, made a hot blush rush to Lone
Eagle's cheeks. The mere mention of her bed made
Lone Eagle's heart skip a beat as passion built inside him.

But when she lowered her eyes, the spell that was
weaving between them was broken. Quickly he slid
his hand down beneath her chin and lifted her eyes
back to his. "Never humbly lower your eyes for any
reason," he said thickly. "You felt comfortable
enough to come to me. Feel comfortable enough to
speak freely to me when you wish to . . . about
anything."

"But . . . ," Zondra began, wanting to explain what
she had meant about offering him her bed. She had
not meant that she would be a part of that offering.

"It is time to sleep now, not talk," Lone Eagle said.
He swept an arm around her waist and led her to the
pallet of furs, then walked away from her.

Her pulse racing, even more in awe of this man's
gentleness, Zondra watched him as he settled down
onto a pallet of blankets far across the fire from her.
He stretched out on his side, his back to her. She then
quietly laid her bag aside and stretched out herself.
She sighed with pleasure at the softness of the pelts
against a body that was tired and sore from the long
ride. The blanket she pulled over her was so warm,
so comforting.

She couldn't help but think about Ralph out there

somewhere, all alone in the cold, perhaps injured . . .
perhaps dead! She squeezed her eyes closed. No! She
wouldn't let herself think the worst about Ralph. Perhaps the cat might come to this very village, seeking
shelter and food. Yes, that was what Zondra would
continue to believe. She would be reunited with her
precious cat. They had been together for so long, it
wasn't fair that fate would separate them now just
as Zondra had been brave enough to seek freedom
for herself.

Her heart lurched as Lone Eagle suddenly rose
from his blankets. It was obvious that he couldn't relax
and sleep just yet. She watched him tend to things at
the far side of the lodge . . . straightening his arrows
in his quiver, rolling and rerolling some blankets.

But she couldn't keep her eyes on those things. His
long hair was so beautiful, sweeping the floor of the
tepee as he moved from place to place. Zondra leaned
up on an elbow. "I love your hair," she suddenly
blurted out, surprised at herself for speaking when she
had not truly intended to.

But now that she had said that much, she continued
when he turned and gazed in wonder at her. "Your
hair is so long, glossy, and beautiful," she said softly.
"It's so thick. I . . . I noticed that the women in your
village wear their hair much shorter than the men.
Why is that?"

Lone Eagle's eyes widened with surprise. "To know
that the Crow women wear their hair differently from
the men means that you have to have seen them, and
how could you have done that when you came to my
lodge this late hour and all of the women are already
asleep?" he asked, his heart thumping inside his chest,
knowing that she must have been somewhere close by,
spying on them.

Had she done this earlier today, before her arrival? Or had she done this some other day, perhaps as she had been horseback riding with her father?

But seeing how his questions created such alarm in her eyes, and recalling how she had eluded his queries earlier, he did not wait for her to respond this time.

"A Crow woman's hair is not allowed to compete in length with her lord's," he explained. "The women are obliged to wear their hair much shorter." His gaze went to Zondra's long, wavy black hair, then he gazed into her eyes again. "If you, Zondra, were my woman, you would be required to cut your hair shorter than you wear it now, for Lone Eagle would be your lord."

Zondra's eyes widened in disbelief. "I see," she said, her voice weak.

Aghast that the Crow warriors would put themselves in a much higher standing than their women, and abhorring the very thought of ever being made to cut her beautiful long hair, Zondra suddenly felt ill at ease in Lone Eagle's presence.

Having sensual feelings for him threatened the sort of future she had mapped out for herself, which was to be free of *all* men. Knowing it would be easy to fall in love with Lone Eagle and stay with him forever should he ask her, and wanting no man ever to be her "lord," having been "lorded" over by men all of her life, she decided that it was not in her best interests, after all, to stay in Lone Eagle's lodge. She must find safety and shelter elsewhere.

She did not have to work hard to force a yawn, for she was still as sleepy as she'd been before.

"I see your yawn," Lone Eagle said softly. "We will talk more tomorrow. I will return to my blankets and stay there this time so that I will not disturb your sleep. You return to yours."

"Yes, I am so terribly tired," Zondra murmured, settling back down on the pelts, drawing the blanket back up to her chin. She watched him get comfortable again on his bed of blankets. She continued to watch him until he went to sleep. Then she tossed aside the blanket that covered her. She crawled from the make-shift bed, then wrapped one of the warmest pelts around her shoulders. She grabbed up her travel bag and started to leave, then stopped long enough to take one last look at Lone Eagle as he slept so peacefully beside the glowing coals of the fire.

Never could any other man be as handsome, she marveled to herself, as though she were looking at him for the first time. For certain, she had feelings for him that she wished she didn't have. If it could have been another time, another life, they might have been able to work things out and have a life together.

But now? The odds were stacked against them. Sti-fling a sob behind one of her hands, knowing that she was leaving something that might have been too wonderful to imagine, she sneaked away from the lodge.

She hurried to the horses and saddled Speedie, took him from the corral, slung her bag in place, then rode onward into the inky blackness of night, downhearted, frightened, and full of despair.

She looked all around her, still hoping that she might find her cat. Until now, Ralph had never let her down.

Now it seemed that all of life was against her!

Chapter Seven

Remorse is cureless—the disease
Not even God can heal.

—EMILY DICKINSON

His long, lanky legs stiff from a joint ailment, Harrison Lester ambled toward the corral. His eyebrows arched with puzzlement when he didn't see his sleek white stallion standing at the gate, where he always waited in the early morning for Harrison.

Cursing the bright sunlight, Harrison blinked and looked toward the corral again, blaming the sun for having blurred his vision. But after blinking his eyes and getting even closer to the corral, his heart skipped a beat, for he *still* didn't see Speedie.

"Damn whoever took my horse for a ride this morning without my permission," he growled as he stamped in his shiny leather boots toward the bunkhouse, where he could see the cowhands just emerging from their living quarters. "The nerve! I'll horsewhip him, that's for sure!"

Someone spoke his name behind him, and his heart lurched when he recognized her voice and knew for damn certain it wasn't his wife. Harrison turned with a start.

He gaped openly at Zondra's mother as she ran

toward him, crying. He had told Ada countless times not to come to him out in the open like this. Thus far, as far as he knew, the cowhands didn't know about his relationship with her.

He wasn't about to allow these men to realize the truth about Ada, nor Zondra, for it wasn't any of their damn business that he had a black mistress with whom he shared a white-skinned daughter.

But seeing how distressed Ada was, the tears flowing down her lovely black cheeks, he quickly forgot who might see them together. Something was terribly wrong or Ada would not be crying, nor would she have approached him openly. She knew the rules.

Harrison hurried to her. Taking her gently by an elbow, he ushered her into the barn, out of sight of the cowhands *and* his wife, who was surely just rising and preparing for her morning bath and coffee. He did not want Sylvia to see him with Ada, even though he knew that she knew about their secret trysts. She most certainly had guessed, long ago, that Zondra was a love child conceived by Harrison and his mistress.

But Sylvia guarded this secret well. She had been embarrassed enough back in Mississippi that most everyone knew why a white child mingled with the blacks!

"Honey, what's wrong?" Harrison asked, placing his hands gently on Ada's waist. He wanted so badly to draw her into his embrace and kiss her. He could never get enough of her. He truly loved her with a passion he could not control.

His eyes swept quickly over her. When he saw nothing visibly wrong with her, he gazed questioningly into her eyes. "You don't look ill," he said softly. "So are your tears for Zondra? Ada, is our daughter ill?"

Her sobs catching in her throat, Ada could hardly

speak. "I'm so sorry to have to come to you like this when I know you don't want us bein' seen together," she cried. She gazed up at Harrison with her wide, dark velvet eyes. "But I had to, Harrison. I *have* come to you about Zondra. Oh, Harrison, I promised her I wouldn't tell you, but I can't keep it to myself. Zondra . . . she . . . left last night."

"What?" Harrison said, taken aback by the news. "What do you mean . . . she *left*?"

"She's been thinkin' 'bout doin' this for some time, Harrison, but I didn't believe she'd do it," Ada said, her voice breaking. "You know how a child can wish for things but never do nothin' 'bout it."

"What things?" Harrison said, dropping his hands away from her. He frustratedly raked his long, lean fingers through his thick golden hair. "Ada, tell me everything. Stop pussyfooting around. My daughter is out there someplace, perhaps lost. Surely frightened as hell!" He inhaled a deep, agitated breath. "How could you allow our daughter to leave? Why didn't you come and tell me earlier so I could stop her?"

"Don't you see, Harrison?" Ada said softly. "This is the way Zondra wanted it. She wants her freedom . . . and she's afraid of Guy. Guy carries a deep hatred inside his heart for that beating you gave him over Zondra. Zondra's afraid of what he might do. He might not stop at raping her next time. He might kill her."

"She's that afraid of her half brother?" Harrison breathed, having tried to forget the confrontation he had had with Guy after he caught his son with Zondra in such a compromising position. He had hoped that both of his children had also forgotten it.

The remembrance of that day when he found Guy close to raping his precious daughter stung every time he allowed himself to think of it. He had wanted to do more than whip the younger man that day. He had wanted to kill him!

"Not only Guy, Harrison, but also the cowhands you've hired here at your ranch," Ada murmured. "Haven't you seen them leering at our daughter? Don't you see how they consider her fair game, since it's obvious she don't belong in the fields with the rest of your slaves? They each and every one of them lust after her. Zondra couldn't bear any more of it."

"I've been too busy to notice my cowhands sinning in their minds as they stare at Zondra," Harrison said, sighing. "Had I, I would've taken them down a notch or two with my whip."

"I promised Zondra I wouldn't tell you I knew anything about her leaving, Harrison, but the more I thought about our precious daughter being out there all alone, I had to tell you," Ada blurted out. "I beg you to go for her. Make sure she is safe. Oh, Harrison, bring her back to me."

She paused, then placed her hands on her hips and looked up at him with fire in her eyes. "And, Harrison, shame on you for not treating your children equally," she scolded. "You know as well as I that Zondra should've been allowed to share all that your other white children have enjoyed. Then Guy wouldn't have been given cause to see Zondra as someone beneath him, as someone to use . . . to rape."

She swallowed hard, then said one more thing. "She's seeking her freedom from not only Guy, but everything else unfair about her life, especially . . . especially you," she said, her voice drawn. "Harrison, she wasn't even allowed to have her true last name when she was born. She's carried that shame inside her heart since the moment she was old enough to know that the name Poole was *my* last name, not her father's."

Guilt clutched Harrison's heart. Not caring anymore that someone might come into the barn and see him with his mistress, he swept Ada into his arms, wanting to make things right between them.

"Oh, Ada, yes, I know you're right," he said throatily. "And should I find Zondra, she *will* be taken into my home and treated the same as my other children, even though I know they will abhor the very idea of her being under the same roof as they."

He brushed soft kisses across her beautifully shaped lips. "Oh, Ada, how I love you," he whispered huskily. "How I need you."

Her pulse racing, needing and loving him just as much, but knowing now wasn't the time to think of themselves, Ada slipped out of Harrison's arms and looked up at him. "My love, thank you for seein' what's best for our daughter," she murmured. "I only hope it's not too late."

"It's not too late," Harrison said, his jaw tightening. "I *will* find her. I *will* bring her home. I'll give her a beautiful room with a closet full of beautiful clothes. And perfumes! Ah, how she'll enjoy the best of perfumes and jewelry. Darling Ada, it'll be a thrill when you see our daughter decked out that first time in Paris's finest!"

"It'd be a dream come true, not only for Zondra, but also me," Ada said, tears flowing from her eyes again. "But, Harrison, you know it's not that easy. There's . . . there's . . . your wife, Sylvia. What about Sylvia?"

"Although she pretends not to, Sylvia has known all along about you and the children born of our love. She just likes to act as though none of you ever existed," Harrison said bitterly. "All Sylvia cares about is having her jewels, furs, fancy clothes, and French perfume. She doesn't truly care about me. We haven't shared the same bed since the birth of our last child. She doesn't allow me to touch her, accusing me of getting her pregnant every time I hang my breeches on the bedpost."

"She's so foolish," Ada said softly. "If I could be there in that fine home with you, I'd never let you out of my bed." She giggled. "Cain't you just imagine how it'd be, Harrison? All the talk we'd arouse?"

"I wish I could take you into my home," he said thickly. He lowered his eyes. "But we both know it can never happen."

"Yes, and I've accepted that," Ada said, reaching over to take one of his hands. "Oh, Harrison, how I treasure our moments together. I wish we were at our cabin now. How I'd love to be in your arms, makin' love."

"After I bring Zondra back, we'll go and make crazy love for a full day and night," Harrison said huskily. "But now? We've got Zondra to think about. I've got to find her."

"Harrison," Ada said, gently touching his cheek. "If I could have any wish I wished granted, our children who were sold elsewhere would still be here with me," she murmured. "It was unfair of you, forcin' me to give them up. But I'll be forever grateful that you didn't force the same fate on our precious Zondra. Yet should the color of our children's skin have made that much difference to you?"

Harrison took her hand and kissed the palm, then again swept her into his arms. He pressed his face into her luxurious black hair. "Forgive me, Ada, for having sold away our children," he said humbly. "I wish now that I had never done such a horrible thing as that. I promise, Ada, that I'll somehow find a way to make this up to you."

She clung to him, then yanked herself free and ran from the barn, sobbing. Harrison stepped to the door and watched her until she went into her cabin. Then, with a tight jaw and flashing eyes, he grabbed his whip from a shelf in the barn and strode across the yard with it clutched tight in one hand. Entering the house, he let the back door bang shut behind him. He took the servant's stairs at the back of the house up to the upstairs corridor and went to Guy's closed bedroom door.

He would have known that Zondra had left mainly because of Guy without Ada telling him. And Harrison now knew who had taken his horse. Zondra. She knew she'd get farther and could depend on Speedie. And he would never hold that against her. He was sure that when he found one of them . . . Zondra *or* the horse . . . he would have them *both* back!

Without knocking on Guy's bedroom door, he kicked it open. Growling, his eyes flaring, and ignoring that he was interrupting his son and daughter-in-law's lovemaking, paying absolutely no heed to the fear in their eyes caused by his abrupt entry, Harrison went to the bed and grabbed Guy by his throat.

As Guy's wife, Lenora, cowered and grabbed a blanket to cover her nudity, Harrison towered over his son and glared down into his eyes.

"You are lazy, useless, spoiled . . . ," Harrison hissed from between clenched teeth as he held Guy immobile, his hands tight around his throat. "You never turn a hand to do anything but cause trouble and satisfy your sexual urges!"

Gagging and choking, Guy grabbed at his father's hands as Harrison dragged him from the bedroom. The young man's bare heels and rear end banged hard against the steps as his father continued to drag him down the back stairs. His wind practically cut off by his father's powerful hands, Guy couldn't even plead to be set free. His father continued to drag him until he had him outside, still nude, and finally released him just outside of the barn.

Sobbing, Guy scrambled away from his father on his knees, his face red with humiliation as the cowhands gathered and watched as his father caught up with him with his whip. Guy cried for mercy and fell to the ground with the first snap of the whip. The piercing pain spread through him as the whip came down across his back and bare rump, not once, but ten times.

The whipping finally over, Guy lay still on the ground, his face buried in the thick green grass. Even though he was glad that the whipping was over, the pain did not end. He was aware of the wetness of blood on his back, where the sting was almost unbearable.

Sobbing, Guy swore beneath his breath that he would find Zondra. *She* was the reason he'd gotten two beatings now from his father's whip. He knew that Zondra was missing—his father had shouted this at him as he had whipped him.

He didn't even turn over when he heard the thundering of horses' hooves as his father and the cowhands rode off in search of Zondra. Hearing nothing but silence now, glad that the men were gone, Guy stumbled to his feet. Ignoring his mother's deep sobs as she reached out for him as he passed her on the steps, he went on inside and back to his bedroom, where his wife was waiting for him, weeping.

"Why did he do that?" Lenora cried, staring disbelievingly at the bloody welts on her husband's back. "Twice, Guy! He's done this horrible thing to you twice now!"

"Just shut up and get some water and a soft cloth,

and the ointment you used after my last beating," Guy grumbled. "Take care of my back, wife, and then I'm leaving."

"Where are you going?" Lenora sobbed as she ran to their bedside table and poured water into a basin.

"I'm going to find Zondra," Guy said, easing down on the bed as Lenora came to him with the cloth and water. "When I find her, I'm gonna kill her!"

"Zondra?" Lenora said, her voice strained. "Is this all about Zondra?"

"Just treat my back, wife, and don't ask any more questions," Guy snorted. "That bitch. She's caused me enough trouble."

"Oh, Guy, why are you so obsessed with that half sister of yours?" Lenora sobbed. "She's nothing but a whoring slave. You know that. Yet . . . you . . . lust after her like a dog lusts after a female dog in heat! Leave it alone, Guy. Forget her."

"I can't," Guy said, his voice tormented. "I . . . just . . . can't."

"Please do nothing foolish," Lenora begged.

"She's gone and I'm going to be the one to find her," Guy said with conviction.

"She's gone?" Lenora said, stepping around to face Guy. "What do you mean?"

"She ran away," Guy said, his eyes gleaming. He smiled wickedly. "And mostly because of *me*."

Lenora took a deep, gasping breath, then continued to make her husband more comfortable while trying not to feel like she was second in his life—second to a slave. The mere thought of her own husband cavorting with a lowly slave, much less his blood kin, made her skin crawl with disgust.

Chapter Eight

The whole of me, forever,
What more the woman can,
Say quick, that I may dower thee
With last delight I own!

—Emily Dickinson

Stretching and yawning, Lone Eagle slowly awakened. When he was finally totally awake, he recalled how he had found Zondra in his tepee the prior evening and that she had stayed the night.

With a jerk he turned his head and peered over the cold coals of his fire. His heart skipped a beat when he saw that she was gone.

Thinking that she might have gone outside to get a cool drink from the nearby stream, or might even be bathing there, Lone Eagle left his pallet of furs, slipped on his moccasins, then pushed the entrance flap aside to step outside and join her.

He stopped and stared when he saw something lying on the ground just outside the buckskin flap. His eyebrows lifted in wonder as he stared down at a deer mouse that lay lifelessly at his entranceway, beheaded.

He looked around and saw several other dead deer mice. They were the dreaded creature of all Crow people because the deer mice constantly raided the Crow's cache of corn and other vegetables they stored away each year for the long, cold days of winter. To the Crow people, the deer mice were a calamity! They seemed impossible to stop.

Lone Eagle bent and studied the mice. Each had its head removed.

"Why?" he whispered. "Who?"

His eyes widened when he noticed a movement out of the corner of his eye. He looked quickly to his right side, just in time to see Zondra's cat scamper into view.

Being the friendly cat she was, Ralph approached Lone Eagle and began rubbing herself against the Indian's leg, purring contentedly.

Lone Eagle scarcely breathed as he stared down at this tiny cat creature. He had never seen anything like it before. The only cats he was familiar with were the large mountain lions and panthers. This small cat's sudden appearance at his lodge seemed steeped in magic and mystery!

"Where did you come from?" Lone Eagle asked softly. He started to squat to study the cat more closely, then stopped and watched as it leaped away and went behind his tepee, returning soon with another dead deer mouse in its mouth.

Stunned speechless, Lone Eagle watched as the cat left, then once again brought another dead mouse and deposited it with the others. Pride showing in her eyes as she gazed up at Lone Eagle, Ralph's tail made slow swipes back and forth. Her soft purring sounded like the contented drone of bees to Lone Eagle.

Now Lone Eagle realized where all the dead mice had come from. This small cat creature was responsible!

Smiling, Lone Eagle bent down and picked Ralph up. He held the cat out before him and looked directly into her sharp green eyes. "Where have you come from?" he asked softly. "And what sort of musical sound is that coming from inside you? How do you make it?"

Mad Buffalo came and stood next to Lone Eagle. He had been standing just outside his own lodge watching the cat. He, too, had found several dead deer mice just outside his lodge entrance.

"My son, is this small cat creature not something to behold?" Mad Buffalo murmured, slowly stroking Ralph's fur as Lone Eagle held Ralph close. "Surely the creature has been sent to our village by *Ah-badt-deadt-deah,* the Great Spirit, to rid the Crow's lives of the destructive deer mice."

When several village dogs came and began barking at Ralph, the cat leaped from Lone Eagle's arms. She hissed and raked a paw across the pointy muzzle of one of the dogs, sending it and the others in a fast retreat, yelping.

Stunned to see how the tiny cat had the power to frighten the large, aggressive dogs, Mad Buffalo was even more convinced that Ralph was special, that she had been sent to his people by the greater power above.

"To have such courage, that it would go against dogs in such a way, it surely is a male cat," Mad Buffalo murmured. "Pick him up. Turn him over, Lone Eagle. Check and see."

Lone Eagle swept Ralph up from the ground. He turned her and saw no sack between the cat's hind legs. He looked up at his father again. "No, the cat is not male," he said. "It is a she-cat with much spirit and courage."

His attention was drawn elsewhere as Two Braids, one of the village women, came to Lone Eagle with a large pot of stew that she had prepared for him.

When Two Braids saw the cat, she stopped short and started backing away.

"Two Braids, do not be afraid of the small cat creature," Mad Buffalo said, reaching over to take the cat from Lone Eagle. "It has come to us for a purpose. Do you not see the many deer mice the cat has brought to both mine and Lone Eagle's lodges as proof of why she has come to us?"

Two Braids gazed around her at the dead mice, shuddered visibly, then walked on past Lone Eagle and Mad Buffalo and took the pot of stew inside Lone Eagle's lodge and hung it on the hook of a tripod over the fireplace.

When Lone Eagle and Mad Buffalo went into the lodge, Two Braids already had a good fire going beneath the food. She turned to them and smiled, gazed questioningly at the cat again, then turned and rushed from the lodge.

"I think Two Braids still fears the small cat creature," Mad Buffalo said, settling down on a pallet of furs beside the fire. Lone Eagle sat down beside him.

"Only because the small cat creature is a thing of mystery to her, as it is to us," Lone Eagle said, ladling some stew into a wooden bowl. "In time Two Braids will grow accustomed to its presence in our village, as will everyone else."

"Except for the deer mice," Mad Buffalo said, chuckling as he watched Lone Eagle set a bowl of food rich in venison meat and juices on the mat before Ralph. "They will learn to run from the small cat creature with fear."

"Since the cat seems loath to *eat* its kill, I will offer it food as a reward for what it has done for us," Lone Eagle said, pushing the bowl of stew over closer to his father.

He watched Mad Buffalo put Ralph down beside
the bowl of food, then smiled as the cat started lapping
up the juices. She grabbed a thick chunk of venison
meat and began to chew it.

"Deer mice meat did not look as appealing as venison meat to the small cat creature," Mad Buffalo said,
again chuckling. He reached over to stroke Ralph's
fur as the cat continued to eat.

"I wonder if there are more like her?" Lone Eagle
said, then looked toward the bed of blankets upon
which Zondra had slept, his thoughts on her again,
wondering why she had not returned to his lodge by
now. Did it mean that she had gone farther than the
stream? Or that she had left his village?

If she was truly gone, he must accept the fact that
she had plans that did not include him. She seemed
driven by some hidden force.

He wondered what he might have done to make
her take flight again in this land that held dangers for
a lone woman, not only from two-legged animals, but
also four.

He wanted to leave right away to look for her, but
he didn't want to look foolish in the eyes of his father
over a white woman who for a brief time had shown
an interest in him. If she was gone, she had stayed
only long enough to rest up for her continuing
journey.

It hurt him to think that she could not trust him
enough to stay the whole night, nor share the morning
meal with him.

Perhaps he was jumping to conclusions. She might
still return to his lodge. She might still share a meal
with him, and if she did, he would try to convince her
of the foolishness of leaving at all.

He wanted her as he had never wanted any other woman. His heart ached to hold her . . . to kiss her. . . .

"Son, where have your thoughts taken you?" Mad Buffalo asked, holding a wooden dish of stew out toward Lone Eagle. "You seemed far away from this place and time. Where were you, my son, in your thoughts?"

Feeling caught, almost trapped, Lone Eagle smiled awkwardly at his father and gently took the proffered bowl of stew. "Where?" he said, now accepting a wooden spoon from Mad Buffalo. "My mind wanders sometimes to a particular woman."

"A woman?" Mad Buffalo said, ladling out stew from the large pot for his own wooden bowl. "What woman? You have not spoken of any particular woman to your father for many moons now."

Lone Eagle glanced at the entrance flap when it suddenly fluttered, his heart lurching inside his chest to think it might be Zondra, preparing to enter. But then he realized it had only been the morning breeze rippling the buckskin covering, and a keen disappointment assailed him. She had been gone way too long now. He did not expect her to appear again. At least not this morning.

He hoped she might reconsider being out there on her own and return to him so he could protect her forever!

He wanted to go and search for her and bring her back, by force, if necessary. But he could not do that. He had never forced anything on any woman before. He wouldn't start now. Not even if it meant that he would never see her again. Whatever was meant to be would be.

He would just have to start looking elsewhere for a

woman. It was time—he had been alone in his blankets long enough! And he so craved a son!

"My son, again your mind wanders," Mad Buffalo said, once more drawing Lone Eagle's thoughts back to the present.

"*Ahh*, yes, I know," Lone Eagle said, nodding.

"Do you wish to share whatever it is that is bothering you with your father?" Mad Buffalo asked.

"Perhaps later," Lone Eagle said quietly. "But for now I must feed the hunger that is gnawing inside my stomach."

Mad Buffalo nodded and ate in silence with Lone Eagle. They both smiled when Ralph curled up on a blanket beside the fire and went to sleep, her purrs filling the silent spaces of the tepee.

When both wooden bowls had been emptied three times, Lone Eagle and Mad Buffalo put them aside. "Let us talk of things fathers and sons talk comfortably about," Mad Buffalo said, crossing his legs before him, resting his hands on his knees. "My son, do you plan to avenge White Bead's pride tonight?"

"Yes, tonight," Lone Eagle said, nodding. A slow smile played across his lips. "If I could be a small deer mouse for one moment of my life, it would be when Red Moon awakens and finds a lock of his hair lying beside him."

"The message will be clear enough to him that he has wronged our beloved prophet," Mad Buffalo said, his eyes taking on an angry gleam. "If this had happened in my father's time, not only a lock of the enemy's hair would be removed. His whole scalp would hang from my father's scalp pole."

"Those times are long past," Lone Eagle said dryly. "Never will we display scalps in such a way again. To do so is a disgrace. It is *not* a thing of honor as our ancestors thought. It was such deeds that caused the whites to nickname red men 'savages.' "

"A disgraceful name that is most hated," Mad Buffalo hissed out. "Too often it is the men with white skin who are the true savages!"

Lone Eagle's mind again went back to someone with white skin . . . to Zondra! He was glad that he hadn't told his father about her having come into his lodge last night, for he now knew for certain that she was gone.

Yes, it was good that Lone Eagle had not mentioned her name to his father and bragged about her having come to him for protection, when it was obvious that something had changed her mind. Apparently she cared nothing for him at all, nor did she trust him.

He could not help but ponder again why she had left him. Was it something he said? Had he done something that was offensive to her?

But how could that be? he despaired to himself. He had treated her like a lady. He had not even approached her as he had so wished to!

In her eyes he had seen that she cared for him in ways women care for men before sharing kisses and embraces. Was it those feelings that had made her flee? Had she been afraid of her emotions? Or was she afraid of him because he was a man with red skin? Was she afraid of his people?

He doubted he would ever know the answers to any of those questions, for he did not think that he would ever see her again. He wondered if he should even want to.

No! He would *not* go and search for her. She had left because she wanted nothing to do with him. So be it!

Chapter Nine

The heart I cherished in my own
Till mine too heavy grew,
Yet strangest, heavier since it went,
Is it too large for you?

— EMILY DICKINSON

Having bathed in a stream, her hair and her body smelling fresh and clean, Zondra sat beneath a cool sheltering of cottonwood trees, eating breakfast from her food supply. Cheese, crackers, and an apple satisfied her hunger for now.

She craved something more substantial, but knew that she would have to be on this same sort of rationed diet until she reached her destination—hopefully a home where she would be paid to help the woman of the house with her chores.

After she had accumulated enough money, she would travel farther, then book passage on a riverboat that would take her to parts unknown. It was exciting to think about such an adventure, yet her heart ached to know that she would never see Lone Eagle again.

For too long she had fantasized about him. It hurt to know that it had all been an impossible dream, she would never be able to share even a small portion of her life with him.

"My 'lord,' indeed," she whispered sarcastically. She would never allow anyone to "lord" over her again.

She would never be anyone's slave again. When she found work, she'd be paid for it.

It made her sad to think about her beloved mother, who had been a slave all of her life. And even though Zondra's mother was in love with her master, and had even borne him more than one child, she was still his slave, and would be until the day she died.

"Unless I can take her away from that life that degrades her," Zondra whispered to herself as she finished up her meager breakfast.

She knew that she had to be reasonable about that and face the reality of the situation. No matter how much she wanted to believe she could take her mother away from slavery, she knew that was impossible. Wherever her mother went, she would still have the skin color that would show proof of her status in life.

"Once a slave, always a slave," Zondra whispered bitterly to herself. Then she smiled. "Well, that no longer applies to *me*. My skin is white. I can pass for white. No one will ever be the wiser."

They most certainly would never know that she had also been a slave since she was born. They would never know that she had a "mammy" for a mother!

It shamed her to think that she would not henceforth claim her mother as hers, especially if she were to be taken in by some wonderful white family that agreed to share bed and board with her.

"Mama, I am so ashamed," Zondra said aloud, tears rushing to her eyes. "Oh, Mama, if you only knew where my thoughts just took me, you'd disown me as yours."

Tired of wrestling with her thoughts, so torn over her feelings for not only her mother, but also Lone Eagle, Zondra rose to her feet.

Hurriedly she washed her hands in the stream,

folded the blanket upon which she had eaten her meal and returned it to her travel bag, then swung herself into her saddle and rode off again into land unknown to her.

Never before had she felt this alone or so empty.

"Ralph," she whispered. "Where are you? You were to be my traveling companion."

She knew that each mile she traveled put more distance between her and her beloved cat. If only she knew how Ralph was, if she was still alive, even. That would be enough for her. Zondra could even tolerate this aloneness. "But I'll never know," she murmured, brushing tears from her eyes with the back of a hand.

She traveled onward beneath the hot sun, the occasional breeze welcome on her cheeks. She sought the shelter of trees whenever possible, the coolness that swept toward her from their deep shadows a momentary reprieve from the dull heat and oppressive air.

She rode into a cool thicket of trees that was a mixture of hardwoods and statuesque pines that were surely centuries old. The pine smell was heavenly, as was the aroma of forest flowers that dotted the land on all sides of her with shades of pale blue, white, and yellow.

Then she was forced to leave all of this behind and again travel in the sun, with tall, green, waving grass stretching out on all sides of her.

Suddenly she saw something up ahead as the brisk wind bent the grass first one way and then another. Her heart seemed to stop and her throat went dry when she saw a pack of white wolves standing around something, devouring it, snarling and fighting over the kill.

Afraid of the wolves, seeing how vicious they were in their hunger, Zondra drew her reins tight and stopped. She was suddenly keenly aware of not having a firearm to protect herself.

She had heard about the white wolves in this area and how they were always foraging for food. When buffalo were plentiful in this area, the wolves were known to follow the herds of shaggy animals. The predators were known to feed on the carcasses of those that fell because of weakness or hunger.

Now that the buffalo were scarce, she wondered what the wolves fed on. What were they feasting so hungrily on today?

A thought sprang to Zondra's mind that sickened her through and through.

"Ralph?" she whispered, her voice catching at the possibility of her cat being the wolves' meal today. "Oh, Ralph," she cried, tears spilling from her eyes. "What if it *is* you?"

Suddenly a flock of buzzards swept down from the sky, squawking. The wolves scattered, soon disappearing over a rise of land.

Her heart pounding, wanting to go and see if the wolves had been feasting on her beloved cat, Zondra sank her heels into the flanks of her horse and rode onward, shouting, sending the buzzards off in a quick, frenzied flight.

When Zondra reached the animal that the birds and animals had been fighting over, a keen relief flooded her senses. It wasn't her cat, but rather a calf that had strayed from someone's ranch.

Zondra could hardly stand the sight of the half-eaten calf. She felt a bitterness rising into her throat. She fought back the nausea, then rode onward, urging her horse into a hard gallop to get away from the kill, and to put as much distance as she could between herself and the wolves.

One positive thing came out of this experience today. She knew that if there was a calf out there in this stark wilderness, there had to be a ranch somewhere nearby. For the first time since leaving her father's ranch, and briefly at Lone Eagle's village, she had hope of finding some semblance of humanity again.

She needed to get settled before her father had a chance to find her. If he found her, she knew he would force her to return with him. And *this* time, the conditions she would live under would be way worse than before.

She doubted that her father would ever go horseback riding with her again. She *knew* that he would have her guarded, day and night. She would never be allowed an ounce of freedom again!

Those thoughts made her urge her horse onward at an even faster gallop. Her eyes searched the horizon for a place of refuge, for signs of life other than her father and fierce, hungry animals!

Chapter Ten

A solemn thing it was, I said,
A woman white to be,
And wear, if God should count me fit,
Her hallowed mystery.

—EMILY DICKINSON

Searching for Zondra alone, not wanting the interference of his cowhands, and still not feeling comfortable about enlisting help at Fort Bass, afraid those
in charge might visit his ranch and discover his throng
of slaves, Harrison rode up to the bluff where he and
Zondra had gone together in the past to look down
at the Crow village. As he recalled those times spent
with his daughter alone, treating her as a daughter
instead of a slave, he felt a lump of regret in his throat,
knowing that was exactly why she had left—because
he only allowed her those few moments with him as
her father, and because he had treated her so differently from his other children, who lived under the
same roof with him.

"By God, when I find her it'll be different," he
swore to himself as he drew a tight rein close to the
edge of the bluff where he had a clear view of the
Crow village.

Yes, her leaving had made him realize how wrong
he had been to make Zondra live and work as a slave,
while in his heart he loved her even more than his

other children! It had just been too hard to accept this truth.

Harrison was always afraid of someone discovering who her mother was. He knew that his wife would never allow Zondra to be passed off as hers. Her pride would stand in the way. That had left Harrison with only one alternative—the one he had chosen the day Zondra was born.

"How could I have been so weak that I would care more about what others would say than about my daughter's well-being?" he whispered into the wind, his voice breaking.

And Ada—how he loved his Ada! With every fiber of his being, he loved that woman with the smooth black skin and dark eyes that melted him with a glance.

"Somehow, Ada, I'll even make things right with you," he vowed aloud. "My wife . . ." He laughed sarcastically. *Wife?* he thought bitterly. Sylvia had not been a true wife for so long it was hard for him to remember when they had shared a bed. He scarcely even hugged her now. He most definitely didn't kiss her. The thought of kissing someone whose heart was so cold made him shiver as though someone had splashed ice water on his face.

"Yes, Ada, at long last you will have your proper place in my life," he whispered, then concentrated on the Crow village and those who came and went from their lodges. He had come to see if Zondra might be here, seeking help against a heartless father and a life of slavery. Or perhaps the Crow had abducted her, taking her there by force?

Neither possibility seemed likely. Surely Zondra wouldn't trust Indians so easily that she would go to them willingly. As far as Harrison knew, she had never even met one face-to-face. And it was a known fact that Chief Lone Eagle did not make a habit of taking white captives.

Still, Harrison had to find out if by chance she was there. If not, he would search elsewhere, hoping that wherever she was, she was safe.

Seeing nothing amiss in the Crow village, yet not able to give up on the idea that Zondra might be there, or that one of the Indians might possibly have seen her as she traveled across the countryside toward God knew where, Harrison rode down from the butte and toward the Indian village.

To his surprise, no one came out to stop him. He entered the village as though he had done so many times before, as though he were someone familiar to them.

As he made his way among the conical lodges, women lifted their entrance flaps and stared at him. Dogs barked and children stopped to gape openly at him. Keeping a stiff upper lip, Harrison kept his eyes riveted on one thing—the large tepee that he knew was Chief Lone Eagle's.

Harrison had seen the young chief coming and going from his lodge many times as he and Zondra shared those precious moments on the bluff. It was good to know that, for the most part, this young chief held no deep-seated grudges against whites.

Of course, there had to be *some* dislike for them, since white people like himself seemed to be moving daily onto land that was once solely the Crow's. But so far Chief Lone Eagle accepted this change without going to war with the whites to try and keep them out. He even knew that Lone Eagle spoke English, making it possible to carry on a conversation with him.

Harrison had seen Lone Eagle at the local trading post, trading precious pelts for supplies for his people.

Harrison's deep thoughts were interrupted when Lone Eagle stepped from his tepee and stood waiting for him. The rancher smiled awkwardly at Lone Eagle and gave him a clumsy mock salute. His smile waned when Lone Eagle offered no smile in return, and certainly no salute. His arms were folded across his bare, broad, muscled chest. His legs were slightly spread, his breechclout whipping against his muscled thighs.

Feeling uncomfortable being stared at by this young chief, and wanting to get a quick glance around the village to see if there were any signs of Zondra, Harrison glanced away from Lone Eagle and scanned the area around him, yet still saw nothing that even hinted at Zondra having been there.

When Harrison reached Lone Eagle, he drew a tight rein and slid out of his saddle. He hesitated when a young lad came to take his horse from him, then felt he had no choice but to surrender the animal if he was going to have council with Lone Eagle. This was surely a courtesy shown any visitor to the village, not an attempt to take away his mount.

"*Kahe,*" Lone Eagle said to Harrison in the manner he addressed all arriving visitors. He folded back his entrance flap. "Come inside. You have come for a reason. We can speak about it beside my lodge fire."

"Thank you," Harrison said, slipping past Lone Eagle through the entranceway. Once inside, he looked slowly around him, fascinated by everything. The drawings on the inside walls of the lodge, the weapons, the pelts—everything that showed just how differently the Crow lived from whites.

"Sit," Lone Eagle said, motioning toward a soft pile of furs beside the fire. He sat down across from Harrison. He did not have to ask this man why he was there. He was searching for Zondra.

Lone Eagle had to wonder if Zondra might have mentioned him to this man who was her father, yet doubted that she had. Lone Eagle did not think that Zondra discussed much of anything with this white man.

"Lone Eagle," Harrison said tightly. "My name is Harrison Lester. I own property not too far from your village. I have come today to see if you or any of your people might have seen my daughter Zondra. She is riding a white stallion. She's alone. If any of your people saw her, surely they would remember."

"Your daughter?" Lone Eagle said, slyly playing a game with the white man by acting as though he didn't know Zondra, and especially that he didn't know she had left her home. "You say her name is Zondra?"

Deep inside Lone Eagle's heart he wanted to protect Zondra, at least in this way, since he knew this would be the way she would want it. She had fled this white man who sat across the fire from him for a reason. Lone Eagle would not be the cause of Zondra being forced back to the life she had fled.

Harrison's eyes wavered. "Surely you would remember having seen a white woman alone on a white horse, wouldn't you?" he asked, his voice drawn. "Wouldn't your people? Lone Eagle, Zondra is riding my white horse. And she is so alone. I doubt she even has a weapon with which to defend herself."

Harrison swallowed hard. "None of my weapons were gone, and I know she would not be able to get one otherwise," he said. Harrison drew a handkerchief from his front vest pocket and nervously dabbed it across his perspiration-laced brow. "Have you seen my Zondra?" he asked anxiously. "Has anyone in your village told you about having seen her?"

It was not an easy thing for Lone Eagle to lie; he was known for his honesty. But now? With Zondra's well-being at stake? Yes, a lie would slip across his tongue as easily as a star suddenly falls swiftly from the sky.

"No, I have not seen a white woman and none of my people have talked about having seen one," Lone Eagle said, once more folding his arms across his chest.

"Would they have told you had they seen her?" Harrison prodded, slowly refolding his handkerchief. "Could I ask around about her?"

"It is not necessary for you to question my people about your daughter, for yes, if they had seen a white woman riding alone, they would have brought news of such strange behavior to me. It is not a usual thing for white women to ride alone in Indian country, is it?" Lone Eagle said, his eyes narrowing when he saw a look in the white man's eyes that revealed his doubt.

"No, at least not my daughter," Harrison said warily. He slid his handkerchief back into his pocket. "Zondra never rode alone."

Harrison could not help but think that this Indian seemed too sure . . . too smug . . . about what he was saying. Could he be trying to hide something from Harrison, like knowledge of Zondra's whereabouts?

Harrison hadn't studied the horses in the corral. Speedie might even now be grazing among the Crow's many horses.

Suddenly Ralph scampered into Lone Eagle's tepee. Harrison paled at the sight of the cat. With a slack jaw and wide eyes he watched in disbelief as Ralph went and settled down comfortably on the chief's lap, purring.

Harrison watched Lone Eagle lovingly pet the cat. Now he knew for certain that Lone Eagle had been lying about Zondra. Her cat, the very one Harrison had given to her when she was a child, was proof of her presence there.

But afraid to openly call this powerful Crow chief a liar, and knowing that he must find another way to get Zondra away from this village, Harrison was careful not to give himself away by letting the chief know that he recognized the cat, and knew to whom it belonged.

Harrison was glad that after he gave the cat to Zondra, he had shown no more interest in it. If he had, Ralph would have come to him today instead of Lone Eagle. Lone Eagle would have known that his lie had been detected when Zondra's cat showed fondness for her father!

Yes, he had to play this smart in order to get out of this village alive, for one wrong move, even showing that he recognized the cat, might be his last.

"I truly must be going," Harrison said, working hard at keeping his voice steady. He especially didn't want to reveal the loathing he felt for this Indian, who was obviously playing games with him. "I have many miles to travel today, it seems, if I am to find my daughter."

Still holding the cat in his arms, loving how it purred with contentment, Lone Eagle rose from the floor as Harrison got to his feet. Without even glancing Harrison's way, he waited for him to leave the tepee, then followed behind.

"Little Cloud, go for the white man's horse," Lone

Eagle said to the young brave who stood dutifully waiting outside the lodge for his chief's command.

"I appreciate the time you took today for council with me," Harrison said, begrudgingly holding out a hand toward Lone Eagle for a handshake, but relieved when Lone Eagle ignored it. He jerked his hand back down to his side. "If by chance you do see my daughter, or hear any of your people talking about having seen her, would you bring word to me?" He nodded in the direction of his ranch. "My ranch is due west from here. It is not even a half-day's ride, Lone Eagle."

Harrison looked slowly around him, once more glancing from one tepee to another for any sign of Zondra. When he still saw nothing to indicate his daughter had been there, he frowned and gazed at Lone Eagle. "Will you do this for me?" he said, his voice drawn. "Would you send word if you see my Zondra?"

"If she is seen, yes, word will be sent to you," Lone Eagle said, realizing that this was not a lie, for he truly doubted he would ever see Zondra again. He would not go looking for a woman who, for whatever reason, chose not to stay with him. It was her decision. He would not fight it.

Nor should this white man, who seemed hell-bent on finding a young woman who did not wish to be found.

When Harrison's horse was brought to him, he grabbed the reins and swung himself into the saddle. He gazed at Lone Eagle again, their eyes locking in what seemed a strange sort of silent battle. Then he gave a quick salute and wheeled his horse around and rode away. He made a deliberate left turn so that as he continued on his way he went past the corral. His eyes searched through the horses for Speedie, his heart sinking when he didn't see him. But surely if Zondra were being kept hidden, so would the horse, he argued to himself. The horse's presence would prove the girl was there.

Although Harrison had wanted to avoid Fort Bass at all cost, he knew for certain now that he had no choice but to go there and ask for their help. They could come back later to the Crow Indian village with the cavalry. He rode determinedly onward in the direction of Fort Bass.

Lone Eagle watched the white man with keen interest as Harrison rode into the distance. He did not feel good about their meeting, especially the last moments. The man's mood had changed from pleasant to wary.

But finding all white men strange, Lone Eagle shrugged off his misgivings and in his mind began making plans for tonight, when he would finally avenge White Bead's embarrassing, degrading encounter with Red Moon.

High above the village, on the butte, Guy watched his father ride from the Crow village. Guy knew that if anyone could find Zondra, his father could. Harrison Lester loved his daughter with all his heart. Yes, surely his father would eventually lead Guy directly to her.

Guy left the butte and kept far enough away from his father so that Harrison wouldn't be aware of being followed.

Guy traveled onward, passing one of the large grazing lands of the Crow's vast herd of horses. He was awestruck. Never before had he seen so many horses in one place! Unfortunately, they belonged to the mangy, savage Crow!

What he wouldn't give for a herd of horses like these! He envisioned himself free of his father's control, an owner of vast herds of horses, and vast land. Guy saw himself owning the Crow horses and the Crow's land. He could imagine one day owning everything that was his father's. He would discard his useless, whining wife and have hordes of women falling at his feet.

But first and foremost, he would kill Zondra! She was responsible for the scars on his back. Laughing sadistically, he rode onward.

Chapter Eleven

Wild nights! Wild nights!
Were I with thee,
Wild nights should be
Our luxury.

—EMILY DICKINSON

Another full day was behind Zondra as she traveled onward. She warily watched the sun sink slowly behind the distant mountains. After seeing the dead calf, she had hoped to find a settler's home soon.

She had known for some time that she'd gone in the wrong direction. So far all she had seen were trees, tall grass, distant mountains, canyons, and all sorts of animals . . . and snakes.

She had been especially careful to watch for snakes, knowing that if one spooked Speedie, Zondra could be thrown from the horse and injured. Thus far, the snakes had seemed as afraid of Zondra as she and Speedie were of them. They had slithered away into the bushes or taller grass.

Zondra was very aware of another danger—the night, and the chill that came with it. Even now she was shivering as the breeze picked up, seeming to blow directly down from the higher reaches of the mountains.

While packing her belongings, the one thing she had forgotten was adequate clothing for the night hours.

The knit shawl she had stuffed into her bag just wasn't enough. It was so thin and tattered from being washed so often on her mama's scrubbing board it resembled a spider's web.

"I've got to find a place to make camp," she whispered, her eyes searching for a place that offered her as much shelter as possible.

She wished that she could build a fire! One thing she *had* remembered to bring was matches that her mama used each night to light their lone kerosene lantern. She hadn't considered that she would be too frightened to build a fire, knowing that its light could guide her father to her.

She still didn't feel confident enough to build one, for once her father started searching for her, he would not stop until he found her.

"Papa, why did you force such a life on me?" Zondra asked out loud, her voice catching emotionally in the depths of her throat. "I loved you. Why couldn't you have loved me as much as your other children?"

She knew that he did love her, but just not enough. She was still a slave . . . *his* slave!

No, she didn't want to get married, *ever*. No man would ever rule over her again! No matter how hard she tried, she couldn't get what Lone Eagle had said out of her mind. It plagued her through the day when her mind would drift to him, how he had spoken of the Crow warriors being looked upon as lords by their women.

Although Zondra couldn't brush aside her intrigue with Lone Eagle, or the strange, sensual stirring just thinking of him caused in the pit of her stomach, she could never allow herself to love a man so much she would bow to him and call him her . . . lord.

Suddenly one of Speedie's hooves sank into a gopher hole, pitching Zondra sideways from the horse. When she landed hard on the ground, her head hit with a bang, rendering her momentarily unconscious.

When she came to, she was keenly aware of an aching in her body; the back of her head throbbed unmercifully, too. Moaning, she reached back and felt a lump rising on her scalp. She was relieved to find no blood, which meant that the skin had not been broken.

A soft neighing sound quickly drew her eyes to Speedie. He had steadied himself enough not to have taken a fall, but it was obvious by the way he limped as he turned and gazed down at Zondra that he had been lamed by the accident.

With a sinking feeling in the pit of her stomach, Zondra realized that Speedie was no longer able to continue with the journey. He was too lame to carry her any further. That meant that Zondra would be traveling on foot—now it might take her many days to find someone who could offer her help!

And what of poor Speedie? If he had become lame while Harrison was riding him, her father would have taken out his rifle and shot him.

"At least for now you are spared such a fate," Zondra whispered as her eyes met the stallion's soft pleading eyes. "I don't have a gun, Speedie, and even if I did, I couldn't be that quick to condemn you to death."

Achingly, she pushed herself up from the ground and went to the stallion. "Oh, Speedie, I'll miss you so," she murmured, hugging him around his neck. She stroked his snow-white mane. "If I turn you back in the direction of Father's ranch, can you find your way home?"

He neighed softly and nuzzled her neck as though he had understood. "If you do make it back there, I hope Father has mercy and doesn't shoot you, but instead uses you for studding," Zondra said. "You are a fine specimen of a horse. Just think of the foals that could come from your mating."

Downhearted over Speedie's accident, and afraid for herself, Zondra removed her bag from the horse, and even the saddle, for the less weight burdening the stallion on his long journey back home, the better his chances were of getting there.

She gave Speedie one last affectionate hug, then turned him in the direction of her father's ranch. "Speedie, for the moment you are the master of your own fate," she said, then gave him a gentle slap on his rump, sending him in a limping gait away from her.

She almost burst into tears when he stopped and gave her one last glance, then ambled on his way again, into the darkening shadows of night.

"Good-bye, Speedie," Zondra whispered, then shivered when she heard the distant cry of a cougar.

She suddenly recalled the white wolves and the merciless way they had attacked the calf carcass. "Oh, Lord, I hope I'm not sending Speedie to such a fate as that," she whispered. She looked heavenward. "God, please keep him safe. Please let him find his way back home."

The cougar screamed again, sending goose bumps up and down Zondra's spine. "Lord, keep *me* safe," she also prayed.

With her travel bag heavy in her left hand, and so downhearted she couldn't help but cry, she walked onward. Deep down inside, she wondered if it wouldn't be best if she turned back herself and went back home *with* Speedie.

Yet she just couldn't. She was finally free. Free of

all bonds. Free of being labeled a slave when her father was one of the richest people in America.

"I will make a new life for myself," she whispered, determinedly wiping the tears from her face with the back of her hand. "I *will*."

Her chin lifted; she walked on with quickened steps.

His spine stiff, his eyes on the soldiers who were watching him ride across the courtyard at Fort Bass toward their colonel's quarters, Harrison scarcely breathed. This was the last thing he had wanted to do. Once he made contact at the fort, who was to say how long it would be before someone would come snooping around his ranch, finding the slaves working in the garden?

He would certainly not offer any information. He would not mention that he owned any slaves to the colonel in charge, or the fact that he had settled on a huge tract of land. He would tell the colonel only what was necessary—that he was a settler in these parts and that his daughter was missing.

The moon was high in the sky, giving off enough light for Harrison to see the many soldiers stationed at the fort, and the grand way in which their colonel lived. His quarters was a huge, sprawling, two-storied log structure. A garden with an assortment of flowers stretched along the front of the house behind a neat white picket fence. Soft lamplight glowed from many of the windows on both floors of the house.

Past the house was a long row of cabins which Harrison assumed were the soldiers' barracks. They were as neatly kept as the house, indicating that the colonel in charge at this fort was someone who wanted exactness and order in his life.

A tall palisaded wall surrounded the fort. Sentries

could be seen walking on patrol, the barrels of their guns picking up the shine of the moon. Those in charge at the wide, tall gate had questioned Harrison enough to know that he was no threat and had allowed him to enter.

Now outside the colonel's house, Harrison dismounted and swung his reins around the hitching rail. Before he could step through the gate of the picket fence, a tall man with shoulder-length blond hair, dressed in casual clothes instead of a uniform, appeared on the spacious porch.

Harrison knew that one of the soldiers had ridden on ahead of him and told the colonel of his arrival and his purpose for being there, so he assumed that Colonel Lloyd Brennan was expecting him.

Harrison went up the steps and accepted the colonel's firm handshake.

"Sorry as hell about your daughter," Colonel Brennan said. He gestured toward the open front door. "Come on inside where we can be comfortable while we talk. My wife Alice has already retired for the night, but my maid Winnie will serve us tea."

"Thanks," Harrison said, moving on inside the house. "I appreciate your taking time for me tonight, instead of making me wait until tomorrow when you would be at your office."

"My work is never done," Lloyd said, chuckling as he led Harrison into a massive living room, where a roaring fire was burning in the stone fireplace at the far end of the room.

Lloyd gestured with a hand toward an overstuffed chair that sat before the fire, then sank down in a plush chair beside Harrison. "Now tell me where you think your daughter has gone," Lloyd said, while smiling a cordial thank-you to a Negro maid who brought a tray that held a tea service and two gold-rimmed china teacups.

Harrison was stunned into a moment of silence by the appearance of the black maid. But now that he had seen her, Harrison felt more comfortable around Colonel Brennan—but not comfortable enough to tell him that he, also, had black people working for him. There was a difference. He believed that the colonel paid this woman, whereas Harrison owned those who labored for him.

Harrison slowly looked around, seeing the grand interior of the room, the many overstuffed chairs, the oak tables, and the expensive oriental rug in the center of the floor.

"Now, about your daughter," Lloyd began, offering Harrison a cup of tea. "Tell me when you last saw her."

Harrison accepted the tea, then tried to explain Zondra's disappearance without giving away why she would have left, or the sort of life she had been forced to live.

"I've seen it before," Lloyd said, settling more comfortably in his chair as he set his teacup aside. "Restless teens. I imagine seventeen is the worst age for both boys and girls who are not yet married."

Lloyd glanced over his shoulder at the door that opened into a foyer where the wide, spacious staircase led to the upstairs, where his very pregnant wife was already asleep for the night.

Then he frowned at Harrison. "My wife should be delivering anytime now," he said, his voice drawn. "Our first child. I wish we were closer to civilization, where a doctor could be summoned when one was needed. As it is, when I was stationed here, I had no choice but to comply with my orders and accept the absence of such conveniences as doctors."

"I wish you the best with your first child," Harrison said, clearing his throat as he thought of his own children and how they had been given the best possible care by his slaves.

All but Zondra and those he had sold at auction!

Guilt weighed on his heart like a heavy stone.

"I dread dealing with my children when they reach the age of your daughter," Lloyd said, offering Harrison a cigar from a gold cigar box.

"Yes, they do tend to get restless," Harrison agreed, accepting the cigar. He leaned toward the match Lloyd held out for him.

"But restless enough to go out on their own in this vast wilderness?" Lloyd said, then stopped speaking for a moment to light his own cigar. "Lord, man, what could have caused your daughter to be this reckless?"

Harrison ducked his head and took a long draw from the cigar, then looked up at Lloyd and gazed into his piercing blue eyes. "Hell if I know," he said, the lie causing a bitter taste as it passed across his lips. "I haven't yet told you, Colonel Brennan, where I think she might be," Harrison then said guardedly.

"Lloyd," Colonel Brennan said. "Call me Lloyd. Now tell me what you mean. Where do you think she is?"

"I went to the Crow village and asked Chief Lone Eagle if he might have seen my daughter in the vicinity," Harrison said, heaving a heavy sigh as he recalled his visit there.

"And?" Lloyd asked, raising an eyebrow. "What did Lone Eagle say?"

"He denied ever seeing my Zondra," Harrison said thickly.

"I have a feeling you thought he lied to you," Lloyd said, tapping ashes from his cigar into an ashtray on the table beside his chair.

"Yes, I do believe he lied," Harrison said stiffly, his eyes suddenly two points of fire. "Goddamn it all to hell, Lloyd, when I was sitting with the chief, Zondra's cat came into his lodge. I know it was her cat. I gave it to Zondra when she was a young girl. And if her cat was there, surely Zondra was there. Maybe she's being held as a hostage. Or maybe she sought refuge there for the night before she continued her foolish journey. I only know that cat is my daughter's."

"Cats are cats and most look alike, especially cats of the same color," Lloyd said blandly. "What color did you say your daughter's cat was?"

"I didn't," Harrison grumbled. "But it's black. As black as midnight."

"Then that says it all," Lloyd said. "All black cats absolutely look alike, unless there are some small markings of white on their fur. Does your daughter's cat have some identifying marks on its fur?"

"I know Zondra's cat, and that was Zondra's cat," Harrison said icily. "That *was* her cat, which means that Zondra must be with the Crow."

Lloyd took the cigar from between his lips. He rested it on the ashtray. "That's impossible," he said dryly. "Chief Lone Eagle has never taken white captives. Nor would he now, for why would he? There is peace between the Crow and the whites. He'd be downright stupid to take a captive."

"Then she must be hiding there," Harrison said, growing impatient with this man's assumptions.

"Had she been there, Lone Eagle wouldn't have lied about her," Lloyd said, hiding a yawn behind his hand. He sighed. "Chief Lone Eagle wouldn't do anything that would stir up trouble between his people and whites."

"If that's what you believe, then I'm wasting my time here," Harrison said, rising abruptly from his chair. "Thanks for nothing, Colonel Brennan."

He stamped from the house and stood for a moment in the shadows of the porch as he tried to regain his composure. He had come to the fort for help, and all he had gotten was rhetoric!

"Damn him," he whispered, doubling his fists at his sides.

Having grown tired of waiting for his father to leave the fort, Guy headed back home as empty-handed as his father as far as Zondra was concerned.

But Guy vowed to himself that he wouldn't give up. He would find Zondra. Some way, somehow, some-day, he would find his half sister.

Suddenly he was aware of a movement in the trees to his right. Before he could draw his pistol he found himself surrounded by rough-looking, whiskered men.

Guy winced when one of the men yanked the reins from his hands and pulled his horse up short as the others drew tight rein in a circle around him.

"What do you want?" Guy gasped out, ashen. "Why did you stop me?"

"You don't recognize outlaws when you see 'em?" the one who seemed in charge said as he edged his horse closer to Guy's. "Billy Feazel's the name." He chuckled. "You don't need to bother tellin' me your name. I already know it, and I know who your father is. You're from a damn rich family, ain't you, sonny boy?"

"What of it?" Guy dared to say back to him.

"What of it, he asks," Billy said, throwing his head back in a loud roar of laughter.

Then Billy leaned close to Guy again, his whiskey breath almost sending Guy reeling. "We've been watchin' your house," he said icily. "I've seen how rich your pa is. Rich pas pay lots of money to get rich sons back, don't you think, sonny boy?"

"You're going to abduct me . . . and . . . f-f-force my f-f-father to pay ransom to get me released?" Guy stammered, his eyes wide with fear.

"Don't take much to make you understand, now, does it?" Billy snarled. "You're goin' with me and my friends to our hideout, then we'll see just how anxious your pa is to have you back. I bet he'll pay a bundle for a rich, snobbish son of a bitch like you."

Guy was too alarmed to say anything else. He was surrounded by gruff, filthy men who made sure he couldn't escape as they took him to their hideout deep inside a canyon.

Once there, he was appalled at the squalor in which they lived. The cabin was filled with a stink that made Guy sick.

When he tried to back away from the cabin door, Billy grabbed him by the throat and threw him back inside, then tied him to a chair where roaches crawled back and forth over his booted feet.

"Now don't get too comfy," Billy teased. "We'll surely be releasin' you real soon. As soon as we get a bundle of money from your pa, you'll be as free as a breeze."

Guy doubted that was true. He could not help but believe that he was taking his very last breaths.

Chapter Twelve

Had I, a humble maiden,
Whose farthest of degree
Was that she might
Some distant heaven,
Dwell timidly with thee.

—EMILY DICKINSON

The moon was high in the sky, bright and mystical.
Lone Eagle was dressed in a breechclout. So that
he could blend with the darkness of night, his face
and body were covered with black ash from the colder
coals of his fire pit. He carried with him in his buckskin
parfleche bag a weasel skin stuffed with buffalo hair,
something he brought along on all jaunts against an
enemy.

Lone Eagle had been riding for some time beneath
the brilliance of the moon; he knew that he should be
arriving at Red Moon's village soon. Although he did
not travel this way often, for he never wished to be
in the presence of his clan enemy unless he had to,
Lone Eagle knew his way there well enough. He had
made sure of it, in case he and his warriors were
forced to go against their enemy.

Lone Eagle was alone tonight, without his group of
warriors. This vengeance was his alone! Oh, what
pride he would take in shaming Red Moon for what
his enemy clansman had done to White Bead.

Yes, it would bring great pleasure to Lone Eagle to cut the long lock of hair from Red Moon's scalp.

Lone Eagle only hoped that while he was there, lurking in the shadows of Red Moon's lodge, he wouldn't be tempted to take all of his enemy clansman's hair—although it would serve him right, for Red Moon's tongue had been loose with wrongful words one time too many!

Never having taken anyone's scalp, Lone Eagle did not plan to begin such sordid deeds now. He would not give Red Moon reason to send his warriors to Lone Eagle's camp to seek vengeance on his beloved people.

No, he would do no more than take the one lone lock of hair, for this retribution was simply one man taking care of another man's wrongful deeds.

Finally, stretched out before him on a wide expanse of land beside a stream, he saw the Crow village. Lone Eagle reined in his horse in the darker shadows of the forest that lay a short distance from the village.

Quietly he dismounted and tethered his horse to a low limb of a cottonwood tree. As he watched guardedly for any activity in the village, or along its outskirts where sentries might be posted, Lone Eagle removed the weasel skin from his parfleche bag.

Still watching Red Moon's village, Lone Eagle was surprised that his enemy neglected to post sentries in strategic places on the outskirts of the village. As egotistical and self-righteous as Red Moon was, the young Crow chief was foolish not to realize that Lone Eagle would not allow him to get away with shaming White Bead.

Still smiling at Red Moon's foolishness, Lone Eagle unrolled his weasel skin, which had been smoked with incense back at his lodge. He stretched it out between his hands and held it toward Red Moon's village as he said a prayer to the Great Mystery above.

"Help guide my hand, *Ah-badt-deadt-deah*, Great Mystery, as I slide my knife through Red Moon's hair," Lone Eagle whispered. "Let it be as soundless as sliding a knife through honey. Lead me safely then back to my horse, so that I might ride free again toward my village, back to White Bead to tell her that the sin against her has been avenged."

As always when praying to the Great Mystery, a peace so gentle and warm it made him relax and feel assured of that which he was about to do settled over Lone Eagle. He smiled heavenward and nodded a silent thank-you toward the sky, then rolled up the weasel skin and placed it gently back inside his travel bag.

After removing his knife from the sheath that he had secured to his left thigh, Lone Eagle moved stealthily, like a silent shadow, going to stand between two lodges. He looked again for sentries. This time he saw two warriors posted just outside Red Moon's large tepee.

He was not as careless as I thought, Lone Eagle thought to himself.

But his enemy clansman had not chosen warriors wisely. Those who sat with folded legs on the ground on each side of Red Moon's entranceway had not kept alert, as their chief would have wished. Their heads were hanging. They were asleep.

Wanting to be sure that the warriors were in a sound enough sleep not to hear him cutting open the back of Red Moon's buffalo hide lodge, Lone Eagle stood motionless for a moment longer, watching the two sentries. But they slept on, unaware of any sound or movement around them.

Smiling, Lone Eagle moved stealthily again through

the moon-splashed night to the back of Red Moon's lodge. He had observed Red Moon's lodge before and had not seen anyone who might share the chief's tepee with him. For certain there was no wife. As far as Lone Eagle knew, Red Moon was true to his passionate feelings for White Bead.

Lone Eagle pushed the tip of his knife through the buffalo hide, then shoved his knife completely through the tough fabric, slowly cutting his way downward until he had made a space large enough to slip through.

When that was done, Lone Eagle waited long enough to take a deep, quavering breath, then holding his knife at his side, he edged his body through the opening and found himself standing over Red Moon. The glowing coals in the fire pit gave off just enough light for Lone Eagle to make sure he and Red Moon were alone. When he was certain that they were, and he saw that Red Moon was sleeping soundly, he fell to his knees beside his enemy and cunningly, carefully, silently lifted one long lock of Red Moon's black hair with his left hand.

Making sure not to tug on the man's hair, which would quickly awaken him, Lone Eagle cut off a long lock of the enemy chief's hair.

Feeling victorious, and savoring how it felt to shame his enemy in such a way, Lone Eagle held the heavy length of hair in his hand for one more moment. Lone Eagle had been taught early on by his proud chieftain father that it was a disgrace to have one's hair cut by an enemy. One would rather die than suffer this sort of indignity!

Tonight it felt good to Lone Eagle to recall his father's teachings, for his father had surely been thinking about his future enemies while instructing Lone Eagle how to disgrace them.

"It is done, Father," he whispered beneath his breath.

Feeling as though he had stayed too long gloating, Lone Eagle hurriedly laid the lock of hair beside Red Moon's face so that when he awakened it would be the first thing he would see. Red Moon would understand very well why his hair had been removed, and by whom!

Smiling smugly, Lone Eagle was careful not to make any noise as he left the lodge and made his way back to his horse.

As he rode off into the moonlight, he knew that the next thing that must be done was to find a body of water far enough away from Red Moon's village so that he could stop and rest and remove the black ash from his body before returning to his people with the news of his victory.

He was so happy about having gotten the best of Red Moon that Lone Eagle felt as though he were flying!

Worn-out and bone-weary, and so frightened her knees were weak, Zondra continued to walk in the moonlight. She was still trying to find a safe haven for the night. She had heard too many night sounds all around her since the sun had set. She had to keep moving onward—if she gave in to her need for sleep, or her need to rest her swollen, aching feet, there might not be a tomorrow for her. She might become food for some four-legged animal.

She couldn't forget the sight of the half-eaten calf. She would never forget how she had been afraid that her precious cat might have suffered the same fate. Oh, Lord, she didn't want to suffer the same fate herself.

"I must travel onward," she told herself, forcing her feet to keep moving, one step after the other. "I must not stop. I must stay awake all night if that's what it takes to survive until morning."

Her travel bag seemed to get heavier by the minute, and Zondra shifted it from one shoulder to the other, yet it felt no less heavy no matter which shoulder she placed it on.

She was tempted to remove some of her belongings in order to make the bag lighter, yet she couldn't think of anything she didn't need. She had planned so carefully for so long what should be taken. She needed everything. All of her possessions, as meager as they might be, were precious to her.

Stumbling onward, the chill of the night seeping more deeply into her bones, making her feel strangely stiff, Zondra groaned.

She fought to keep her eyes open. She fought the dryness in her mouth, having not found a stream for some time now to quench her thirst. But still she moved onward.

It seemed that one hour blended into the next, until she wasn't sure how long it had been since it had turned night. She gazed heavenward, looking for any signs of daybreak along the horizon. She wished she knew how long it would be before morning came. When it did, she would finally take the time to get some badly needed rest. With the light came some security. Animals didn't roam about as readily during the day as they did at night. Except wolves, she reminded herself. Hadn't those white wolves feasted on the poor calf while it was daylight?

I hope they are nowhere near, Zondra thought worriedly.

Suddenly she saw a movement a short distance

away, where there was a thick growth of trees. A stark
fear grabbed her in the pit of her stomach. The motion
was surely caused by an animal lurking there that
might at any moment jump out and feast on her.

When she heard a soft neigh, her heart lurched with
excitement, for she knew that the animal standing
amid the shadowed trees was a horse.

She moved onward and finally was close enough to
see the horse. It was a lovely, muscled black mustang,
tethered to a low tree limb. Her heart skipped a beat
and her excitement over having found the horse
waned, for she knew that where there was a tethered
horse, a rider was somewhere nearby. Thoughts of
outlaws and renegade Indians rushed through her
brain. She knew that she must not chance waiting to
see who the horse belonged to. It might be someone
who could take advantage of her in a sexual way, for
surely men who were out here all alone in the wilderness would have been without women for many weeks,
perhaps months!

She would have to steal the horse before its owner
returned. She trusted no one. Absolutely no one! If
her own half brother could attempt raping her,
wouldn't a stranger?

When she saw no one nearby, she ran with a pounding heart to the mustang, uncoiled the reins, and
swung herself into the saddle. After hanging the strap
of her bag over the pommel of the saddle, Zondra
urged the horse away in a quiet trot, thankful that the
tall grass muffled the sound of its hooves.

Then when she felt that she had put sufficient distance between herself and the owner of the horse, she
sent her mount into a hard gallop for a while, then
slowed to a steady lope.

Riding along beneath the moonlight, she studied the

Mexican saddle, and then the parfleche bag hanging at the side of the beautiful black mustang. It all seemed familiar to her, but why?

Then it came to her. She had seen Lone Eagle riding a magnificent black horse. She even recalled his special saddle. It was exactly like this one!

Then she scoffed at the notion that this horse belonged to Lone Eagle. It *couldn't* be his, for what would Lone Eagle be doing this far from his village, all alone in the night?

Unless Lone Eagle was looking for her, she suddenly thought to herself.

"Is he searching for me?" she whispered, a part of her hoping that he might be, for it was impossible for her to shake her feelings for him. At the same time, another part of her knew that they weren't meant to be together. They each had a different way of life. And she wanted no man for a husband—especially not Lone Eagle. She deplored the very thought of being at the beck and call of a "lord."

Yet this certainly did look like Lone Eagle's horse. She had seen it often enough. She believed this steed did in fact belong to the man of her midnight dreams. And although she didn't like to think of leaving Lone Eagle stranded, if this *was* his horse, she knew that he had a better chance of getting through the night alive without a horse than she did. She must be concerned only with herself. She rode onward.

Still wondering if Lone Eagle was back there all alone, she took a long look over her shoulder. "I'm sorry, Lone Eagle," she whispered. "But I think you'd understand."

Chapter Thirteen

We are as clouds that veil the midnight moon;
How restlessly they speed and gleam, and quiver,
Streaking the darkness radiantly—!

—PERCY BYSSHE SHELLEY

His face and body washed clean of the black ash, his spirits still high from having bested Red Moon, Lone Eagle returned to where he had left his horse tethered.

He stopped dead in his tracks when he saw that his horse was gone . . . a horse that it had taken him several weeks to master. While he had been bathing in the stream, a horse thief had come along and stolen his beloved steed!

His jaw tight with anger, his eyes filled with fire, Lone Eagle gazed down at the crushed grass that marked the spot where he had left his horse tethered. In the dewy dampness of the grass, it was easy to see the path along which the horse had been led away.

Being a skilled tracker and one of the fastest of the Crow, Lone Eagle began following the crushed grass, the moon's glow giving him light. He hoped to catch up with the culprit when the person stopped to rest.

Lone Eagle knew that it was only one person who had turned horse thief tonight, for there was only one set of tracks.

"When I catch up with you, you will pay for the terrible crime of horse stealing," Lone Eagle whispered, his gait steady as he ran onward through the night.

He knew that daybreak would soon appear on the horizon. If the guilty party *had* stopped to sleep until morning, but then left again at a gallop upon awakening, he doubted he would ever catch up with the thief. So he had to continue running hard tonight. He couldn't allow anyone to get away with stealing his valuable, well-loved horse.

"*Ahh*, yes, the thief will pay," he hissed through clenched teeth. "No one steals from Lone Eagle!"

His heart skipped a beat when he saw something in the dark shadows of a thick stand of trees. And when he heard a soft neighing, his heart jumped with joy. He had found his mustang. Apparently he had recognized Lone Eagle approaching in the moonlight.

Lone Eagle ran onward, then stopped, his eyes wide with disbelief when he saw who was curled up asleep on a blanket on the ground beside his tethered horse.

Zondra!

Stunned over finding her with his horse, he stared down at her for a moment longer. Then it came to him in a flash that since she was with his horse, *she* must have stolen his steed. *She* was a horse thief, the worst of all thieves among men!

"And now *women*," he grumbled to himself, for when it came to stealing horses, it did not matter if the thief was a man or a woman. The crime was no less serious just because the criminal was a woman.

Squatting on his haunches, his position of rest, Lone Eagle studied Zondra's still form. It was obvious that she was all right, but how was it possible that she had come out of nowhere and stolen his horse?

Where had she been since she fled his tepee? Wandering aimlessly through the stark wilderness, with no true destination? And surely she had fled her home on a horse. Where was it? Had it run away from her? Was that what had forced her to become a horse thief tonight, leaving him to fend for himself on foot? Had she known that it was Lone Eagle from whom she was stealing? Or had she not bothered to look and see to whom the horse belonged?

Surely all that mattered was that she had come upon an unattended tethered horse in the night. She had seen it as her means to escape the life she had left behind at Harrison Lester's ranch.

Lone Eagle's heart melted as he gazed at Zondra, forgetting for a brief moment that she had actually stolen his horse. In the moonlight she was a vision of loveliness with her flawless features, her night-black hair spilling all around her on the ground like a dark halo.

He could not help but think how innocently sweet she looked. For certain, she was a woman who needed someone to care for her.

Yet no matter how sweet and beautiful she was, or vulnerable, it didn't change the fact that she had stolen his horse. But he was unsure what he'd do about it when she awakened. He certainly couldn't let her think she could steal something as valuable from him as his horse and get away with it.

Yes, he thought to himself, Zondra *must* be taught a lesson; she must understand the wrong in what she had done tonight. Then once she understood, he would make it up to her for the moments of distress he caused her by how he chose to make her pay for her crime.

What he truly wanted to do was to reach out and

run his fingers across her beautifully shaped lips. He ached to draw her into his arms and whisper to her how much he loved her. But that would only send the wrong message to her. He must make her believe she was being punished for stealing his horse.

As Zondra rolled over, turning her face away from Lone Eagle, he continued to watch her without awakening her.

There was no doubt that there was something about the girl that he admired even more than her loveliness. Although stealing horses was a terrible crime, he could not help but think that this young woman had remarkable courage, setting out on her own to seek a new life for herself.

At this moment, as he watched her lying there, so alone, so beautiful and vulnerable, he knew that he must have her, not only because he had deep feelings for her, but because he wanted to protect her for the rest of her life.

But for now he must push his tender, sensual feelings for Zondra to the farthest recesses of his mind. He must do what he could to make her realize the wrong in what she had done tonight, so she would never again consider stealing anyone else's steed. After tonight she would realize that a man's horse was sacred to him!

Rising to his feet, he went to his horse and took a moment to stroke its sleek black mane. "For a while you held an angel on your back," he whispered to his horse. Giving his mount a fond hug, he took a rope from his parfleche bag.

Going back to Zondra, he fell to his haunches again before her. As he leaned over to tie her wrists, he jumped with a start and jerked the rope away when she rolled over again, her face once again visible to him in the moonlight.

He hesitated before reaching for her wrists again, thinking that she might be awakening.

When she again seemed to be sleeping soundly, Lone Eagle began to loop the rope around one of her wrists, but stopped when her eyes suddenly opened and she gazed questioningly up at him.

"Lone . . . Eagle . . . ?" Zondra asked softly, not sure if he was truly there or if it just might be a figment of her imagination.

She had just been dreaming about him, about those moments she'd shared with him in his lodge before he had spoken the word "lord" to her, which had quickly changed everything between them.

In the dream, he had been holding her. His lips had come to hers in a sweet, soft, quavering kiss. Her mind had been reeling with rapture.

But now that she was certain that she was awake and she knew without a doubt that he was there, that he had found her, she smiled at him.

But that smile was short-lived as she became aware of what he held in his hand, and what he might have been ready to do with it. She recalled now how, when she had awakened, he had leaned quickly away from her.

Surely he had been ready to wrap the rope around her wrists, and there could only be one reason for him to be doing that—to take her captive. He obviously considered her a horse thief!

Now instead of being glad that he was there, a stark fear clutched at Zondra's heart.

Chapter Fourteen

We conceive or reason, laugh or weep,
Embrace fond woe, or cast our cares away.

—PERCY BYSSHE SHELLEY

"Sylvia, just leave me alone," Harrison growled as he sat at the dining table, not even hungry, staring at the large silver trays of breakfast food that sat before him on the massive oak table. "You know damn well that you don't care what happens to Zondra, so don't pretend to care by asking questions about her."

He tilted his cup to his lips and drank the last of the coffee, then slammed the cup onto the table and glared across the table at his wife, who was already fancied up this early in the morning in a silk dress, and with diamonds flashing on her fingers and jeweled combs fitted into her upswept hair.

"Wife, you know that all you care about is those damn diamonds and fancy clothes," Harrison said, his voice breaking. "If the truth be known, I imagine you'd have to confess to not even loving your *own* children, much less my bastard daughter."

"That's not so," Sylvia said, a flush of red rushing to her fat cheeks. "I love my children. *All* of them."

"Yes, I believe you just might in your strange sort of way," Harrison said, still studying Sylvia, trying to see something about her that had drawn him into marrying her all of those years ago, when in his heart all he had ever truly wanted was Ada.

He *had* loved the flash of Sylvia's red hair. He had marveled over her large breasts. But as for anything else? No. There wasn't much else to enjoy about her, nor had he felt any true attraction to Sylvia. She had just been available, someone to have around to act as his wife at the many social functions they held back in Mississippi.

Those days were over now, and things were soon going to change. He planned to send Sylvia packing and bring Ada into his home. He would make things right for her as he should have after their first child was born.

"I declare, Harrison, you've been in a strange mood these past weeks, and *way* before Zondra chose to escape like so many slaves have a tendency to do," Sylvia said, fanning herself with her white, lace-trimmed napkin. "Had I known moving here would change you this much, I'd have downright refused to agree to the move." Her full lips curved into a pout. "Had I known there would be nobody to have tea and embroidery with, I'd have said a flat no to your proposal of moving north," Sylvia said in her Southern drawl. Tears filled her eyes. "I've never been so lonely in my entire life, Harrison, as I've been since our move to this godforsaken land."

"You'll survive," Harrison spat out, pushing his chair back and rising when he heard a loud knock on the front door. His butler appeared and announced that a stranger had arrived, asking for him.

Saying a silent prayer to himself that someone had brought news of Zondra, and that it was good, not bad, Harrison walked briskly to the front door, then

took an unsteady step backward when he saw the un-
kempt man with soiled, frayed clothes and heavy
whiskers standing there. Surely the man was a drifter
stopping by for a handout.

Harrison swallowed hard and stepped up to the
door. "What is your business here, young man?" Harrison said, his voice strangely hollow.

"I've brung you a message from my boss," Taylor
Horsley said, his eyes gleaming.

"A message? From your boss? Who *is* your boss?
What *is* the message?" Harrison blurted out, wanting
to get this over with so that he could order this filthy
man from his property.

"The message is written here on this paper," Taylor
said, slipping a folded piece of paper from his front
breeches pocket. "I cain't read, so's you'll have to do
the readin'." Taylor handed the note to Harrison and
laughed throatily. "Of course, I know what's in the
note. It's a ransom note. Read it, then give me your
answer."

"Ransom?" Harrison said, paling. Knowing it was
surely about Zondra, yet wondering who would know
that *he* would pay to get her back, Harrison's fingers
trembled as he tried to get the paper unfolded.

His eyes widened and he was taken aback when he
saw just whom the ransom note was about. It most
certainly had nothing to do with Zondra!

"Harrison, what does this man want?" Sylvia asked
as she came and stood beside her husband. She eyed
the note that he was reading. "What's that you are
reading?"

"A ransom note," Harrison said thickly.

"Lord a'mercy," Sylvia said, placing a hand to her
throat. "A ransom note? Oh, Lord, Harrison, who is
the note about? Who's been abducted?"

Ignoring her, Harrison gazed intently into Taylor's beady, shifty eyes. "For all I care, you can take this note and shove it up your behind," he said, forcing the piece of paper back into the man's grubby hands. "And hear me well when I tell you that no one will blackmail me to get my money. Let Guy die. He's worthless to me, anyhow."

With the mention of Guy's name in the same breath as blackmail, and knowing now that her son had been kidnapped—and worst of all that her husband was going to do nothing about it—Sylvia fainted dead away on the floor.

Harrison gave her a brief glance, then glared at Taylor again. He waved him away with a hand. "Get out of here, you son of a bitch," he said, his eyes narrowing angrily. "And don't chance coming back here with any more of your notes—not unless you want to have your behind filled with buckshot."

Slack-jawed with surprise over Harrison caring so little for his son, Taylor gave him another quizzical stare, then turned and raced down the steps and mounted his horse.

Harrison's eyes wavered as he watched the outlaw ride away, hoping that he hadn't done the wrong thing. He *did* love his son, yet he had no respect for him. He hoped he hadn't just signed Guy's death warrant.

But no matter what, he couldn't let someone come here and make such demands on him. If word spread that one man got paid a good sum of ransom money, others could play the same game. Before long, Harrison would be as poor as he had been when he lived with his parents all those years ago. He had been born into the worst sort of poverty along the Louisiana bayou.

Yet deep down inside, he knew that had that note been about Zondra, he would have paid the money in a minute! She had already suffered enough injustice. He would not have allowed any more.

Sighing, he gazed down at Sylvia. Filled with regret over having no feelings whatsoever for her, he bent low and swept her into his arms and took her upstairs to her bed. When a maid came to check on her, Harrison left the servant to tend to his wife.

He went to his study and tried to busy himself with his journals. He kept glancing over at the safe, in which most of his wealth was stored. More money was hidden in the garret over his bedroom. He wondered if his son would be set free even though the ransom money had not been paid. Those who had sent the note would surely realize that it would gain them nothing to kill an innocent man.

I have to believe that's what they'll do, he thought, again working on his journals, trying to block out all thoughts of Zondra . . . of Guy . . . of ransom money . . . of two mothers who now had children missing.

"Oh, Ada, I wish I could give you better news about Zondra when I see you," he whispered to himself. "But I can't. I doubt now we'll ever see her again."

He gazed toward the window, in his mind's eye still seeing the black cat at the Indian village. Surely he had been mistaken. Surely it wasn't Zondra's cat. The colonel was right. All black cats looked alike.

"He refused to pay the ransom?" Guy shouted, eyes wide with disbelief. "My very own father refused to do what was required to set me free? I didn't know he hated me *this* much."

Sitting on a chair in the center of the drab, stinking

one-room cabin, his hands tied behind him, Guy
strained and wrestled with the rope in an effort to get
free. But he had already done this countless times
before since being placed there, succeeding only in
rendering his wrists raw and sore from the ropes dig-
ging into them the more he strained against them.

Guy looked desperately from one man to the other,
unable to read their expressions, not sure how they
had taken the news. Were they going to take him
outside and kill him now, and leave him as food for
the wolves?

"I plead with you to release me," he said, his voice
breaking. "I promise not to tell anyone who you are,
or where your hideout is. I'll just forget this ever
happened."

Billy Feazel spat a thick wad of phlegm over his
shoulder; it landed in the muddy floor behind him. He
placed his hands on his hips and glared down at Guy.
"I ain't sure just yet what I'm going to do with you,"
he said in a slow drawl. "Damn it all to hell, I expected a father to care enough for a son that he'd pay
any amount of money to get him back."

"As you see, you were wrong," Guy said dryly, still
finding it incredible himself that his father could be
this coldhearted. Had it been Zondra, he'd have paid
the money in a minute!

A plan came to Guy, lighting his eyes up with hope.
"I've got a deal for you," he said, his eyes dancing.
"Just listen. Believe me, it's too good of a deal for
you to refuse."

"Tell me," Billy said, placing a cigarette between
his yellow teeth. "I'll listen. If I'm game, I'll tell you.
If not, I'm going to let Taylor here take you out and
kill you however he chooses to."

"Let me be a part of your gang," Guy said breathlessly, glancing from Billy over to Taylor. He went cold inside when he saw a strange sort of anxiousness in Taylor's eyes, and knew it was because he was impatient to do some killing today.

"What's that you say?" Billy asked, his eyebrows arching. He idly scratched his head and laughed throatily. "I ain't never seen anyone use that angle to get his hands untied."

"I'm serious," Guy said. "Let me be a part of your gang. I'll steal my father's money and split it down the middle with you."

Billy threw his head back and gave a harsh, ringing laugh, then he gazed with narrowed eyes at Guy. "Do you think I'm a fool, or what?" he hissed out. "The minute I set you free, you'd run back to your pappy and come with him gunnin' for me." He dropped his cigarette to the floor and ground it out with the toe of his boot. "No, I don't think so. And if that's all you have to say, Taylor here'll be takin' you outside."

"No! Listen! I'm serious!" Guy shouted, his eyes wide with fear. "Don't you see? My father hates me. I hate my father even worse. How could I not hate him when he doesn't care enough about me to save my life? Give me a chance. I'll show you just how rich I can make you. I know where he keeps his safe. I even know the combination. Lord, man, if you knew what was in that safe you'd not hesitate to agree to my plan."

Billy sighed deeply as he studied Guy's expression, then laughed. "I ain't never before met such a family as yours," he said. "How can a father and son hate each other so much?"

"Take off my shirt and see the stripes made on my skin by my father's whip and you'll see just why such hate is shared between us," Guy said dryly. Then he laughed. "And you think my family is peculiar? Well, you've only seen half of its lunacy. My half sister has a Negro mother!"

There was a strained silence in the room as the outlaws stared at Guy for a moment, then Billy nodded at Taylor. "Untie him," he said. He took another cigarette from his pocket and jammed it between his lips.

"You believe him?" Taylor said, his eyes wide. "You actually believe he's goin' to ride with us . . . be a part of us? Do you truly believe he'd go against his very own father and steal from him and throw half of it in our direction?" He laughed sarcastically. "I don't think so, Billy."

"I give you my word that what I have said is true," Guy said, anxiously looking from Billy to Taylor. "Don't you think that I know you won't allow me to escape? I'd be stupid to try. Trust me. I do hate my father enough to go against him. Give me the chance. What can it hurt? If you see that I'm not telling the truth, you can shoot me."

"And I would laugh while doin' it," Taylor said, giving Billy a questioning look. "Do you really want me to untie him?"

"That's what I said, ain't it?" Billy replied, taking another cigarette from his pocket. He held it in his hand until Guy was free, then offered it to him.

Guy eagerly took it and leaned into the flame of a match that Billy held out to him.

"I think a toast is in order to welcome this man into the gang," Billy then said as he smiled smugly at Guy. "A man who's going to make us richer than sin." He nodded toward Taylor. "Get a bottle of whiskey. Pour everyone a shot. Then we can get down to the business of Guy's father's safe."

As Guy took a deep drag from his cigarette, he rubbed his raw wrists. The thought of finally having a way to best his father made his heart race. He welcomed the small glass of whiskey and downed the burning liquid in one swallow.

Chapter Fifteen

Her cheek was pale, and by and by
It flashed forth fire,
As lightning from the sky.

—WILLIAM SHAKESPEARE

Zondra couldn't believe that Lone Eagle could treat her so heartlessly. She had always thought that he was kind and gentle. Instead, he was actually leading her behind his horse, her worn-out, sore feet aching badly, as he rode haughtily on his steed. She winced as the rope he had tied around her wrists tugged painfully as she was made to walk onward through the dimness of early morning.

She reminded herself that he looked upon himself as a lord over women, so why wouldn't he be this angry over a woman getting the best of him by stealing his magnificent black steed?

"Lone Eagle, what plans do you have for me next?" Zondra suddenly said hatefully, breaking the silence between herself and the handsome Crow chief. "Are you going to kill me?"

Lone Eagle was surprised that Zondra had suddenly decided to talk, since she had refused to say a word to him during their slow trek toward his village. She certainly hadn't apologized for having stolen his horse, or explained why she'd done it.

He turned his head and gave her a quizzical stare. Of course, he had figured out on his own that probably the horse she had been riding had either been crippled by some mishap or had abandoned her. But no matter what her excuse was, he still had to teach her a lesson about thievery. One just did not go around stealing horses as though it were a normal thing to do. Horse thieves to the Crow were the worst sort of criminal and deserved the worst of punishments!

"Well, do you or do you not plan to kill me?" Zondra asked hotly. "I think I deserve to know what my final fate will be, don't you? Or are you going to make me suffer more humiliation by making me wait until you either plunge a knife into my heart, shoot me, or hang me?"

"It has never been my practice to kill White Eyes," Lone Eagle said, his voice calm.

It rankled Zondra's nerves even more that he was so calm and sure of himself in what he was doing to her.

"But I do not hesitate to punish them if they steal from me," Lone Eagle quickly added.

"As if I didn't know," Zondra hissed, holding her tied wrists up for him to see.

"In the past I have taken horse thieves captive," Lone Eagle said, the lie sliding across his lips like honey. He saw her lovely brown eyes narrow even more with anger. "As *you* are now my captive."

Zondra felt some relief in knowing that might be his only way of punishing her. There was no denying how sorely tired she was. But she'd show him. She had fled from him in the dark once. If the good Lord above was willing, she would again!

This time she wouldn't stop at just taking a horse. She would steal one of his weapons, then let him come after her again. She would never allow him to take her captive a second time.

She most certainly would never bow down to him and call him her lord. She would die first!

"You are my captive for as long as I want to be bothered with you, that is," Lone Eagle continued. He smiled gleefully when he saw how that added bit of information made her eyes widen in dismay.

Then he looked away from her quickly and kept his horse going at a slow yet steady pace. A part of him was amused about being able to make her pay in this way for having stolen his horse. Yet another part of him felt somewhat ashamed for taking advantage of the moment by humiliating her in this way. It was not something he normally would enjoy doing. But he knew that she would think twice before taking anything from Lone Eagle again.

Zondra's heart and her spirits sank when she realized just how short-lived her longed-for freedom had been. She realized she wouldn't get the chance to escape from him as she had hoped. Surely he would keep her well-guarded, both day and night!

What had he meant when he said that he would keep her captive for only as long as he wanted to be bothered with her? Then what would he do with her? She knew that he did not mean that he would set her free. No, he was too angry for that.

Here she was, a slave again so soon, and to a man she had fantasized about many nights while lying lonely in her bed in the slaves' quarters. And when she had actually met him, face-to-face, how he had mesmerized her. He had been so kind . . . so soft-spoken.

How *could* she have been so wrong about him? He wasn't a nice man after all. He was a roguish savage!

A quick anger overtook her. "I won't be enslaved again," she hissed. "No matter how hard you try to keep me in captivity, to do whatever you think you are going to do to me, you won't get away with it for long. I will flee you as I did slavery!"

Lone Eagle yanked hard on his horse's reins and stopped his black steed. He turned sideways in his saddle and gave Zondra a questioning stare. "Where have you been incarcerated as a slave?" he asked dryly. "It was your father who came looking for you, not a man who boasts of owning you as a slave. No father labels his daughter a slave."

Believing now that Lone Eagle didn't know that those black people he had seen hoeing in her father's garden and working around her father's ranch were slaves, perhaps not even understanding that white men held black people in bondage as slaves, Zondra gave a low, bitter laugh. But she still didn't explain any of this to him, especially the part that included her.

Just let him stay confused, she thought angrily to herself. It served him right to not know these things about her. Anyhow, she would flee from him at her first opportunity. She had succeeded in doing it once. She could do it again.

He then took her aback somewhat by asking a question that seemed to come from nowhere. "Why are you not married?" Lone Eagle asked, slowly looking her up and down, his arms aching to hold her. Again he looked directly into her eyes. "The Crow girls are married before puberty," he said softly. "The girls' playmates even poke fun if a girl is still single at the time of her menses. Surely your menses has been with you for several winters," he said. He noticed in her eyes a shocked embarrassment that he had never seen before. "Are you not perhaps seventeen winters of age?"

Scandalized by a man speaking of such things as a woman's monthly blood flow, and by Lone Eagle treating her like she was some old spinster at the age of seventeen, Zondra glared at him. "Why aren't *you* married?" she blurted out. A slow, taunting smile quivered on her lips. "Aren't you man enough to bed a woman?"

When she saw a quick anger leap into his eyes, and he urged his horse onward into the dawn, purposely yanking the rope, making Zondra fall hard to the ground, she wished she had been more careful about what she had said to him. She might have just tightened the noose around her own neck. Perhaps he *might* kill a white person for the first time in his life. When they stopped to rest, he might even rape her to prove to her how much of a man he was. . . .

As Lone Eagle stopped his horse to give Zondra a chance to get back to her feet, he turned to watch her.

Seeing how tired she was, and how angry, he was tempted to stop this game right now, for it was gaining him nothing, it seemed, but the deep loathing of this beautiful woman. And that was the last thing he wanted to achieve from this lesson he was trying to teach her.

He wanted, ultimately, to make her love him.

But lessons taught about horse stealing came before lessons of love, and he would teach her later just how much he loved and wanted her. His gentleness then would erase all the hate she felt for him now.

A few shared gentle embraces and kisses, and surely she would forget how much she, for just a while, had hated him. . . .

Chapter Sixteen

My heart would wish it broke before,
Since breaking then, since breaking then,
Were useless as next morning's sun,
Where midnight frosts had lain!

—EMILY DICKINSON

Guy was dressed in clothing much different from his usual expensive suits. Now, by choice, he was wearing frayed homespun pants, shirt, and roughed-up boots. Out of anger over how his father had betrayed him, Guy had burned his fancier clothes in the fireplace at the outlaws' hideout. The act symbolized his rejection of his sorry past life.

Filled with an angry contempt for his father, Guy was riding with the outlaws toward his father's ranch. Recently Guy had spied on his father while the older man had been putting money in the safe in his study. He now knew the safe's combination by heart, having known that day, while lurking in the shadows, that he would one day want to escape his father's bitter tongue and hurtful whippings.

After Guy left the ranch house today, his father's wealth would be diminished by many thousands of dollars. He would also take as many of the family jewels as his father kept hidden in the safe.

Guy cast a quick glance at the horizon. Dawn was breaking too quickly for him to feel entirely comfortable about the morning's plans. But he knew the habits of his father and the cowhands. Guy had at least two more hours before anyone would be stirring in the huge ranch house, or in the bunkhouses.

He did expect that some of the slaves might be up, though, preparing their morning meal before their day's chores would begin all over again. If any of the slaves saw Guy coming and going from the house, surely they wouldn't offer this information to his father, for they hated him as much as Guy did for his cruel ways.

Except for one slave, Guy thought bitterly to himself. He knew about his father's rendezvous with Zondra's mother, Ada, in the cabin deep in the forest. He had followed them there more than once and had spied on them through the window.

It had excited and sickened Guy at the same time to see his father's large hands groping the woman's black breasts. He had been captivated, though, by how skilled the woman was at making love. She gave her all to her man, that was for sure.

Guy had even secretly lusted after Ada himself, but knew that if he attempted to be with her sexually, his father would not stop at whipping him, he would kill him. For no one touched Ada but his father—especially not the son he loathed.

That, too, was why Guy was so eager today to best his father, even if his father never knew who had robbed him. Just the fact that he could get inside the house and open the safe and remove the riches was enough for Guy to gloat about.

And if Ada should happen to catch him in the act, he would take her with him back to the hideout. There, with all of the outlaws for protection, Guy would be safe to act out the fantasies he had had about the woman.

But he would rather she didn't see him, for at the moment he had another woman on his mind. Ada's daughter. Yes, Guy would find Zondra one day and she would pay for causing the scars on his back. She would pay for being responsible for his father not caring enough about him to pay a ransom for his life.

"There it is," Guy said, catching his first glimpse of his home in the distance. He turned his eyes to Billy. "We've got to be careful. Since we chose to come this time of morning instead of at night, we've got to be doubly on our guard."

"I thought you said your father and his cowhands didn't get up for at least two more hours," Billy grumbled. "Are you telling me now that you aren't sure?"

"They *don't* usually get up until later, but that doesn't mean they aren't stirring and might not be awake enough to hear us," Guy grumbled back. "We'll leave our horses tethered in the forest and go the rest of the way by foot."

"Only me and you, Guy," Billy said, giving his cohorts a look over his shoulder as they followed on their steeds. "More than that would certainly create too much commotion. And by damn, I don't want to get caught stealin' a few measly diamonds and coins. Until I was forced to move to this wilderness to hide from the law, banks were my specialty, not safes in private homes."

"I'm telling you, you'll cart away more stash here than you probably did from most banks, 'cause Billy, my father don't believe in banks," Guy said, chuckling. "He's always kept everything at his home. Don't you know how much he's worth? God, Billy, he's one rich son of a gun."

"You'd better be right about that," Billy warned. "If not, you're dead."

"You don't mean that," Guy said, paling. "You'd kill me that easily?"

"If you are worthless to me, yes, I'd kill you as quickly as I'd swat a fly on my supper table," Billy said, his eyes narrowing. "Now let's get on with this. You'd better hope I don't have to treat you like no fly."

Afraid now that perhaps his father's jewels and money might not be enough to appease this outlaw's lust for riches, Guy felt cold inside. He hadn't guessed that this outlaw was so heartless that he could kill so easily. But Guy had gotten himself into this mess by volunteering to help rob his father's safe. He had to do the best that he could and pray to God that it would be enough, or he could be living his last moments on this earth.

He rode onward, Billy close at his side. When they reached the outskirts of the ranch and could see the tall pillared house standing like a jewel in the early morning light, they reined in their horses, dismounted, and studied the house for a moment to make sure no one was up and around yet.

Guy hoped he'd soon be laughing and joking with the outlaws as though they were fast friends. But he knew that would come later—if he proved worthy to them today. His only fear was that after he led them to his father's riches, they might kill him anyway, because his usefulness would have run out.

His knees trembling with fear, wishing he were anywhere but here, Guy turned to look at Billy and found Billy staring at him questioningly.

"Well?" Billy asked. "How do you think it looks?

Should we go on to the house now, or perhaps wait until tonight?"

Wanting to get this over with, Guy looked at the house one more time, then nodded at Billy.

"Let's go," he said, his hand resting on the pistol Billy had loaned him for the heist with a warning not to try and use it on him. Billy was known for his fast draw. He'd plug Guy in a second if he felt threatened by him.

Both men grabbed the leather bags that had been hanging from their saddles. And while the others stayed behind, Guy and Billy ran quickly through the dawn.

When they reached the house, they crept up the back steps to the porch. Stopping to catch their breath, they rested a moment before entering the house.

"Let's do it now," Guy said anxiously, reaching over to turn the knob on the back door.

Quickly, quietly, they stepped into the back corridor that led to the kitchen, and then onward to the other rooms on the lower floor of the house. Moving past the servants' quarters, Guy was relieved to see that the cook had not yet risen to begin preparing the morning meal. He nodded at Billy and led him to his father's study.

There was enough light now coming through the windows for Guy to make out the safe that sat against the far wall. He looked over at Billy, who was already staring at the safe, then nudged him in the side with an elbow, nodded, and both of them went on over to the safe.

But only Guy knelt down before it. As he turned the dial on the safe, remembering the numbers well, Billy busied himself rifling through Guy's father's desk drawers.

Guy looked up just as Billy lifted Harrison's pearl-handled derringer from one of the drawers. Billy winked at Guy as he slid the derringer into one of his rear pockets, then knelt down beside Guy as he swung the safe door open wide.

Billy's green eyes lit up as the light coming through the window picked up the sparkle of the diamond necklaces and bracelets.

"Man, you knew what you were talking about when you said your father was rich," Billy said, beginning to scoop up the jewels, sliding them into his leather bag.

Billy's eyes took in the tall stacks of bills rubber-banded together, and the gold coins that were stacked neatly along the sides of the safe.

"Except for one other time in my life, when I robbed a jewelry emporium in Kansas City, Missouri, I ain't never seen such a sight as this," Billy said. "How can one man be so rich?"

"Sugarcane and cotton," Guy mumbled, recalling the huge fields of those crops back home in Mississippi. "And slaves to harvest them for my father."

"It beats the hell outta me why you'd be anxious to leave such a life as this," Billy said, giving Guy a questioning look. "Wouldn't you inherit your father's riches one day?"

"It's not what I'd inherit then," Guy said bitterly. "It's what I was getting now. You saw the scars on my back. That should be explanation enough. I gladly best my father today. I only wish I could be a little mouse in this room when he finds his safe empty. Seeing his expression and hearing his rage would be the delight of my life."

"Just be sure and get everything you can in your bag as I scoop the rest of the jewels into mine," Billy said. "The good Lord sure did bless me when he led me to you. Lord a'mercy, I sure did strike it rich, Guy. And believe me, you'll get more than your share. It would only be fair that you do." Billy swallowed hard. "You see, I had a miserable father, too," he admitted. "He tried to beat the living hell outta me. As soon as I was old enough, I stood up to him and cursed him as he hit me. But he beat me up one time too many. It was the last time. I was all grown up. I laid into him and didn't stop hittin' him until he was dead."

Billy then got a look of regret in his eyes. "My poor mama, when she came into the room and saw what I'd done," he said softly. "I'll never forget the look on her face. I couldn't get outta there fast enough. And I never looked back. I'm not sure if my mama is even still alive. She was poorly those last weeks I lived with her. Yes, she was of poor health, but do you think my father cared? Nope. He womanized every night as my mother lay in bed crying because she knew it."

Guy stared disbelievingly at Billy. "Christ, your life was way worse than mine," he said.

"In a sense," Billy said, shrugging. He snapped his bag closed. "Come on. Let's get outta here."

His bag heavy with money, Guy hoisted it from the floor. Together he and Billy fled the house without being caught. They even got across the yard and the wide pasture without anyone seeing them.

Laughing, so glad to have achieved what he had thought would be impossible, besting his overbearing father in the way that would hurt him the worst— taking his money and jewels—Guy rode off with the other outlaws.

They rode until they were far enough from the ranch to feel safe, then drew a tight rein and dismounted. The gang, ten men in all, were awestruck

by the riches that were humped on the ground for
them to see. They looked at Guy with admiration,
seeing him as a great addition to their gang.

Guy felt important for the first time in his life. But
still, one thing was missing.

He had to find Zondra to show her who was boss.
This time it wouldn't be her white father. It would be
her half brother!

Chapter Seventeen

O, that a war of looks was there between them!
Her eyes, petitioners, to his eyes seeing.

—WILLIAM SHAKESPEARE

With too many more miles to travel before he would reach his village, and feeling guilty when he saw how truly tired Zondra was, Lone Eagle took pity on her and stopped to make camp, even though daylight was now fully upon them.

He had pushed Zondra beyond her limits, especially knowing that she couldn't have had much time to sleep before he had caught up with her and his horse.

Zondra's heart skipped a beat when she saw Lone Eagle rein in his black mustang. She scarcely breathed as he slid from his saddle and stopped to look at her. She had no idea what to expect from him next, for in his eyes, she was an enemy!

"We have stopped to make camp for a while so that we can both rest," Lone Eagle said, seeing that what he said seemed to make her spirits lower rather than making her grateful that he was thinking of her welfare.

Surely Zondra knew that if it were not for her, he would travel onward until he reached the comfort of his lodge, instead of setting up a temporary resting place many miles from his home and people. None of his people yet knew how things had gone for him at their clan enemy's village, whether or not Lone Eagle came away from there safely.

If he was gone too long, his warriors might become alarmed and go to Red Moon's village and confront the enemy chief. That would be the wrong thing to do. Red Moon must be given the time to work through his anger over losing his lock of hair before facing any more clan enemies.

As for Zondra, had she expected him to release her this soon? Was that what she had hoped when he stopped? His jaw tightened, for he knew that he still had to make her truly understand the seriousness of horse stealing.

"I will build a fire and we will sleep for a while before moving onward," Lone Eagle said, loosening Zondra's ropes so that she could sleep more comfortably.

He took her gently by the elbow. "Come and sit on the ground while I make you a soft bed of willow limbs and blankets to sleep upon," he said. "When we arrive at my village, I will see that you have food, for I am certain that you are hungry."

Too disheartened over still being his captive, Zondra didn't offer any conversation. She sat down on the ground and watched as he snapped several long branches from a willow tree, then meticulously laid them one by one in a crisscross pattern. He then spread two blankets over these, making what appeared to Zondra to be a soft and comfortable bed.

"It is done," Lone Eagle said. He gestured with a hand toward the makeshift bed. "*Di-a,* go ahead. Come. Sleep."

Still stubbornly refusing to talk to Lone Eagle, and

most certainly fighting sleep, because once he was asleep she would grab the opportunity to escape from him, Zondra went to the bed and stretched out on it. She gave him a wavering look as he gently spread a blanket over her, up to her chin.

"It is best that you put your stubbornness aside and allow yourself to get some rest," Lone Eagle said, realizing that she was purposely not talking to him.

He could almost read her mind. She was planning to try an escape while he slept.

Sighing, he built a campfire, then spread his blanket a few inches from Zondra.

He saw her look of anger when he took the rope that was tied around her wrists, although more loosely now, and tied the other end around his right wrist.

"Yes, I am tying us together. I do not trust that you will not sneak away from me while I rest," Lone Eagle said, truly not enjoying this game he was playing with her. He was afraid the longer he played it, the greater the chances she would hate him for eternity.

But this was a chance he must take. In the end, however it would turn out between them, she would have learned a hard lesson of life.

Her jaw tight, her eyes flashing, Zondra turned over, her back now to him.

She fought the sleep that was burning in her eyes. She fought the sluggishness of her body. Knowing that she had to put many miles between herself and Lone Eagle as soon as he was asleep, she tried not to feel the aching in her feet and legs.

She fought the sensual feelings she still had for him, especially intense now with him lying there so close behind her, his handsomeness so unnerving. If she did not hate him yet for what he was doing to her, she knew she never could. When one loved as deeply—

and as quickly—as she loved Lone Eagle, it was not something tossed aside just because it was for the best.

Although she did not plan to ever see him again once she was free of his captivity, he would be with her always in her heart and memory. And in a sense, that would make her Lone Eagle's prisoner no matter where she went, or what she did.

Once he was asleep, she planned to remove the shackle from around her wrists. She would be careful not to tug on the rope as she struggled with it. Although he had loosened the knot, it had not been enough for her to easily slide the rope off.

Suddenly, a coyote howled in the distance, long and eerily. In a flash, Zondra saw in her mind's eye the white wolves circling the calf, hungrily yanking at its bloodied body. She wasn't even aware of gulping out loud with terror until Lone Eagle looked quickly at her and saw the fear in her eyes. He knew what frightened her when the coyote howled again and he saw her stiffen.

"Do not be afraid of Little Brother Wolf," Lone Eagle said softly. "That's what I call the coyote, kin of the great wolves. Little Brother Wolf is a friend, not an enemy, to mankind."

He waited to see if Zondra would say something, but soon realized that she was too stubborn to. He ignored her silence and spoke again.

"One morning long ago, when I was a young brave and new with firearms, I was hunting deer with a black powder rifle. The fog was so thick it was a visible presence in the pitch-dark of the predawn. I sat down underneath a mesquite tree to wait for deer and daylight."

Lone Eagle placed a log on the campfire, stirring the orange embers. "I do not know which of us saw the other first," he said, chuckling. "He looked a little embarrassed when he realized how close this Crow brave had managed to get to him. He then quickly executed a clever fade-into-the-fog vanishing act."

Lone Eagle gazed into the leaping flames of the fire and at that instant saw the coyote's dark eyes as though it were there now, daring him. "For an insane moment that morning I almost shot at him," he said. "I did not shoot, though. Even if I had, I would not have hit him. He was, as all coyote are, the master of stealth and speed, of purposeful motion. It is good that I did not kill him. I would still feel ashamed."

When Lone Eagle realized that Zondra still wasn't ready to join the conversation, he sighed and stretched out on his blanket again.

Zondra had been totally captivated by Lone Eagle's story, yet she did not want to give him the satisfaction of knowing it, so she still ignored him. She watched him as he curled up on his side and closed his eyes.

Hoping to soon have the opportunity she needed to make her move, Zondra waited, then smiled when she heard him breathing evenly and saw no twitching beneath his eyelids. Finally he was asleep!

She kept her eyes on Lone Eagle as she gently tugged and struggled with the rope. When she found it harder to remove than she'd expected, she struggled harder.

When her hands were finally free, and she was able to lay the rope gently on the ground between her and Lone Eagle, she smiled triumphantly. Slowly she rose to her feet.

Watching Lone Eagle's eyes, she backed away from him until she reached the tree where his black mustang had been tethered. She untied the reins from the limb of the tree, and trying to be as quiet as possible, she edged the horse into the shadows of the forest, where his hoofbeats were muffled by the thick bed of dried leaves left there last autumn.

When she thought she was far enough away that Lone Eagle couldn't hear the horse's hooves, she mounted the steed bareback and rode away.

But when she heard a shrill, sharp whistle behind her, and the black mustang stopped so abruptly that Zondra found herself sailing over his head, she knew that Lone Eagle hadn't been asleep after all. He had purposely allowed her to get far enough to get her hopes up, then whistled to his horse, apparently a command he had taught his steed that was guaranteed to bring the horse back to him quickly.

As she lay on the ground on her back, she watched in amazement as the mustang whirled around and headed away from her at a fast gallop, back in the direction from which they had come.

Sore, angry, and humiliated, Zondra was still sprawled on the ground when Lone Eagle rode up on his horse. She gave him an angry glare when he reined in the mustang and gazed down at her with amusement in his dark eyes.

"*Again* you steal my horse?" Lone Eagle said, their eyes locked in silent battle. He then reached out a hand for Zondra.

"You'll have to drag me back to that campsite," Zondra said sourly, refusing to take his hand. "I'm most certainly not going anywhere with you willingly."

"If being dragged is what you want, it can be arranged," Lone Eagle said, shrugging, now more determined than ever to see this thing through to the end.

Thus far Zondra had ignored all lessons he was trying to teach her. She had proved that to him by stealing his horse a second time. And although his heart went out to her, so badly wanting things to be different between them, he stayed firm in his decision to make her realize, and admit, that she was wrong to steal someone's horse.

Certain that he would do as he said, Zondra scrambled to her feet. "You certainly are enjoying yourself, aren't you?" she hissed as she brushed dirt from her skirt. "I can't believe you are doing these things to me. You even played possum so that I could steal your horse again, didn't you? You . . . you . . . savage rogue! If I had a gun, I would . . ."

She stopped short of saying that she would shoot him, for in truth, she knew that she wouldn't.

What *were* his feelings for her now? Did he hate her this much? Or was it all to make her pay for what she'd done?

She paled when he slipped a rifle from his gun boot and started to hand it to her.

"What . . . are . . . you doing?" she gasped out, her hand at her throat.

"Here is a gun," Lone Eagle said, their eyes again locked. "Is that not what you want? To have a gun? To shoot your captor? To shoot a savage?"

"N-n-n-o . . . I . . ." Zondra stammered.

She stopped speaking and turned with a start when she heard a loud roar behind her and discovered that her argument with Lone Eagle had awakened a bear from its den. It was standing on its hind legs in a threatening manner, and again gave a tremendous roar.

Zondra was scared to death of the huge animal. She was amazed that neither Lone Eagle's horse nor Lone Eagle himself seemed bothered by it.

The Indian chief said nothing, just stared at the bear

until the animal settled back down on all four legs, turned around, and lumbered off into the forest again.

Zondra was amazed that Lone Eagle had not shot the bear when it seemed so ominously ready to pounce on them, and wondered why he now so confidently slid his rifle back into its boot.

She was so in awe of Lone Eagle's courage in the face of danger that she didn't fight him off when he reached down and swept an arm around her waist and lifted her onto his horse, settling her down in front of him.

She didn't even flinch when he slid an arm around her waist and held her against him as they rode back in the direction of their campsite.

"I don't understand," Zondra said, as she gazed over her shoulder at Lone Eagle.

"You do not understand what?" Lone Eagle said, feeling such strong emotions for Zondra at this moment, when their bodies were touching, that he almost forgot why he was treating her like a captive. It was easy to forget that moments ago she had called him a savage.

It would be so easy to forget that he needed to teach her a lesson and to just be with her as he had that night back at his village. When they had talked then, he had known from her eyes and what he heard in her voice that she had deep feelings for him.

Yet he remembered how she had run from him that day that he had come upon her resting beside the stream, and how she had later fled his lodge.

Yes, there was so much about her that was a mystery . . . a mystery he hoped to unravel.

"I don't understand why neither you nor your horse were afraid of that bear, or why you didn't shoot it," Zondra said softly, enjoying this brief time with him when bitter words were not being exchanged between them. "The bear was so close. It could have mauled all of us to death."

"To the Crow people, bears are a forbidden animal," Lone Eagle said. "After all, do bears not walk upright like a man?"

He was enjoying this lighthearted talk between them, if only for a moment. Once they were back at the campsite, he would have to tie her up again with the rope until he could convince her that she was still his captive!

"To kill a bear, except in self-defense, is very bad medicine," he said. "To the Crow, to actually eat the flesh of a bear is the equivalent of cannibalism."

"You appear to have more respect for a bear than *me,* and I am a human being," Zondra said sarcastically, breaking through that quiet, soft moment they had briefly shared.

"I cannot recall any bear ever stealing horses from Lone Eagle," he said, frowning at Zondra as she flashed him an incredulous look.

Zondra sighed heavily. She knew that trying to talk to Lone Eagle about anything right now was a waste of breath, for it was obvious that he could see no farther than her being a horse thief!

But at least one thing was in her favor. For now, he allowed her to ride on his horse with him instead of leading her by a rope behind him like an animal.

No matter, though, her pride would not allow her to thank him.

Chapter Eighteen

The birds rose smiling in their nests,
The gales indeed were done;
Alas! how heedless were the eyes
On whom the summer shone.

—EMILY DICKINSON

As the morning light spiraled down through the smoke hole in his tepee, settling on his face, awakening him, Red Moon stretched and yawned, then slowly opened his eyes.

As he turned to check on his fire, to see if there were coals in it that were still smoldering, making it easier for him to start his morning fire, he jumped with a start when he found something lying beside him on his pallet of furs and blankets.

His eyes widened and he gasped as he bolted to a sitting position. His hand trembled as he reached toward the thick, long lock of hair that looked as though it were alive, mocking him.

His hand had almost reached the lock of hair when he drew it back again and did not touch the lock. Instead, as his heart pounded, he lifted that hand toward his head.

Closing his eyes and grimacing, he searched his scalp for the missing lock of hair, moaning with despair when he finally found from where it had been removed.

"No!" he cried, feeling cold and violated. Sick inside, he hugged himself as his whole body began to shake and tremble. Without a full head of hair he would be humiliated in the presence of his people!

Someone had purposely come and degraded him with one quick slice of a knife. How could he face his people? They would know that someone had been able to come in the night to Red Moon's lodge and succeed at cutting his hair without awakening him.

It was a disgrace. It was a humiliation so keen Red Moon was not sure if he could ever leave his lodge until the hair grew back.

His eyes narrowed angrily as he looked toward his entrance flap. No. Whoever came as a ghost in the night and removed his hair would not have risked entering through the front of the tepee. That had to mean that . . .

With a jerk of his head, he turned and gazed with wide eyes at the long slit that had been made in the buffalo hide at the back of his tepee. Now he knew how the intruder had managed to get into his tepee without being detected. But he still did not know who the culprit was!

Who would dare do this to a powerful Crow chief? And why . . . ?

Anger clutched at his insides, for he suddenly thought of someone cunning enough to move this quietly and stealthily through the night to do something like this and not be caught.

Lone Eagle!

And Red Moon knew why. It was done to avenge his humiliating remarks to White Bead in the presence of her people.

Red Moon had expected some retaliation, but not something as severe or as devastating and degrading as this.

He looked quickly toward the entrance flap again, recalling having ordered warriors to stand guard all night. Apparently Lone Eagle had come in the back way to elude them.

Although angry over what Lone Eagle had done to him, Red Moon was filled with many regrets today and he became lost in thought.

Right after his father died, Red Moon had tried to change things for his people. He wanted peace, not war, yet there was still conflict between his clan and the clan of Lone Eagle, mainly because the old grudges between two clan enemies were kept alive by Lone Eagle's father, who still lived as a reminder of things past.

Lone Eagle's father was a man of peace, yet when it had come to Red Moon's clan, Mad Buffalo could not seem to forget how Red Moon's father had gone against all his efforts at peace between the Crow clans.

In time, too, Red Moon had learned to enjoy coming up with ways to best Lone Eagle, which kept the feud going between the two after Lone Eagle was appointed chief of his Crow clan.

Even now Red Moon could not help but want revenge against the man who removed his lock of hair, but knew that if he did retaliate, the feud that had begun so many moons ago would never end.

Red Moon sighed as he gazed sadly down at his precious hair. Yes, it was time to stop this age-old feud. Red Moon was tired of challenges between two men who should look to one another as brothers. Clans should stay together as though they were of one heartbeat, not snort and snarl like animals when one looked the other in the face.

He stroked his fingers through his long, thick hair, grimacing again when he came to the empty space on

his scalp. Until his hair grew out, he would just comb
it a different way.

Yes, the sin could be that easily hidden.

And perhaps in time he would have a chance to
make things right with White Bead. He wanted to
apologize to her—something that came hard for this
man of pride.

His thoughts lingered on White Bead. He could envision her lovely face, her gentle countenance. He
couldn't believe that he had done such a terrible thing
to her. If only he could go to her and make things
right between them today.

He felt so bad for having gone so far in humiliating
her. He shivered as he remembered what he had said.
It was disgusting and definitely a nontruth, for never
had he met anyone as pure and sweet as she.

He wanted her so badly he ached.

When someone stepped up to his entrance flap and
announced their presence, Red Moon started to grab
the lock of hair and hide it, then didn't. He knew who
the morning visitor was. It was his best friend, Possum.
They always ate their morning meal together. Red
Moon and Possum liked to discuss the plans for the
day before they went into council with the rest of
the warriors.

Today Red Moon and Possum would have more to
discuss than matters of their people. Possum would be
shown the lock of hair. Together they would decide
what to do.

"Red Moon, it is I, Possum," Possum said through
the closed flap.

"Come," Red Moon said. He held his chin high and
folded his legs before him. He rested his hands on
his knees as Possum, a large, muscled Crow, entered
the lodge.

When Possum came close enough to Red Moon to see the empty space on his chief's scalp, and then as quickly saw the lock of hair that lay beside him, he took an unsteady step away from him, his eyes registering the shock that he felt over knowing his chief's humiliation.

"Who did this to you?" Possum gasped. He looked at the lock of hair, and then looked again at Red Moon.

Seeing the horror in his friend's dark eyes, Red Moon quickly explained how it had happened, and why.

"You will avenge such a cowardly act as this," Possum hissed, facing Red Moon as he settled down on a blanket across the fire pit from him.

Red Moon said nothing for a moment. Instead he worked on his lodge fire until flames were lapping at the logs that he laid in a crisscross fashion in his fire pit.

Then he lifted the lock of hair and held it between his two hands, gazing at it mournfully. "This is the most humiliating thing I have ever suffered," he said thickly. "In the past I would have gone for Lone Eagle's scalp. But now? It is my decision to prove to Lone Eagle that I wish for the feud between our two clans to be over."

"You will allow him to get away with this?" Possum asked incredulously. "What he did deserves the worst sort of punishment."

"You know why he did this and you can still say that?" Red Moon asked.

"What he did to you is way worse than what you did to White Bead," Possum growled. "We must seek vengeance, my chief, not peace."

"One vengeance leads to another and another and

another," Red Moon said, sighing heavily. "I will just wear my hair differently so our people cannot see where the one lock was removed."

"But, my chief, our people are astute. They will see how differently you will be wearing your hair," Possum persisted. "They will want to know why. What will you say? How will you explain why you will not seek vengeance for such a terrible act against you, their proud chief?"

When Red Moon heard footsteps approaching outside his lodge, he ignored Possum's troubling questions and quickly covered the lock of hair with a blanket. He then reached up and repositioned several locks of hair over his bald spot.

He smiled as though nothing was wrong when Apple Blossom, a young maiden, came into the lodge carrying a pot of stew, her young, sweet face brightening up the lodge as she smiled from one man to the other.

"Thank you, Apple Blossom," Red Moon said, taking the heavy pot from her and hanging it on a tripod over the leaping flames of his lodge fire.

"I will return soon with your morning water," Apple Blossom said, pausing long enough to stare at the strange way her chief had arranged his hair today, one long lock crisscrossing strangely at the side of his head.

Red Moon saw her quizzical stare, then got to his feet and took her gently by an elbow and ushered her outside. "Get the water," he said, his voice drawn.

She took one last look at his hair, smiled shyly up at him, then walked away.

When Red Moon returned to his lodge, Possum gave him a smug "I told you so" look.

"I will not explain anything to my people; especially

I will not tell them that one of their clan enemy came like a thief in the night and removed my hair," Red Moon grumbled. "At least Lone Eagle did not steal it to show it to his people, to laugh at my humiliation. He left it in my possession."

"It is good that he did not take it, for the longer you have it in your possession as a reminder of what Lone Eagle did, the greater the chances you will change your mind and make the man pay for what he did to shame you," Possum said sourly.

"Do you forget you are in the presence of your chief, talking down to him?" Red Moon said, his eyes narrowing at Possum.

Possum humbly lowered his eyes.

"I would have been disappointed in Lone Eagle had he *not* come and avenged what I did to White Bead," Red Moon then said. He got two wooden bowls from his supply of dinnerware and handed one to Possum. "If Lone Eagle had left White Bead's humiliation unavenged, I would have seen him as a coward," he said.

"And how do you think he will now see you?" Possum asked, avoiding Red Moon's angry glance when the chief paused as he ladled food into Possum's bowl.

"Say no more, Possum," Red Moon said sternly. "Or no more morning meals will be shared with your chief. I will choose another warrior to sit with me in your place, at least until I find a wife who will sit and eat with me."

"It is hard not to speak my feelings to you today when you have always allowed me to do so in the past," Possum said guardedly.

"This is now, not the past, and it is because of something *I* did that was wrong that I lost my lock of hair, so I no longer wish to talk about it, now . . . or ever. . . ." Red Moon said bluntly. "If you cannot accept that, leave and do not come back ever again for council with your chief."

Possum became quiet and began eating the large chunks of stew meat from his bowl with his fingers. "It is good to be here with you," he then said as he chewed. "I will say nothing more that upsets you."

Red Moon plucked a piece of cooked wild carrot from his bowl and popped it in his mouth and began chewing as he became lost in thoughts.

Ahh, yes, ways must be found to prove to Lone Eagle that Red Moon wished for the feud between their two clans to be over, he thought to himself. And if that could be achieved, perhaps there might be a chance of his having White Bead as his wife after all. There was no denying that he had seen her look his way with much favor.

And eyes did not lie.

In the depths of her beautiful dark eyes she had silently revealed to him that she still cared for him the way she had as a child. That's why he had persisted in going to Lone Eagle's village and making a fool of himself over her.

When White Bead lashed back at him this last time it was because she had not yet been ready to put her life as her people's prophet behind her. But he knew that in time she would. Someone that beautiful and with so much to offer a man could not live the life of a spinster forever. Eventually, White Bead would hunger to have her womanly desires fulfilled.

And I will be the one to fulfill them, he thought determinedly to himself.

But a lasting peace must come first between himself and Lone Eagle. Without that, he knew that he would never have the opportunity to hold White Bead in his arms.

Chapter Nineteen

Taste the high joy none but the blest can prove,
There thou or joinest the immortal quire
In melodies that even Heaven Fair
Fill with superior bliss, or, at desires.

—JOHN KEATS

It was midday when Zondra and Lone Eagle arrived at the outskirts of his village. As they entered the village, and Lone Eagle began to wind his way around the conical lodges, all of his people's chores and all of the children's play halted as everyone stopped to gawk at Zondra.

Trying her best to ignore their stares, Zondra looked slowly around her. Although she had seen the village many times from the bluff, and had been there briefly that one night, she was no less in awe of the Crow tepees, which were said to be the most elegant of all Indian lodges.

They were so huge, Zondra surmised that each had been made from at least a dozen buffalo hides. Surely it took the Crow women many days to make one lodge.

Zondra noticed that all of the tepees had their own distinct drawings on the outside, but soon realized that one animal in particular dominated the paintings on all of the tepees—the buffalo, the animal that gave the clan its name.

Her gaze moved to the many children in the village. Her heart melted when she saw how beautiful they were, the young boys as well as the girls. Their lovely copper faces, with wide, dark eyes, and their lustrously thick black hair were so endearing, she had an instant picture in her mind of how a child born to herself and Lone Eagle would look. With her mixed ancestry of white and black and Lone Eagle's copper skin, oh, how beautiful a child born of their love would be.

When a warrior came running to Lone Eagle, his eyes shining as he smiled at his chief, Zondra's thoughts of foolish things fled from her mind. She felt Lone Eagle's arm tighten around her as he reined in and stopped.

Lone Eagle saw in Two Chances's eyes just how relieved he was to see him. Lone Eagle regretted having worried his people by not arriving home sooner from their clan enemy's village.

Yet, even so, he would not change anything. Finding Zondra, although in a much different way than he would have chosen, was like a miracle sent from the *Ah-badt-deadt-deah,* the Great Mystery above. After Zondra had fled his lodge in the middle of the night like a frightened deer, Lone Eagle had given up on ever seeing her again. And then there she was, seemingly put there for him to find, as though fate had drawn them together again for a purpose.

It was destiny. Even while they both were only tiny seeds growing inside their mothers' wombs, it was planned for them to find one another and be together for eternity—on earth, and much later in the hereafter, when they would walk among the clouds holding hands.

"The deed is done," Lone Eagle said quietly. "Entering Red Moon's village and lodge under the cover of night was easy, especially since Red Moon's guards carelessly slept the whole time I was there." Lone Eagle laughed softly. "Even now, while we speak, I am certain Red Moon is gazing upon his lock of hair, knowing who took it from his scalp, and why," he said, his eyes gleaming.

"I would like to be a deer mouse in Red Moon's lodge, watching him mourning the loss of his lock of hair," Two Chances said, chuckling. "I shall go and tell White Bead her embarrassment and humiliation have been avenged."

Lone Eagle saw how Two Chances's gaze shifted to Zondra, then moved back to Lone Eagle, a questioning in their depths. Lone Eagle ignored his friend's way of silently questioning him about Zondra. He wanted more time alone with her before he explained her presence to his people.

Lone Eagle nudged his steed's flanks with the heels of his moccasined feet, and gazed straight ahead as he rode onward through the throng of people, which parted to make way for the chief to go to his lodge.

Zondra's mind was awhirl with questions about the lock of hair that had been cut from some warrior's scalp, and about who White Bead was. For Lone Eagle to have put himself in danger by going into another man's lodge and cutting some of his hair to avenge something the man had done to White Bead surely meant that he had to think an awful lot of the woman.

Zondra could not help but feel a pang of jealousy at the thought of Lone Eagle caring so much for another woman that he would risk his life for her.

She looked slowly around her, through the crowd, and searched for a particular woman who might be paying more attention to Lone Eagle, her eyes filled with pride over him having done something solely for her.

But Zondra saw no woman looking more proud than the others. Each seemed as taken by their chief as the next, old and young alike.

Yes, he would be this admired, Zondra thought to herself. Lord, she was so entranced by him herself, she found it hard to continue being bitter toward him for having treated her like a horse thief, when deep inside his heart he surely knew that her reason for taking the horse was a valid one, that she might not have survived another night without the means to travel onward in search of a safe haven.

Yet here she was. No matter that she was no longer being forced to walk on her sore, aching feet, but instead was riding with him on his proud steed, she was still no less his captive.

What were his plans for her now that they had arrived at his village? she wondered despairingly. Surely he had a plan formulated in his mind.

Would she be forced to serve him as a menial servant—a white slave? Would he insist that she call him her lord? Or was that title only used by wives?

The very thought of having to bow down to Lone Eagle, after having left another sort of enslavement, made a renewed anger grow inside Zondra. And while she felt this way, how could he expect a civil tongue from her?

No! No matter how much he tried to force her, she would not be his slave—love, or otherwise.

She had regained her pride after having escaped her father's stronghold. She would not let another man take it away. Not even a man she had more than once envisioned making love to. From here on out she had to fight off such foolish notions as that. Yes, at her first opportunity, she was going to leave, even if it meant leaving her heart behind in the process.

She swallowed hard and grew tense as Lone Eagle stopped before his tepee. The chief slid from the saddle and reached his arms out for Zondra. "I will help you dismount," he said, hating it when she got that determined, stubborn look in her eyes and locked her arms across her chest.

He dropped his arms to his sides. "Come down alone, then," he said impatiently. "But do not think I will tolerate this stubbornness for long. You are here because I brought you here. You will do as I say, or—"

"Or *what*?" Zondra snapped back before Lone Eagle could finish his warning.

Lone Eagle sighed, then reached up and grabbed her by an arm. "Come now or I will jerk you down into my arms and carry you inside by force," he said, his eyes flashing up at her.

Knowing that she had no choice but to do as he said, or risk being humiliated in front of all of his people, Zondra removed his hand from her arm and slid from the saddle to the ground.

But she went no farther than that. She would show him that she wasn't going to take being bossed around by him that easily.

"Now what?" she said icily. She again folded her arms across her chest.

"Are you going to make me tell you everything to do, one thing at a time, as though you are someone with no means of thinking for yourself?" Lone Eagle said, his jaw tightening.

When she still stood her ground, he leaned down into her face. "Go inside," he said dryly. "*Di-a*, do it!

I will carry you if you do not go there on your own two feet!"

"Oh, all right," Zondra said, turning on her heel and stamping on inside his lodge as he held the buffalo hide entrance flap aside for her.

Although she tried her hardest to still appear strong-willed and unafraid, Zondra felt a growing fear as she stood inside Lone Eagle's lodge, alone with him. Although she had been there before, there was a difference. Then, she was treated kindly. Now she was a captive and was not sure what to expect next from a man who seemed adamant about hating horse thieves. Perhaps she should feel lucky that he hadn't already hanged her.

Zondra watched Lone Eagle guardedly as he came into the tepee. She expected to be tied up again to ensure that she couldn't escape. She was so relieved when Lone Eagle didn't force this on her.

"Sit on the cushions and be comfortable," Lone Eagle said gently, gesturing toward the pillows beside the fire. "After the long ride I am sure you will not argue about that."

Bone-tired and hungry, Zondra didn't have to be asked twice. She gladly went and sat down on the soft cushions. The delicious smell of meat and vegetables wafting toward her from the huge pot that hung over the fire made her stomach growl. Lone Eagle sat down against his willow backrest, which was strung with sinew that was suspended from tripods and covered with buffalo hides.

Zondra looked up quickly when an elderly, bent woman came into the lodge carrying an armful of firewood. Wide-eyed, she watched the woman kneel beside the lodge fire and slide wood into the flames.

The woman then turned and sent a questioning gaze toward Zondra, and then Lone Eagle.

"Singing Star, the woman you see in my lodge today is called by the name Zondra," Lone Eagle said as he spoke to the elderly lady while keeping his eyes on Zondra, making her stir uncomfortably. "Zondra, the woman who questions you with her eyes is named Singing Star."

Zondra returned Singing Star's curious gaze, her eyes slowly sweeping over the elderly Indian. The woman was dressed in a long, flowing, fringed buckskin dress, with beautiful beads around her neck and twined into the one long braid down her back.

Her thin, frail shoulders were bent, and her skin was so thin, it was drawn tautly like leather across her bones. Her eyes were so pale they hardly held any color in them.

Zondra could not believe how the elderly lady seemed duty-driven to carry Lone Eagle's wood for him and tend to his fire!

"Is Singing Star related to you?" Zondra blurted out. "Perhaps your . . . aunt?"

"No, she is of no relation to Lone Eagle," he said, smiling up at Singing Star as she stood quietly studying Zondra.

He knew why she stared this incredulously at Zondra. Singing Star had never before seen a white woman in her chief's lodge and wondered why one was there now.

Singing Star would soon know, but not just yet. Because Lone Eagle was her chief and had many decisions to make, Singing Star had learned to wait for answers about things her still-active mind questioned.

Zondra was ready to blurt out how shameful it was that Lone Eagle allowed the elderly woman to wait on him like a slave, but had barely opened her mouth to speak when he continued to explain who Singing Star was.

"In every Crow lodge there is an unattached old woman who sleeps beside the entrance, makes up the beds, wards off intruding dogs with clubs, and relieves a childbearing woman of the heavier labors," he said, reaching a hand to gently touch Singing Star's arm. "She also brings in wood and water, and cooks. The food now hanging over the fire was made by Singing Star because she knew I would return soon to my lodge."

Something made Zondra keep her feelings to herself about how appalled she was by this practice. She had second thoughts about scolding him, for if she kept her opinions to herself and kept a civil tongue, just perhaps she would be treated more civilly . . . at least until she managed to escape and could continue her trek toward total freedom in her life.

She now realized that no matter the risks out there, she *must* go on with her quest for freedom, and on her own.

"White woman, do you have a husband?" Singing Star suddenly blurted out.

Zondra was taken aback by the abrupt question. She took a deep, quavering breath, then responded. "No, I have no husband," she murmured. "Why . . . do . . . you ask?"

Singing Star ignored Zondra's response. Instead she looked quickly at Lone Eagle. "This white woman's age is greater than the age at which women marry," she said, her voice deep, almost masculine. "Since she is not married, surely she is a prophet! A *white* prophet! Lone Eagle, she must be treated special.

Surely the Great Mystery purposely placed her in your path!"

Lone Eagle gave off a low, mocking laugh. "Singing Star, she is no prophet," he said, his eyes dancing as they held Zondra's. "She is a *horse thief.*"

Singing Star stifled a gasp with her hand as she stared at Lone Eagle, then turned and looked questioningly at Zondra. She backed up to the entrance flap, then turned and hurriedly left the lodge.

"You certainly enjoyed that, didn't you?" Zondra spat out, unable to keep her feelings to herself.

Then she remembered something that puzzled her. She was too curious not to ask Lone Eagle about it. "If Singing Star is the elderly woman who serves you, who is supposed to even sleep in your lodge, then where was she when I was in your lodge earlier . . . when I came to you for a night's shelter?" she asked guardedly.

"Singing Star was ill," he said, tossing another log onto the flames of his lodge fire. "She was at Medicine Fox's lodge."

"Who is Medicine Fox?" Zondra asked warily.

"He is our people's shaman," Lone Eagle said. "Our wise healer."

Zondra resisted the urge to shame him about having the elderly lady waiting on him like a slave, especially now that she knew the woman had recently been ill. She thought better of saying such things to him when she had already crossed the line by saying too much.

Instead, she grew quiet as she waited for him to make his next move, his decision about *her,* all the while starving, but too proud to ask him for food.

Chapter Twenty

He touched me, so I live to know
That such a day permitted so.

—EMILY DICKINSON

More than once, Lone Eagle had seen Zondra hungrily eyeing the pot of food that hung over the flames of his fire. He had even heard her stomach growling. Thinking that she might be too stubborn to accept his offer of food, he hesitated doing so.

Perhaps by holding back he might make her stubbornness wane, allowing her sweeter side to surface. He knew she had such a side by having been with her before.

But seeing her so hungry, her gaze now locked on the food, her eyes eager, he could not be so cruel as to make her wait any longer to eat. His own stomach was painfully empty.

Even if Zondra refused to eat, he was not going to make himself suffer any longer by not eating in her presence. He was going to fill his belly with Singing Star's delicious stew.

He knew that Zondra's eyes had turned to him as he rose and went to his supply of eating wares. Instead of choosing utensils made of rawhide, stone, or soapstone, he chose those he knew would be more like what she was used to.

He took two wooden bowls and spoons from his supplies and went back and sat down beside her on the cushions. His heart raced as he felt her eyes watching him ladling the stew into both bowls. He could almost feel her eagerness as the bowls were filled with the wonderfully rich smelling stew made from venison and wild vegetables.

Zondra was so hungry she was light-headed. Never had her stomach felt so empty. As she gazed at the bowls of stew her mouth actually watered, yet she wished that she had the strength to refuse the stew when he offered her a bowl. She wanted to tell him that she wished nothing from him except her freedom!

Yet as the delicious smell wafted from the bowl that he had placed close to her, nodding to her in his silent way to tell her to take it and eat, she had to fight hard to resist.

Lone Eagle saw her hesitance and could not help but admire her strength, although it was foolish at such a time as this when she needed nourishment so badly.

Not meaning to add to her self-imposed torture, he began eating the stew from his bowl in great gulps, hardly stopping to chew the food, as she hungrily watched him, her lips slightly parted.

Even when his bowl was empty he saw that she still had not attempted a bite. He wondered just how much longer she could hold back from eating. How could she be *this* stubborn?

Sighing, he set his bowl down and lifted hers in one hand while picking up the spoon with his other. "Do you want to be force-fed?" he said irritably. "You need nourishment. You *will* eat."

"And why should you care?" Zondra blurted out, tears rushing into her eyes. "All I am to you is a

captive. Why should you care if I die by starvation?
Won't it make it easier for you? That way you won't
have to hang a vicious horse thief like me."

"I have never met anyone as stubborn as you,
or . . ." Lone Eagle's voice wavered; he was taken
aback when she suddenly grabbed the bowl of food
and spoon and ravenously began gobbling the stew
down as though there were no tomorrow.

Glad to see that Zondra was finally coming to her
senses, and comfortable himself from having eaten,
Lone Eagle went to the back of his lodge and got his
long-stemmed pipe and small leather pouch of
tobacco.

Smiling when he saw Zondra filling her bowl a second time, Lone Eagle opened his tobacco pouch and
shook some into the bowl of his pipe. With his teeth,
he pulled the string on the small pouch closed again,
laid it aside, then took his filled pipe and propped
himself comfortably against his willow backrest beside
the fire.

He lit the pipe and smoked in silence for a while,
the pungent smoke drifting over to Zondra. His eyebrows arched when he saw her fill her bowl a third
time with stew. When even that was eaten and she
pushed the bowl aside, Lone Eagle asked her a question that had been troubling him from the first moment he had seen her.

"Are you a breed?" he blurted out, resting the bowl
of his pipe on his bare knee.

Stunned by the question, Zondra gazed with wonder
at him.

After only a moment of thought she realized why
Lone Eagle might think that she was a half-breed. Her
skin was white, yet her eyes and hair were dark like
an Indian's. *And* he had noticed that she wasn't al-

lowed to live in her father's big house with the other white people. No wonder he thought she might be a breed, for she had heard how breeds were shunned by white people, and sometimes even Indians!

Since he had been kind enough to give her all the food she wished to eat, and was now being gentle and thoughtful to her, Zondra decided to answer his question. She'd give him only enough information to make him know that she wasn't a breed. She wasn't going to go as far as to tell him how it was that she might look like one, that it had nothing to do with Indians. She wasn't ashamed of her black heritage, just afraid that he wouldn't understand. She still found it hard to understand herself, how white people held such power over blacks.

Oh, how she hated slavery! All kinds! If Lone Eagle was forced to live on a reservation, wouldn't he then also be enslaved by whites?

"Yes, in a sense I am a breed," Zondra murmured, then went quiet again. She waited for him to seek more answers from her.

Lone Eagle was puzzled by what she might mean by saying that she was a breed "in a sense." Either a person was, or they weren't.

But he could tell that she didn't wish to say any more about it, so he would be patient, for in time he would know everything about her. She didn't know it yet, but she would be his woman.

He looked quickly over at the entrance flap as it was shoved aside. He smiled at his father as Mad Buffalo sauntered slowly into the tepee. He was glad that the older man had chosen this moment to arrive, for it would save the awkwardness that had just fallen between Lone Eagle and Zondra.

"My son, Singing Star came to me and told me

about the white woman in your lodge," Mad Buffalo said, moving on into the tepee, moaning as he stiffly sat down on a mat beside Lone Eagle. "I had to come and see for myself this woman who Singing Star thinks is a white prophet."

"Father, she . . . ," Lone Eagle began, but went quiet when Ralph scampered into the tepee and went right up to Zondra and leaped onto her lap, purring as she licked Zondra affectionately on her cheek.

Zondra couldn't believe it. Ralph! Her precious cat was alive, and so familiar with the surroundings it was as though she had been there forever!

Thrilled to see her cat, Zondra swept her into her arms and hugged her to her bosom.

As Ralph snuggled against Zondra, obviously glad to see her, Zondra wasn't aware of being studied intently by both Lone Eagle and Mad Buffalo. For the moment she was in another world, one that did not include Crow Indians. She was that little girl again who had been so happy when her father had placed the small kitten in her arms, telling her it was hers to keep. Her cat had helped her through many lonely moments as she struggled to understand a father who treated her as a lowly slave instead of a daughter.

"Do you see how quickly the small cat creature bonded with the white woman?" Mad Buffalo said, shocked, his old eyes wide as he watched their affection for one another. He looked quickly over at Lone Eagle. "My son, I have already seen that the small cat creature was sent from the Great Mystery to rid us of the dreaded mice. This woman has surely been sent to us for a special purpose, also."

Except for Ralph's gentle, contented purring, the lodge was suddenly quiet.

Zondra had seen this elderly man more than once

as she observed the Crow people from the butte. She had wondered if he was related to Lone Eagle, since he came and went so often from the chief's lodge. Now she knew. The man was his father.

She looked in awe at Mad Buffalo because of what he had said, then slid her gaze to Lone Eagle. She was not at all surprised when she saw an incredulous look in *his* eyes as he gaped openly at her, and then his father.

Lone Eagle started to say something but stopped when his father continued. . . .

"My son, Singing Star is *right*," Mad Buffalo said, again staring at Zondra. "This woman *is* a prophet. Do not treat her as a thief any longer. Do not treat her as a captive!"

Lone Eagle was too stunned to speak, for it had been a long time since his father had given him a command, certainly not since Lone Eagle had become chief of their people. And now? To demand something so ridiculous?

It was hard for him to fathom how both his father and Singing Star could be so wrong about Zondra. She was anything but a prophet. And he would have to make sure he convinced his father and Singing Star that she wasn't, for prophets did not marry, and he wanted Zondra as his wife!

Lone Eagle rose to his feet. Towering over Zondra, he placed his hands on his hips as he glared down at her. "Why did you not tell my father the truth?" he said, his voice drawn. "You are no prophet. And confess to me about the cat. The cat is yours, is it not? Admit to me that it is not by coincidence that you are so familiar with one another."

Sheepishly Zondra smiled up at him and nodded. "The cat has been mine since I was a little girl," she said softly, although she knew that she could continue this charade with him that his father had begun, and disown Ralph.

But she saw Ralph as a way to break through this wall that she felt was there between her and Lone Eagle. If she could use the cat to get on Lone Eagle's more tender side, perhaps he would release her and allow her to go on her way to seek the freedom she so badly wanted.

"The cat's name is Ralph," she quickly added.

Lone Eagle's eyebrows rose upon hearing the name she had chosen for her cat. It most certainly deserved a name that matched its gender.

Zondra could tell by his reaction that Lone Eagle was very aware that the name she had told him did not fit the gender of the cat. She giggled.

Lone Eagle heard her giggle and understood why. Surely she had named the cat before she knew that it was a female and had become too accustomed to the name to change it once she discovered the truth about it.

A low rumble of laughter he tried to keep from surfacing suddenly erupted from deep inside him.

It was infectious.

They both joined in a good-natured laugh as Ralph looked from one to the other, purring contentedly.

Chapter Twenty-one

> *As from the darkening gloom a silver dove*
> *Upsoars, and darts into the Eastern light,*
> *On pinions that naught moves but pure delight,*
> *Regions of peace and everlasting love.*

—John Keats

Having not gotten enough satisfaction from stealing his father's money and his mother's jewels, Guy was pacing back and forth in the cabin hideout. "It just isn't enough," he said. "Damn it, it just isn't enough. There's got to be something else I can do to get my father's goat. I want him to pay over and over again for turning his back on me."

Billy Feazel chewed on a cigar as he sat at the table watching Guy. "Think, man," he urged. "What else can we take from him that's valuable?"

"I'd say my half sister Zondra would be the next thing, but she's gone, damn it," Guy mumbled, just loudly enough for Billy to hear. "Or perhaps his black wench, Ada. If she came up missing, my father would split a gut."

Guy's eyes wavered as he stopped and gazed down at Billy, the light from the lamp on the table casting an evil sort of glow in the outlaw's eyes. "But I'm not going to bother with Ada," he said dryly. "If anything happened to his black mistress, Father wouldn't stop until he found the guilty party. I sure as hell don't want to be the one who'd pay for the crime. My father's rage would be deadly."

Guy yanked a chair out from the table and sat down. In his mind's eye he saw Zondra riding with his father when they had no idea they were being observed. "I wish I knew where Zondra was," he spat out venomously. "She took my father away from me *and* my brother and sisters. Once she had my father in her spell, he didn't even remember having other children."

"I don't understand how that can be, and even if it's so, what does it matter?" Billy said, arching an eyebrow. "Man, *you* lived in the mansion, with all the opportunities of the rich. If you say Zondra wasn't allowed to live with you in your house, doesn't that mean that she lived in the slaves' quarters with her black mammy?"

"Yeah, but that was only a smoke screen to make it look as though Zondra wasn't nothing to my father," Guy hissed out. "It wasn't ever a secret like my father thought it was. Hell's fire, even the cowhands know about Zondra and what her black mama is to my father." He tossed his head back in frustration. "It's so damn embarrassing!"

"All right, *now* I can understand this grudge you have against your father," Billy said, again chomping on the end of his cigar as he recalled his own abusive childhood. "Think, man. Come up with something we can do that will make your pa pay for what he's done to your brain."

"My brain?" Guy said, looking quizzically down at Billy. "What do you mean by that?"

"If you don't know by now that your brain has been messed up by your pa and his lousy treatment of you, then, man, you'll never know," Billy said, reaching across the table for a half-empty whiskey bottle. He poured a glass full and handed it to Guy. "Take a slug. That'll clear your head. Then we'll talk later about this. I want to go and check on things outside with the guys. Some of the herd have come up lame." He chuckled. "We've got to find a way to build our herd of horses back up or be robbin' from your rich father and everyone else on *foot*."

Billy rose from the chair and started for the door, but Guy went and grabbed him by an arm, stopping him. Billy turned and eyed him quizzically.

"I've got it!" Guy said, his eyes dancing. "You need horses? By damn, we'll have horses."

"Your father's?" Billy asked, raising an eyebrow.

"No, not my father's," Guy said, dropping his hand to his side. He went to the table and grabbed up the glass of whiskey. He tipped it to his mouth and emptied the glass in one large swallow, then slammed the glass back down on the table and turned gleaming eyes back to Billy. "No, we won't steal my father's herd. We'll multiply it!"

Billy sighed and shook his head slowly back and forth. "Like I said, your father has played mind games on you too long," he said somberly. "Too often you show that you ain't playin' with a full deck. Why in the hell would we multiply your father's herd? It's us needin' horses, not your father."

Then Billy laughed throatily as he thought of what Guy might have in mind. "You mean swap your father's horses for ours and add a few of ours that are agin' to his?" he said, watching Guy's expression change to that of someone who was very frustrated by Billy's inability to understand what Guy had in mind.

"No, goddamn it," Guy shouted. "That's a stupid-ass idea, Billy. Give me more credit than that. My brain is as set in place and maybe even quicker than yours." Guy leaned close to Billy's face. "Listen to my plan, Billy, *then* tell me I've lost my marbles," he snarled.

"All right, tell me, Guy, but it'd better be good," Billy warned. "I've wasted enough time jawin' with you today. I don't like it when someone wastes my valuable time."

Guy shuffled his feet uneasily, then placed his fists on his hips and, with confidence, told Billy his plan. After he had told him everything, Guy waited breathlessly for Billy's reaction.

"By damn, I think you've got it," Billy said, laughing throatily. "After we steal a few of the Crow's horses for ourselves, that is."

"No, that shouldn't be a part of the plan," Guy argued. "We don't want Indians seeing *us* riding Crow horses. We'll get our payment in time after a range war breaks out between the Crow and the whites, and all because the Crow will think my father stole their horses. That would make the Crow not trust *any* whites. They would surely retaliate. And when they do and leave blood spilled everywhere they go, blood from *whites,* first the settlers will run scared from the area. Then when the cavalry intervenes and chases the Crow from the territory for having killed whites, perhaps even placing the redskins on reservations, all of the wild horses in the area will be ours to take to market in Texas for bundles of money. Don't you see? The Crow will be gone. The settlers will be gone. The cavalry won't see a need to stay if the Indians are gone. Everything will be ours, Billy. Ours!"

"All right, let's run through this again," Billy said, slowly kneading his chin. "Our gang will round up several Crow horses and mingle them with your father's. The Crow will think your father stole them and will retaliate."

"Yeah," Guy said, smiling evilly. "That will start the ball rolling. We'll just stay in hiding until things cool off after the Crow are jailed on a reservation and the settlers and the cavalry are gone. Then we'll move in and lay claim to everything . . . land *and* horses."

"I've thought of something else that might rile the Crow even more," Billy said, his eyes sparkling. "You know how the Crow revere their squaws. If one of their squaws came up missing and the Crow found the woman's discarded clothes on your father's property, wouldn't your father be blamed for the missing squaw?"

"I'm not sure I want to do that," Guy said, frowning. "I'd hate like hell getting caught with the squaw."

"Okay, for right now we'll just think about that," Billy said, clapping Guy on the shoulder. "Come on. Let's go and tell the boys what we're plannin' to do."

Guy nodded, proud that Billy had agreed to his plan. Yet in the darkest recesses of his mind, he couldn't get Zondra off his mind. Soon he must resume his search for her. He was still determined to find her and make her pay for all the hurt she had caused him.

"Who could've done it?" Harrison said angrily as he gazed down at Colonel Lloyd Brennan. He had ridden to the fort as soon as he realized someone had stolen not only his wife's jewels from his safe, but also his money. He felt he had no other choice but to seek the colonel's help, for this was something way too large to try to solve alone.

"You said you didn't share the combination to the

safe with anyone, not even your wife?" Colonel Brennan asked as he slowly closed the ledger on his desk.

"No, no one," Harrison said, sinking down into a chair in front of the desk. "Yet someone had to know. The safe wasn't forced open."

"There's an outlaw gang that works this area," Colonel Brennan said, plucking two cigars from his gold cigar box, offering one to Harrison. "Surely they got word about the valuables in your safe. That's the only thing that makes sense."

"Like I said, the safe wasn't forced open," Harrison repeated, shaking his head and waving off the offer of the cigar with his hand. "And I don't need to be told about outlaws. My son is still missing. Some damn outlaw abducted him."

Lloyd nodded, then replaced the cigar in its box and lit his. He smoked it for a moment as he went through what Harrison had told him in his mind, then took the cigar from his lips and looked at Harrison with narrowed eyes. "Are you certain that your son was abducted?" he asked warily. "Could it be that he . . . ?"

His face flushed hot with a quick anger, Harrison jumped to his feet. "Are you accusing my very own flesh and blood of faking his own abduction, then stealing from me?" he shouted, his eyes filled with rage.

Lloyd shrugged. "Just a passing thought," he said, again puffing on his cigar.

"Then forget it," Harrison growled out.

"There isn't much that can be done about the outlaws if they *are* responsible for the theft," Lloyd said, resting his cigar on the edge of an ashtray, the smoke spiraling slowly from it. "They're very smart at eluding the cavalry. Their hideout is well hidden. I promise

you, though, that my soldiers will keep an eye out for
them. I just don't want to waste time, money, and
valuable horses sending the cavalry out to look for a
gang that's too skilled at eluding them. Especially not
for only one man's problems. Now if it happens to
several other settlers, we'll . . ."

So angry at the colonel he was about ready to hit
him, Harrison left before Lloyd could finish what he
was saying. As he swung himself into the saddle he
cursed the day he decided to leave Mississippi, where
he had always been able to control his own destiny—
at least until gossip of warring over slavery had ruined
his life!

He rode out of the fort and urged his horse into a
fevered gallop. When he was near his ranch, he reined
his horse to a shuddering halt when he saw something
that caused a quick sinking feeling in the pit of his
stomach.

"Speedie?" he whispered, watching his white stallion hobbling along the trail, its one leg lame. He
stared blankly at the empty saddle, a deep remorse
rushing through him when he realized that something
horrible must have happened to Zondra.

He rode up to Speedie and dismounted. Tears
streaming from his eyes, Harrison gave Speedie a desperate hug. "Where is Zondra?" he whispered. "Oh,
Lord, Zondra, what if you are dead?"

He wiped the tears from his face and checked his
steed's lame leg to see if he had to put his horse out
of its misery. He was relieved to see that the stallion's
life could be spared. Although no one would ever ride
Speedie again, his horse could live a useful, happy life
as a stud.

"Come on, boy," Harrison said as he grabbed
Speedie's reins. "Let's go home." He chuckled. "Yep,

Speedie, I think you're going to like your new lot in life." He swung himself into his saddle and rode on toward the ranch at a slow trot, Speedie dutifully following.

After he arrived home, he was walking Speedie into his stall when Ada rushed breathlessly into the stable, her eyes wide with fear as she stared at the horse. She knew that Zondra had fled on Speedie.

Harrison saw the fear in Ada's eyes. He went to her and drew her into his arms.

"Our daughter, Harrison," Ada sobbed. "What's happened to our daughter?"

"I'm not sure," Harrison said thickly. He held her for a moment longer, then afraid someone might come in and see the affection he was showing one of his slaves, he eased her away from him.

"Go to our cabin," he said, his eyes wavering as he saw Ada's deep sadness. "I'll be there real soon."

Nodding, Ada wiped tears from her eyes with the back of a hand, then turned and ran from the stable.

Harrison placed a bucket of oats beneath Speedie's nose, then left for the secret cabin in the woods.

When he was finally there with Ada, where he had made a pretty place for the woman he truly wished were his wife, he held her and comforted her. "I'll resume my search for Zondra," he said, his voice drawn. "I'll not stop this time until I find our daughter, Ada. I promise. I will find her and bring her home."

"But Speedie came home without her," Ada cried. "That surely means that something terrible happened to Zondra."

"I know it looks bad, but we can't give up hope just because the horse came home without her," Harrison said, framing Ada's face between his hands, their eyes holding. "Don't lose hope, love. Zondra is still out there somewhere. I'm not going to give up on her. Nor should you."

"Just hold me, Harrison," Ada said, flinging herself into his arms. "Hold me and tell me how much you love me."

He swept her up into his arms and carried her to a bed covered with a lacy bedspread upon which were piles of pillows covered with the same lace.

All around the room were delicate, pretty things that Harrison had brought to Ada as gifts. Furniture covered with plush, flowered fabric was arranged before a stone fireplace. A braided rug so thick Ada could curl her toes in it stretched across the wooden floor.

And ahh, the mattress on the bed . . . It was filled with feathers and felt wonderful to a woman who normally slept on a thin, hard thing in her lonesome, drab cabin.

"You smell of lilacs," Harrison whispered, sniffing the long, delicate column of Ada's throat where she had sprinkled perfume before his arrival at the cabin.

"Love me, Harrison," Ada whispered, pushing his breeches down as he lifted the plain cotton skirt of her dress. "Just love me."

She took a quavering breath of ecstasy when he deeply filled her. For a moment everything ugly in her life turned beautiful.

Chapter Twenty-two

On which, as one in trance up borne,
Secure o'er woods and waves I sweep
Rejoicing like a cloud of morn:
Now 'tis the breath of summer's night.

—PERCY BYSSHE SHELLEY

The morning air was sweet as it blew under the rolled-up bottom of Lone Eagle's tepee. Several days had passed since Lone Eagle had brought Zondra to his village. While several of the Crow women were busily butchering animals outside, up to their elbows in entrails, each trying to lay claim to the choicest cuts and most desirable organs, Zondra was inside Lone Eagle's lodge, straightening the mats and folding blankets.

Zondra was surprised that, although Lone Eagle still kept her well-guarded, only allowing her out of sight of her guards when she went to the river with a group of women to bathe, she no longer felt like a captive.

She hadn't been able to keep from falling even more in love with him. He treated her with respect, never approaching her sexually even though she still shared his lodge with him and slept so close they could reach out in the night and touch one another.

By the way he looked at her, though, she knew that he wanted her as badly as she wanted him.

Every time she was near him she was conscious of

her crazy heartbeats. Sometimes, while in his presence, her knees became so weak from passion she could hardly continue standing. But she fought her feelings, as she knew he fought his.

Yet there was still the fact that she *was* his captive. He *did* have her guarded, one way or the other. The first time Lone Eagle had sent several women with Zondra to the river for a bath, it had infuriated her. Until then she had never before bathed in the presence of anyone but her mother.

But after the first few times, she had found a strange sort of camaraderie with the women as she listened to them laughing and talking while bathing, some even splashing each other playfully. When one of them had suddenly splashed her, she had not been sure how to react. But soon realizing it had been done in fun, she had splashed the pretty Crow woman back, a friendship beginning as innocently as that.

Zondra had been stunned to learn with whom she had become friendly. White Bead, the village prophet.

White Bead had told her that day how Lone Eagle had avenged her humiliation at the hands of Red Moon on the very night Zondra had stolen Lone Eagle's horse.

When Zondra first heard about Lone Eagle going to such extremes for this woman, she had been instantly jealous. But after getting to know White Bead, recognizing her sweetness, and knowing that her relationship with Lone Eagle was only that of a cousin's, Zondra had grown fond of the young Crow woman. She was in awe, actually, of her, and how she was so special to her people.

That day, after Zondra and White Bead had bathed and then lain in the sun wrapped in soft white doeskin towels, White Bead had explained what her title of prophet meant, that she was a chosen holy one for her people, a woman untouched by any man.

That day, after White Bead had talked so openly with Zondra about many things, Zondra had been convinced that White Bead loved a man, yet could not bring herself to admit such feelings to her.

It was the way White Bead had talked of one day being married and having children that made Zondra realize that White Bead's days as a prophet were numbered . . . that the woman wanted more from life than to be a spinster.

Zondra wore one of White Bead's dresses today. She gazed down at it and admired anew the beautiful pink beads sewn in the design of flowers across the front. She loved the way the fringes at the hem swished and swayed against her ankles as she walked, a caress, as though someone's fingers were there, touching her.

White Bead had explained to Zondra the procedure for tanning the hides for clothes. The new skins were immersed for a few days in lye made from ashes and water, until the hair could be removed.

Those hides were then stretched upon a frame, or upon the ground, with stakes or pins driven through the edges into the earth, where they remained for several days with elk brains spread upon them.

The tanning procedure was finished by "graining." Women used a sharpened bone, the shoulder blade of an animal, to scrape the fleshy side of the skin, drying and softening the skin and making it ready for use.

In a short period of time, Zondra had grown close to the Crow people. She had become intrigued by everything about their lives—so much so that were the guards removed today and she given the chance to flee, she doubted she would.

She no longer wanted the sort of freedom she had been seeking the day she left her father's ranch. Now she wanted the freedom to love.

To love Lone Eagle.

She wanted to be able to whisper sweet nothings in his ear, to float on clouds of rapture with him when they made love.

She could feel the sexual tension growing between them with each sunset and sunrise. Surely he would soon grab her and kiss her. She wondered, if he did, how she could keep from sliding from his wondrous arms in a dead faint.

Even now, while kneeling beside the slow-burning flames of his lodge fire, as she closed her eyes and allowed herself to feel his presence and to smell the outdoorsy smell of his flesh and hair, and to pretend he was there, holding her, his lips pressed sweetly against hers, she felt all giddy and warm inside.

Something strange had awakened in another part of her body these past days when she was with Lone Eagle. There was a gnawing, sweet hunger at the juncture of her thighs, a place she knew men touched and caressed when they loved you.

She was startled out of her thoughts when Singing Star came into the lodge carrying a heavy bag of water. Zondra quickly took it from her.

"I know you've heard me say it before, but Singing Star, I still don't think you should be carrying something this heavy," she said, thinking to herself that this was surely how the old woman's back had become so bent. "At your age, you should be sitting somewhere comfortably sewing."

Zondra saw the look of frustration in Singing Star's eyes over her insistence that the old woman give up such hard labor. Zondra thought she knew what was best for the elderly woman. She had grown close to her these past days, even felt protective of her. She was glad that Singing Star thought as much of her, showing it by the gentle way she talked to Zondra and treated her.

"Do not fret so over this old lady," Singing Star said, smiling at Zondra. "Have I not told you that I do what I do because it not only makes Lone Eagle and Mad Buffalo happy, but also myself? I feel useful."

She reached a hand out toward Zondra and gently placed it on her cheek. "Do you not know, my child, that now I also want to make *you* happy, as does Lone Eagle?" she murmured. Then she sighed. "Ah, my young chief Lone Eagle. I know how disappointed he must be to know that you are a prophet, for you are the sort of woman who would make my chief a good wife."

Zondra had gone along with Singing Star's and Mad Buffalo's insistence that she was a prophet, thinking that by doing so she was assured a more comfortable stay at the Crow village.

She had come so close, so often, to telling Singing Star that she wasn't anyone's prophet, that she was just an ordinary girl with ordinary dreams. But when she was on the verge of confessing the truth, she had stopped just short of saying the words that she knew would disappoint Singing Star. Zondra could tell that Singing Star *liked* thinking this white woman and her cat were special . . . sent there by the Crow's Great Mystery.

Zondra just shrugged and accepted it when Singing Star insisted that she was this prophet who had happened along and was now a part of the Crow people's lives.

"Singing Star, why hasn't Lone Eagle ever married?" Zondra asked as the elderly woman used a stick to stir the hot coals in the fire pit.

"Lone Eagle loved a woman some winters ago, but she was taken captive by the Blackfoot," Singing Star said, her voice sad. "Lone Eagle and his warriors searched many months for the Blackfoot who stole his wife from him. Finally he gave up. The hurt of losing his woman was so severe he vowed never to take another wife. He does not dare to love again."

She dropped the stick into the flames, then settled down onto a mat and rested awhile before venturing back outside again to resume the chores she believed made her look important to her people.

Zondra couldn't help but feel a sting of jealousy inside her heart, knowing that Lone Eagle had been in love before. But she forced the jealousy aside, for although she ached for Lone Eagle to hold her and make love to her, she *still* did not want him as her husband . . . to be owned by him . . . to be lorded over by him!

"I will never be any man's wife," Zondra said stubbornly. "No man will ever own me again."

The moment the word "again" slipped from Zondra's lips she regretted having said it. Surely Singing Star would think that she meant she had been married before, when in truth it was Zondra's father to whom she had been referring. And by saying this, surely Singing Star would no longer think she was special . . . a prophet.

"My child, what do you mean when you say you were owned by someone?" Singing Star gasped, raising a shaggy gray eyebrow.

Zondra was silent. She wanted no one to know that she had been a slave, although in a sense being a captive meant almost the same thing. *She* knew the difference, and she abhorred the very thought of how her father had treated her.

She wondered now, even having escaped the life of slavery, if she could ever put it behind her, for talking about it brought it alive again in her heart and memory. It made her feel so cold and miserable inside to know that her mother was still a slave . . . called a "darkie" by some.

Zondra tried to explain away what she had said. "I used the wrong word when describing how I felt about a father who treated me as though he owned me, who expected too much from me," she blurted out. "That's all, Singing Star."

She didn't want to feel bad about not being completely truthful with Singing Star, but in a sense she *wasn't* telling a big lie. She was fleeing just the sort of father that she had described to the elderly woman. She was glad when she saw that this explanation seemed to satisfy Singing Star.

"Since you are now one of us, there is much for you to learn about what is expected of Crow women," Singing Star said, going to sit against Lone Eagle's willow backrest. She sighed as she leaned back against the soft sinew and willow. "As I told you before, to make clothes, women spend days tanning and smoking the necessary deer skins. Once this is completed, the finished buckskin is fashioned into such apparel as shirts, leggings, dresses, and moccasins. The finished decorative touches are also the woman's task."

"I have so admired the women's porcupine quill embroidery, the beadwork, and the men's bows of elk and mountain sheep horn," Zondra said softly.

"Some of the men's bows are covered with the skin of rattlesnake," Singing Star said. "You have seen

Lone Eagle's quiver. I decorated it myself with the
sketching of a quill rosette."

"Yes, I saw it," Zondra murmured. "It is so lovely."

She looked to her right and once again wondered
about the sacred shield that was wrapped so that no
one's eyes would touch it unless Lone Eagle gave permission. She wanted to ask Singing Star to tell her
more about the shield, but assumed that she wasn't
allowed to talk about it, so she looked away from it
again as Singing Star resumed talking about the duties
of the Crow women.

"We Crow women always sun-dry chokeberries,
wild plums, bullberries, and serviceberries so that
when winter is upon us, there is something sweet to
fill our bellies," Singing Star said, watching the entrance flap, having heard Lone Eagle's voice. He was
involved in a conversation as he approached his lodge.
"And after a hunt, Zondra, meat is cut into strips and
placed in the sun to dry. When it is dried, some of it
is pounded until it becomes quite fluffy in texture and
it's then packed, along with lumps of tallow, into rawhide cases."

Knowing that Lone Eagle would arrive at any moment and want private time with Zondra, Singing Star
slowly pushed herself to her feet. "Another thing
about food, Zondra," she said, stopping for one more
moment before she left. "We women always make
sure to leave enough meat from the hunt for strips of
dried jerky."

"Thank you for sharing all of this with me," Zondra
said, scarcely aware of what she was saying, for she
knew that Lone Eagle would be in his lodge momentarily. She had heard his voice as he walked toward
the tepee. He was no longer talking, which had to
mean that he would soon appear in all his noble hand-

someness, so breathtaking it was becoming harder and harder to be alone with him without him reading her thoughts, knowing that her need for him surpassed her need to eat or sleep!

Oh, Lord, she despaired to herself. *Feeling this way about Lone Eagle, one kiss would be enough to keep me here forever!* She knew she would never want to take a step out of his village for fear of never being held by him again.

"Zondra?"

Zondra had been so lost in thought she had not even noticed that Singing Star had left and Lone Eagle had come in and was now standing over her, staring in wonder at her, his voice filled with questions when he spoke her name.

Blushing, she looked quickly up at him.

"You were thinking so deeply about something," Lone Eagle said, going to sit down. "Do you want to tell me about it? You did not even say good-bye to Singing Star."

"I . . . I . . . was thinking about . . . ," she stammered, the heat of her cheeks burning, for she dared not tell him the truth about what she *had* been thinking. It would condemn her, not in *his* eyes or heart, but in her own, for she so wished she had more control over her feelings for him. Her loving him was a complete denial of what she had wanted so badly for so long— to be free and clear of all men!

"Yes?" Lone Eagle said, leaning closer, an eyebrow arched. "You were thinking . . . about . . . what?"

Zondra searched quickly through her mind for something to say that might make sense. Her gaze fell upon the shield. Yes! The shield! It was no lie that only moments ago she had been wondering about his sacred shield.

"Singing Star was teaching me some customs of your people," Zondra blurted out, casting a quick look his way. "I . . . wanted . . . to ask her more about your sacred shield but didn't think I should. It seems to be such a personal item. Surely Singing Star isn't at liberty to talk about something that personal."

"It would not be so much that she would betray me by talking about it," Lone Eagle said, remembering Zondra's earlier curiosity about the shield yesterday when they had been eating and a ray of sunshine slipped through the overhead smoke hole and settled on his covered shield. "It is just that she would leave such things for me to tell you about when *I* choose to."

"Would you tell me now?" Zondra asked, so glad that she could turn her thoughts of moments ago to things a bit less intimate.

"*Ahh*, yes, I will *show* you," Lone Eagle said, thinking that the more open he was about things that were divine to him, the easier it would be for her to open up to him about her true feelings for him. He could see even now, as he had before, that his presence was causing an anxious pulse in the hollow of her throat. He could see the flush of her cheeks. He could even see how her hands were trembling. Those were all signs of a woman who was battling deep inside herself to hold back her feelings for a man she desired. As he now, in her presence, was fighting his own sensual feelings for her. She had shared his lodge now for too many nights. He had been forced to lie there and fight off the aching in his loins that seeing her so beautifully sweet, both awake and asleep, had caused. He had wondered how she would react if he would have gone to her and drawn her into his arms and told her how much he loved her. Would she have fought off his kiss? Would she have run from the lodge?

"Lone Eagle?" Zondra murmured when she noticed how quiet he had become, and how his thoughts had strayed. Although he was now kneeling beside his sacred shield, he seemed lost in thought as he gazed at it.

Zondra's voice brought Lone Eagle out of his reverie. He smiled awkwardly over at her. "It was my turn to daydream," he said softly.

"About what?" Zondra dared to ask, her breathing anxiously shallow, for what if he had thoughts about her as she had about him? If so, just how much longer could they be together like this in his lodge without him kissing her?

"About you," Lone Eagle said huskily, but hearing her low gasp, he thought it best to wait longer before revealing his hunger for her.

Zondra didn't ask him any further questions. She was afraid where her curiosity would lead them. She was glad when he turned his eyes from her and got involved with something else. She was puzzled, though, that he did not get the shield, as promised. What he was doing instead seemed strange.

"I cannot unwrap the buckskin from the shield and show you the sacred shield yet," Lone Eagle said. "First I must take some embers from the fire and place them on a rock."

With wonder she watched him do this. She then watched him go to a bag at the right side of his lodge and remove the root of a carrot from it, placing it on the live ember on the rock.

"The carrot root creates an incense that I will use on my shield before unwrapping it," Lone Eagle said, going now to get the shield. He raised it just a little bit above the smoke, so the smoke could surround it. Then he raised the shield just a little more as he held it in the smoke, lowering it again, then once more raising it, a little higher than before. He repeated this ritual four times.

Only after having gone through these preparations did he finally sit down beside Zondra and slowly unwrap the buckskin covering from around the shield.

When she saw the lovely designs painted on the shield, she reached over and touched it. It was made of some strong fiber that was smooth to her touch. It was fringed with eagle feathers, quills, and slung with a broad leather strap that, when worn, crossed the man's breast.

The paintings on the shield seemed to depict many of the Crow's customs. Most prominent of all, as usual in this village, were paintings of buffalo.

"Have you carried this in many battles?" Zondra asked softly. "Has it kept you alive?"

"I am a man of peace so, no, I have not warred enough to be forced to carry my shield when I travel away from my village," Lone Eagle said. The drawings of the buffalo seemed to come alive in his eyes as the flames cast dancing shadows along his sacred shield.

"But this shield has seen warring," he continued. "My grandfather battled many enemy tribes for possession of land and horses, and sometimes just for the pleasure of warring. If you look closely enough you will see some denting and scarring. The marks were made by enemy Blackfoot and other tribes my grandfather encountered in battle."

"Did he fight whites?" Zondra asked warily.

"He fought anything that came within a certain distance of our village on horseback," Lone Eagle said. "I am certain there were some whites who dared to cross the land of the Crow when my grandfather was chief. If so, I am sure their scalps hung from my grandfather's scalp pole."

"Scalps?" Zondra gasped, a shiver running up her spine.

Not wishing to get into a discussion that could turn Zondra against any notion of wanting to stay with the Crow, Lone Eagle said nothing more about scalps or warring.

He held the shield closer to her so that she could see it better. "The shield is made of the skin of the buffalo neck, hardened with glue extracted from the hooves and joints of the same animal," he said. "When cooled and cut into the desired shape, it is painted with our people's totem, the buffalo, which will guard and protect the shield's owner from harm."

"It's very impressive," Zondra murmured. "I'm glad, though, that you don't have to use it. . . . I mean I'm glad that you aren't involved in warring with anyone."

"You care enough for this chief that you do not want him to fight battles with enemies?" he said, covering the shield and placing it back in its resting place.

He went to her then, and reaching down, gently took her by the wrists. As their eyes locked, he urged her to her feet. His eyes searched hers, then he wrapped her in his muscular arms. "I can wait no longer to kiss you," he said huskily, his lips quivering as he lowered them to hers.

As they kissed, delicious, wonderful feelings of ecstasy swept through Zondra, making it impossible for her not to respond to him. Moaning with pleasure, her pulse racing, she twined her arms around his neck and returned his kiss twofold.

Again she was aware of the strange feelings at the

juncture of her thighs. The aching, sensual throbbing was almost unbearable. She needed something else, but she knew not what!

Unaware of doing so, she pressed her body against his, and when she felt something long and hard pushing against her through the thin fabric of his breechclout and her dress, her breath caught with an even stranger sort of rapture.

Oh, Lord, now she knew what was straining against her. It was the part of a man's anatomy that made women out of girls!

And as he moved his manhood seductively up and down against her body, rubbing against that part of her that she had recently realized was capable of such wonderful feelings, she felt light-headed and dizzy from the intense pleasure he was giving her.

Something, like an unseen force inside her, made her lean her body even closer to his, so that his manhood could pleasure her even more fully. This same force even guided her hand down there so that she dared to touch his hardness, her hand jerking back when she felt something wet on the buckskin fabric of his breechclout.

Suddenly afraid and, oh, so breathless, Zondra jerked away from him. Gasping for air, she turned her back to him. "Please don't," she said, a sob catching in her throat.

"You do not want me to awaken more feelings inside you that are women's feelings?" Lone Eagle asked huskily.

"No, please don't," Zondra repeated, doubling her hands into tight fists at her sides, for everything she was saying now was a lie. Oh, Lord help her, she wanted to undress and give her all to this man.

But she just couldn't allow herself to give in to her feelings. She was too afraid to be owned again.

Hurt by her rejection, hardly able to resist drawing her into his arms and shouting at her to stop fighting her feelings, Lone Eagle walked away from her and left the lodge.

He went straight to the deepest part of the stream that led out into a river, dove in headfirst, and swam and swam until his body was cooled of sensual feelings.

Then he went and sat on a high bluff that overlooked his village. He had to find a way to make this woman stop being afraid to give herself to a man. More and more he saw how her past had been a troubled one. He was beginning to doubt that she could ever feel free to love him, to love *any* man.

"She must!" he whispered, raking his fingers through his long, thick hair. "She must love me. I will make her forget the wrong other men have done her!"

Sobbing, her whole body aching with needs that were new to her, Zondra sat down beside the fire and drew her knees up, hugging them to her.

"What can I do?" she murmured, tired of fighting feelings that she now realized were too delicious to live without. "I want him so badly. I can't hold out much longer. I . . . must . . . have him. I must know the ultimate pleasure, which surely he can give me. I . . . want to give pleasure back to him."

She stopped whispering to herself when White Bead suddenly came into the lodge and sat down beside her.

"Zondra, you will never meet another man as kind and good as Lone Eagle," White Bead said, taking Zondra's hands, holding them gently. "He has been lonely for too long. He waited a long time for his wife to return. When she did not, and he heard that she was married to a Blackfoot chief, Lone Eagle felt as though a part of his heart had been torn from him. The betrayal of his wife seemed complete, even though she had been forced into marriage with the Blackfoot. Once a Crow woman sleeps with an enemy, she is the same as dead in the mind of the Crow. He mourned for his wife as though she were dead. Only recently has he cast this mourning aside. Only after he met you."

"I didn't know," Zondra said, now understanding so much more about the man she loved. She gazed deeply into White Bead's eyes. "Did Lone Eagle send you to me?" she asked softly. "Did he ask you to explain these things to me?"

"No, he did not send me, nor does he know that I am here, unless he has seen me from the bluff where I saw him go after his swim in the river," White Bead said. She squeezed Zondra's hand affectionately. "When he returns to his lodge, welcome him. Do not continue shunning him. He is a man of much pride. And he is a man who can give much to a woman. Accept his gift of love. You will not regret it."

"You speak of it as though you, yourself, shared your blankets with Lone Eagle," Zondra dared to say.

"No, not I," White Bead said softly. "But I was Lone Eagle's wife's best friend and she shared her experiences with me. *That* is how I know."

"I see," Zondra murmured, jealousy for that first wife again plaguing her.

She said nothing more, nor did White Bead, except a quiet farewell as White Bead left.

With an anxious heart Zondra awaited Lone Eagle's return. She undressed as she waited, so that upon his first sight of her he would know that she welcomed him in ways that she had earlier denied him, in ways that she had denied herself.

She could wait no longer to ride the waves of ecstasy with the man she loved. Her thoughts of being enslaved by him were pushed back into the deeper recesses of her mind.

She wanted him.

She must have him.

That was all that mattered now.

Chapter Twenty-three

> *She is a woman, one in whom*
> *the spring time of her childish years*
> *hath never lost its fresh perfume.*
>
> —JAMES LOWELL

After having communed with the *Ah-badt-deadt-deah*, Great Mystery, about how Zondra had rejected him after their embrace and kiss, Lone Eagle had returned from the bluff realizing that no matter how badly he wanted Zondra to stay with him and be his wife, it was wrong to keep her. Even though he had felt that she loved him by the response of her lips and body, it was how she had behaved afterward—turning her back to him—that made him finally conclude that she truly wanted no part of loving him.

Yes, it was time to release her and allow her to resume her search for the life she wished to have, which most certainly was not with him.

As he led one of his strongest steeds, already saddled with his most comfortable Spanish saddle, up to the entrance of his tepee, he knew that he must, in at least this way, make her travels more comfortable. He had already asked the women of his village to prepare two parfleche bags of smoked, dried foods for Zondra's journey. He would give her an escort at least for the first few miles of her journey.

He was going to go inside his tepee now and tell her that she was free to go. He would even wish her well, for he did want her to do what would make her the happiest.

As he watched two women bring wrapped bundles of Indian bread and dried fruits and meat to his horse, slipping them gently inside the parfleche bags that hung from the saddle, he nodded and smiled a silent thank-you to them.

Sighing, so hating to see Zondra go, Lone Eagle shoved the entrance flap aside and stepped into his lodge. He stopped for a moment to let his eyes adjust to the dimmer light. His heart skipped a beat when he thought he saw Zondra sitting beside the fire without any clothes on.

Surely his eyes were playing tricks on him. Surely what he was seeing was an apparition!

He blinked his eyes.

Then his heart beat thunderously, for he now knew for certain that what he was seeing was not an apparition.

Zondra *was* sitting beside the fire.

She *was* nude, her young breasts round and firm, the pinkish-brown nipples beacons beckoning his hands to them.

His pulse running wild now, Lone Eagle still could not move. He was too stunned by seeing her there nude, smiling, her arms outstretched for him. He was in awe of her creamy white flesh, of the tantalizing cleavage of her breasts and her slim, supple, exquisite waist. His hands could already feel the softness of her long, smooth thighs.

He swallowed hard when his gaze stopped at the muff of hair that hid her womanhood beneath it like a dark crown of silk.

Although he wanted to fight his arousal, he could not. Seeing her there, her body gleaming in the dim interior of his tepee, he was aware of the heat that was growing in his manhood, filling it, expanding it to its full length beneath his breechclout.

He ached unmercifully to have her, yet he was still too puzzled by having found her this way to go to her and hold her, when only a short while ago she had taken flight over a mere kiss.

"Why?" he found himself asking her, the word passing across his lips without any prior thought.

"Because I love you," Zondra murmured, tears of joy rushing to her eyes as she finally said the words she had fought saying for so long.

She *did* love him. With all her heart.

She *did* want him. She never wanted to leave him.

She had to believe that if he loved her as much as she loved him, surely he would never demand that she call him lord. He seemed too gentle a man to subjugate the woman he loved.

When Lone Eagle still did not make a move toward her, nor said anything in response to her confession of love, even when she'd gone so far as to behave in a way she knew was wanton, the fear of having been too bold came to her in a flash. If he saw her as a shameful hussy because she had taken her clothes off and was inviting him to sleep with her, she had surely caused him to deplore, not love her.

Her heart pounding, she reached for a blanket with which to cover herself, but stopped when he quickly came to her, placing his hands at her waist and lifting her up into his embrace.

"You have always loved me?" Lone Eagle whispered against her lips, his arms holding her close, her breasts feeling hot and wonderful pressed against his bare chest.

"Always and forever," Zondra whispered back to him as he brushed soft kisses across her lips, and then her closed eyes, and then her lips again. "I . . . just . . . was afraid to love a man."

"What changed your mind?" Lone Eagle asked softly, drawing away from her a bit as he gazed deeply into her dark eyes.

"My bleeding heart," Zondra said, her breath catching in rapture when his hands slid up and cupped her breasts. When his thumbs rolled over her nipples, a sensual shiver traveled her spine.

"Your body is ready for a man?" Lone Eagle whispered huskily, his heart beating so hard she could not help but hear it. To him it was like distant drums pounding in the depths of his ears.

"Yes," Zondra whispered, her shoulders swaying in her building passion as he swept a hand down across her belly, leaving ripples of pleasure along her flesh in its wake. Never had anything felt so wonderful as his warm hands on her body.

And now, as he touched her with his fingers, slowly caressing her at the juncture of her thighs, her head swam with a sweet, wondrous passion.

"Those feelings you are experiencing are only the beginning of the pleasure I will give you," Lone Eagle said, very aware of how she was becoming awakened to new feelings . . . feelings that were making her blossom into a woman.

"Please . . . please. . . ," she gasped, throwing her head back in ecstasy as he thrust a finger up inside her, moving it rhythmically within her.

Then a new feeling, a sharp pain caused by his

thrusting finger, made her wince and cry out. Her eyes opened and she gazed at him questioningly.

"The brief pain was necessary to open the way for your full pleasure," Lone Eagle said, drawing her against him, cradling her close. "It will soon pass. Then I will teach you the true meaning of love, of sharing a love so intense you will never want to leave me."

"I already feel that way," Zondra murmured, twining her arms around his neck, his lips seeking hers.

As he kissed her long and deep, his fingers once again caressed her. The pain had changed to a delicious, tingling splendor. Zondra took a deep breath, awaiting the pain, when he again thrust his finger inside her.

Instead she felt something soft and wonderful that seemed to build within her, as though a spinning light were spreading throughout her, followed by an exploding pleasure so keen she felt as though she might faint from it.

Glad that he had given her pleasure first, acquainting her with what she could look forward to as his wife, Lone Eagle smiled and drew quietly away from her.

Stunned by the feelings that had overwhelmed her, Zondra gave Lone Eagle a soft questioning look. Her body still trembled with ecstasy.

She started to ask him why he had withdrawn from her, then stopped, her breath catching as he suddenly dropped his breechclout away from his body. It fell to his ankles, and he kicked it away from him, along with his moccasins.

Never had she expected a man to be this handsome and virile unclothed. Lone Eagle's muscles were evident down the full length of his lean copper body. His wide shoulders tapered to narrow hips. His stomach was flat and hard. His legs were long and firm. And . . . his . . . manhood was thick and long and thrust out away from his body, shiny yet velvet-looking in texture.

When he slid a hand over his manhood, flicking a pearl drop of something away from the tip, Zondra's heart leapt and her knees went weak, for when he touched himself there, it seemed the most sensual thing he could have done, arousing her to even greater heights.

When he reached for one of her hands, she hesitated, then twined her fingers through his, scarcely breathing as he led her hand to his erect manhood.

"Feel the heat," Lone Eagle said huskily, wincing with pleasure when her fingers circled his throbbing member. His hand covered hers and he taught her how to move her hand on him. She was an astute student, for she pleasured him so skillfully, he had to clench his teeth and fight hard to keep from going over the edge into total ecstasy.

He closed his eyes and enjoyed her caress for a moment longer. Then, trembling, he took her hand away and wrapped her in his arms. With his body pressed against hers, he eased her downward until she was stretched out beneath him on the pelts and blankets beside the fire.

Afraid of disappointing this man she adored, not knowing the first thing about making love, Zondra tensed up when she felt his hardness pressed against her body. When he kissed her, her body pliant in his arms, she was aware of one of his knees spreading her legs apart.

She sucked in a wild breath of pleasure when one of his hands went back to her throbbing center, parting her curly mound of hair and for a moment caressing her with his fingertips.

Having been readied in that way for the ultimate pleasure, her head already reeling with ecstasy, Zondra gasped with a sensual shock when she felt Lone Eagle enter her.

She was euphoric as he began to move rhythmically within her, his lips stilling her moans of pleasure as he kissed her, his tongue probing between her lips, flicking in and out.

As he pushed ever deeper inside her, her gasps became soft whimpers. She locked her legs around his waist when his hands swept around her hips and lifted her closer.

Lone Eagle's ears were roaring now as his heartbeat quickened. He was overwhelmed with pleasure, yet still held back so that Zondra's first time with him would be unforgettable.

He wanted her to lie awake at night thinking of how it was between them.

He wanted her to awaken each morning wanting more.

He wanted to teach her the ultimate in lovemaking by using his skilled hands, lips, tongue, and mouth on her body.

He wanted her to learn how to use *her* tongue, hands, and lips on *his* body. Theirs would be a love all-consuming!

He again gave her a desperate, hungry kiss, his body stilled for just a moment, resting before he took the one last, deep plunge that would bring them together in a magnificent finale of lovemaking this first time.

Later he would take it much more slowly with her. He would make it something beautiful and sweet.

But now? He could wait no longer. He ached from having waited too long.

"I love you," Lone Eagle whispered against Zondra's lips, then plunged deep inside her as she arched toward him.

Zondra's breath was stolen away as the most ultimate of pleasures soared through her. She clung to him as his body quivered against hers.

When they came down from the clouds of rapture, Lone Eagle rolled slowly away from her and stretched out on his back, breathing hard.

Too stunned to speak, still feeling the wonders of their lovemaking, Zondra snuggled close to Lone Eagle, then welcomed Ralph when her cat scampered into the tepee and came to them, purring.

"How wonderful it was," Zondra murmured as she laid her cheek against his chest. She was very aware of how hard his heart was pounding, as was hers.

"As it will be for always between us," Lone Eagle said, placing an arm around her waist, drawing her even closer. He laughed throatily when Ralph tried to snuggle between them.

"I think Ralph is jealous," Zondra said, giggling. Then she became serious. "Lone Eagle, I don't want to leave you, ever," she said, leaning up on an elbow as she gazed at him. "But I . . ."

She stopped short of saying that she could never call him lord, thinking this was not the best time to mention that. It would spoil the magic of the moment.

"But . . . ?" Lone Eagle said, arching an eyebrow.

"Oh, nothing," Zondra said, shrugging. "Just let's lie here and enjoy being together. I have wanted this for so long."

He twined his fingers through her long, lustrous hair and drew her to him. He gave her a long, soft kiss as the sun set behind the distant mountains and night came over the village in a stilled blackness.

While everyone in the Crow village rested around their fires, some telling stories to their children, others making love in the privacy of their lodges, while still others sat peacefully making bows, or sewing, Guy and his outlaw friends were rounding up several Crow horses.

They took them and mingled them with Harrison's herd, then rode off into the night, laughing.

Chapter Twenty-four

The cope of Heaven seems rent and cloven
By the enchantment of thy strain,
And o'er my shoulders wings are woven.

—PERCY BYSSHE SHELLEY

When Zondra awakened and found herself snuggled against Lone Eagle's warm, naked body, she was thrown back in time, to the prior evening, when she had found paradise in her lover's muscled arms.

The fact that she had spent the entire night sleeping with him, rather than lying on the far side of the lodge fire with resentments building in her mind, made her heart soar.

She regretted now that she had not given in to her feelings earlier. To think that she had lost even one night of such wondrous lovemaking due to her determination to be free of all men made her heart ache.

But now everything had changed. She was dedicated to loving this wonderful man.

She hated admitting to herself that she lived for his touch, his kiss, his hands upon her body, when she had so recently wanted to be free of a man's powers over her. The only thing that took away from the joy of the moment was her dread of his demand that she refer to him as her lord. She still knew that she couldn't do that!

Living with a man who shared your love was different from living with a man who lorded over you. Surely Lone Eagle would understand her feelings and not demand anything of her but her devoted love. She even knew now that he had saddled a horse for her last night and provided bags of food prepared by the Crow women for her exit from his village. He had actually decided to release her from captivity and allow her to continue her search for freedom. She had come that close to being totally free again.

She knew, though, that had he told her before they made love that a horse awaited her, she would not have gone to it. She had already decided that she would stay. She had already undressed for Lone Eagle's return to his lodge.

Ralph awakened and crept up Zondra's bare legs, the soft, furry paws tickling her flesh. Zondra giggled, picked up her precious cat, and gazed into her beautiful green eyes. "It's so good to be with you again," she whispered, then drew Ralph down against her bosom and cuddled her close.

As Ralph purred, Zondra softly stroked her black fur. Zondra's eyes were on Lone Eagle as he slept. She had hoped that he would awaken before her and rouse her with soft kisses along her body. Even now she felt shamelessly brazen for thinking such thoughts.

Until she had fallen totally and completely in love with Lone Eagle, she had not spent any time thinking about men, or how they could make a woman feel so wonderfully alive. Most of her deep thoughts had centered on escape, on finding a life away from sordid slavery.

But after having seen Lone Eagle that first time, she knew that things were beginning to change in her life. She had dreamed dreams that made her face turn hot when she remembered them.

Although she had never been with a man before sexually, or knew how they made love, in her dreams it had been so easy to imagine. Yes, the dreams had been wonderfully sensual, but the real thing was many times more passionate and rapturous than any dream.

Her pulse racing, her heart thudding, so badly wanting him to awaken and begin anew what they had stopped just prior to sleeping, Zondra was tempted to reach out and stroke that part of him that lay limp and seemingly asleep itself.

She was amazed at how that part of his body could expand to such limits and then shrink again to something so different in size and length. But while it was swollen and thick, ah, how wonderful it was to know what it could do to her.

A voice outside the lodge drew Zondra out of her sensual thoughts. The man's voice came through the buckskin fabric of the entrance flap, saying in a singsong fashion, "I sing for you!" Zondra could hear him singing the same small phrase at the next lodge, which was Lone Eagle's father's.

"As I explained to you last night, Elk Sitting's wife requests our presence today for a *iruk-oce waraxu-a,* Cooked Meat Singing Festival," Lone Eagle said, bringing Zondra's eyes quickly to him. Apparently the warrior's song had awakened him.

"The warrior singing outside the lodge was Elk Sitting?" Zondra asked breathlessly, closing her eyes with ecstasy when Lone Eagle reached over and filled his hands with her breasts, his thumbs tweaking the nipples into a gentle hardness.

"Yes, that was Elk Sitting," Lone Eagle said, now sliding his hands down the front of her body, stopping when the fingers of one hand splayed across the crown of hair at the juncture of her thighs. "I hunger for you, my woman, but this hunger must be fed later, not now. We cannot even take the time to eat or bathe before we go to the festival. Elk Sitting's wife awaits everyone's arrival. Singing Star and Father will sit with us at the festival, as will White Bead."

Zondra looked quickly around the lodge, only now realizing Singing Star's absence. "Where did Singing Star sleep last night?" she asked, looking again at Lone Eagle.

"From now on she will sleep in Father's lodge," Lone Eagle said matter-of-factly. He gently lifted Ralph out of the way, then slid Zondra beneath him.

His body moved seductively over her, sliding slowly up and down, the friction causing his manhood to swell against Zondra's silken skin.

He closed his eyes and sucked in a breath of wild pleasure, then leapt up away from her and hurriedly dressed.

"With you lying there so beautifully nude, it is hard not to forget the festival and make love," he said huskily, his eyes gleaming with hungry intent. "But others come first today, my woman, our pleasure second."

Breathing hard, having to fight off her own arousal, finding it so hard to realize that she was this sensual a person, Zondra pushed herself up from the bed of blankets and pelts and reached for one of the beautiful doeskin dresses that White Bead had given her. This one was as white as snow, and the red beads that decorated it were like rosebuds in the snow.

She had always wondered about her mama, and why she was so eager to go and meet Zondra's father, knowing nothing would ever come of it but perhaps more children who would be sold into slavery.

Now Zondra understood. She now loved a man as much as her mother loved *her* man!

Dressed, her hair brushed with a porcupine quill brush, and her feet tucked into soft moccasins, Zondra watched Lone Eagle tend to his ground-length, lustrous hair. He smoothed buffalo grease into it, which made it shine, and then he twisted it around into a big knot at the back of his head and secured it with wooden combs.

She loved his hair when it was long and loose. It made him look even more majestic and noble! But today she would accept anything he did, for she was lost in her love for him. Everything today seemed to be more brilliant and wonderful than any other day in her life.

"I do love you so," she murmured as he finished his morning ritual of preparing his hair.

He went to her, swept his arms around her waist and drew her hard against him, giving her a long, deep kiss, his hands clasped against her buttocks as he urged her against his hardness.

She went breathless when he again moved his body in a seductive up-and-down fashion against hers, awakening rapture anew inside her.

When he drew away again, both of their faces flushed hot with arousal, Zondra came close to pleading with him to not go to the festival . . . to stay and make love to her all day.

But she knew that might shock him even more than he might already be shocked by her wanton behavior, hoping he knew that she had never done this with anyone else, that she had saved herself . . . *all* of herself . . . for the man she loved.

"We must go now or we will not go at all," Lone Eagle said huskily, his eyes dancing. "But tonight, my woman, when we return to my lodge, we will make up for what we are denying ourselves this morning."

"Today will be so long," Zondra said, curling her lips into a pout as she waited for him to get a parfleche bag at the back of the lodge.

"What's in the bag?" she asked, now feeling privy to whatever Lone Eagle did. And why not, for she was now a part of his life, and not as a captive, or intruder. As his *woman*.

It was wonderful to think of herself as his woman, his lover, and even his future bride, something she never thought possible, no matter *who* the man might be. Now it only seemed natural that she would be everything to this man, and he, everything to her!

"Sacred rocks," Lone Eagle said, slinging the bag over his right shoulder.

"What are they for?" Zondra asked, leaving his lodge with him.

"They are a part of the festival ceremony," Lone Eagle said, saying no more when he saw the excitement across the way, where everyone was already sitting in a wide semicircle just outside Elk Sitting's lodge.

"Elk Sitting's wife's name is Soft Sky," Lone Eagle said, giving his father and Singing Star a nod of welcome as they came from Mad Buffalo's lodge and joined Lone Eagle and Zondra on their way to the festival.

Zondra spoke a quiet greeting to both Mad Buffalo and Singing Star, and then White Bead as she joined them. Zondra smiled at them all somewhat shyly when she saw that they each gave her a knowing look, surely because they knew that Lone Eagle had changed her from a girl to a woman last night.

She quickly looked away from them and tried to keep her focus off such thoughts. "The sky is blue, Lone Eagle," Zondra said, giving him a questioning look. "So does that mean that Soft Sky's eyes are blue?"

"Yes, her eyes are blue," Lone Eagle said, his eyes meeting and locking with Zondra's. "Her father was white. He forced himself on her mother many moons ago when the white pony soldiers first arrived on our land."

He paused, then said, "Soft Sky's grandfather even now keeps her father's scalp in his collection, those which were taken during a time when scalping was something ordinarily done against enemies," he said, his voice quiet.

Zondra paled and said nothing, so glad when they reached the crowd of people who greeted all of them with loud hellos and smiles of welcome.

Suddenly Zondra was aware of being treated differently now. It was as though they all knew that her status in their village had changed . . . that she was no longer considered a captive, but instead their chief's woman!

This made her blush, realizing that everyone probably knew that she had spent last night with Lone Eagle in a much different capacity than the previous nights. The tribe surely knew that she had shared his bed and of their lovemaking.

She tried not to be self-conscious, and soon found it easy to relax, for once the festival proceedings began she became totally immersed in the excitement, glad that she partially understood each facet of it. Last night, just before she and Lone Eagle fell asleep, he

had told her that he was going to take her with him
to the Cooked Meat Singing Festival today.

He had explained to her that such a festival was
prompted by a woman's dream. The person who
dreamed it would be the hostess of the festival. The
woman's husband would be the host. The festival
would be made up of a medley of social and ritualistic
customs, in which sacred rocks, *baco-ritsi-tse,* and a
bear image played an important part.

Lone Eagle had further explained to Zondra that
once this woman, a wife of one of Lone Eagle's most
powerful warriors, had dreamed about the ceremony
and told her husband about it, he had gone around
the village notifying the guests. Everyone who lived
in the village was invited.

Each woman had then taken mashed bones and
cooked meat to the hostess, who boiled the bones in
a large kettle to extract the grease, then thoroughly
soaked the meat in it. The meat was then shaped into
loaves, cooked, then carefully stowed away until the
festival.

Elk Sitting had come around today, announcing the
festival again, so that everyone would come to his
wife's party and she would be proud of a large
attendance.

Zondra noticed that a buffalo calf skin was spread
between the huge outdoor roaring fire and those who
sat before it.

She also noticed that a smaller fire had been lit just
in front of Elk Sitting, and that all of the men held
beautiful rocks in their hands. Their wives sat beside
them.

She nodded a silent thank-you to Lone Eagle as he
led her to a place reserved for him and his loved ones.

After they were all comfortable on blankets on the

ground, the ceremony began. Lone Eagle sat at Zondra's right side and White Bead at her left.

Zondra watched a beautiful middle-aged woman sit down beside Elk Sitting, and from the blue color of her eyes, she knew that the woman was Elk Sitting's wife. Zondra studied the woman more closely and saw that Soft Sky had many features that spoke of white kin. Her nose was tiny. Her cheeks were not pronounced. Her skin was a much lighter shade of copper than that of everyone else of her village.

But it was her eyes that set her apart the most from those around her. They were so piercing a blue they seemed to be the reflection of the blue sky overhead today.

Zondra realized that she was staring. She looked away and awkwardly cleared her throat, then sat quietly with her legs crossed beneath her dress.

She watched as the men, beginning at the left of the half circle, one by one passed their stones from hand to hand until they reached Elk Sitting, who then took them and laid them on the skin and smoked them over the fire with wild carrot root incense until he had treated all of the stones the same way.

Elk Sitting then smoked a round rattle with incense, gave it to his chief, and asked him to sing. Elk Sitting also gave Lone Eagle a pipe of tobacco to be smoked.

Before singing and smoking, Lone Eagle gave Soft Sky a present that he took from his parfleche bag. Zondra looked closely at it and saw that the gift was a small buckskin bag, the likes of which she had seen Lone Eagle wear at his waist for the purpose of carrying his tobacco, or his smaller sacred rocks. She wondered what Soft Sky might carry in this bag. Perhaps beads for sewing? Or some lucky charm?

Zondra looked quickly away from the small bag

when Lone Eagle began to sing. She was awed by his deep, resonant voice as he sang songs connected with war, or of sacred, mythical Crow characters.

After Lone Eagle stopped singing, the man next to him gave his own gift to Soft Sky. It was a tiny carved figure of a buffalo that made Soft Sky's eyes light up.

She thanked him with a smile and set the gift aside with the one she had received from Lone Eagle. They all listened to the man singing his songs of conquest after the rattle was passed to him.

This ritual continued until each man had given his gift, had partaken in a smoke from the pipe, and had taken a turn singing. And after the rattle and pipe made the rounds among the warriors and returned to Elk Sitting, Zondra watched the husky middle-aged warrior rise and take the pipe and rattle to a man who appeared to be at least eighty years old. He was so wrinkled it was hard for Zondra to find his eyes among the deep folds of his face. His hand shook terribly as he lifted it to accept that which Elk Sitting so gently offered him, and he said, "*Aho,* thank you," in a voice so gruff and deep it was hardly understandable.

When Lone Eagle glanced over at Zondra and saw her looking so contemplatively at the elderly medicine man, he leaned closer to her. "The old man is Medicine Fox, our people's sacred medicine man, a man with both bear and buffalo medicine," he whispered, just loud enough for her to hear. "It is now time for Soft Sky to distribute the meat loaves to the women who shared their meat and bones with her. You will be given a loaf, for meat and bones were given to Soft Sky by Singing Star in your name."

"Truly?" Zondra said, her eyes wide as she turned to Lone Eagle. "When did she do this?"

"On the very day you arrived with me at my village as my captive," Lone Eagle said. "It was on that day that I told Singing Star that in time you would be the woman of my lodge instead of a white prophet."

"Yes, I am your woman and I adore it," she murmured.

"You will be my wife," Lone Eagle said thickly. "Soon."

Zondra's eyes wavered, for the word "wife" could mean so many things to Lone Eagle. She prayed that he would understand her feelings about being subjugated, for she just could not be degraded in such a way again!

She quickly looked up when the elderly medicine man began singing something in the Crow tongue, accompanied by the sacred rattle that his quivering hand was shaking. Soft Sky began distributing the loaves of meat to her guests.

When Soft Sky came to Zondra and held out a loaf of meat to her, Zondra smiled and thanked her and took it, amazed that, up close, it looked exactly like the meat loaf her mama had always made whenever meat was available in their poor, tiny cabin.

Tears came to Zondra's eyes at this reminder of her precious mama, knowing where she surely was at this moment . . . with the rest of the slaves doing their assigned chores.

Of late, Zondra had become concerned about her mother having to work out in the hot sun in the large garden. Her only reprieve was those times she was allowed to go to the pretty cabin deep in the forest to be her lover's mistress. Her mother had taken Zondra there once. She knew that with its pretty things, the cabin was something akin to heaven to her mother.

"It is over," Lone Eagle said, drawing Zondra out of her troubled thoughts.

Zondra jumped, startled, then smiled awkwardly over at Lone Eagle. "What did you say?" she asked softly.

"The festival is over," he said, placing a gentle hand to her elbow to help her up from the ground. "As you see, everyone is returning to their homes and their chores."

She was surprised to see that White Bead, Singing Star, and Mad Buffalo were no longer there, nor were Soft Sky and her husband. Most everyone was gone, except for Lone Eagle, who had waited to speak with several warriors who had problems to discuss with him.

"I . . . was . . . lost in thoughts of my mama," Zondra said apologetically. "I didn't even notice."

"I cannot return to the lodge with you or bathe with you," he said. "There are problems. Several of my warriors wish to meet in council to discuss one thing or another."

"I hope the problems aren't serious," Zondra said, frowning.

"No, most have to do with children who are giving mothers and fathers difficulties," Lone Eagle said. "During stressful times like these, when the red man is losing so much dignity because of the intrusion of evil, greedy white settlers, the children are the ones who suffer the most. They are confused. This sometimes leads them to disrespect their parents. It must be stopped now before it worsens."

"If so much is wrong among your people because of whites, how can they look at me and smile?" Zondra asked, swallowing hard. "I have even been allowed to join them today in their meat festival." She dropped her eyes to the loaf of meat. "Soft Sky was generous enough to give me a loaf of her meat."

"There are bad and good in red- *and* white-skinned people," Lone Eagle said. "It is not hard to separate the good from the bad. In my people's eyes, you are good because they know I would not bring someone bad among them."

"I hope I never give them cause to regret having befriended me," Zondra said, hoping her father would not come and cause trouble once he discovered she was there.

"That is not something that you should concern yourself with," Lone Eagle said, placing a gentle hand to her cheek. "Just be yourself. That is enough."

He looked toward the council house where the men were filing in, one by one, then gazed down at Zondra again. "I really must go," he said. "I will return home soon. We will go and bathe in the river. We shall have our noon meal. And then we will tie the ties at our entrance flap and make love."

A sensual tremor raced up and down Zondra's spine as she smiled, nodded, then watched him walk away from her.

Her heart was filled with such a wondrous, peaceful joy as she went to his tepee. "Nothing is going to happen to ruin this for me," she whispered. "Nothing . . . no one."

When Ralph came to her sniffing, having caught the scent of the meat, Zondra tucked the loaf safely in a parfleche bag away from her.

"You'll get your share soon," Zondra said, bending to stroke her cat's thick fur. She laughed softly. "For certain you don't have to depend on deer mice for your meals."

When she heard a noise behind her, she turned with a start, puzzled when she found no one there.

"I've got to quit being so jumpy," she whispered. "I am safe here."

But something still made her feel uneasy, as though someone might be somewhere close by, spying on her.

She picked Ralph up and left the tepee. She went behind the lodge and stared up at the bluff. She was relieved when she didn't see anyone, but knew that if her father stood watch for any period of time, he would see her there.

She wondered what he would do if he did.

Chapter Twenty-five

Round western isles with incense blossoms bright,
Lingering, suspends my soul in its voluptuous flight.

—PERCY BYSSHE SHELLEY

Harrison almost spilled his coffee on the dining room table's sparkling white linen tablecloth when someone started pounding on his front door. He knew that something must be terribly wrong for someone to come at this ungodly early hour, disturbing his breakfast.

Not even paying attention to his wife, who was whining about who might be at the door, always afraid, on the lookout for outlaws and renegade Indians ever since her precious jewels had been stolen from the safe, Harrison beat his butler to the door and yanked it open.

He started to give whomever it was a cussing, but stopped and got a cold feeling inside when he found his lead cowhand there, his eyes wild, sweat pouring from his brow even though the morning air was still chilly.

"I just went out on the range to check our herd and, Christ, boss, it's almost doubled through the night," he said, taking a red handkerchief from his rear pocket, mopping up the sweat as it streamed down into his gray eyes. "I came and reported back to you as soon as I could."

"Our herd has doubled? That doesn't make any sense, Al," Harrison said, reaching over and taking his gun belt from a peg on the wall beside the door. He swung it into place around his waist, then grabbed a leather jacket and jerked his arms into the sleeves.

"And that ain't all, boss," Al said, scratching at his stained denim breeches, and then his whiskered face. "They have the markings of being Crow horses."

"God, no," Harrison said, paling. "If those are the Crow Indians' horses, the Indians could retaliate because they will think *we* stole them."

He hurried from the porch and headed for the stable, still ignoring his wife as she screamed at him, asking him what was the matter.

"Lord almighty, Al," he grumbled as the cowhand walked beside him. "How'd the Crow horses get in with ours, especially if there are as many as you say?"

"Boss, I think someone is out to get you by planting the horses there, trying to get you in hot water with the Crow," Al said, huffing and puffing as he kept up with Harrison's long-legged stride.

"It's probably the work of the goddamn outlaws," Harrison rumbled, yanking the stable door open. "Since I refused to pay money to get Guy back, they probably mixed the Crow horses with ours to send me a silent message."

"What *are* you going to do about Guy?" Al asked guardedly as Harrison took his horse from its stall and quickly saddled it.

"I'd hoped the damn outlaws would release him once they saw they'd not get a plugged nickel out of my pocket for him," Harrison said thickly, his eyes wavering as guilt swept through him anew over having not lifted a finger to help his son.

Harrison had hoped that by not paying ransom for Guy, it might teach his son a valuable lesson. When Guy returned home, which Harrison had hoped would have happened by now, he'd have been taught an important lesson and would henceforth be the son Harrison wanted him to be. Useful!

Harrison was beginning to worry now that the outlaws might not release Guy unless the money *was* paid. And if it wasn't . . . ?

"Round up several men," Harrison shouted, swinging himself into his saddle. "We must get the horses returned to the Crow. We've got to prove to them that we are innocent of horse thievery. If not, I'd hate to think what they will do to us. I'm sure they won't stop at just burning down my house!"

As he edged his horse through the stable door, he gazed at the slaves' quarters where his Ada was feeling safe and secure, then at his house where his wife was standing, trembling and wringing her hands, on the porch.

"Al, make sure some of our cowhands stay behind to keep a watch on things," Harrison said, then rode away at a hard gallop toward his pasture.

When he arrived there he saw that some of his cowhands had already started cutting out the horses that didn't belong to him. He drew a tight rein and studied the horses.

Yes, damn it, they *were* Crow horses. They were of a larger breed than those Harrison had bought from a man who had come to these parts from Texas. Wanting to have a full-fledged ranch, Harrison had purchased the horses shortly after arriving from Mississippi. The man he bought them from had established a ranch many miles from here along the Yellowstone River, where he had thought he was far enough from Indians to be safe.

Word had come to Harrison only recently that this man and his entire family had been slain. His house and outbuildings had been burned. His cattle and horses had been stolen.

The fact that cattle had been stolen as well as horses made him think it was the work of outlaws rather than Indians, for as far as he knew, Indians hated cow meat and would have never burdened themselves with them.

"The ones who killed that family are probably the same outlaws who abducted Guy, and who placed the Crow horses among mine," Harrison mumbled, unable to deny the fear that was creeping in around his heart at how all of this might end. "I've got to get those horses back to the Crow."

He smiled smugly when another thought came to him. In a sense, these horses arriving when they had might be in his favor. They gave Harrison an excuse to go to the Indian village again to see if Zondra was there. He just couldn't get the black cat that he had seen there off his mind and accept that it wasn't Ralph. Yet he hadn't felt safe enough to return just yet to the village for another meeting with Chief Lone Eagle.

Now he could without it looking as though he had something besides the horses on his mind, truly believing they *were* planted there among his for a purpose.

Wanting to get the horses back where they belonged as soon as possible, Harrison joined his men at rounding them up, then rode with them toward the Crow village.

When they got close enough that they could see it in the distance, plumes of smoke spiraling upward into the sky from the smoke holes of their tepees, Harrison couldn't deny how leery he was of what was to come next. What if the Crow didn't believe him . . . ?

Suddenly several Crow warriors on horseback plunged from their hiding places behind thick brush and surrounded Harrison and his men.

Harrison reined in his steed as he gazed warily from Indian to Indian. Their rifles were drawn. There was a look of mistrust and hate in their eyes as two of them began riding through the herd, checking their markings, yet already realizing the horses were theirs and were in the possession of white men.

"What are you doing with horses that belong to Crow?" Two Chances asked, his eyes narrowing angrily as he stared at Harrison. "We came up short the exact number that we see are with you."

"We found your horses mingled with ours this morning," Harrison said, his hands not close enough to a pistol to use one if it should become necessary. The Indian's rifle was aimed directly at Harrison's heart. One pull of the trigger and Harrison would be dead.

"You say you found them?" Two Chances asked, forking an eyebrow. "How can that be? Our horses do not stray."

"No, I'm sure they don't," Harrison said. "That means that someone had to have stolen them from you and put them among mine purposely. I vow to you that none of my men did it. Someone else did it to make it look like we stole the horses to get us in trouble with the Crow."

"And you expect me to believe that?" Two Chances asked, chuckling under his breath.

"If it were not true, why then would you see us bringing them back to your people?" Harrison said reasonably. "If we had stolen them, wouldn't they still be in my pasture, scattered among my own horses?"

Two Chances kneaded his chin as he thought through Harrison's explanation. Then he nodded. "I will take you to my chief and he will decide what must be done about this," he said flatly. "But know this, white man, the Crow make horse thieves pay dearly for their crime."

"I imagine you do," Harrison said, taking a deep, nervous breath.

"Come with us," Two Chances said, motioning with a nod of his head toward his village.

He then rode on ahead of Harrison.

Harrison watched Two Chances ride into the village. He was joined by another Crow, and the two warriors on horseback sat waiting for Harrison to ride up with their horses. From this vantage point, Harrison could tell that the other Indian was Chief Lone Eagle. He recognized his flowing hair and his noble countenance.

Realizing that his plan to go into the Crow village a second time to look for Zondra might not work out, since the chief was waiting at the very edge of the village, Harrison's spirits fell.

When he did reach Lone Eagle and the man failed to invite him into his village, choosing instead to question Harrison on the outskirts, Harrison assumed that it was because the Crow thought that he *had* stolen the horses in order to give him a chance to bring them back as a mock gesture of friendship with the intent of snooping in his village for Zondra.

"You say you did not steal the Crow horses—then who might you suggest is the guilty party?" Lone

Eagle asked, looking at Harrison, and then past him at the horses.

"I have an idea, but I'm not sure," Harrison said. He looked beyond Lone Eagle, trying to see the women in the village, to see if one of them might have white skin.

He jumped with alarm when Lone Eagle edged his horse to one side and purposely blocked Harrison's view.

"Who do you lay the guilt on?" Lone Eagle prodded, smiling to himself when he saw the frustration he caused by blocking the man's view. He was not going to give Harrison the opportunity to see if Zondra was in the village.

"Outlaws," Harrison said flatly.

"And why would they do this?" Lone Eagle asked, nodding to his warriors to take the horses and return them to their rightful place.

"I believe it was done to frighten me," Harrison said, not wanting to get into the details of how he truly felt.

"And did it?" Lone Eagle taunted, knowing this man must be evil through and through for Zondra to have fled him.

Harrison's lips tightened and he refused to answer Lone Eagle, for he could tell that for some reason the Crow chief was purposely mocking him.

"Am I free to go?" Harrison blurted out instead.

"Yes, you are free to go, but if this happens again, I will not look at it as a ploy on anyone's part except yours," Lone Eagle said, then swung his horse around and rode back into his village.

When he arrived at his lodge and went inside, he found Zondra tense, her eyes wide with questioning.

"You knew he was here," Lone Eagle said, placing gentle hands on her shoulders.

"Yes, someone told me that you were taken from council, and why," Zondra murmured. "Where is he now?"

"He is returning to his home," Lone Eagle said, seeing the relief knowing that caused his woman. He drew her into his arms and held her close. "He will never know you are here. You are safe."

Zondra clung to him, then melted inside when he swept his arms around her and carried her to his bed of blankets and furs. "Wait here," he whispered, brushing a soft kiss across her lips. "I shall secure the entrance flap and then return to you."

Her pulse racing, she was unsure of why he suddenly wanted to make love. Was it to assure her that he was there for her? Or was it to remind her that she was *his*? Her father had reminded Lone Eagle that she had been a part of another world before they met.

No matter why he chose to make love now, she wanted it, too, to prove to him that she had placed her other life out of her mind, that she was there, to be his woman, for as long as she had breath enough to tell him.

When he came back to her, his breechclout and moccasins already removed, he slowly undressed her until she was kneeling nude before him, her breasts heaving in sensual excitement as his eyes swept over her with a silent, urgent message.

When he reached for her and pushed her down beneath him on his bed, blanketing her with his powerful, lithe body, she writhed in response.

"Take me," she whispered, her arms twining around his neck as she urged his lips to hers.

As he kissed her with a fierce, possessive heat, he

plunged his manhood deep inside her. The pleasure was so intense, Zondra drew a ragged breath and lifted her hips higher so that he could fill her more deeply.

Dipping his head, Lone Eagle flicked her nipples with his tongue, then sucked on them one at a time as he drove his throbbing hardness into her, withdrew, and drove into her again, his lean, sinewy buttocks rhythmically moving.

He slid his hands up and filled them with her exquisitely rounded breasts, his mouth again on her lips, the kiss long, deep, and passionate.

Aware of the heat building within her, Zondra clung and rocked with Lone Eagle. Her whole body was quivering with anticipation of experiencing again that same explosion of ecstasy that he had introduced her to.

"My woman," Lone Eagle whispered huskily against her lips. "How fiercely I want you."

"I want you as badly," Zondra whispered back to him, her warm breath mingling with his.

His mouth closed over hers as he kissed her again, the fires of their passion raging between them.

Lone Eagle paused for a moment, then plunged again inside her. He cradled her close when their bodies trembled, the explosion of their needs leaving them shaken and weak.

As they lay beside each other while the lodge fire burned soft and low, Lone Eagle considered once again how his horses had happened to be among the white man's. Harrison had sworn that he hadn't stolen the animals, so that meant that someone else was guilty of the crime.

But who?

If it was outlaws, why hadn't they just gone ahead and taken the horses for themselves?

No. None of it made any sense, yet Lone Eagle was not going to bother Zondra with it. Their relationship was good. He did not want to do anything to spoil it. He did not want to fill her mind with all sorts of questions, not now that she seemed content with the way things were between them.

"Hold me," Zondra murmured, cuddling closer to him. "Before you have to return to council, please spend a few more moments with me."

"Are you feeling lonely?" Lone Eagle dared to ask.

"No, just the opposite," Zondra said softly. "I have never felt as content as I do now."

He lowered his lips to hers and kissed her, vowing to himself that he would never give her cause to feel any other way than how she was feeling now. He would let no other man near her to threaten her stability. Especially not the man who came today with what Lone Eagle guessed were lies!

Chapter Twenty-six

Thine eyes glowed in the glare
of the moon's dying light;
As a fen-fire's beam on a sluggish stream
Gleams dimly, so the moon shone there.

—PERCY BYSSHE SHELLEY

Having agreed to carry out a plan to abduct one of the Crow's women, hoping to cast guilt Guy's father's way since it didn't seem as though the Crow had been convinced that his father had stolen the horses, Guy and the outlaws were looking down through the darkness at the Crow village from the butte.

Guy stared at the largest tepees in the village. There were two. Surely one of them housed the chief. Guy and the outlaws had decided that to truly direct anger Harrison's way, they would steal the most valuable woman in the village. The chief's wife!

Yes, since the horse idea had backfired, Guy had to make sure his plan worked this time. After the woman was abducted, several pieces of her clothing would be spread out in Guy's father's pastureland. When the Crow began searching for the woman they would find the clothes.

Suspecting how the Crow would retaliate, Guy smiled. The savages would burn all of his father's out-buildings, the mansion, and perhaps take many white captives.

The only regret he had about seeking vengeance against his father was that his mother would also be a target of the Crows' fury. But not recalling many times when his mother had stepped in and spoken up on his behalf, perhaps it was best that she was taught a lesson as well. In any event, Guy was finally free of their abuses.

Billy Feazel drew his men close around him. "Men, as best I can tell, there ain't no sentries posted around the village. But you keep a close watch while Guy and I go there," he said darkly. "If you see warriors snooping about after we get inside the tepee, you'd better come and make sure they are silenced before the whole damn village discovers we're there."

"We've never gone against Indians like this before," one of the men said nervously. "I ain't ready to lose my scalp over this stranger here who you've suddenly taken a liking to."

"That stranger, as you call him, is responsible for us being way richer than we were before we abducted him," Billy hissed. "Now if you want to hand over your portion and leave, do it. If not, shut your mouth and do as you're told."

"All right, boss, I'll stay," the man grumbled. "But I sure as hell don't like what your plans are tonight. I've heard what Injuns do when they're on the warpath." He shuddered visibly. "They don't just scalp a man." He covered his private parts with a hand. "They dismember a man and stuff it in the dead man's mouth."

"That's a lot of hogwash," Billy said, laughing throatily. "And even if it were true, you can bet your bottom dollar whoever they did it to deserved it. I've heard what the cavalry has done to innocent Injuns. It ain't somethin' to brag about."

"Still, I—" the man began, stopping when Billy drew his pistol on him.

"Either ride out of here or shut up. If you insist on complainin', I'll just plug you and get it over with," Billy snarled. "Then you won't have to worry about what a redskin might do to you. I'll let the white wolves take care of your carcass."

The man paled and edged his horse back from Billy. "I ain't sayin' nothin' else, Billy," he said, gulping hard. "But, damn it, man, go on. Get it over with so's we can hightail it outta here."

Billy's lips tugged into a mocking smile as he gazed a moment longer at his friend, then twirled his pistol around a finger, slid it into his holster, and dismounted. "Come on, Guy," he said, motioning with a hand. "Let's go and get us a pretty lady to have some fun with before the Injuns realize she's missin'. Then we'll kill her and put her someplace for them to find her. But not before she knows what it's like to have several white men mounting her."

Guy's eyes gleamed at the thought of having a redskinned woman to rape. While doing it he would pretend it was Zondra. That would appease him at least for a while, until he found Zondra and finally showed her what it was like to have a man inside her breeches.

He followed Billy until they reached the area behind the tepees. Their eyes searched the night for anyone who might be wandering about, or for sentries they hadn't seen from the butte. When they neither heard nor saw anything except for the shine of a screech owl's eyes as it rested on a branch of a tree above them, they moved stealthily through the dark toward the tepee they had chosen to enter.

When they finally reached it, Guy stood aside and watched Billy slowly and quietly run his knife down the back side of the buffalo skin covering until he made a slit large enough for them to enter.

Billy smiled crookedly and nodded as he held the buckskin back for Guy.

Never one to be brave, Guy's insides quaked with fear as he put his head through the slit in the buckskin to check things out before going on inside. He wanted to make sure they didn't step on someone as they entered.

From what he could tell by the glow of the burning embers in the fire pit, there were two people sleeping in the lodge. What seemed strange to him was the fact that they slept totally apart from one another. One was asleep beside the entrance flap. The other was asleep only a few inches from where Billy had made the slit in the buckskin. If these two were man and wife, why didn't they sleep together? From the way they were snuggled into their blankets, it was impossible to tell anything about them.

Billy nudged Guy in the ribs. "Go on, damn it," he whispered, glowering at Guy as Guy turned a quick glance his way.

Guy nodded, then stepped inside. Billy quickly followed after him.

Unable to control the trembling of his hands, absolutely terrified of being caught by redskins, and knowing what they would do with him and Billy were they found inside their chief's lodge, Guy watched as Billy fell to his knees and slowly drew back the blanket from the Indian that slept at the back of the lodge.

When Billy gave Guy a surprised look, Guy dropped down beside him and took a look himself. He had heard that the chief was a young man. This man was elderly!

Billy replaced the blanket and nodded for Guy to go and check the other sleeping figure.

Swallowing hard, now wondering what they had gotten themselves into, Guy tiptoed over and slowly drew back a corner of the blanket. He was taken aback when he found an old woman, her skin drawn taut like shoe leather over her facial features.

He looked over his shoulder at Billy and shook his head back and forth, knowing for certain that this couldn't be the young chief's wife.

Replacing the blanket, Guy went back to Billy. "It has to be the other tepee," he whispered. "You know. The other large one that sits next to this one. This must be the young chief's father."

Mad Buffalo suddenly sat up, his eyes wide as he looked from Guy to Billy.

Before he could utter a sound, or cry out for help, Billy had his knife plunged into the old chief's heart, killing him immediately.

Guy swayed as a keen light-headedness came over him at the sight of the old man's eyes growing large and wild as the knife entered his heart . . . and how quickly those same eyes became locked in a death stare.

Guy had never seen anyone murdered before. He had hardly seen anyone dead. Back in Mississippi, when kin had died, he had begged out of going to their wakes. He had only gone when a close cousin his age had died and his mother forced him to serve as a pallbearer.

Feeling the urge to vomit, Guy rushed from the lodge. As he hung his head and the vile bitterness rushed across his lips, he said a silent prayer that the old woman wouldn't awaken. He knew that Billy would end her life just as quickly as he had taken the old man's.

He wanted to run away and hide and pretend this hadn't happened. He absolutely wanted to forget his role in the murder.

But when Billy came from the lodge, wiping blood on the legs of his trousers, then went immediately to the other large lodge and made the same sort of slit in its buckskin as he had in the first tepee, Guy knew that there was more to come. Billy was here for a purpose. He would not leave until it was accomplished.

The slit gaping open, Billy came to Guy and grabbed him by an arm. "Get a hold of yourself," he whispered harshly. "Damn it, man, you're actin' like a sissy. I can see now why your pa didn't want you back. You were probably an embarrassment to him. He learned early, I'm sure, that his son was way less than a man."

"Shut up that kind of talk," Guy snarled back at Billy. He wiped his mouth with the back of his shirt sleeve. "I'm not a sissy. I've just never been part of a murder until tonight."

He reached out and grabbed hold of Billy's shirt collar. "You shouldn't have done that, Billy," he said anxiously. "The whole damn Crow nation will be after our hides."

"After your pa's, don't you mean?" Billy said, slapping Guy's hand away from him. "Now, Guy, if you don't go inside that tepee with me I'll use the same knife on you that I used on that old Injun." He snickered. "But it'll be easier gettin' the knife through your skin since it's so young, not like the shoe leather skin I had to stick it through to kill the old savage."

"We're taking too much of a chance entering another tepee," Guy gulped out. "Come on, Billy. Let's get outta here. I've changed my mind. I don't want to get my father in *this* much trouble."

"Yellow belly," Billy hissed. "That's what you are. A damn scared yellow belly."

Guy's jaw tightened. He stared at Billy for a moment, then went past him and through the slit in the tepee. This time it was easy to make out the lady from the man. Although the light from the glowing embers was too dim to tell what the woman looked like, it was her long, flowing black hair that fell across the blanket that she slept beneath that distinguished her from the man.

Also, the man—a young, virile redskin—was lying there asleep, nude. Thankfully, he was far enough away from the woman so that it would be possible to abduct her without the warrior realizing it. It was apparent that they had rolled away from each other as they slept.

Guy stood quietly by as Billy slipped his knife into Guy's hand. His pulse racing with fear, Guy watched Billy quickly tie a gag around the woman's mouth, then wrap her quickly in a blanket and carry her outside.

Clutching the handle of the knife, Guy stood there for a moment longer, watching for any signs that the young chief might be awakening, his gaze sweeping over the man's well-muscled body.

He could not help but be awed by the man's physique. He noticed how well-endowed he was, where God either gifted a man or cheated him, like Guy had been cheated. He stared at that part of the young chief's anatomy for a moment longer, then continued moving his eyes over him, seeing the smoothness of his hairless, copper skin and everything else that made this Indian way more of a man than Guy knew he could ever be.

Always before he had seen Indians from a distance. Up this close, he could see why they were called the lords of the plains.

This man, with his long black hair lying beneath him like a blanket, and with the sleekness of his muscles and his handsomeness, was all male, causing envy to gnaw at Guy's insides.

Guy had never been blessed with muscles, nor good looks. What he had achieved in life was due to his father's being rich. Guy could buy anything he desired, but that only mattered up to a point.

After his father realized that he had raised a good-for-nothing, lazy son, things had changed, even though it was his father's fault that his son had turned out the way he had.

Guy doubled his free hand into a tight fist at his side. "How I hate you," he whispered as his father came into his mind. The man was everything he wasn't—so strict, so exact, so tall and handsome, and yes, so virile!

"Come on, damn it," Billy whispered to Guy through the slit in the buckskin. "We've gotta get outta here. But first find a dress. This woman's probably buck-naked beneath this blanket. We need the dress to plant on your father's property, anyway!"

Brought back to the moment, Guy nodded and looked around the tepee for a dress.

He was relieved when he saw a white doeskin dress close to where the woman had been sleeping. He grabbed it and rushed from the tepee. He followed alongside Billy as the outlaw struggled to carry his prize up the steep hillside.

When they finally reached the waiting gang, Billy

laid the bundled woman on the ground. Beneath the bright shine of the moon on the butte, everyone stood around, eyes anxiously wide, as Billy slowly unwrapped the blanket. They all knew they were going to have a piece of her, and hoped she'd not be some toothless hag that'd turn their stomachs.

When the woman was revealed to them, Guy took an unsteady step away from her. "Zondra!" he gasped, paling at the sight of her eyes, glaring up at him above her gagged mouth.

Then he smiled smugly. He couldn't believe his good fortune!

He had planned to search until he found Zondra, and here she was like someone had placed her on a silver platter for him. He had achieved more tonight than he had anticipated.

He was puzzled, though. Why had Zondra been in the savage's tepee? Had the Injun abducted her? Or had she become enamored of the handsome warrior and chosen to live with him? Was that why she had left her home? To be with this well-endowed Indian chief?

He battled the jealousy this caused him . . . to think of what she had probably shared with the young chief tonight, and all of the nights since she had been gone.

Well, now she wouldn't be with the young chief again in any respect. Now she had several men who'd pleasure her, who'd receive pleasure from her beautiful body. After having seen the chief's anatomy, Guy felt sure it would take several men to equal the one Indian's skills in bed.

Zondra's heart pounded inside her chest. Her feelings were mixed. She was afraid, yet she was also filled with a terrible anger when she saw who was at least partially responsible for her abduction.

Her very own half brother, Guy.

But why? And who were these other men?

She got a better look as they leaned down closer to her, staring at her while two men held her down. She could see their whiskers and filthy clothes, their guns hanging heavy at their hips, and surmised they were the scourge of the countryside . . . outlaws!

She glanced quickly at Guy. He was dressed as crudely as the other men. He even had a growth of whiskers on his face; in the past he had never been seen without a fresh shave. Since he was with these outlaws, and took part in her abduction tonight, that had to mean that he was part of their gang.

But why?

Afraid they were too close to the Indian village, Billy decided not to remove the gag from Zondra's mouth. He took the time to tie her wrists and wrapped her in the blanket again.

He then placed her on his saddle and swung himself up behind her, holding her and riding hard until they reached their hideout deep in the forest.

Struggling against Billy's hold as he pulled her down from the horse, Zondra tried her best to get away from him. But the blanket still imprisoned her, and although he was a wiry, thin man, Billy was muscled enough for her not to be able to get free of him.

She glared at Guy as he walked beside Billy toward a cabin nestled beneath the trees, hating it when Guy smiled smugly. She could tell that he was pleased with himself, that he had finally found a way to best her, and at the same time, to best his father.

She looked around surreptitiously as Billy carried her inside the dark cabin. She barely breathed as she watched one of the outlaws strike a match, then held it to the wick of a kerosene lantern.

Soon soft lamplight flooded the dark, stinking interior of the cabin. Zondra shuddered at its filthiness, at its total disarray. The smell, a mixture of urine, whiskey, dead animals, and cigar smoke, made her nose curl.

She was glad when Billy finally laid her across a bed on her back and removed the gag.

As she leaned up on an elbow, she glared at Guy. "Why are you doing this?" she asked in a choked whisper. "What are you doing with these filthy men? How did you know I was at the Indian village? Did you spy from the bluff and see me? Why, Guy? What have I ever done to you except be unlucky enough to be your blood kin?"

"Damn it, you know how I feel about you, how me and my brother and sisters have always resented you," Guy blurted out as he stood over the bed, his fists on his hips. "But, Zondra, I had no idea you were at the Indian village. Billy and I came to steal a squaw. When we unrolled the blanket and saw that it was you, it was a total surprise to me."

"But why were you in the village abducting anyone?" Zondra asked warily, very aware of the loathsome, filthy men standing around the bed, looking at her lasciviously.

She was glad that prior to going to sleep tonight, after she and Lone Eagle had made love, she had slipped into a warm, soft doeskin gown White Bead had given to her this morning for the cooler nights they had recently been having. Otherwise the men would be looking at her naked.

"And how on earth did you make it into Lone Eagle's tepee without waking him up?" Zondra continued, although she did remember now that Lone Eagle had complained of being extra sleepy earlier in the

evening. She had teased him about being tired out by
their constant lovemaking. To prove that she was
wrong, he had made love to her again.

Afterward, he had immediately fallen asleep. She
had lain with him for a while, watching him, adoring
him, then had gone and slipped into the gown and
fallen asleep beside him.

Somehow, while they were both sleeping, they had
become separated enough for the outlaw and Guy to
abduct her without awakening Lone Eagle.

"Don't answer any of her questions, Guy," Billy
snarled. "Remember, we've got somethin' else to do
before callin' it a night. Did you get the dress like I
tol' you?"

"Yes, it's in my saddlebag on the horse," Guy said,
not taking his eyes off Zondra. "Perhaps you should
also take this gown she's got on." He chuckled throatily. "It'd be kind of nice seeing her lying there naked
and afraid before we take turns raping her."

Zondra gasped and went pale. Billy gave her a long
look, then shook his head. "Naw, let's leave her be,
at least for now," he said, walking toward the door.
"The dress is enough to prove to the Crow who stole
the woman tonight from the young chief's tepee."

He stopped and swung around. "Since you wanted
her so much, you stay behind and keep watch on her,"
Billy said, frowning at Guy. "We've got more fish to
fry tonight, Guy, after we toss the Indian dress on
your father's property. I don't think you're up to as
many hours on a horse as we plan before comin' back
to the hideout."

Billy went to Guy and grabbed him by an ear. "But
don't touch her until we all get back, do you hear?"
he said, giving the ear a hard yank. "The fun's to be
shared by everyone, not only one man."

"All right," Guy said, cringing when Billy gave his ear one more pull before releasing it. He moaned as he reached up and touched the burning ear, his eyes filled with anger as he watched Billy and the others gathering up several guns before leaving.

"How long will you be gone?" Guy asked.

"Maybe a day, maybe two," Billy said, shrugging idly, then walked out with the rest of the men, leaving Zondra and Guy alone, their eyes locked.

"You've been nothing but trouble for me since the day your dark-skinned mammy brought you into this world," Guy lashed out at Zondra. "Do you know just how much I hate you?"

"I think I have a pretty good idea," Zondra said scornfully, so relieved that Guy had been ordered not to rape her. This would give her more time to get away—and she would. Guy was dumb. He would slip up one way or the other while the outlaws were gone. She would watch his every move and grab the first opportunity to best him.

But first she had to find a way to get him to release her wrists. Her hopes dimmed as he came to her with another rope and tied her ankles together.

"Enjoy your legs being shut while you can," Guy said, laughing mockingly. "Once that rope is untied, baby, your legs will be spread wide apart and the gang will be all over you."

"You are a pig," Zondra hissed out, trying to show her courageous side, while deep within her she knew that the chances were slim of her ever getting out of this mess alive, much less untouched.

Chapter Twenty-seven

Had I no eyes but ears, my ears would love
That inward beauty and invincible;
Or were I deaf; thy outward parts would move
Each part in me that were but sensible.

—WILLIAM SHAKESPEARE

As Lone Eagle slowly awakened, the dawn still breaking, he felt around him for Zondra. When he didn't find her, he smiled. He knew where she was—down at the stream, bathing before he awakened. She would come to him in their bed of blankets this morning fresh and sweet, smelling of river water, her long, lustrous hair shining and softly scented from having dried in the morning breeze.

Needing a bath himself, thinking, too, how wonderful it might be to make love in the water with his woman before everyone else awakened and made their morning trek there, Lone Eagle pushed himself up from the bed and without taking time to dress, ran from his lodge.

Ralph scampering at his heels, Lone Eagle ran to the stream, then stopped abruptly when he saw no signs of Zondra anywhere.

Thinking she might have gone farther, to the point where the stream forked out into the river, Lone Eagle ran there, his heart sinking when he didn't find her there either.

Knowing that she could swim as well as he, he knew that she wouldn't have drowned. And he doubted that she would have gone farther down the river, for there were deep currents there that he had warned her about.

Ralph didn't feel Lone Eagle's alarm. Purring, she slowly rubbed herself back and forth against Lone Eagle's legs, then jumped back from him with alarm when the Indian broke into a hard run back in the direction of the village, his eyes locked on his tepee.

Lone Eagle prayed that he would find Zondra there. Perhaps she had gone somewhere else this early in the morning, when the sun was still hidden behind the distant mountains. If she'd simply slipped into the shadows of the forest to relieve herself, by now she would be back inside his lodge.

If so, she might be concerned about *him* by now, for it was not a usual thing for him to leave without first awakening her. Their mornings invariably started with lovemaking.

He could smell smoke and knew that some of the women were now awake and starting their morning cook fires. He was even aware of some of them drawing back their entrance flaps to see who was running past their lodges. He did not look their way or he would have seen the shocked look on their faces, for he had forgotten that he hadn't stopped to dress before leaving his lodge for the morning swim. He'd known that it was safe then, for no one else had been awake.

But this was now. Many were awake. Many knew that their chief was alarmed by something by the way he was running nude through their village.

But no one came out and questioned him. As soon as they saw that he was undressed they dropped their entrance flaps back in place, for they did not want to embarrass their young chief.

Panting, his cheeks flushed hot from the hard run, Lone Eagle rushed inside his lodge.

He grew cold inside when he saw that Zondra still wasn't there.

And now, as daylight spread across the valley, brightening everything in the village with its sweet white light, Lone Eagle saw something about his tepee that made his heart lurch with alarm inside his chest. He saw the long slit in the buffalo skins. It was large enough for someone to slide through . . . and back out again!

He sucked in a quavering, frustrated breath. He wove his fingers through his long, thick hair. "Why, Zondra?" he whispered painfully to himself. "Why?"

He walked dispiritedly to the back of his lodge and ran a finger up and down the long slit, puzzled anew over why it was there. He had thought that Zondra no longer had any notions of leaving him. He had trusted that she cared enough for him to never want to. More than once she had told him that she loved him and wanted to stay with him.

"Forevermore," he whispered, that word like a thorn piercing his heart. "She said she wanted to be a part of my life forevermore!"

He turned his back to the slit in the skin. He lowered his eyes and closed them, the pain of Zondra having betrayed him so deep he felt he could not bear it.

How could he have been so wrong about her? he despaired. When he kissed her, her lips revealed to him that she loved him. The way she surrendered herself to him when they made love had convinced him that it was not a pretense. No woman could love as wholly, as completely, as wonderfully as Zondra, and not mean it!

She had truly seemed so happy with him, even with

his people. She had become good friends with White Bead.

Had that been just a ploy on her part to look content until she had the opportunity to escape? he wondered, his jaw tightening. His hands closed into fists to think that he had allowed a woman—a *white* woman—to make such a fool of him. To make such fools of his people.

It was especially wrong of her to have betrayed White Bead, his people's precious, beloved prophet!

And although it seemed undeniable that she had betrayed them all, he was not sure what to do about it. Should he go and find her and make her a true captive this time? Or should he just let her go and forget her?

It made him cringe to think that only two nights ago he had lifted the sentries that had been posted at strategic points in his village to make sure Zondra didn't escape.

She had been clever enough to stay with him, pretending to be in love, until he trusted her enough to leave her unguarded.

His heart ached to think that she could be this devious, when she had seemed as sweet as the scent of roses in the spring.

And when they made love, ah, how wonderful it had been to see her blossoming into a woman.

His hands . . . his mouth . . . his tongue . . . had taught her so much!

"The skills she will now use with another man!" he cried, so overwhelmed by the betrayal that tears flooded his eyes.

And although she had proved to be untrue, he knew that he could never love as deeply as he had loved her.

He doubted that he would ever take another woman

to his bed. None of them were trustworthy. They were all deceitful!

His spirits low, he turned to the slit again and ran his hand along it, knowing that a knife had to be keenly sharp to penetrate the thick coverings of buffalo hide. It had to be that sharp, also, not to have made a sound as it cut through the hides.

"Mine is as sharp," he murmured, his eyes narrowing. "She stole my knife. She used it to gain her freedom!"

Angrier by the minute, his hatred for Zondra building inside him, he went to his cache of weapons. He sorted through them to find the perfect weapon to carry with him as he sought her out, to frighten her with when he caught her. No woman betrayed Lone Eagle. Not even the woman he loved with all of his heart.

His heart stopped dead-still inside his chest when he found his sharp, thick-bladed knife in its leather sheath, right where he had left it. Had Zondra used the knife, she would not have taken the time to return it to its rightful place. She would have taken it with her for protection.

As well as one of my firearms, Lone Eagle thought, his heart skipping a beat when he noticed that none were missing. He knew that surely he had been wrong about Zondra. She had spoken of having been afraid as she fled her old life because she had not had any firearms for protection. This time she would have made sure she took something with which to protect herself!

Ralph came and rubbed against Lone Eagle's bare ankles again, purring.

"The cat!" Lone Eagle said, gazing down at Ralph. Zondra would have taken her cat. She adored Ralph!

He hurried back to the slit in the hides. He checked it more closely, his pulse racing when he realized now, upon closer inspection, that a knife had been used to cut from the outside in, not the inside out.

Someone had come like a thief in the night and made the slit in the skins from the outside in. That meant that someone had come and abducted Zondra while Lone Eagle slept.

Pangs of guilt for having allowed himself to think that Zondra could be so conniving tugged at his heart. And knowing now that someone had come and taken her away made a quick anger rush through him.

"Her father," he whispered harshly. "Her father is responsible for this."

Suddenly, screams and wails rent the morning quiet. His first thought was of Zondra. What if someone had found her and she was *dead*?

A feeling of despair, so deep and painful inside him, made Lone Eagle's feet seem frozen to the mats beneath them.

Then as the cries became even louder, as more of his people joined in, he was shaken from his fear. He yanked on his breechclout.

Hysterical, Singing Star came into his lodge. She went to Lone Eagle and clutched at his arms, her eyes wide with grief, tears flowing from them.

"What causes you such deep emotion?" Lone Eagle asked gently, taking her hands, holding them affectionately. "Singing Star, calm yourself. Tell me who . . . has . . . died?"

Her body racked with sobs, Singing Star lowered her eyes.

He knew now that she was avoiding telling him because she knew that whoever had died was so important to him. His heart cold with fear, Lone Eagle

placed a hand beneath her chin and forced her eyes
up so that she looked directly at him.

"Who . . . died . . . ?" he asked again, his heart
thumping like pounding drums inside his chest.

"Someone came in the night and . . . while I slept
soundly in your father's lodge . . . they . . . ," Singing
Star began, then trailed off, as she found the words
too hard to say.

"Are you saying that someone came into my father's lodge and . . . and . . ." Even Lone Eagle could
not find the courage to say what he now knew must
be true. Not only had his woman been abducted in
the night, his father had been slain.

"No!" he cried, dropping Singing Star's hands. Lone
Eagle rushed past her. He left his lodge. He pushed
his way through the crowd of wailing people and entered his father's lodge.

He stopped when he saw his beloved father lying
on his blankets, so lifeless, his eyes locked in a
death stare.

And when Lone Eagle saw the blood that had
pooled around his father, and still lay wet and shining
beside him, Lone Eagle had to fight the nausea that
rose bitter and warm into his throat.

Trying to get over the initial shock of what had
happened, Lone Eagle stood for a moment longer just
looking at his beloved father, whose life had been
needlessly drained from him.

Anger soon helped Lone Eagle momentarily put his
grief aside. He went to his father and inspected the
wound, realizing that it had been made by a knife.

He looked quickly behind his father and saw the
long slit in the buffalo hides, his insides growing cold
with fear when he saw the same type slit that had

been made in his own lodge. Obviously whoever came and abducted his woman also killed his father.

That meant that Zondra might have been killed, or was even now at the mercy of a madman!

Apparently the person who killed his father had come for Zondra. But why? How were these fiendish acts connected? Why would anyone see the need . . . the logic in killing the old man?

Then it came to him! Wasn't it likely the one who came for Zondra was her father? Surely he sneaked into Mad Buffalo's lodge and forced answers from him about Zondra's whereabouts, then killed him to silence him . . . and *then* came and got Zondra!

The need for vengeance like a hot poker inside him, scalding him, Lone Eagle rushed from his father's lodge. As his people went silent and watched him, he went to the huge outdoor communal fire and reached his hands into the deep bed of cooler ashes around the edges. As he smeared his face and body with the ash, he shouted commands to his warriors.

"Ready yourselves to ride!" he cried. "Ready yourselves, as I have, for war! Blacken your faces, then get your weapons! We will not let one day pass without avenging my father's death . . . and the abduction of my woman!"

He gazed at the young braves who stood around in groups, watching and listening to their chief.

"Go and prepare many horses!" he shouted at the young men. "Bring them to us. Quickly!"

The braves ran to the corral, readied the steeds, then took them back to Lone Eagle and the waiting warriors.

Hatred and hunger for revenge flashing in their dark eyes, Lone Eagle and his warriors rode from the village. Zondra's father's ranch was their destination.

Chapter Twenty-eight

He sees her coming and begins to glow,
Even as a dying coal revives with wind.

—WILLIAM SHAKESPEARE

Zondra felt lucky to have made it through the night
without Guy raping her. She knew that the outlaw
called Billy meant what he said when he warned Guy
not to touch her yet—not until they all returned from
their night of pillaging as they wreaked havoc across
the countryside.

After having been taken outside to see to her personal duties, Zondra was again in the outlaws' cabin,
the stink now somewhat camouflaged by the smell of
coffee and bacon cooking on a wood-burning cook-
stove not that far from where she was sitting at a
crude kitchen table, her wrists and ankles once again
bound.

She watched Guy putter about, amazed at his cooking skills when she knew that he had never lifted a
finger while living in the lap of luxury at his parents'
home. Zondra watched him turn the bacon in the large
skillet as he whistled contentedly, suddenly yelping in
pain when the grease spattered onto the tender flesh
of his hand.

Zondra's pulse raced as an idea formed inside her

brain. Grease. It was scalding hot! It would quickly disable a man if enough was spilled on him.

Or splashed purposely, she thought to herself, smiling.

She gazed at her tied wrists, then back at Guy again. She *must* get him to remove the ropes from both her wrists and ankles for her to be able to make her move toward freedom. She was so close to the stove she could make a lunge for the handle of the skillet before he realized what she was doing.

If she could get to it and splash the grease on his face, he would be in too much pain, perhaps even too blinded, to go after her.

She *must* get free so that she could return to Lone Eagle. By now he had to know that she was gone. If he thought that she had left because she wanted to, he would most surely believe that everything she had said to him, that she loved him and wanted to stay with him forever, was a lie.

"Sure as hell didn't mean for that old Indian to get killed last night," Guy said, sending Zondra a downcast glance. "Damn it all to hell, all I wanted to do was get a squaw. I sure as hell didn't want to kill anyone in the process."

"Old . . . Indian . . . ?" Zondra asked guardedly, her heart sinking, guessing what he meant. In the process of abducting her, Guy and Billy must have killed some old person in the Crow village.

"What old Indian?" she quickly repeated.

Guy sat down across the table from her. He toyed with a salt shaker, jumping with a start when he accidentally knocked it over, spilling salt in all directions.

"Guy, who did you kill?" Zondra prompted, although she was afraid to know. It could have been anyone. Perhaps Singing Star? Or Mad Buffalo? Or any old person who might have come across Guy and Billy making the long slit down the back of Lone Eagle's lodge. His or her life would have been quickly snuffed out to silence them.

"Damn it, Zondra, I think it might have been the young chief's father," Guy said, his eyes wavering as he blurted this out to her. "You see, we came to steal a woman away from the Crow, with plans of making it look like Father did it so we could get him in trouble with the Crow. We thought the best way to rile the Crow was to steal the chief's wife. Not knowing that much about the Crow, or who lived where in the village, or even if the young chief was married, we saw the two larger tepees and surmised the young chief lived in one of them."

"You're saying that you chose the wrong one first," Zondra said, paling, as in her mind's eye she saw the fiends entering the back of Mad Buffalo's lodge, soon discovering the mistake they had made.

"Yes, and the old man woke up and discovered us there," Guy said, shakily taking a breath. "Billy slammed his knife in the old man's chest before I could stop him."

"No," Zondra said, swallowing hard as she fought the urge to cry. "He didn't kill Mad Buffalo! He was such a kind man."

Then another thought came to her that made her heart skip a beat. "There was an old lady sleeping in Mad Buffalo's tepee," she said warily. "Please don't tell me that Billy killed her also."

"Her life was spared, but only because she didn't wake up and witness what was going on," Guy said, envisioning the old lady lying there, still peacefully asleep when they fled the lodge.

"I don't understand the logic in any of this," Zondra

said, sighing heavily. "How on earth did you think stealing a Crow woman could end up being blamed on Father?"

As Guy got up and went back to the sizzling bacon, lifting one strip and then another out of the skillet with a fork, placing them on a plate, he tried to explain things to her.

Then he turned and faced her, a crooked smile on his face. "And that's not all we did to make the Crow think Father was responsible," he said, chuckling. "We put Crow horses in Father's herd to make the Crow believe Father stole them."

"How could you hate him so much?" Zondra gasped, remembering her father coming to the Crow village with the horses and his explanation about finding them with his.

She knew that Lone Eagle hadn't altogether believed him. She could hardly wait to tell him the truth about everything that had happened . . . especially who killed his father!

Guy went to the back of the lodge and brought out a saddlebag. He unfastened it, turned it upside down, and dumped its contents on the table for Zondra to see. She gasped as the lamplight picked up the shine of the diamonds from the bracelets and necklaces glittering before her eyes.

She couldn't believe the amount of money that lay on the table beside the jewelry. "Where on earth did you get all this?" she questioned. Her breath was almost knocked from her when he answered.

"From Father's safe," Guy said, shrugging.

"Father's safe?" Zondra softly breathed out, totally stunned by Guy's vindictiveness. She now knew how deeply he hated their father. To have joined an outlaw gang to get back at their father was proof enough. But to steal? To kill?

She dreaded even more what he had planned for her, for *she* had caused him to get whippings from his father. Because of that, he surely hated her even more than their father. She *had* to get free, or suffer the worst of consequences from a brother whose heart was dark with the need for revenge.

"Guy, I'm so hungry," Zondra said as he swept the jewels and money back into the saddlebag. For now she had to put all he had told her out of her mind and concentrate on getting free. She felt lucky that he had been afraid enough of Billy to have obeyed him and left her untouched until he and his gang returned. She didn't even want to think about the gang rape that Billy had in mind!

"You'll live," Guy said sarcastically as he carried the bag to the back of the cabin and tossed it with several others. "At least you're no longer among the savages. How could you have stayed in that savage's tepee? Now that I know you were there because you wanted to be, it makes me want to puke."

He came back and bent low over her, laughing sarcastically. "But now you're with me and I'll allow you to live a while longer," he said darkly. "After Billy and the guys get back and we all get through with you, you'll beg to be dead."

Trying not to envision the horror of how it would be if she didn't get out of there before Billy and his men returned, Zondra persisted in making Guy believe that she was truly starving.

The truth was that food was the last thing on her mind. Even if she *did* eat, she knew she would choke, for after all that Guy had said, especially about how

Mad Buffalo had died so needlessly, the very thought of food made her sick to her stomach.

"Please, Guy?" Zondra said, purposely whining, watching his eyes waver as he heard the pleading in her voice. Never had she asked him for anything! She had always avoided him as much as possible.

The softness of her voice, the pleading in her eyes, went straight to Guy's heart, for there was no denying that no matter how much he tried to hate this half sister of his, in truth he had always had a crush on her and would have gone to great lengths to have her as his mistress. He would have built her a cottage far away from the ranch so they could meet there like his father met with Zondra's mother.

But it had been evident for some time how much Zondra loathed Guy; he had no choice but to return the feeling.

That day he'd almost raped her, it had been to put her in her place, but not because her mother was a darkie. It was because Zondra had treated him like dirt since the day they had realized they were blood kin.

"Guy?" Zondra persisted, noticing that she had struck a nerve in him, for he was suddenly quiet. In his eyes there was a softness that she hadn't seen for many years. She had known since the time she started budding into a young woman, with breasts evident beneath the bodices of her plain cotton dresses, that he desired her as a man desired a woman, forgetting that she was his half sister.

Today she saw that same look he'd cast her way the first time he had seen her as an object of desire.

Afraid of that look, seeing something else in the depths of his eyes that she had seen when whites watched the Negro women working in the fields, she had fled from him that day and had avoided him as best she could ever since.

"Guy, please feed me before the others return," Zondra asked softly. "You know that once they return, they'll have other things on their mind than me eating. Please, Guy? The bacon smells so good. I'd even like one of those eggs lying there in the bowl if you could be so kind as to—"

"Oh, all right," Guy said, going to the stove. "I'll give you a decent breakfast." He chuckled and gave her a sly look. "That's what they do in jail, don't they? Feed the prisoners before hanging them?"

"If that's the way you want to look at it, yes, Guy, the law has the decency to feed those they are about to kill," Zondra said, shivering to have to think about such things.

"I'd better hurry," Guy said, flashing a look toward the door. "I expect them home early today. They'll not forget you're here. I imagine it's been a long spell between women for most of them."

Seeing that Guy was still planning on being a part of the gang rape, Zondra's hate for him strengthened. She glanced down at her tied wrists, then held her similarly bound ankles out in front of her.

She *must* make him understand how important it was to be able to eat while untied, at least this last time before she suffered the injustice and humiliation of rape. If he had any feelings for her at all left inside his heart . . .

Guy broke several eggs into the hot, spattering grease. "Didn't know I was a cook, did you?" he said, pride in his eyes as he looked over at Zondra. "Just wait until you eat my bacon and eggs. I'll eat with you. It might be a while before both you and I'll get the chance to eat again."

Zondra scarcely breathed as she watched Guy flip the eggs over and then slide them onto the plate alongside the bacon.

When he brought the heaping platter of food over to the table and set a plate and fork before Zondra, and then poured two cups of coffee, placing one of the filled cups beside her plate, she waited for him to realize that she couldn't eat while her hands were tied.

He had been in his chair for only a moment when he looked over at her and saw her sitting so quietly, the platter of food sitting between them untouched.

"Well, aren't you going to eat?" Guy asked, raising his eyebrows. "Lord, Zondra, all that complaining and you're now refusing to eat?"

"How can I?" Zondra murmured, lifting her shackled hands for him to see.

"Damn it, I forgot," Guy said, scooting his chair back, coming around the table to Zondra.

"Please release my ankles, too, Guy," Zondra asked in a voice she made soft and pleading. "My feet are numb. I think the ropes have cut off the circulation. Please, Guy, remove the ropes at least until after I've eaten. Then tie me back up before the outlaws return. I wouldn't want you to get in trouble."

Guy leaned down and gazed directly into her eyes. "I can't believe that," he said dryly. "That you don't want me to get into trouble with the outlaws. Zondra, you'd love to see me hanging from a rope now, wouldn't you?"

"Guy, I don't know what has made you hate me so much, but should I ever get the chance, I'd try to make things different between us," Zondra said, the lie slipping across her lips so easily, it almost even fooled her. "It's all because of Father . . . how he made things so different between us. Guy, please let's be friends. I'll do anything I can to make things up to you."

Guy's face became flushed with an anxious heat. His eyes filled with hope. "Zondra, you aren't just saying those things to fool me?" he asked throatily. "If you truly can forgive me for what I've done, can we be friends? I'd do anything for you, Zondra. If you'd let me, I'd take you far away from this life that's been so hard on you. In another town, who'd know you had a colored mammy? Who'd know we were kin? It's only half and half, Zondra, half black and half white. Can you forget? I'd not touch you until you said you were ready. Zondra, I've loved you for so long. Truly loved you."

"I . . . didn't . . . know," Zondra said, her eyes widening, really having never known that he felt this way about her. She was so stunned, she almost forgot her plan of how she would regain her freedom today.

"If I released you, would you leave with me now, Zondra, and go somewhere and make a fresh start together?" Guy asked huskily. "You saw the diamonds and the money. There's enough there to pay for our transportation clean across the country. When we find a place we like, I'll build you a beautiful home. I'll give you everything you were denied as a slave, Zondra. Everything."

"Truly?" Zondra murmured, so stunned by all of this she found it hard to think clearly. Of course she didn't love him and never could. It was just how much he was ready to offer her in order to have her that was so unreal!

But her reverie was abruptly brought to an end when he suddenly covered her mouth with a wet, slobbering kiss, his hands in a frenzy on her breasts.

She knew by this that he was still the despicable,

loathsome creature she had always known him to be. It was hard, but after he drew away from her she tried not to show the loathing in her eyes, or allow him to hear it in her voice.

"Guy, I truly believe I can learn to love you," she said softly, fighting back the urge to spit in his face. "Please release me. I'm still . . . so . . . hungry."

She held her feet out to him. "Oh, please, first release my feet," she begged. "The circulation. Guy, if it's cut off for much longer I'll . . ."

She didn't have to finish what she was saying. She held her breath as he bent to a knee and untied the ropes at her ankles and tossed them aside.

She forced a smile when he stood up and hurriedly undid the ropes at her wrists.

As soon as they fell away from her she raised her knee and jammed it hard into his groin.

Crying out with pain, grabbing at his injured private parts, holding himself with both hands, Guy fell back away from her, giving her the room she needed to get to the stove.

Her pulse racing, so afraid he was going to reach out and stop her, yet relieved that he was still temporarily disabled, Zondra jumped to her feet and grabbed the skillet of hot grease from the stove.

Without any further thought of the damage she was inflicting on him when she did it, truly not caring, she tossed the hot grease from the pan into his face.

Guy screamed in shock and agony, and she went pale when she realized that so much of the grease landed in his eyes. She might have just blinded him.

Zondra stared at him for a moment longer, then ran from the cabin, panting.

Grabbing the first saddled horse that she came to, she swung herself into the saddle and rode off in a hard gallop. To get to the Crow village she knew that she must ride past her father's ranch, but she would take the chance of being spotted. She must get to the village and tell Lone Eagle who had killed his father. She also wanted to be by his side in his time of heartbreak over having lost his father in such a hideous way.

As she thought of the grief he must be going through at this moment, tears came to her eyes.

"My beloved, I'm coming," she whispered, her hair flying in the wind as she leaned even lower over the horse in an effort to gain even more speed.

She watched for things around her, a cluster of trees, a valley, a familiar butte, to lead her back to her home, and then on to Lone Eagle's village. She had become acquainted with the lay of the land these past days, hopefully enough to get her where she desperately needed to be.

She sank her heels into the flanks of the horse, urging it on. She rode and rode, then began seeing more things that were familiar to her and knew that she was near her father's ranch. Her pulse raced to think that her father or some of his cowhands might spy her and try to stop her!

Chapter Twenty-nine

His broad, clear brow in sunlight glowed,
On burnished hooves his war-horse trode—

—ALFRED, LORD TENNYSON

Sitting tall in his saddle, his face black with ash, Lone Eagle drew a tight rein and brought his horse to a shuddering halt when he came in sight of Harrison's ranch.

"Surround the ranch!" he shouted at his warriors. "Now! Let no white man get past you! Kill if you must!"

In force, crying the war cry and waving their rifles over their heads, Lone Eagle and his warriors rode onward, some moving out away from Lone Eagle to his right, others to his left, until the whole ranch was surrounded.

Harrison was awakened by the war cries and the thundering hoofbeats approaching his house. When he leapt from the bed and looked from the window, he was puzzled as to why the Indians were arriving in such force, their faces painted, their cries of war like arrows piercing his heart.

He knew, however, that this was not the time to stop and ponder anything, not with this many Indians apparently on the warpath.

"Harrison, I'm so afraid," Sylvia cried, running after him out into the corridor.

"Sylvia, I don't know why, but I do know that in a matter of moments you and I, and everyone else at the ranch, could be dead," Harrison said, racing down the winding staircase in his monogrammed satin pajamas. "Sylvia, get the children. Take them and hide in the cellar. I knew something like this might happen in Indian country."

"But, Harrison, there are spiders and . . . and . . . all sorts of things down there," Sylvia cried down at him from the second-floor landing.

"God, woman, would you rather be spider-bit or riddled with Indian arrows like a pincushion?" Harrison shouted at her over his shoulder.

He grabbed his rifle and headed for the back door. He intended to go to the bunkhouse to join his men in fighting off the Indians as best they could. He thought unhappily of Ada, who was so alone at a time like this.

Harrison's heart pounded in his chest as he rushed out the back door. He stopped dead in his tracks on the porch when Lone Eagle and his men rode up and came to a halt only inches away from him.

His eyes locked with Lone Eagle's, Harrison dropped his rifle and waited to be shot, wondering if he would take his dying breath not knowing why.

A voice crying Harrison's name—and then Lone Eagle's—made Harrison turn to stare in wonder. It was Zondra! He could see her riding toward the house. He was stunned to see her there, when he had spent sleepless nights wondering where she was, or if she was still alive. And suddenly there she was. What had brought her home?

As Zondra had ridden past her father's house and seen his ranch surrounded by Crow Indians, her heart had seemed to stop. Afraid of what it meant, she had made a quick turn toward the house. She saw Lone Eagle was holding her father at bay with his rifle. His face was covered with something black. It made him look vicious, as though he had painted it that way for warring.

Lone Eagle turned and watched Zondra. Now he knew that she had not been taken by this white man and imprisoned in his house. She had come from somewhere else, which meant that someone other than her father had abducted her and killed his father!

"Lone Eagle," Zondra said, breathing hard as she reined in beside him.

Everyone was quiet as she breathlessly explained where she had been, with whom, and why.

"I thought your father was responsible," Lone Eagle then said, his voice drawn.

"No! No!" Zondra insisted. "He isn't. It was all my half brother's plan. Everything bad that has happened to both our families lately was because of Guy. He is a man with a twisted mind. He's *mad*."

Harrison stepped closer to Zondra. Their eyes met and held.

Then she heard a voice so dear and precious to her, tears sprang into her eyes. Turning in the saddle, she watched her mother run from her slave cabin toward her. Zondra rode to her, dismounted, and hugged her close.

Lone Eagle watched Zondra with the black woman; he had heard her call her Mother, and he was confused by it. He watched as they talked and hugged and talked some more. "Mama, I can't stay," Zondra murmured, gently wiping tears from her mother's cheeks with the palms of her hands. "I must return with Lone Eagle. His father was killed. I must be with Lone Eagle as he goes through his mourning period . . . and the funeral. I plan to marry him, Mama. He is my soul mate, my intended. It was fate that brought us together. It was our destiny to meet and marry."

"Come and talk to me more about it later, Zondra," Ada said, a sob lodging in her throat. "I want to know everything. I'm so happy for you."

"I couldn't be any happier," Zondra said, then hugged her again before mounting her horse and going to Lone Eagle.

"Let us go home," Lone Eagle said, reaching a gentle hand to Zondra's cheek.

"Yes, home," Zondra said, ignoring her father's loud gasp behind her as she rode off with Lone Eagle at her side, the warriors following dutifully behind their young chief.

Never had she been as proud to be with anyone as she was to be with Lone Eagle. She was also proud to have reached him before he had done something he would have regretted. He was free now to return home and prepare his father for burial. He was free to mourn for him. And he had Zondra there to help him through all of this.

Oh, how she loved him. With all of her heart she loved him. She would do anything for him.

She glanced over at him, wondering if he was ever going to tell her that she must call him her lord.

She hoped not. She still wasn't willing to do that for anyone!

And as for her brother Guy, he and the outlaws would pay for what they had done. Tonight had proved just how determined Lone Eagle was to have his vengeance.

Harrison stared at Zondra as she rode away from him, then forced himself to look away from her. His time of interfering in his lovely daughter's life was truly over. It was evident that she was with the Indian because she wanted to be, not because she'd been forced.

He had to wonder when it changed between his daughter and the Indian chief, when she became more than a captive to him, for surely she was with him at first as his prisoner.

He had to believe that she'd been there both times he had gone to the village. It gave him a strange feeling in the pit of his stomach to envision Zondra there, hiding from him. He knew now just how much he had wronged her, but it was too late to think about that. He had lost her forever.

He thought then of Guy, and what his son had done against him. He had robbed him. He had stolen Crow horses and mingled them with his father's to make it look as though he had stolen them, in order to bring the wrath of the Crow down on him.

He had also gone into the Crow village and killed an elderly man, as well as stolen a woman, who just happened to be Zondra, in a plot to turn the Crow on his father.

"And he almost succeeded," Harrison whispered to himself.

How could he have raised a son who hated him this much? he despaired. From the beginning there had been something lacking in the relationship between him and Guy. He had just never figured out how, or what, to improve on it. When he had tried, Guy just disappointed him again.

As he saw it now, Guy was no longer his son. However the Crow chose to make him pay for what he'd done, so be it.

Harrison and Ada exchanged glances, then they both turned and went their separate ways . . . she to her small, ugly cabin, he to his mansion.

Chapter Thirty

It's all I have to bring today,
This, and my heart beside,
This, and my heart, and all the fields,
And all the meadows wide!

                                        —EMILY DICKINSON

When Billy and the other outlaws returned to their hideout, they found Guy sprawled across one of the beds, moaning with pain. When Billy stepped closer, he saw the red, raw blisters on Guy's face. His eyes were swollen shut.

Then Billy quickly became aware of something else. As he swept his gaze around the cabin, he saw that Zondra was gone. He frowned down at the ropes on the floor, then turned an angry glare back at Guy.

"You son of a bitch," Billy hissed. "You let 'er get away. How could you have allowed it?"

"Don't you see my face?" Guy said, his voice edged with pain. "She got the best of me, Billy. She threw hot grease on my face! Go for a doctor. I don't think I can stand the pain much longer. Go! Please! Find a doctor and bring him back here with a painkiller!"

"I ain't goin' nowhere lookin' for a dumb-ass doctor, especially not for someone as stupid as you," Billy said, laughing. "You got yourself in that fix. Squirm your own way out of it."

"You just don't know how convincing she was," Guy groaned. "I thought I could trust her."

"Now you know you cain't believe anything a broad tells you," Billy said, grabbing a glass and pouring whiskey into it.

He went to Guy and tapped him on the shoulder. "Sit up," he said. "Down this rotgut. Maybe it'll help with the pain."

"Give me the whole damn bottle," Guy said, shivering as he pushed himself to a sitting position. He winced when he placed the glass to his mouth, the pain when it touched his burned, swollen lips almost making him black out.

After he drank several swallows, he reached out for Billy and found his arm. He clutched it. "We've got to get outta here," he said anxiously. "Zondra's going to lead the Crow back to the hideout. They'll come here with vengence eating at their guts over the death of the chief's father."

"Naw, they won't be comin' for a while," Billy said, pouring another glassful of whiskey for Guy. "They'll take time to bury the elderly man and go through their mourning rites. That could take several days, perhaps weeks. This will give me time to round up enough outlaws in the area to band together against a Crow attack."

"You can't be sure," Guy said, the sting of the whiskey warming his gut and finally easing the pain somewhat.

"Let me tell you, Guy, many Crow will die before Billy Feazel takes *his* last breath on this earth," Billy said darkly.

"Please, Billy, let's leave," Guy said, his voice breaking. "Let's find a place to hide until this all blows over."

"Guy, you're even dumber than I thought," Billy said, slamming the half-emptied bottle on the table. "Don't you know that there's no place *to* hide from the Crow now that they have hate in their hearts? No. We won't hide. I'll not die a coward's death."

"Why on earth did you kill him?" Guy whined, slowly lying back down on the bed. "You should've known they'd find out who did it."

Billy frowned down at Guy, then went outside and lit a cigarette and smoked it as he slowly surveyed the land around him. He had slipped up this time. He truly had slipped up. This time he and his whole gang might die.

Chapter Thirty-one

O! how nigh was night to thy fair morning!

—John Keats

Zondra sat solemnly beside Lone Eagle as he prepared his father for the hereafter, having begun by placing his father's feather fan in his right hand, then resting both hands over his heart.

Zondra had sat by, eyes wide, watching Lone Eagle paint his father's body with vermilion and the other colors of a great chief.

She had sat there as Lone Eagle meticulously dressed his father in his best clothes.

Earlier she had watched him cut away a part of his father's tepee covering, and now saw why he'd done it. He was wrapping Mad Buffalo in the yellow part of the tepee cover she now knew was called the *acde-cire*.

His father's body totally wrapped now, Lone Eagle twined buffalo sinew around him to secure the *acde-cire* before taking him to his burial place.

"It is time," Lone Eagle said thickly as he turned and gazed with sad eyes down at Zondra, his face blackened with ash for mourning.

He wore only a breechclout and moccasins.

His hair hung long and lustrous to the mats on the lodge flooring.

"Go and get those who are waiting to help carry my father's wrapped body from the lodge," Lone Eagle said solemnly.

Tears welled up in Zondra's eyes to see Lone Eagle so devastated. But he was so brave that he never lost his composure.

She rose to her feet, gave him a warm, reassuring hug, then left the lodge, returning soon with three warriors who were also painted with colors of mourning.

She stepped aside as they lifted Mad Buffalo's wrapped body and carried him out of an opening at the back of the lodge much wider than the slit that had been made there by Guy and Billy Feazel just prior to killing Mad Buffalo.

Earlier Lone Eagle had explained to her that a corpse was carried out from wherever the last breath of the deceased had been drawn, and that a corpse was never taken out of the lodge's regular entrance or someone else who lived there would die soon after. That would be Singing Star.

Solemnly, tears streaming from her eyes, Zondra followed Lone Eagle from the lodge.

When she stepped outside, she found all the people of the village standing in a large circle. They had been waiting for the body to be brought from the lodge. Their mourning for Mad Buffalo had been continuous since they discovered that he had died.

The wails had softened to a sort of rippling song that was repeated over and over again, building in strength now, as Mad Buffalo's body began its last journey on earth. Lone Eagle and his warriors slowly carried the old man toward his final resting place.

Zondra had been with Lone Eagle when he had gone into the forest and prepared a tepee for his father. He had explained to Zondra that a great chief was honored with a new lodge in which his body would be laid.

She had stood back and watched Lone Eagle put together a tepee smaller than what his father had lived in during his lifetime. This was a tepee only large enough for a four-pole platform and body.

Once the lodge was finished, looking all new and white against the dark shadows of the dense forest, Zondra had watched Lone Eagle paint the buffalo-skin covering with horizontal red stripes.

She could see it now as everyone walked in a solemn cadence through the hovering shadows of the forest. The sun was just beginning to lower behind the distant mountains, making it seem even more ominous among the trees where a dead man would be left to decay.

Zondra swallowed back the urge to cry again when they reached the small burial lodge. She hung back when Mad Buffalo's body disappeared inside the small tepee, to be placed on the four-pole platform that had been prepared for him.

Lone Eagle and the others stepped back out from the lodge. Tears brilliant in his eyes, Lone Eagle then tied the entrance flap closed. He was heartbroken to realize that he would only see his father again when they were joined as father and son in the hereafter.

Zondra knew that it would be hard for Lone Eagle to think about leaving his father there to slowly decompose along with the lodge.

She still stayed back from the others when Lone Eagle fell to his knees beside the lodge, lifted his arms heavenward, and cried out: "You are gone, Father!

We wish you farewell along your trail to the hereafter!"

Everyone was quiet and solemn as they turned and walked slowly back toward their village.

Besides Zondra, there was only one person left who still grieved openly. His head hung, and choking off sobs, Lone Eagle knelt on his knees beside the lodge.

Zondra went to him and knelt beside him. She slipped a hand over one of his, their fingers twining. "I wish I could be of more comfort to you in your time of sorrow," she murmured, a sob escaping from the depths of her soul. "Tell me what to do, Lone Eagle. Please tell me."

He turned tear-filled eyes toward her. "You are here," he said thickly. "That is my greatest comfort." He drew her quickly into his arms.

She held him and for a moment he forgot that he was a powerful chief who had been taught the art of restraint by his father. He clung to Zondra and cried hard, his tears soaking through the buckskin fabric of her dress, wetting her breasts, as he buried his face against her bosom.

"Let it all out," Zondra whispered, stroking her fingers through his thick, long hair. "My love, oh, my love." She closed her eyes and slowly rocked him back and forth against her.

In her heart she felt somewhat responsible for his father having been killed. Had she not been the cause of so much of Guy's rage, which had built up inside him through the years, just perhaps he would not have come to the Crow village with his sordid plan to get back at their father.

Yet she knew that if anyone was responsible, it was their father. Had he treated his son as a son, instead of a thing to be used and ordered around, surely Guy would not have grown up with such bitterness in his heart.

He would not have wanted to make Zondra pay for the sins of his father.

Nor Mad Buffalo . . . , she thought sadly to herself.

"Let's go home," she whispered, gently framing Lone Eagle's face between her hands, lifting his chin gently so that they could look into each other's eyes.

"Yes, home," Lone Eagle choked out. He took her by the hand. Together they rose from the ground.

They took one more long, last look at the lodge, the shadows building behind it as the shroud of darkness crept more deeply into the forest.

Holding Zondra closely at his side, his arm around her waist, Lone Eagle walked slowly from the dark forest into the village.

Zondra noticed that everyone but those who were dismantling Mad Buffalo's lodge were inside their lodges. And when she and Lone Eagle went inside his own tepee, Singing Star sat there beside the fire, her shoulders bent in sorrow.

Lone Eagle went to her. He sat down beside her and drew her into his arms.

"He is only gone from us for a little while," he tried to reassure her, as Singing Star clung to him, sobbing against his powerful bare chest. "We will all one day join him, and you know that time is such a fleeting thing. We will all be together again, Singing Star. We will laugh and sing. We will dance. We will embrace."

Zondra turned when she heard someone else enter the lodge. When she saw that it was White Bead, she went to her and embraced her.

"We are all sad, but tomorrow will bring smiles again, for when one makes it into another day, that

alone is cause for smiling," White Bead said, easing
from Zondra's arms.

She went to Singing Star and gently touched her
shoulder. "Come with me, Singing Star, and stay in
my lodge," she said softly. "Do for me what you did
for Chief Mad Buffalo. I would enjoy your company."

Her eyes eager, Singing Star looked quickly up at
White Bead. "I can cook your meals and carry your
wood?" she asked, her tears drying on her cheeks. "If
I cannot do for someone, I will die a useless old lady."

"No one ever sees you as useless," White Bead said,
bending to take one of Singing Star's hands. "When
you were young, did you not make a good wife to
your husband? Did you not bear two sons?"

"My husband joined his ancestors in the sky long
ago. My sons are gone," Singing Star said, lowering
her eyes. "They . . . deserted . . . their mother."

"They have followed the path of white men elsewhere, seeking dreams we hope they have found,"
White Bead said, helping Singing Star up from the
floor. "One day you will see them again."

"It will not be the same, seeing them in the hereafter, as it would be to see them here in flesh and
blood," Singing Star mumbled. "This old woman's
arms ache to hold her children again."

"But remember, Singing Star," White Bead said as
she led the elderly lady toward the entrance flap,
"they are not children any longer. They are grown
men who shun embraces from a mother."

"Lone Eagle is a grown man and he does not shun
my embraces," Singing Star argued softly.

Before stepping outside, White Bead smiled at Lone
Eagle and Zondra over her shoulder. "Sons behave
differently than chiefs toward a mother," she tried to
explain as Singing Star gazed up at her, listening.

"Sons feel as though they look weak if mothers coddle them. Chiefs never look weak."

"*Ahh*, yes, that is so." Singing Star nodded, looking over her shoulder at Lone Eagle. She smiled, then went on outside with White Bead.

"They are both so special," Zondra said. She sat down beside Lone Eagle and sighed as he slipped an arm around her waist and drew her close.

"No one is as special as my woman," Lone Eagle said, then stared into the fire, his thoughts on the emptiness inside his heart from knowing his father who would never be there for him again, to talk, to embrace, to love!

"Those who are responsible for my father's death must pay," he growled out. "And soon, my woman. Soon."

Zondra's insides tightened, for she knew that Lone Eagle would not rest until those who killed his father had paid in the worst way possible.

But to achieve vengeance, one must place oneself in danger! She shuddered at the thought of something happening to Lone Eagle. It just couldn't be! For the first time in her life she was at peace with herself, because she had found her soul mate. Surely fate hadn't drawn them together to know and love one another for such a short time!

She wanted a lifetime with him! Not just this brief encounter.

Chapter Thirty-two

*'Tis very sweet to look into the fair and open
face of Heaven—to breathe a prayer full in the
smile of the blue firmament.*

—JOHN KEATS

"Now is the time to seek vengeance for my father,
not later," Lone Eagle suddenly blurted out,
causing Zondra's breath to catch in her throat, knowing that he would be placing himself in danger sooner
than expected, and might even die seeking revenge in
the name of his departed father.

"You aren't going to wait until your mourning period is over?" Zondra choked out, afraid for him to
leave. She must be with him for a few more days
before he faced danger that might end his life. She
wanted to cling to him and hold him close to her heart
while she could.

Lone Eagle turned to Zondra and placed a gentle
hand on her cheek. "My woman, do you not see the
logic in what I must do?" he asked, his eyes searching
hers for understanding. "Those who needlessly killed
my father will not expect a retaliation for the crime
this soon. Those who know anything about the red
man know that when someone as beloved as a past
chief, as beloved as a *father*, dies, there is a mourning
period for the deceased, and it would be expected to

last several weeks. This time lapse would give the outlaws a chance to double the number of them awaiting
our arrival at their hideout. If enough outlaws come
together against the Crow, many of my warriors could
be killed in the battle."

His eyes narrowed into two points of fire. "Or the
mourning period, if observed, might give the outlaws
time to flee the country and the wrath of the Crow in
a cowardly way," he hissed out.

"Yes, they might," Zondra murmured. "But if they
don't leave, and they are caught off guard by you now,
the chances are that more of them would die than
your warriors."

"Yes, that is so," Lone Eagle said, nodding. "Lone
Eagle will not take the normal time for mourning as
is usual among my people when someone as important
and cherished as my father dies. Avenging my father's
death is more important than mourning. My father
would want it this way. He would not want his son
sitting idly by, his grief unbearable, his thoughts
clouded with sadness, while those who killed him
would be making plans to achieve more victories over
the Crow. Also, my father would understand that
fighting and killing the evil white men could help work
out his son's grief."

"I am so afraid for you," Zondra said, flinging herself into his arms.

He held her close. "Nothing will keep me from this
fight," he said hoarsely. "Especially not fear. Mine
or yours."

He held her gently away from him. "My face," he
said thickly. "I must have the mourning ash removed
so that before I leave with my warriors to seek vengeance, I can place fresh war paint there in its place."

"I shall wash your face for you," Zondra said, easing to her feet.

She went to the side of the lodge and got a wooden wash basin, then went to the buffalo hide pouch that hung just inside the door and poured fresh water from it into the basin.

After taking a soft doeskin cloth from the supplies of washcloths and towels, she went and knelt down before Lone Eagle and gently, lovingly washed his face free of the black ash until all outward signs of mourning were gone.

After she took the basin of water and dumped it outside behind the tepee, she went back in expecting Lone Eagle to be choosing the weapons he would take with him for the battle. Instead she found him undressed and reaching his arms out for her.

"This is the last time, for a while, that you and I will have private time together," he said, walking toward her. "I must take memories of our moments together into battle with me."

When he reached her he took the wooden basin from her and set it aside, then lifted her into his arms and carried her to his bed of blankets and pelts at the back of the lodge.

Lone Eagle slowly, reverently removed Zondra's buckskin dress and moccasins, then pressed her down onto the bed with his body, the touch of her soft flesh like rose petals against his.

As he gave her a long, deep kiss, he gently nudged her legs apart with a knee, her soft folds opening like a flower opens to the beckoning sun. He shivered with ecstasy as her warmth surrounded his throbbing manhood. He groaned with pleasure as he moved within her, thrusting powerfully.

Zondra responded in kind, her hips moving with

his. She tried not to think of what the next hours might bring. She forced thoughts of warring from her mind and allowed herself to become lost in the soft, wondrous world of ecstasy that came with making love with her beloved.

When he slid his lips down and his tongue flicked across her nipples, Zondra's breath quickened and delicious shivers of rapture raced up and down her spine.

She moaned throatily when his mouth swept lower as he moved gently from within her and knelt beside her, his hands and mouth everywhere, teasing, taunting, arousing her to an almost mindless bliss.

And when his tongue went where her heartbeats seemed centered, where the flowering nub of her womanhood throbbed with need, she sucked in a breath of almost unbearable ecstasy.

She closed her eyes as his tongue flicked across her throbbing center, and then he sucked it as though it were another nipple grown taut with a life of its own.

The warm wetness of tongue, the wondrous spiraling of rapture were so overwhelming to Zondra, she had to fight against going over the edge into total ecstasy. She wanted to prolong it, to savor it. . . .

Sensing that Zondra was nearing the point of no return, and wanting to ride that same wave of rapture with her, Lone Eagle again rose over her and made one deep thrust that threatened to bring them both the wild, exuberant passion they sought.

But wanting more, groaning huskily, Lone Eagle anchored Zondra fiercely still against him as he continued to dive deeply into her with his throbbing hardness, her body responding as she lifted her hips to meet his every thrust with an eagerness of her own.

His mouth hot and urgent, he kissed her, his tongue surging between her lips. As one of his hands slid between them, Zondra sucked in a wild breath of pleasure as he cupped a breast, his eager fingers kneading.

Feeling himself ready to spill his seed inside Zondra, Lone Eagle's body tightened. He slowed his pace within her, then made one last, deep plunge and brought them both to wondrous heights of bliss.

Breathing hard, his pulse racing, his body trembling, Lone Eagle rolled away from Zondra. He stretched out on his back, his eyes closed as his heartbeat slowed to something more normal.

Zondra was as breathless, yet she didn't want to say good-bye, and she knew that was surely only moments away. She caressed Lone Eagle's muscled chest with her fingertips, then reached up and brushed a soft kiss across his lips.

Her eyes closed in ecstasy when one of his hands swept over her sensual center, his middle finger sliding easily into her wet, hot, soft folds. She sighed throatily as he moved his finger inside her, his fingertips brushing against the most tender part of her, threatening to send her into another mindless moment of pleasure.

"I wish we could lie here like this all night," she whispered, scarcely recognizing her voice, it was so husky with passion.

As Lone Eagle turned on his side and faced her, she turned to him and pressed her breasts against his chest. His finger still moved within her, bringing her closer . . . closer . . .

Suddenly her whole body became engulfed by wondrous spasms of joyous bliss, her mouth eager as his lips came to hers in a frenzied kiss. She gasped with intense ecstasy as he pushed himself into her again and began his rhythmic strokes, until they again shivered and quaked against the other, the pleasure never ending between them.

But this time he pulled totally away from her and left the bed. As he went to the pouch of water and poured some in his hands with which to wash his private parts, Zondra lay there, watching him.

She was breathless from being loved so intensely tonight. It was as though they both sensed it might be their last time together this way. Zondra was frightened when she allowed herself to think of where he was headed when he left his lodge, and why.

"I hope the outlaws are far gone by now," Zondra blurted out, moving from the bed to draw her dress over her head.

"They cannot have yet gone far," Lone Eagle said, slipping into his breechclout. "Not far enough to elude the Crow!"

He went to her and, placing an arm around her waist, drew her against him. "I must leave you now," he said, his eyes serious.

"So soon?" Zondra gasped. "You are leaving now, this very minute, to gather your men together for warring?"

"No," he said.

"Then . . . where . . . ?" she stammered out.

"I go to commune with the Great Mystery before the fight that comes tomorrow," he said, his voice drawn. "I must go and pray for guidance as I lead my warriors into battle against the evil white men."

"Can I go with you?" Zondra murmured, wanting so badly to be with him every moment that she could before he left her, perhaps for the very last time.

"A chief's praying must be done in private," he said softly. "You do understand, do you not?"

"Yes, I understand," Zondra said, swallowing hard. "How long will you be gone? Where are you going to pray?"

"I will be at my private prayer place for as long as it takes for me to feel the presence of the Great Mystery, even my father's spirit," he said seriously. "You have your own God. You might pray to yours as I pray to mine for my people's victory tomorrow against evil brought into our camp by whites."

"Yes, I shall pray," Zondra said, flinging herself into his arms and holding him one more time before he left. "I will pray for so many things, my love. For your victory, for your safe return home, and for our future together."

"Those, too, will be among my many prayers," Lone Eagle said, easing away from her.

He went to his robes and blankets and chose a robe that once was his father's. It had been made from many mink pelts by Lone Eagle's precious mother's delicate hands especially for her husband.

With the mink robe wrapped around his shoulders, he gave Zondra one last kiss, then left the lodge.

She sat beside the lodge fire, and Ralph cuddled onto her lap, purring.

Lone Eagle went far into the forest, to his special place, where a hill rose above the highest tips of the trees so that he freely saw the sky all around him.

He sat down and listened to wolves howling in the distance while he relived the precious moments of his life with his father, from Lone Eagle's childhood until the night his father died, and along with him, a corner of the young chief's heart.

He could feel his father's presence as he began praying for solace in his time of sorrow, and for the strength and power that he needed to achieve the vengeance he sought.

As eagles soared overhead, and as the wind spoke to him in gentle whispers, and as he saw white buffalo in the shapes of the white clouds overhead, he knew that all would be well with him soon, for his *Ah-badt-deadt-deah,* Great Mystery, and his father's spirit had just blessed him.

"Things will soon be as things should be again," he whispered as tears spilled from his eyes. "And, Father, oh, Father, my love for you . . . my devotion to you . . . shall never, never die!"

Chapter Thirty-three

As when a cloud the golden moon doth veil,
Its sides are tinged with a resplendent glow,
Through the dark robe oft amber rays prevail
And like fair veins in sable marble flow.

—JOHN KEATS

Zondra watched Lone Eagle preparing himself for warring. It seemed only moments ago that she had washed his face free of black ash, and now he was covering it with war paint.

"I'll be so glad when this is all behind us and we can live normal lives," Zondra murmured as Lone Eagle, his face now fully painted with warring symbols, went back to his cache of weapons. Dressed in a fringed buckskin outfit, he lashed his sheathed knife to his upper left thigh, then secured a quiver of arrows on his back.

He grabbed his huge bow, clutching it tightly as he turned and gazed at Zondra. "Tonight we will share blankets again," he said thickly. "The act of vengeance will be behind us, yet inside my heart it will not go away as quickly. It will lie there like a wound, paining me. Time is a healer, though, and will one day help me accept what is, and what should have been."

"I still can't help but feel responsible for what has happened," Zondra said, stifling a sob behind a hand. "Had I not . . ."

Wanting to ease her guilt, Lone Eagle quickly slid his bow over his left shoulder, then went to Zondra and drew her into his arms. "Never blame yourself for the sins of others whose twisted minds lead them into doing wrongful, ugly deeds," he said softly. "Were you not the focus of this madman who came and assisted in my father's death, someone else would have found their way into my village, killing a man with red skin for whatever reason some men do these things against men whose skin color does not match their own. It is something I have never understood . . . how people of one skin can so loathe someone else of another color. You have not been touched personally by such offensive behavior. You were born into a white world. White people are not chastised as are red-skinned people."

Those words leapt into Zondra's heart like someone splashing cold water on her face. She suddenly remembered she'd never explained her heritage to Lone Eagle—that she was not altogether white. So many things had gotten in the way of talking of such things to him that she had been able to forget it must eventually be said!

"You see me as white," Zondra murmured, gently drawing away from him. She reached for one of his hands and brought it to her face. "To you, my skin is white, yet . . ."

"Yet what?" Lone Eagle asked, forking an eyebrow. "What are you trying to say?"

"That I am not completely white," Zondra said guardedly.

Lone Eagle remembered Zondra embracing a black woman and calling her Mother, and his eyes swept over her, stopping at her black hair. He reached over and twined his fingers through her hair. "Your hair has always made me think you are perhaps a breed," he said. He gazed intently into her eyes. "As did your dark eyes. Yet you said that you are *not* a breed."

"When you asked me if I was a breed, don't you recall my saying that in a sense I *am*?" Zondra said, hating having come to the moment of truth, worrying about his reaction to her revelation.

In the white community, if someone was known to have a black mother or father, they were considered more black than white. And the fact that her father had placed her in the fields with the slaves whose skin was black proved to most who saw her exactly what her heritage must be—that she had a father and mother whose skin colors were different.

"*Ahh*, yes, I remember, but then you said nothing more about it," he said, again recalling her embracing the black woman. His thoughts had become so clouded with grief and problems, everything else had slipped from his mind.

"And I remember now that the woman you called your mother has a skin that differs from yours in color," he said, taking her hands, holding them as he saw the warring that was going on inside her. "Her skin was black."

"Yes, the woman you saw me embrace and call Mother *is* my mother," Zondra said softly. "It's just like it is when Indians and white people marry and have children. The color of the children's skin will always be in question until the child is born to them."

"Your mother is black-skinned and your father is white," Lone Eagle said softly.

"Yes, my mother, Ada, is black, and my father, Harrison, is white," Zondra said, swallowing hard. "But they are not married, nor do they share the same home. I am their link—along with the love they feel for one another."

"If they love each other, why do they not marry and live together?" Lone Eagle asked, getting more confused by the minute.

"Because my father has a wife," Zondra said, lowering her eyes.

Feeling her pain, her embarrassment, Lone Eagle placed a gentle finger beneath her chin and lifted it so that their eyes could meet and hold. "How . . . *why* . . . does a man marry a woman he does not love?" he asked, searching her eyes for answers. "Why does he place the woman he loves in a house that does not even compare with the lodge of a red man?"

"Because my mother was bought by my father at a slave auction," Zondra said, the words like poison as they crossed her lips. "She is a slave to him. As I am also a slave to my very own father."

"A . . . slave . . . ?" Lone Eagle said, gasping. "You are your own father's slave?"

"It's true and it pains me so to admit it," Zondra said, a sob catching in her throat. "He has never even allowed me to use his name. I am Zondra Poole to everyone. Not Zondra Lester."

Lone Eagle slid his arms around her and drew her gently into his embrace. "You are no longer anyone's slave," he said softly, being as gentle and understanding about this as Zondra had hoped he would be.

He brushed a soft kiss across her lips. "And you have a man who loves you and who will soon marry you," he said huskily.

"You have given me a new life," Zondra said, clinging to him. "You have given me hope for mankind. Until everyone realizes that skin color makes no difference, the world will be torn apart by prejudice."

She eased from his arms and gazed up at him. "Lone Eagle, in a sense I am no different from you," she murmured. "My having been born into slavery, and you, being a man with red skin, a man who is too often labeled a savage by ignorant white people, both of us shunned by the white community, aren't we both, you and I, captives in a world that is dominated by whites?"

He placed his hands on her shoulders. He frowned down at her. "I have never been anyone's captive nor are you anyone's captive or slave," he said firmly. "Always remember this, my woman. One's life is what a person makes it."

"I want nothing but you," Zondra said, flinging herself into his arms, clinging to him again.

They drew apart quickly when they became aware of the thunderous sound of many horses' hooves approaching the village.

"Lord," Zondra gasped, paling. She turned frightened eyes up at Lone Eagle. "What if it's the outlaws? What if they've had enough time to get other outlaws to join their cause and are arriving to attack the Crow village before you and your warriors can attack them? No doubt Guy told Billy Feazel that I could identify them and get them hung if the law catches up with them. He must have warned the outlaws that I know how to lead you to their hideout!"

Seeing this all could be possible, Lone Eagle went to his weapons and grabbed and loaded a rifle, then rushed back to the entrance flap. "Stay inside where it is safe," he said, giving her a look that made what he had said a command.

When Lone Eagle saw how his command had affected Zondra, who was visibly shaken and shocked by it, and recalling how her life up to now had been spent—in slavery, where she had been made to live under strict rules of slavery—he gave her a silent look of apology. He reached out and slid an arm around her waist and walked her outside with him.

Just as they got outside he saw who it was arriving on horseback, now stopped at the very outskirts of his village, his warriors holding them at bay with their rifles.

"It's Indians, not outlaws," Zondra gasped out, aware suddenly of how shallowly Lone Eagle was breathing as he stared with narrowed, angry eyes at those who had arrived just outside their village.

"My clan enemy," Lone Eagle hissed out. "Cutting a lock of his hair has not stopped him from coming again to taunt and embarrass White Bead. I see now that it is going to take more than that warning to teach him a lesson. This time I will take his scalp!"

"His *scalp*?" Zondra said, shocked.

Lone Eagle walked away from her in determined steps toward the waiting enemy clan.

Zondra quickly caught up with him and walked beside him. "Is that Red Moon?" she asked, remembering now that was the name of the man whose hair had been cut to avenge something he had done to White Bead.

"Yes, that is Red Moon and he does not come alone this time," Lone Eagle spat out. "And he has made a mistake by coming now when my warriors are already prepared for warring inside their hearts! It would be so easy to take advantage of my warriors' seething anger and their painful grieving. All I would have to tell them is to fire at the enemy Crow and the enemy would finally be gone from all of our lives!"

"But you aren't going to do that, are you?" Zondra asked, gazing up at him anxiously.

"No, but I must warn them to leave quickly or I

can't be responsible for what my warriors will do against those who they have always seen as enemies," Lone Eagle said. He stopped when he came to Red Moon's horse, his enemy sitting stiffly in his saddle, his gaze not wavering as he looked down into Lone Eagle's angry eyes.

"Lone Eagle, word was brought to my people about your father's death," Red Moon was quick to say, since he felt endangered by Lone Eagle's obvious anger and the many guns aimed at him and his warriors. "I have come with my warriors to offer assistance in finding the ones responsible for your father's slaying."

There was an awkward moment of silence as disbelief leapt into Lone Eagle's eyes. He was stunned by the offer, wondering if it was sincere, when in his mind's eye he was recalling the very instant he had cut the lock of hair from Red Moon's scalp.

Lone Eagle saw now how Red Moon had brushed his hair in an unusual way so that the empty space where the lock had been removed was no longer visible to the naked eye . . . his shame hidden from the world.

Seeing that Lone Eagle was at a loss for words, perhaps finding it hard to believe the sincerity of Red Moon's offer, Red Moon again spoke to Lone Eagle. "Allow me to help in finding the men who came like ghosts at night into your village and killed a man loved by your people," he said softly.

Red Moon reached a hand of friendship out toward Lone Eagle. "Lone Eagle, accept my friendship," he said. "Is it not time that we forgot our hostilities . . . old and new? It should be now as it should have been those many years when feuding tore our clans apart. Lone Eagle, let me remind you that the word clan is *ac-ambare-axia,* a word meaning a lodge where there is driftwood, meaning that clansfolk should cling together as driftwood sometimes lodges at a particular spot in the river. Lone Eagle, your clan and mine should come together as one force against those men who are the scum of the white community."

Red Moon swallowed hard. "Lone Eagle," he continued, speaking in an even softer, more sincere tone, "I always admired Mad Buffalo. So did my father. And although it appeared as if my father and your father were the bitterest of enemies, there was always a mutual respect and admiration between the two powerful chiefs."

Lone Eagle weighed each of Red Moon's words in his heart. He had never seen Red Moon this humble and sincere, his hand still held out in a true gesture of friendship. And the fact that he had come today, seemingly touched deeply by the wrongful death of Mad Buffalo, made it hard for Lone Eagle not to believe him. No Crow would speak with a forked tongue to another Crow at a time such as this.

This alone made Lone Eagle believe that Red Moon had thought deep and hard about his decision to come today with offers that could bring two enemy clans together in friendship, to behave henceforth as one family of Crow instead of two.

Zondra's pulse raced as she gazed up at Lone Eagle. She could see that he was battling his feelings about this man who, up to today, had been his enemy. She had listened intently to what Red Moon had said, weighing each of his words, trying to find fault with them, finding in the end that they all seemed spoken with sincerity.

She waited breathlessly for Lone Eagle's decision, for everyone who witnessed this today knew that whatever he said would affect many lives in the future.

She prayed that he would see the good in what Red

Moon was trying to achieve today and accept his friendship. In the end, such a friendship would benefit them not only today, when they would be searching for outlaws, but in the future, when it might be necessary to pull together as one people to fight off the white cavalry, should the government decide that they would take possession of land that had been the Indians' since the beginning of time.

Zondra's eyes widened when Lone Eagle slowly lifted his right hand, then reached it out for Red Moon's, clasping it, the bond of friendship that quickly sealed, forged more strongly than some treaties that seemed so easily broken.

"In the name of my father, and yours, and for our people's benefit, both your clan and mine, I accept your offer of friendship today," Lone Eagle said, scarcely aware of someone coming to stand by his side as White Bead slipped up next to him, her eyes filled with tears of joy as she gazed up at Red Moon, whom she loved with all her heart and soul.

Now it would be possible for her to declare her love for him. She had lived her life as her people's prophet up till now but she wanted more out of life than that. She wanted a husband. She wanted children.

She was filled with joy when his eyes slid down and locked with hers. She recognized his hesitancy, for she knew that he must feel it was dangerous to pay her any attention at a time like this, when friendship was finally being achieved between enemies.

"You see the warring colors on my face, and on my warriors'," Lone Eagle said, drawing Red Moon's eyes back to him. "Had you arrived moments later, you would have come after the Buffalo Crow left to war with the enemy who downed my father. If you wish to join the fight, we will wait for you to color your faces for warring. Then we can ride together as one unit and down the enemy!"

Lone Eagle's hand stayed clasped with Red Moon's. "And when we return victorious, I will offer you my pipe of peace," he said warmly. "I will offer you and your men food and lodging for the night. We will join in the celebration of victory. We will join in the celebration of friendship!"

Red Moon's grip tightened. "All that you speak of will be done," he said confidently. "It is good to come together as one in friendship . . . as *brothers*."

Zondra was very aware of how happy Red Moon's offer of friendship made Lone Eagle. She had to wonder just how long the feud between them had been going on, when it was evident that they each had such fond feelings for the other.

And she was glad that Red Moon wasn't showing any harsh feelings toward her for being the woman of Lone Eagle's choice, even though her skin was white.

But Zondra could tell by the way Red Moon had glanced down at White Bead with deep emotion evident in the depths of his eyes that he still had feelings for her. It concerned Zondra that even though White Bead was a prophet and was unable to marry, and even though Red Moon had already suffered an embarrassment because of this woman, he still could not help but reveal his feelings for her in a mere glance!

Zondra was worried that that alone could tear asunder all that had been achieved today by Red Moon's offer of friendship . . . and Lone Eagle's acceptance of it.

She was afraid that old enemies could never be new, lasting friends!

Chapter Thirty-four

That I shall love always,
I offer thee
That love is life
And life hath immortality.

—EMILY DICKINSON

Zondra had used a stick to draw a map in the dirt to show the route Lone Eagle should take to the outlaws' hideout. She was choked with fear as she watched him ride from the village with the throngs of warriors, their faces painted, headbands holding their hair in place, and strips of shells and feathers woven into the manes of their horses.

Zondra and White Bead went silently back to Lone Eagle's lodge where Singing Star sat solemnly beside the lodge fire, the sadness in her eyes revealing how much she still mourned for Mad Buffalo. Her sorrow was twofold now as she awaited Mad Buffalo's son's return. If he should die, also . . .

"Singing Star, why don't you go to my lodge and lie down and rest?" White Bead asked as she knelt down beside Singing Star. She was feeling the elderly lady's pain, for White Bead had been filled with the same sadness over Chief Mad Buffalo's death, her heart troubled now over whether or not her chief and dear friend Lone Eagle would return alive.

She also had much fear in her heart for Red Moon.

It would not be fair if Red Moon died during the battle with whites just as he had made peace with the Buffalo Crow, opening the door for White Bead to finally be able to reveal her love for Red Moon to her people.

"Yes, I will go and rest in your lodge," Singing Star said, her voice low and sad.

Ralph went to Singing Star and leapt onto her lap before she rose from the soft cushion of blankets. This brought some sparkle to the older lady's eyes, and a slight smile fluttered quaveringly across her lips.

"If you wish, take Ralph with you," Zondra murmured. "She can be good company. The very sound of her gentle purring can ease one's pain."

"Yes, the small cat creature, who has rid our village of the dreaded mice, is, as I see it, a small prophet," Singing Star said, gently sweeping Ralph into her arms. She rose slowly to her feet and gazed at Zondra. "But I believe the small cat creature should have an appropriate name."

"If you wish, you can rename her," Zondra said, reaching over to stroke her cat's soft fur. "You could get used to being called something else, couldn't you, sweet cat?"

"I will soon give her a new name," Singing Star said. "Something feminine." She snuggled Ralph close to her bosom and left the tepee.

"She is such a sweet woman," White Bead said, sitting down beside Zondra near the fire. "But of late she shows her age more than before. Too much sadness does add to one's age."

"Yes, I know," Zondra murmured, sometimes feeling forty instead of eighteen.

Her eyes widened when she realized that, yes, she

was now eighteen. Having been so immersed in her new life, she had forgotten her eighteenth birthday.

But, she thought sadly, it would have been no different back at her father's ranch. She had never had a birthday cake, like her brothers and sisters who lived in the mansion. And there never were any gifts except for something her mother might sew for her out of rags she got from Zondra's father's servants.

"I realize how time does pass you by, and I have decided to seek from life what my heart desires. I may never have the chance again," White Bead said, drawing Zondra's eyes quickly to her.

"What does your heart desire?" Zondra asked softly, noticing how White Bead shyly lowered her eyes.

"It is a man I wish to have as my very own," White Bead said, still hiding her eyes from Zondra. "I wish to give up the title of prophet and become his wife."

Zondra recalled now how Red Moon and White Bead had exchanged glances; she'd wondered even then if there was more between them than White Bead resenting having been humiliated by Red Moon. Zondra believed that most of the conflict between them was the result of sheer frustration over not being free to marry!

"His . . . name . . . ?" Zondra dared to ask.

White Bead smiled shyly over at Zondra as their eyes met and held. "It is Red Moon," she murmured. "He has had my heart for many moons now, yet I could not speak of it because I was the prophet for my Buffalo clan."

"But, White Bead, I know about the hair that was cut from Red Moon's scalp," Zondra said. "How did you let it go that far if you loved him?"

"I had no choice but to keep my silence about the

vengeance my chief sought in my name," White Bead said, swallowing hard. "At that time I saw no hope of Red Moon and I ever getting together. I never thought that he would humble himself to come as he did and make friends with his enemy clansman. That he has speaks much of his character, do you not think? That he is someone to be admired?"

"Yes, and I'm so glad that he came and made peace with Lone Eagle," Zondra said, leaning forward to add a piece of wood to the slow-burning embers of the lodge fire. "It made me uneasy to know that Red Moon and his warriors could come at any time and make trouble for Lone Eagle. Now they can work together for the betterment of your people as a whole."

"Soon also to be your people," White Bead said, placing a gentle hand on Zondra's arm. "For do you not plan to marry my chief soon? Do you not plan to get heavy with his child soon? It is apparent that his love for you is strong. He will marry you, Zondra, if you say that you will marry him."

"Yes, I want nothing more than to be his wife and to bear him children," Zondra said, in her mind's eye seeing herself holding their first child, perhaps a son in his father's exact image.

"Being a wife and bearing children is also what I now want more than anything in this world," White Bead said, seeing herself making love with Red Moon for the first time. She knew that he would be as gentle as the butterflies that flit from flower to flower on a spring morning.

"I no longer wish to be labeled a spinster," White Bead quickly added. "Birthdays come and go too quickly for a woman who has no man to love her."

"But both of our men must first live through today's

battle," Zondra said, swallowing hard as she came back to the reality of the moment.

"The men will be victorious," White Bead said, nodding. "The Great Mystery will make it so."

Zondra looked toward the entrance flap. She wondered just how long she and White Bead would have to wait to see whether or not the men they loved would return to them.

Having pushed their horses into a hard gallop, much land was crossed in a short period of time, and finally Lone Eagle knew that he was almost at the outlaws' hideout.

He drew a tight rein and brought his horse to an abrupt halt. He turned and gazed at his men as Red Moon stopped and waited for his own men to rein in their mounts.

After all of the warriors had edged up close to their chiefs, Lone Eagle spoke for both himself and Red Moon, for while traveling toward the enemy's hideout, they had made their combined plans of attack.

"We will not attack in silence!" Lone Eagle shouted. "Nor will we wait until night falls. We will attack now in full force!"

He gestured with a hand toward a deep valley a short distance away. "As my woman's drawings showed us, in that valley stands the hideout," he said. "When we begin the fight, do not stop until all white men are dead! Today, if you desire to, you have my permission to take scalps! We will hang them at the door of my father's burial tepee!"

There were low rumbling chants as the warriors clasped their rifles and held them up over their heads, then waved them in the air.

"Ayyy!" Lone Eagle suddenly cried, waving his own

rifle over his head. "Now, warriors! Let us go and attack!"

All of the warriors, singing their cries of challenge, sent their horses into a gallop behind their chiefs toward the valley, where cedar trees clung to the sides of a bluff that rose high on one side of the deep stretch of land that the Crow now entered, and a forest of hardwoods stretched out on the other.

"Come, white men!" Lone Eagle cried at those who might be in the cabin that he spotted a short distance away. "Come! *Chien,* sons of dogs, find your deaths today!"

Suddenly, having heard the Crow approaching on their thundering steeds, and having had time to ready themselves for the fight, the outlaws began firing at the Indians from their hiding places among the trees.

Clever in battle, the Crow began firing into the trees, yelps of pain evidence that their arrows and bullets were finding targets.

The fight continued until there was a sudden silence. The outlaws who had not fled the rage of the Crow lay dead on the ground, with only a few Indians wounded, none mortally.

Slowly, victoriously, Lone Eagle and Red Moon rode through the bloody aftermath of the battle as their warriors dismounted their steeds and saw to their wounded brethren.

Lone Eagle had seen Guy only one time from a distance. That had been before Lone Eagle and Zondra had met and talked that first time when Lone Eagle had come to her in the forest.

It was on that day that he had seen the white man, whom he now knew was called Guy, at the mercy of a father who was unmercifully slicing his back open with a whip. All that Lone Eagle had seen was Guy's bloody back as the man crawled back into his house.

But his face? No, he had not gotten a good look at his face, so he did not know now whether or not Guy was among the dead white men who lay sprawled on the ground. They all looked the same to him, thickly whiskered, disheveled, dirty, and bloody.

Suddenly a lone blast of gunfire rang through the air from a thick cover of bushes. Lone Eagle's eyes widened and his body lurched with the impact as he felt the sting of a bullet entering his chest.

Red Moon looked at Lone Eagle with a puzzled dismay that soon turned to horror as he watched Lone Eagle clutch at the wound, then slide from his saddle to the ground, unconscious.

Another blast of gunfire rent the air. Red Moon heard the bullet whiz past his head, then turned just in time to see a man standing in the bushes, loading his rifle again to take another shot at him.

Realizing this white man, whose eyes were strangely swollen into blistered slits, had shot Lone Eagle, and had even shot at him, Red Moon took steady aim with his rifle and shot him before he had the chance to get another round of gunfire off at him.

When Red Moon's bullet entered just beneath Guy's heart, he dropped his firearm, clutched at his bloody chest, then fell face first to the ground.

But Guy wasn't dead. When he heard the Indian ride up and look down at him, Guy slowly rolled over and stared up at him.

"You shot Chief Lone Eagle!" Red Moon cried when he saw that the man was still alive. "You take away my friend!"

Guy's eyes widened in horror and he gasped as Red Moon knelt over him, the Indian's one hand now filled with Guy's hair, the other a knife. "Lord, no!" Guy cried, then took his last breath as Red Moon sliced his scalp from his head.

The scalp dangling from his left hand, Red Moon went to his horse. He tied Guy's scalp to the pommel of his saddle, then went to Lone Eagle and knelt beside him. He reached a hand to Lone Eagle's throat, relief rushing through him to know that Lone Eagle was still alive.

"Warriors!" he cried. "Make haste in constructing a travois for my friend. We must get Lone Eagle home!"

Lone Eagle awakened momentarily and smiled up at Red Moon, then slid back into the void of unconsciousness—but not before Red Moon heard a faint whisper of Zondra's name on his friend's lips.

Chapter Thirty-five

Now was she just before him as he sat,
And like a lowly lover down she kneels.

—WILLIAM SHAKESPEARE

Zondra and White Bead had fallen asleep beside the fire while awaiting their loved ones' return. Zondra was now awakened by the sound of many horses' hooves pounding in the distance. Her heart racing, she reached over and gently shook White Bead awake. "They're home," she said, pushing a blanket aside as she jumped to her feet.

White Bead hurried to her feet, too, but instead of going outside, she reached over and took one of Zondra's hands, stopping her.

"What's wrong?" Zondra asked, her eyebrows arching. "Let's go, White Bead. Let's greet them as they enter the village."

"Do you not notice the silence of their return?" White Bead said, her voice guarded and quiet as she gazed at Zondra.

"I hear the horses," Zondra replied, slipping her hand from White Bead's. "White Bead, I thought you were as anxious as I am about their return."

She searched White Bead's face, totally stunned by her change in mood. "White Bead, why are you acting so glum?" she asked, her voice shaking. "White Bead, you're frightening me."

"If our warriors' and chiefs' return home was a victorious one, there would be songs and shouts so that our people would hear and be glad along with them," White Bead said, swallowing hard. "If they are not victorious, or if someone of importance has been slain, there would be a strained silence such as you are now aware of upon their return."

Zondra's face drained of color. "What are you saying?" she asked, almost afraid to hear the answer.

"I am saying that someone we love might have been slain during the fight with the outlaws," White Bead said, looking with fear toward the closed entrance flap. "I . . . am . . . almost afraid to find out who."

Now that Zondra understood White Bead's strange behavior and hesitance, her heart skipped a beat. She hurried from the tepee and gazed intently at the approaching Crow warriors, her heart sinking when she didn't see Lone Eagle in the lead, riding beside Red Moon. Instead, she saw a travois with someone stretched out on it being dragged behind Lone Eagle's black mustang.

"No!" Zondra cried, tears flooding her eyes, for she knew that if Lone Eagle wasn't on his horse, and a travois was being dragged by his proud steed, the silence of the warriors' return was because of their fallen chief!

Blinded by tears, unaware of White Bead crying out to her in an attempt to stop her, Zondra ran through the crowd that grew as people came from their lodges to stare and gasp as they also realized that something had happened to their young chief.

When Zondra finally reached the warriors and saw Lone Eagle unconscious on the travois, blood on his chest, she had to fight off the urge to faint. She reached a hand out toward Red Moon. "Please stop," she cried. "Let me see him. Let me see Lone Eagle."

"We cannot stop just yet," Red Moon said, riding onward. "We must get him to his lodge so that Medicine Fox can come and care for him."

"I wish I knew of a white doctor who could come and see to Lone Eagle's wound," Zondra said, her eyes never leaving Lone Eagle as she walked beside the travois, watching his eyes, praying to herself that they would open and prove that he was alive.

"No white doctor is needed. The Crow medicine men are gifted with powers of healing," Red Moon said somberly as he glanced down at Lone Eagle, his heart aching when he saw that his friend was still unconscious. "Medicine Fox's healing powers were given to him in a vision. He can read spirit talk that is woven into dreams. It is through those dreams that he found knowledge of healing."

"Is Lone Eagle going to live?" Zondra asked, swallowing back a sob as she watched for signs of life behind her beloved's closed eyes, still seeing none.

She looked quickly up at Red Moon when he didn't answer her, now truly afraid that Lone Eagle might not survive his terrible chest wound.

White Bead came and placed a comforting arm around Zondra's waist. She walked with her beside the travois. "Lone Eagle is a strong man with a strong will," she murmured, unable to fight back the tears that were streaming from her eyes. "And knowing that you are awaiting him, a woman who wishes to bear his children, yes, he will come back to you."

White Bead looked around her at the grieving crowd. "He will come back to us all," she said, her voice breaking.

"Red Moon, what happened?" Zondra asked, feeling the need to know this now, for soon everyone would be too immersed in prayers for their loved ones to pay heed to one woman's questions.

Zondra had only just now seen how many more injured warriors were riding limply on their horses, their chief the only one placed on a travois. One glance told her that no one was as severely injured as Lone Eagle.

And, thank God, no one had died.

"It was an ambush," Red Moon said with regret and hatred. "The white men were prepared for our arrival."

"And . . . what . . . about *those* men? The outlaws?" Zondra asked, her thoughts going quickly to Guy. In her mind's eye she saw Guy hovering over her that day he almost succeeded in raping her. "Are the outlaws dead?" she rushed out. "All of them?"

"Some fled, but those who stayed behind and continued to fight the Crow are dead," Red Moon said solemnly. "Although they ambushed the Crow, they suffered the heavier casualties."

"Among those men was a man who . . . who . . . is my half brother," Zondra said guardedly, aware that the time for questions was almost over, for the horses were now at the far side of the village where Lone Eagle's large tepee awaited his arrival. "Do you know if . . ."

Her words seemed to stick in her throat as they arrived at Lone Eagle's lodge. Red Moon stopped his horse, then swung it around to face the rest of the warriors who were still approaching. It was then that Zondra could see the bloody scalp hanging from the pommel of Red Moon's saddle. Recognizing whose scalp it was caused a bitter bile to rush into Zondra's throat. She knew the color of Guy's hair well enough to know that it was his!

Realizing that seeing the scalp had caused Zondra's face to turn sheet-white, and knowing that she was ready to faint, White Bead quickly grabbed her and held her in her embrace.

Red Moon had also seen her reaction and knew she was aware of whose scalp he had claimed in battle. Red Moon knew by Zondra's reaction that it surely belonged to this man she had just called her half brother.

"The scalp was taken from the man who shot Lone Eagle and who wounded so many other Crow," Red Moon said, frowning down at Zondra. "The man whose eyes were strangely swollen and blistered will kill or wound no more Crow."

Recalling that she'd splashed the hot grease in Guy's face, knowing that his eyes had surely been affected by it, Zondra found it hard to believe that he could have seen well enough to do this terrible deed today against not only the man she loved, but all of his warriors.

She had thought that she had left him handicapped enough that she wouldn't have to worry about him for at least a little while.

She had thought that the hot grease had blinded him so that he would be incapable of causing her any more harm. Now she knew that she had been wrong not to take a gun and shoot him on the spot. She had left him alive to kill the man she loved!

"We must step aside now," White Bead murmured as she gently led Zondra away. "We must make room so that Lone Eagle can be taken into his lodge. I see Medicine Fox. He is coming. He will make Lone Eagle well again."

While all of the other wounded warriors were helped from their horses and taken to their lodges, Lone Eagle was carried from the travois into his tepee.

Many of the villagers had brought medicinal herbs to the medicine man, wanting to contribute to the shaman's efforts to make Lone Eagle well again. Then as chants began outside his lodge, his people's prayers reaching to the heavens to seek the Great Mystery's blessing, Zondra was made to stay outside Lone Eagle's tepee as Medicine Fox, an old man with gnarled fingers, dressed in skins of the white fox, went into her beloved's lodge.

It seemed an eternity before she was summoned by the old man. White Bead went inside with Zondra. Both knelt beside Lone Eagle's bed of blankets and fur pelts.

Zondra felt as though her heart was being torn from inside her as she gazed down at the man she loved and saw how lifelessly he lay there. A blanket covered him up to his chest, where the wound lay open with a poultice spread over it. His eyes were still closed.

Zondra stifled a sob behind her hand when she noticed how slow and labored Lone Eagle's breathing was.

"The bullet is removed and my medicine, a mixture of buffalo chips and herbs, lies within the wound, and over it," Medicine Fox said as he knelt on the other side of the bed from Zondra and White Bead. "*Leptotaenia-multifida,* the root called bear root because in the summer bears fatten on it, is being used as incense inside this lodge. It will also help cure Lone Eagle's wound."

"He is sleeping so soundly," Zondra said, her voice breaking as she gently touched Lone Eagle's brow, thanking God that at least the man she loved was not being tortured with a fever. His brow was cool to the touch. She leaned over and brushed a kiss across it.

"Sleep brings healing," Medicine Fox said, closing his eyes as he began chanting in a low sort of rumbling sound that came from the depths of his throat.

"I am going to Red Moon and talk with him about what happened," White Bead whispered to Zondra. "Pray, Zondra, that Lone Eagle awakens soon. When he finds you sitting beside him, he will greatly improve."

"I will be here for him always," Zondra whispered back, brushing tears from her eyes with the back of her hand.

As Medicine Fox prayed in his way, Zondra bowed her head and closed her eyes and prayed in her own. Although she had been deprived of attending church along with her white brothers and sisters, she knew well the art of praying to God.

No one had been able to take *that* privilege away from her.

She whispered one prayer after another for Lone Eagle's recovery. They had made promises to each other that must be kept. He was her world. He was her everything.

Without him, life would have no meaning!

Chapter Thirty-six

Full gently now she takes him by the hand,
A lily prisoned in a jail of snow.

—WILLIAM SHAKESPEARE

Weary, so afraid that Lone Eagle would never recover, Zondra sat vigil at his bedside, gently bathing his brow with a damp piece of doeskin. Four days had passed and Lone Eagle had drifted in and out of consciousness, but was never truly awake. He had come to at least enough that Zondra was able to spoon-feed him broth, stiffening each time he sounded as though he might choke on the liquid as it trickled down his throat.

Now, as she had so many times these past few days and nights, Zondra leaned over and brushed a soft kiss across his brow. "I love you," she whispered, hoping that somehow, wherever he was in his unconscious state, he could hear her, or at least sense her presence.

While sitting vigil that second day with Medicine Fox, he had talked of spirits that lived in a camp apart—ghosts that haunted the graves of the dead.

He had told her that when an owl hooted in the trees, it was, in truth, a ghost.

When one saw a whirlwind, they were seeing ghosts. He had told her he always addressed whirlwinds by saying, "Where are you going? It is bad! Go by yourself!"

He had also explained to Zondra that when someone says to a person that he is like a ghost, it is one of the worst insults of all.

Now she turned with a start when she heard someone enter the lodge behind her. She smiled a welcome to Medicine Fox as he came and knelt down beside Lone Eagle, opposite from where Zondra sat.

Zondra watched Medicine Fox check Lone Eagle's wound, relieved when he smiled and nodded.

"It is healing well," he said, then moved a thin, wrinkled hand to Lone Eagle's closed eyes and softly rubbed a finger over one of them. "I feel some movement today."

"You *do*?" Zondra asked, her eyes widening. "Truly, you do?"

"My chief will regain full consciousness today and begin a more vigorous journey on the road to full recovery," Medicine Fox said, smiling as he saw the joy knowing this brought to Zondra's eyes.

And then he saw her eyes as quickly waver, which proved that she might have thought her joy was premature and was not sure whether or not to believe him.

"Do not doubt me," Medicine Fox said gently. "Lone Eagle *will* awaken today. He *will* one day soon leave his bed of blankets and join his brethren in laughter and jokes."

"How . . . do . . . you know this?" Zondra asked guardedly, hoping the elderly man might be right.

"How do I know this?" Medicine Fox murmured. He drew the blanket back up to rest just beneath Lone Eagle's armpits. He smiled over at Zondra. "To the Crow the number four is the mystic number. To every undertaking there are always four trials. Lone Eagle will achieve his today. It is his fourth day of illness."

Zondra hoped that her disappointment didn't show in her eyes, for she now knew that what the elderly man was depending on was pure myth, something surely taught to him as a child by someone who believed in mythical things.

To her, it was just another way for the Crow people to keep up their hope. To her it meant nothing. Absolutely nothing. Only when she saw Lone Eagle's eyes open, only when he smiled at her and told her himself that he was going to be all right, would she know that it was true.

Myths to her were only that . . . myths.

She watched Medicine Fox leave, then she reached beneath the blanket and took one of Lone Eagle's hands. "Darling Lone Eagle, I wish you could prove to me that what your medicine man just said was true," she whispered. "Awake, my love, and I shall never doubt the power of your people's myths again."

She gasped softly and leaned closer to Lone Eagle's face when she saw signs of movement beneath his closed lids. Her pulse raced as she waited for his eyes to open, then despair filled her all over again when he still stayed so quiet, so deeply lost to her in his long, deep sleep. . . .

Hovering somewhere between heaven and earth, Lone Eagle was once again joined with his black mustang as he traveled to the "above world."

When he arrived at the wondrous place where there was no pain or sorrow, he found himself riding beside a river, beyond which he saw a large camp of buffalo-skin tepees.

His hair flying in the wind like wings behind him,

his horse's hooves riding across white, fluffy clouds, Lone Eagle soon arrived at the camp.

He drew a tight rein and looked around him and recognized many faces of those who had died before him. There were cousins, aunts and uncles, and friends.

And when he saw two people so dear to his heart, he felt an inner joy never experienced before by him. He had found his mother and father. Their hands were intertwined as they smiled at him, awaiting his arrival, yet there seemed to be some sort of barrier that stood in his way as he tried to ride onward.

He could hear the singing of praise songs in the village, also loud talking. He leaned his ear closer to those who were singing, his eyes widening when he now made out the words.

"Is that person coming already?" the words of the song said. "Is he coming?"

Then Lone Eagle saw his parents go among the singers, their voices drowning out their songs as they spoke to him, telling him to go back.

"Leave the camp of the dead," his father cried.

"Come another time," his mother said. "Do you not know that we will be waiting forever for you? There is no need for you to come now! You are young. You are vital!"

"Come another time," his father said, holding out his hands toward Lone Eagle, motioning for him to turn around and ride away from the camp of the dead. "Return to your people. You have much to do as their leader! Your mother and I watch over you from above, Lone Eagle. This trial you have just been tested with was necessary for you to come and see the spiritual side of death so that you can return home and teach it to our people. Then they will know there is nothing to fear from death!"

"I miss you so!" Lone Eagle cried, trying to edge his horse closer. "Just one embrace, and then I will return to our people. Mother! Father! Let me feel your arms around me just one more time before I turn away from you until we meet again!"

Suddenly they were gone from his sight and he felt himself and his horse being drawn back away from the place of clouds and the beautiful flowing river.

He no longer heard the voices. He no longer saw the camp. All that he was aware of now was a strange sort of weightlessness, and that his horse was no longer beneath him.

He was being drawn through a vast tunnel of bright light. The light was so beautiful and created such a peaceful feeling inside him that he tried to reach out and catch on to something so that he could linger there longer.

Then his eyes opened and he discovered Zondra sitting there, her head hanging as she sobbed in her grieving for him.

He blinked his eyes as he tried to recall those past moments when he had traveled out of his body and into the world on the other side. It was all so vague to him now.

Now he felt that it had all been a dream, a dream that came with returning to the real world after having been unconscious.

"Zondra?" Lone Eagle said, his voice drawn and weak.

Zondra's heart skipped a beat.

Had she heard his voice, she wondered? Or was she wanting to so badly she had imagined it?

Slowly, she raised her eyes to Lone Eagle, then gasped with pure joy when she found his eyes open and looking at her.

"You *did* say my name," she cried. She leaned over him and wrapped her arms around his neck. "Oh, Lone Eagle, I thought I'd never hear your voice again," she sobbed. "You've been gone from me for four long days!"

Then she suddenly recalled what the medicine man had said about the fourth day, and that Lone Eagle would be awakening. He was right! Oh, Lord, he was right! She would never doubt the old man again.

"Kiss me," Lone Eagle whispered, reaching a hand to her face, touching it as though he thought she might be an apparition.

"Oh, yes, darling, yes," Zondra said, her voice breaking.

She pressed her lips gently to his and gave him a long, sweet kiss, then eased away from him.

She explained to him what had happened, how he had been wounded, and how many outlaws had died. She told him that her half brother had shot him, and that Guy was dead.

She told him about the last four days and how she had been so worried about him, and about how his people had stood outside awaiting news of his recovery.

"I must go and tell them!" she cried, jumping to her feet. "And then I will come back and give you water and feed you whatever you wish to eat!"

Beaming, she went outside and faced the questioning gazes as everyone looked at her with anxious eyes.

"He is awake!" she shouted, tears of joy spilling from her eyes. "Your chief is going to be all right!"

Loud cheers rose into the air, as well as chants of victory.

She watched Red Moon approaching, carrying the scalp he had taken from Guy. She paled and started to ask him to please not take it inside Lone Eagle's tepee, but he was already past her and into the lodge before she had the chance to utter even one word of complaint.

She slipped back inside the tepee and stood back as Red Moon explained to Lone Eagle about the scalp, and why he felt it was necessary to take it.

"I killed the white man for you," Red Moon said, as Lone Eagle stared at the scalp, having never taken one himself from anyone.

"I will leave it with you," Red Moon said, smiling over his shoulder as White Bead entered the lodge carrying a pot of soup. "It is a gift from one friend to another friend."

"Thank you, brother," Lone Eagle said, clasping a hand on Red Moon's shoulder, the word "brother," the honor of it, usually spoken aloud only between clansmen who were true friends and allies.

As Zondra watched, touched by it all, Red Moon and Lone Eagle embraced.

When Red Moon laid the scalp on the floor beside Lone Eagle's bed, she was glad that it was out of her sight, for she could never condone the taking of scalps. Not even from a man she abhorred!

White Bead brought a wooden bowl of soup and handed it to Zondra, then sat down beside her as Zondra began slowly feeding Lone Eagle.

"It is so good to have you with us again," White Bead said, holding back a sob of joy. Lone Eagle smiled back at her.

"It was an interesting venture I was on," Lone Eagle said between bites. Perhaps in time he would reveal his strange journey to someone . . . to his Zondra.

Zondra and White Bead exchanged puzzled glances.

Chapter Thirty-seven

How sweet it were, hearing the downward stream,
With half-shut eyes ever to seem
Falling asleep in a half-dream.

—ALFRED, LORD TENNYSON

His wound healed, only a small, puckered scar left on his chest as proof of having been shot by Zondra's half brother, and well enough, even strong enough now to ride his black mustang, Lone Eagle rode with Zondra beneath the bright moon. Only moments earlier he had shared the magnificence of a feast with his people to celebrate his recovery.

"This is our first time alone since before you left to avenge your father's death," Zondra sighed as she edged the white steed she was riding up next to Lone Eagle's. "I am going to savor every moment of it."

She held her head back and let her hair flutter long and luscious down her back, the night breeze delicious against her face. Earlier today, before the celebration, Zondra prepared for the festivities tomorrow—her and Lone Eagle's wedding—while he had been making special tobacco for the occasion.

White Bead had helped Zondra in her preparations. It had been so exciting to see the beautiful elk-tooth dress that White Bead had sewn for Zondra for the wedding, along with the beaded leggings with red fringe, similar to what White Bead would wear to her wedding when she and Red Moon were married in the near future.

It was wonderful that Lone Eagle's people had accepted Red Moon's friendship and trust so quickly and completely. He was as one with them, as though there had never been ill feelings between them. They no longer looked at one another as the enemy clan.

Zondra had been quite taken with the fur strips and pieces of decorated buckskin that White Bead had brought to her, telling her how beautiful she would be with them tied into her long black hair tomorrow.

"Enjoy the ride tonight, when the air has only a nip to it, for soon the cold-maker will gray the sky and chill our bones with his icy breath," Lone Eagle said, as he looked up at the sky, then looked over at Zondra. "My people have prepared well for the approaching moon of long nights. The storage spaces behind their lodge linings are stuffed with dried meats, pemmican, dried corn, beans, and pumpkins obtained in trade."

He frowned as another thought came to him. He looked past Zondra at the emptiness of the vast land that stretched out on all sides of them. "Many moons ago it was wonderful to see the buffalo herds flow over the hills like a dark, fluid thing," he said, his voice drawn. "The Crow warriors are good hunters and horsemen. They deserve to still have the chance to hunt the buffalo. But there are now only a few, too few to hunt and take from the land they once roamed like black clouds cross the sky."

"It's terrible how the buffalo herds were abused by white people," Zondra said, feeling the pain of his loss as he gazed across the moon-shadowed land. "I have seen how your warriors love the hunt, the pride in their eyes when they return with food for their families. I have admired your women so much. They are such hard workers. And the Crow children, Lone Eagle. They are so polite to their elders and are so well-disciplined."

"Ah, the children," Lone Eagle said, guiding his horse into a sharp turn. "They are the true losers when it comes to the dwindling buffalo herds. It is hard for me to think they will never see the wonders of huge groups of the large, shaggy animals. The young braves will never know the thrill of hunting buffalo. It is shameful that they will see only a few buffalo during their lifetime."

"You adore the Crow children so much," Zondra said, following Lone Eagle's lead, swinging her horse alongside his. "You will make a wonderful father."

She smiled at him surreptitiously, for she had a wonderful secret that she would share with him tomorrow after the marriage ceremony. It would be her wedding present to him—the news that she was carrying his child within her womb. When she had missed her first menses she had not thought much about it. But now she had no doubt that she was with child. And it was wonderful to envision the child inside her, waiting to be held in his parents' loving arms. She only wished it could happen sooner than the eight months they would have to wait for the magnificent event.

"I do love children," Lone Eagle said, nodding. "They are the hope of the Crow's tomorrows, if they have the chance for that tomorrow. So much has changed since I was a child. So much has been taken from my people. I wonder how much will have remained Crow when our son or daughter reaches our age?"

"We can't think of that," Zondra murmured. "We

must concentrate on each day as it comes and feel blessed for what we have. We must teach our children to feel the same, for sometimes blessings come in small packages."

Lone Eagle smiled over at her. "Sometimes blessings come when you least expect them," he said. "After I was shot I experienced something special while fighting for my life."

"What do you mean?" Zondra asked, raising her eyebrows. "What experience?"

"I have not yet told anyone about it," Lone Eagle said, in his mind's eye seeing now how it had been.

"About what?" Zondra asked, edging her steed closer to Lone Eagle's as they rode in a slow trot across land now shadowed on one side by a tall bluff. She could see horses in the distance and knew Lone Eagle was purposely taking her to his herd tonight, yet had not told her why.

"When you were not sure if I would live or die, I traveled from my body for a short time and entered the afterlife," Lone Eagle said, drawing a tight rein, stopping.

Zondra stopped her own horse and listened to his tale of wonder, amazed to learn that someone could travel beyond their body and see life as it would be after death.

"Strength, understanding, and peace are found through inner experiences, whether waking or sleeping," Lone Eagle began.

He paused, then spoke again. "The Crow believe that while they live on earth, they have no spirit, or soul," he said. "As soon as they die they assume that other existence. This soul then enters an ethereal realm where all other Crow who have died are camped."

He paused again, took a deep breath, then continued. "Beyond the individual, the spiritual world is universal," he said. "It infuses the whole of the natural world. It informs earth and skies, breathes life into mountains and waters, and imparts a soul to every living creature born of the earth, each to return to the earth by dying.

"While you sat beside my bed, watching and praying that I would live, I traveled far above myself into the mystical place called the afterlife," he said. "It was so beautiful and filled with peace. I was on my horse, riding across voluminous white clouds. I could hear voices. I could hear singing. I saw cousins, aunts and uncles, and many beloved Crow who passed on before me."

His eyes filled with tears as he reached over and lifted Zondra from her saddle, bringing her over to sit on his lap, holding her close to his heart as he continued his tale of wonder.

"And then I saw my mother and father," he said, cuddling Zondra close as she listened intently. "They spoke to me. They told me to return to earth, to live again among my people. While they were talking of our people, I thought of you and the love we have just begun to share and of the children we would have together. It was as though some magnificent force drew me back from those clouds, from my parents and the other people, to awaken to find you there, waiting for me."

"You actually experienced dying, then came back to life?" Zondra said, her eyes wide as she leaned away enough to be able to look up at him.

"I was not dead," Lone Eagle said softly. "I was somewhere between. You see, Zondra, the Crow people believe that the spirit travels to other realms, returning with guidance that fulfills the secret desires of the soul. That is how I see having been with my parents again. They had been placed there, as had I, so they could guide me back to the world of the living. To *you.* I was given the chance to choose. I chose life over death. I chose earth over a place of wondrous beauty and peace because you were calling out to me from the depths of your heart."

"I am so glad," Zondra said, tears filling her eyes as she thought of how it would have been had he chosen to stay in the other world. "I love you so, Lone Eagle."

He twined his fingers through her hair and drew her lips to his in a long, deep, passionate kiss.

As they kissed, he managed to slide from the horse with her still in his arms. He carried her to a mystical place beside a stream where the moon reflected like many moons in the cool, clear water.

Gently he stretched her out on the thick green grass, his hands quickly up under the skirt of her buckskin dress, stroking her wet center with his fingers.

"I didn't think we'd ever be together like this again," Zondra whispered as his lips slid from hers and he kissed the nape of her neck.

She felt a joyous rapture when he slid his free hand down the front of her dress and cupped a breast in it, his thumb rolling her nipple.

"The horses," Zondra said, having some sense left to worry about them straying.

"Do you not recall how I taught my horse to obey my whistle?" Lone Eagle said huskily as Zondra's trembling hands slid his breechclout down away from him.

"Yes, I remember," she murmured as he kicked the garment aside.

"My horse still knows the command, should it wander."

"But the horse I'm riding tonight doesn't know . . ."

He placed a hand gently over her lips, stopping her worries. "If it wanders, there are many close by you can ride back to our village," he said, his eyes gleaming down at her. "And I would prefer it goes and mingles with the herd anyway."

"Why?" Zondra asked, searching his eyes.

"Because I have brought you this far from our village tonight for you to choose from my vast herd a horse for yourself as a wedding gift," he said. "I want you to choose the one that touches your heart the moment your eyes meet. You will know which one. There is a magic in knowing one's horse. It is like a web that spins from the person's heart to the steed's. It is something wondrous to experience."

Before Zondra had the chance to say anything else, he was kissing her again, his fingers on her womanly center driving her wild with pleasure, especially when he would occasionally slide a finger deep inside her, touching that inner part of her that seemed more sensitive than any other pleasure point on a woman's body.

"I want to touch all of you tonight as we make love," Lone Eagle said, as he reached down and slowly slid Zondra's dress up past her thighs, her waist, and then over her head.

As the stars twinkled like diamonds in the sky and the moon gave off its soft, white light, Lone Eagle lay down over Zondra.

Responding to him, Zondra opened her legs and lifted her hips to meet him as he thrust gently inside her and began the rhythmic strokes that filled her with euphoria. Her head reeling with pleasure, her tongue responded to his when he slid it between her parted lips.

Overwhelmed with the desire that raged through her, she yearned for that moment of completeness, that which had been denied them during his time of healing.

Tremors cascaded down her body when his mouth slid from her lips, across her throat, and then sucked one of her nipples between his lips, his tongue flicking.

Breathing raggedly, the rapture so wonderfully sweet, Zondra ran her hands down his back, across his hips, and then around to the front, where she nestled her fingers in the thick tendrils of hair at the juncture of his thighs.

When he withdrew from inside her and pushed his manhood instead into her hands, she could hear his sharp intake of breath as she began moving her fingers on him, stroking the full length of him, then swirling her fingers across the tip that was wet from his building sexual excitement.

Suddenly he rolled away from her and stretched out on his back. She gave him a questioning look when he gently placed his hand behind her head and led her mouth toward him.

"Love me in that special way," he said huskily, taking a wild breath of pleasure when she understood what he wanted and sank her mouth over him, her tongue swirling, her lips sucking.

He twined her around so that he could pleasure her in kind, all of her swirling with the most wondrous of sensations as she strained against his tongue, one of his hands gently taking himself away from her lips, the ultimate of pleasure too near to continue without being inside her.

Again he turned her beneath him and plunged into

her. As his hands kneaded her breasts, their lips met
and held in a long, deep kiss, their tongues touching.

Suddenly their bodies became still.

Lone Eagle slid his lips from hers and rested his
cheek against hers as he took in deep, quavering
breaths.

Then once again he lay above her, his hands moving
seductively over her body as he pushed into her more
deeply, more wonderfully.

Their bodies trembled and shook in unison as they
found the ultimate of pleasure they were seeking.

And then they lay there clinging together beneath
the stars, their cheeks touching, their hands intertwined above Zondra's head.

"You know horses well, do you not?" Lone Eagle
asked as he gazed into her eyes."

"Yes, Father at least shared his knowledge of horses
with me," she murmured. "Why do you ask?"

"Among all the horses you have seen, which do
you find the most beautiful?" he said, then chuckled.
"Besides mine, that is."

"Of all the horses I have seen?" she said, eyes wide.
She smiled. "I love strawberry roans. They stir something inside me. I have always wanted to own such
a horse."

"Then you will have a strawberry roan from my
herd for your wedding present from the man you will
marry," Lone Eagle said, rolling away from her. He
reached for her, placing his hands at her waist, then
lifted her onto his lap, facing him.

His eyebrows lifted when, beneath the shine of the
moon, he saw tears filling her eyes. "Why do you
cry?" he asked softly.

"Except for the clothes I have worn, my precious
cat, and the dresses and moccasins that White Bead

has given to me, I have never owned anything before," she said, flicking tears from her eyes with a finger. "I am deeply moved when I am given anything, especially such a wonderful thing as a horse."

"I will take you to the herd," he said, smoothing her tears away with his thumbs as they rolled from her eyes. "You can have two horses, even more, if you wish, for your wedding present. You can cut from the herd as many as you wish to own as yours."

Zondra giggled. "One will be enough," she murmured. "I don't want to appear greedy."

He moved her gently, laying her down on her back. Her eyes gazed at the stars as he gestured with a hand toward them. "The Big Dipper you see overhead consists of brothers who transformed themselves into stars," he said softly. "They also recognized other prominent stars, including the sun, which we Crow call either Father or Grandfather."

"I've much to learn about your beliefs," Zondra murmured. "Oh, so much."

"And you shall, because you are an astute student," he said, again gently turning her, but this time beneath him.

"Would I be greedy if I asked to make love with you again tonight before we go for the strawberry roan?" he asked huskily, his hands already stroking her soft, wet center.

"I would be disappointed if you didn't," Zondra said, heaving a wondrous sigh when he covered her mouth with his lips, melting when once again he moved within her, filling her so deeply, taking her once again to that place that only they shared while clinging together as one heartbeat, one soul.

Chapter Thirty-eight

Oh! how I love, on a fair summer's eve,
When streams of light pour down the golden west,
And on the balmy zephyr tranquil rest,
The silver clouds far-far away, to leave
All meaner thoughts and take a sweet reprieve!

—JOHN KEATS

The years have passed so quickly, Zondra thought
to herself as she sat with Lone Eagle just outside
their lodge, watching their three-year-old son, Soaring
Eagle, playing with Fawn, White Bead and Red
Moon's four-year-old daughter. As she often did now,
since she had become fast friends with Soaring Eagle,
Fawn was there to spend a few days with Soaring
Eagle and his family.

White Bead and Zondra had grown so close, White
Bead was like the sister Zondra had been denied while
growing up apart from her sisters who lived in her
father's mansions.

She and White Bead got together as often as they
could, but Zondra was no longer able to travel to
White Bead and Red Moon's village. She was large
with her third child. Sadly, she had miscarried her first
one during her fourth month of pregnancy.

She smiled as Soaring Eagle and Fawn ran over and
stared, wide-eyed, at a group of young braves who
were involved in games. Archery was the most typical

of the braves' games. The young men had gathered
up *pupua* grass for the target, making a bundle about
a foot long, thicker at one end and tied together
with sinew.

Players were divided into sides, and were now wa-
gering their arrows. Each side shot off four or five
arrows and whoever came the closest to the target
took all the arrows.

In the winter the young braves killed as many rab-
bits as they could. When they took their kill home for
their mothers to roast or boil, the one who shot the
rabbit got the best parts for his family.

Some day Zondra's son would join the young braves
in the hunt and games; how proud he would make his
parents as he marched into their lodge with his kill!

Zondra became melancholy when her thoughts returned to her earlier miscarriage. She prayed often
that she carried a daughter in her womb this time. She
wished to have a daughter to share things young girls
and mothers shared—sewing . . . cooking . . .
laughing. . . .

"You seem so lost in thought," Lone Eagle said.
He slid an arm around Zondra's waist and drew her
close to his side.

"I was," Zondra said, turning to him, smiling. "I
was thinking of the child I'm carrying."

She gently laid a hand over her abdomen, which
was so large it reminded her of the watermelons that
had grown in her father's watermelon patches in
Mississippi.

Those were good times, back in Mississippi, for her
father's slaves. They were always given permission to
eat their fill of watermelon after the harvest, for her
father had always been blessed with the best watermelon patches in all of Mississippi!

"I've been so careful with this child," Zondra murmured. "I've done nothing that might threaten it. I didn't even ride my horse from the moment I knew I was with child again. I have lifted nothing heavy nor done any chores that might put a strain on me and make me miscarry. I want this child badly, Lone Eagle. And I want it to be a daughter."

She slid a hand over and twined her fingers through his. "But if this child is another son, I truly won't be that disappointed," she said, smiling softly at him. "I could never be more proud than I am of your son."

"Our son," Lone Eagle said, his eyes twinkling as he watched Soaring Eagle romping and playing, now chasing a chipmunk as it scampered quickly through the grass. His chest swelled with pride. "Our son is going to be a great hunter. Watch how his legs carry him so quickly after that small forest animal."

"And, darling, once he marries, he will be as gentle and kind with his wife as you are with yours," Zondra said, sighing. "That you have never demanded that I call you lord pleases me more than you will ever know. Nor have you ever demanded that I wear my hair shorter than yours, which is the custom of the Crow."

"I do know how that pleases you," Lone Eagle said, sliding his hand from hers and placing it gently on her radiant face. "I understand how you hated slavery and how you could not bear to be lorded over by another man."

He chuckled. "I remember that look of surprise in your eyes when I told you on our wedding day that I had never intended to make you call me your lord," he said. He lifted his hand and brushed a fallen lock of her black hair back from her eyes. "Nor would I have ever asked you to cut your hair. My woman, I respect you too much to make foolish demands of you."

"But you *did* hold me captive for a time," she said, thinking back to those days when she had loved and hated him in the same moment.

"Not really," he said. "In truth, I had never intended to hold you captive. It was all to teach you a lesson."

"But you *did* place sentries around the village and guards just outside your lodge so that I could not escape," Zondra said, a bit sullenly.

"I did, but again, it was all a ploy to make you understand the wrong you did when you stole a Crow chief's horse," he said. "No one, not even the woman who would one day be the chief's wife, should feel free to steal horses. In the white world are horse thieves not hung by their necks until they are dead?"

"Yes," Zondra said, smiling meekly.

"Then do you not truly know how lucky you are that you stole from a man who loved that pretty neck too much to harm it?" he asked, his eyes dancing.

Zondra giggled, then went quiet when she saw her father's buggy arriving at the far end of the village. It was beginning to be dusk, so she couldn't make out who was with him.

It puzzled her that he was there, for it was very rare that he came to the Crow village. He still resented Zondra for having behaved like a runaway slave, escaping her master at her first opportunity.

And she could hardly find it in her heart to forgive him for not having accepted her child as his grandson. She felt that it was because Soaring Eagle was the exact image of his father, in no way resembling his white grandfather.

It saddened her that her mother had not been able

to come and visit as much as Zondra would have liked. Her mother couldn't ride a horse, nor did she own a buggy for comfortable travel to the village.

Zondra had gone as often as possible to visit her mother with Soaring Eagle. It had warmed Zondra's heart to see her son mingle with the slaves' children, seeing no difference in their skins nor feeling awkward because the slave children's clothes weren't as fine as his own fringed buckskin outfits and moccasins.

Zondra had since sewn several buckskin outfits and had taken them to the slaves' children. It had pleased her so much when their mothers had accepted the clothes and allowed their children to wear them on the days Zondra came there with her son.

"Your father arrives again so soon after the time of his last visit?" Lone Eagle said, forking an eyebrow. He helped Zondra up from the blankets. Arm in arm, they walked slowly to meet the wagon.

When the wagon came closer to the leaping flames of the outdoor fire, which gave off enough light for Zondra to see her father's companion, she stopped dead in her tracks and stared disbelievingly at her mother, sitting there so tall and proud beside him.

Her mother was even wearing a beautiful dress and a lovely hat bedecked with artificial flowers. Why, Zondra marveled to herself, she's even wearing beautiful white gloves!

And in her mother's eyes she saw such radiance!

"I don't understand," she murmured, giving Lone Eagle a quick, questioning glance. "Never before has Father allowed anyone to see him with my mother. And especially not in his buggy, sitting beside him as though she were his wife, even dressed as his . . ."

Her words trailed off, her lips parting in a slight gasp when she thought of her father's wife and how

appalled she must have been to see her husband leave
the ranch with a slave at his side.

Not just any slave—her husband's mistress!

"Did Sylvia die?" Zondra whispered, her pulse racing as the buggy drew up alongside her and Lone
Eagle.

"Daughter!" Ada exclaimed, not waiting for anyone
to assist her from the buggy. She climbed out and
rushed into Zondra's arms and hugged her.

"Mama, I don't understand. . . ." Zondra whispered
in her mother's ear as she returned the hug.
"Why . . . ?"

She didn't finish the question, for her father was too
quickly there, easing her mother from her arms.

"Zondra, I see that you are stunned by what you
see today," Harrison said. He placed a possessive, gentle arm around Ada's waist and drew her close to his
side as though she were a prized possession.

"Yes, I am," Zondra said. She looked cautiously
from her mother to her father. She had never seen
them together openly, especially not like *this*.

When Soaring Eagle ran up to Lone Eagle and
clung to his leg, gaping questioningly up at this tall,
thin man who he knew was his grandfather, yet who
never had so much as given him a hug, Zondra
reached down and took Soaring Eagle's hand.

"A lot has changed since I last saw you," Harrison
said, his voice drawn. "Zondra, I received word that
the war is over. All slaves have been set free." A
grave look was evident in the depths of his blue eyes.
"President Lincoln is dead."

Having heard too much too quickly, stunned
speechless, Zondra stared at her father as he continued to explain things.

"As a war measure, Zondra, Lincoln proclaimed the

slaves in the rebellious states free in 1863," he said. "He was assassinated by a man named John Wilkes Booth as he sat at Ford's Theatre in Washington, just days after the Union victory in 1865."

"After achieving freedom for the slaves . . . he . . . was murdered?" Zondra said, placing a hand to her throat. "And the slaves? Are they truly still free?"

She glanced over at her mother, again seeing the fineness of her clothes and the way her father kept his arm around her waist as though she were his beloved wife, not only a mistress.

"Yes, the slaves are free, including mine," he said, sighing. "Although I am far away from the center of things, and could possibly keep my slaves for some time without anyone's interference, it was my own choice to set them free."

"Your father's decision to free his slaves came not because of the war or Lincoln, but because of you, Zondra," Ada said, reaching out to take Zondra's free hand. "Daughter, after receiving word of the war's end, and the freedom given to the slaves, and when your father realized to what length you went to be free of slavery, he saw the true wrong in having slaves. Of course it took some time for him to be brave enough, but finally he has freed them, Zondra. He has freed them."

"Those who wished to stay with me are salaried," Harrison said. "Those who wished to leave got a safe escort to the closest railhead. I paid each of their passage to wherever they chose to go."

"What about Mama?" Zondra asked guardedly, her eyes sweeping over her mother and how beautiful she was in the pale blue silk dress with its matching hat. She even wore beautiful leather shoes, after having gone barefoot for most of her life!

"Papa, what about Mama?" Zondra repeated. "What is *her* status in life? She has no one to go to. For all of her adult life she has never known anything but being a slave . . . and a mistress."

"I took care of that mistake," Harrison said, his eyes meeting and holding Ada's as she gazed proudly up at him. "I divorced Sylvia. I ran her off. I married my first true love. I married Ada."

Left absolutely speechless by this announcement, Zondra couldn't find the words to say how wonderful this news was to her, for she had always wanted so much more for her mother than she had ever been able to have.

And now her mother had everything she had never thought possible. She had been set free of slavery and she had the man she loved!

Sobbing, Zondra rushed to her mother and flung herself into her arms. "Mama, I'm so happy for you," she sobbed. "Oh, Mama, so very happy."

What Harrison said next drew Zondra from her mother's arms. She stared disbelievingly up at her father when he told her that she could now claim her true last name, which was his.

"Zondra, you can now say the name Lester is yours," he said, smiling at her as he awaited her reaction, which he expected to be one of gratitude and joy.

When she didn't react the way he had predicted she would, his smile quickly faded and he took a shaky step back from her.

"Papa, I no longer need your name," Zondra said with firmness and much pride. She gave Lone Eagle a radiant smile. "My goals changed after meeting Lone Eagle. As his wife, all of my ugly past has been erased from my heart." She gave her father a solemn stare. "Even my long-denied true last name."

"I understand," Harrison said, nervously clearing his throat. "I apologize for having waited so long."

Zondra went stiff when Harrison gazed down at Soaring Eagle. She wasn't sure how to react when he reached his arms out for him and asked him to come to him, saying that he was his grandfather. He wished to know him. He wished to love him.

Zondra slipped her hand from Soaring Eagle's so that he would be free to either accept or reject this tall white man who suddenly wished to acknowledge him as his grandson.

Lone Eagle and Zondra weren't at all surprised when their little boy refused to go to Harrison, who up to now had chosen to be a stranger to him.

"Give him time," Lone Eagle said, whisking Soaring Eagle up into his arms. "Come often. Let him know you in that way. And if you wish, we will come to your big house and bring him with us so that he can see that side of life he, until now, knew not existed."

"Yes, I'll do anything you ask," Harrison said, clasping his hands tightly behind him. "Family is important. It just took me a long time to realize that."

"And what of your other children?" Zondra asked dryly, glancing over at their lodge, where Lone Eagle still had Guy's scalp, but not where it was visible. It was kept in a parfleche bag so that their son would not see it and question it.

Her father had taken Guy's death much harder than Zondra had ever thought possible. She believed that was when he began thinking about his life, and how wrong he had been in how he had chosen to live it, forcing everyone else to live as he demanded they live.

"They are gone," Harrison said, sighing. "As soon as their mother left and they saw whom I brought into their house in her place, they had their bags packed and were gone in the blink of an eye. I haven't heard from them since."

"I'm sorry," Zondra murmured, though she really wasn't. It seemed only right that her mother would have a true chance at her new life without the interference of Zondra's snobbish half sisters and brother.

It was hard still, though, to grasp what had happened . . . how things had changed for her beloved mother. It made things change inside Zondra's heart for her father. She would now be able to embrace him and feel something for him that she had long denied herself as his daughter. Suddenly she did feel like his daughter.

And were she not married, she would accept this man's last name as hers. She had wanted it all her life. How could she not still want it now?

"As you know, Zondra, most of our family jewels and a lot of my cash were recovered when the authorities went through the outlaws' cabin," he said thickly. "It was all found hidden in a trunk beneath a floorboard there. I still can't believe that my very own son stole it from me. But that's in the past. It's the future I'm focusing on. I've made out a new will. If I should die before your mother, everything is hers, to be shared with you and my grandson as she sees fit. Should your mother die before me, the will then states that when I die, everything becomes yours and my grandson's."

He looked over at Lone Eagle. "In turn, much of my wealth becomes yours, so that you can do with it what you wish for the good of your people," he said. "I do appreciate the hardships your people have suffered from the interference of whites in your lives. I know that what I have to offer is small in comparison to what you have lost."

"Papa," Zondra said, tears splashing from her eyes as she went to him and fell into his embrace. "Oh, Papa, I knew that part of you that took me horseback riding as a child, and that loved Mama as you loved her, would be revealed somehow to more than me and Mama. I love you, Papa. I've always loved you."

She cherished the warmth of his arms as he enfolded her within his embrace. She melted when he placed a soft gentle kiss on her brow as she gazed up at him, their tearful eyes locking.

"Daughter," he said, the world now hearing him saying it, not just Zondra, "I have always loved you so much. I was wrong to allow my family to stand in the way of voicing my feelings for you aloud to the world."

His eyes slid over to Ada. He reached an arm out for her. Zondra smiled as he drew her against him and openly kissed her.

Suddenly a small voice added to the wondrous events of the late afternoon as Soaring Eagle cried out for his grandmother, wiggling free of Lone Eagle's arms, running to her, and reaching his arms up for Ada.

It was as though he had just this minute recognized her. Until now he had seen her only in thin cotton attire, and barefoot, her hair tied in a tight bun at the back of her head. This woman tonight, dressed finely in rich attire, had seemed different until now, when he'd studied her enough to know that she was the grandmother he adored.

Beaming, Ada moved away from Harrison, kneeled, and swept her grandson into her embrace.

Zondra went and stood beside Lone Eagle. Joyous tears fell from her eyes as she smiled up at him as their son chattered like a magpie to his grandmother.

Then Zondra felt warmed through and through when her father bent to his knees and Soaring Eagle went to him, hesitant at first before giving him a hug, then laughingly embracing him. Soon Harrison was sitting on the ground as his grandson climbed playfully over him, giggling.

"I have never seen such a lovely sight as that," Ada said as she stood beside Zondra, their hands intertwined. "There's a lot of little boy in Harrison that has never been allowed to come out."

"Mama, he *looks* like a little boy, sitting there with Soaring Eagle," Zondra murmured. "I doubt his father ever gave him any attention when he was a child. Surely that is why he never knew how to give attention to his own children."

She smiled sweetly up at Lone Eagle. "You are an excellent father," she murmured. "And soon there will be another child for us all to love and marvel over."

A sudden pain grabbed at Zondra's abdomen, causing her womb to tighten. Her eyes widened as it came again. Then the color drained from her face when she felt her water break.

Her buckskin dress soaked, everyone's eyes wide as they stared at her, Zondra gave Lone Eagle a look of radiance. "Darling, I'm suddenly in *labor*," she said, wincing when another pain came so soon.

Everything then happened so quickly it seemed like a dream. Zondra's mother went with her into her tepee and helped prepare her for the delivery of her child.

And before anyone could catch their breath, Zondra had given birth to a beautiful pink baby girl, her eyes blue, her hair curls of gold.

"She is so lovely," Zondra murmured as her newborn baby was placed into her waiting arms as she lay on the bed of blankets and pelts where the child was conceived.

Lone Eagle knelt down beside the bed. His eyes wide with pride, his trembling hand went to the child's tiny arm.

"She's perfect in every way," Zondra murmured, as she watched Lone Eagle marveling over her. "I would like to call her Singing Star, after Singing Star, who left us a year ago to join her ancestors in the sky. Can we, Lone Eagle? Can we call her Singing Star?"

"Ah, yes, she will forever be called Singing Star," he said warmly. "And be sure that she is near and knows that she is being remembered in such a way."

Ada and two other women cleaned Zondra and the child, then slid a beautiful cotton gown over Zondra's head and placed clean blankets beneath her.

Moments later, Zondra looked past Lone Eagle as her father came into the lodge, his eyes wavering as he looked down at the newborn child resting in his daughter's arms.

He went and stood beside the bed. "Can I hold her?" he asked softly. "I want this grandchild to become acquainted with my voice and how I hold her so that she will know that I loved her from the moment she took her first breath."

Ada went to the supply of baby clothes that she had busied herself sewing these past weeks with the fancy new sewing machine her husband had bought for her. She slid an embroidered shawl from the collection.

She went back to the bed and wrapped the child snugly in the shawl, then handed Singing Star to the waiting arms of her grandfather.

Lone Eagle sat down on the bed with Zondra. She leaned into his embrace. She no longer had empty

spaces in her life, left there by an uncaring, cold father. Today was a day of miracles. Finally, at long last,
everything had fallen into place like pieces in a puzzle.
She could never be any more content than she was
now.

She laughed when Soaring Eagle romped into the
room, all eyes, carrying Zondra's cat, which no longer
went by the name Ralph, but rather Fluffy, a name
chosen by Singing Star before she died. Fluffy had
befriended a stray male not long ago and was now the
proud mother of a litter of six kittens!

"Our baby!" Soaring Eagle said, beaming as he
looked up at Lone Eagle. "Daddy, Mother has given
us a baby!"

"Yes, son, and she is a baby sister," Lone Eagle
said, scooping both Soaring Eagle and Fluffy into his
arms. Smiling, he watched Harrison, who still held his
new granddaughter, cooing baby talk to her.

"Everything is suddenly so perfect," Zondra
thought to herself as she watched Soaring Eagle and
Lone Eagle gazing at the newborn child who had
added another ray of sunshine to their lives.

Touched deeply, and loving Lone Eagle so much,
Zondra gazed at him. Meeting him was the best thing
that could have ever happened to her, for he had
shown her a life that was far removed from the slavery
she had been raised in. She hated even thinking of
how it might have been had she never known him.

She sighed with a blissful, contented happiness.

Letter to the Reader

Dear Reader:

I hope you enjoyed reading *Lone Eagle*. The next book in the Topaz Indian Series, which I am writing exclusively for Dutton Signet, is *Silver Wing*. This is the first book that I have written about the Nez Perce Indians, and I'm excited about the story—the intrigue, romance, and adventure that you will find on each and every page of the book. I hope you will buy *Silver Wing* and enjoy reading it as much as I enjoyed writing about the interesting customs and lives of the Nez Perce.

For those of you who are collecting all of the books in my Topaz Indian Series and want to read more about it, you can send for my latest newsletter and bookmark. Write to:

Cassie Edwards
6709 North Country Club Road
Mattoon, Illinois 61938

For a prompt reply, please send a self-addressed, stamped, legal-size envelope.

Thank you from the bottom of my heart for your support of my Topaz Indian Series. I love researching and writing about our country's beloved Native Americans!

Cassie Edwards

SUSAN KING

☐LAIRD OF THE WIND   0-451-40768-7/$5.99

In medieval Scotland, the warrior known as Border Hawk seizes the castle belonging to the father of the beautiful Isabel Scott, famous throughout the Lowlands for her gift of prophecy. During the battle, Isabel is injured while fighting alongside her men and placed under Border Hawk's protection. As the border wars rage on, the warrior and prophetess engage in a more intimate conflict, discovering their love for the Scottish borderlands is surpassed only by their love for each other.

Also available:
☐THE ANGEL KNIGHT	0-451-40662-1/$5.50
☐THE BLACK THORNE'S ROSE	0-451-40544-7/$4.99
☐LADY MIRACLE	0-451-40766-0/$5.99
☐THE RAVEN'S MOON	0-451-18868-3/$5.99
☐THE RAVEN'S WISH	0-451-40545-5/$4.99

Prices slightly higher in Canada

Penguin Putnam Inc.
P.O. Box 12289, Dept. B
Newark, NJ 07101-5289
Please allow 4-6 weeks for delivery.
Foreign and Canadian delivery 6-8 weeks.

Bill my: ☐Visa ☐MasterCard ☐Amex _____(expires)
Card#_____
Signature_____

Bill to:

Name_____
Address_____City_____
State/ZIP_____
Daytime Phone #_____

Ship to:

Name_____ Book Total $_____
Address_____ Applicable Sales Tax $_____
City_____ Postage & Handling $_____
State/ZIP_____ Total Amount Due $_____

This offer subject to change without notice.